To Isobe
all the
Barb
Bissonette

JUST A BIT OF MAGIC

BARB BISSONETTE

Cover design copyright © 2020 by Niki Lenhart
nikilen-designs.com

Published by Water Dragon Publishing
waterdragonpublishing.com

ISBN 978-1-946907-05-9 (Trade Paperback)

FIRST EDITION

10 9 8 7 6 5 4 3 2 1

This book is dedicated to Eva Carrick,
who is *just a bit of magic* all by herself.

JENNY'S GRIMOIRE

Oh, my. I must have slept. I didn't think I would. I didn't think I could.

This is the day! They are coming today! Joy floods through my very being.

My huge bedroom window faces east, and I love to watch the world awaken in the morning. On the west wall hangs the ancient mirror which has been there for as long as I can remember. It is oval, and the glass is a little frail in places. The outside is carved from the wood of a very old, very wise oak tree. It reflects each morning as the days of my life unfold, relentlessly and without pause. Toby calls it my "magic mirror".

And, on the very rarest of days, I really can see magic in that mirror. If I turn to look out of the window, there is only the expanse of the eastern sky. If I look directly into the mirror, only the reflection of morning is visible. But sometimes I catch just a glimmering — a misty apparition catching at the corner of my vision, niggling at the edge of my waking consciousness. I have thought that they weren't real, these scraps of magic, that they had been evoked from an intense longing deep within me. But years and years have passed. I am older now and I have learned to believe what I see even if it seems beyond belief.

I've caught only glimpses of them for many years. Yet my soul is literally starving for one more such glimpse.

There were times in my life when I wondered if I should just curl up and cease to draw another breath — times when life seemed too real and full of pain to exist in me.

But there remained that incessant stirring of hope, refusing to die inside my spirit. I needed to see them, to feel them one more time. Even if it was just a reflection in my old magic mirror.

And so, I have held on for all these years.

And today is the day.

I can hear the magic spoken in the merest of whispers.

Miranda. Molly.

They are coming today.

1

"All the great stories have witches in them."

I'D ARRIVED AT LAST. I gulped a deep breath as I entered my new place of employment, my heart in my mouth. The café, weathered and grey, appeared warm and cozy enough at first glance: colourful tablecloths and vases of wildflowers perched cheerfully on haphazard tables. The seams of this friendly establishment fairly burst with people eating, drinking coffee, and talking loudly amongst themselves.

I hesitated on the threshold, inhaling resolve. I reminded myself how grateful I'd been to obtain this job. My head still reeled, my heart ached, at the knowledge of my absolute aloneness in the world — a poor student who had wandered miles from home, arriving in this unexpected village. I needed, now, to earn some money and obtain a university education. So, here I was, enrolled in a degree program for early childhood education, in a nearby unknown city.

I announced my arrival to the harried-looking owner, Mrs. Snell. She hustled me into the kitchen, clearly relieved at my presence, simultaneously throwing an apron over my shoulders and thrusting a tray into my arms. All the while, she explained my job description over her shoulder. Her head turned sharply to observe a girl about my age who had slipped into the kitchen. She exuded a defiant air, not overly friendly. Or so it seemed to my uncertain eyes. Her brown hair tumbled down her slim shoulders, caught in a ponytail. Her eyes gleamed like bits of blue ice. She might have been pretty if she'd ventured to smile.

Mrs. Snell regarded us with a quizzical look on her tired face, asking, "There's two of you?"

We looked at each other. Shouldn't she know that?

Mr. Snell entered the kitchen then, nodding a greeting, his brisk demeanor mirroring his wife's.

They appeared to be in their fifties, resembling each other in the uncanny manner some married couples do. The matching blue-checked aprons they wore reinforced this image. Salt and pepper waves of hair adorned faces weathered from years of hard work and ruddy from the kitchen heat. Despite their brusque, business-like personas, they seemed pleasant.

"These are the two new girls, Verna," he said unnecessarily. "I don't know why you had them both start today when it's so busy out there."

"Because it's so busy out there," she answered, motioning towards the people milling about in the café. "We need extra help."

"Of course we do, but who's going to show them the ropes when all these people need to be fed and watered?"

I opened my mouth to say that I could start right now. Before I had a chance to utter anything, the other girl donned an apron, grabbed the coffeepot and headed out the kitchen door with it.

"I guess she's just going to start." Mrs. Snell observed, with approval. Then she turned to me, as if querying why I didn't follow suit.

Mr. Snell, Malcolm as he introduced himself, must have sensed my consternation, because he took my arm, proceeding to explain the setup of the kitchen and my duties.

I followed the other girl — *I must learn her name* — into the café. I began filling coffee cups (the main staple, it seemed) and taking orders. I tried not to feel too nervous. The people here seemed friendly, not in too great of a rush — a type of folk familiar to me from the small town in Prince Edward Island from which I had come.

Several people were reading the paper, a couple worked on laptops, but the bulk of the customers seemed immersed in conversation.

One grey-haired woman, with beady eyes and a hooked nose, looked up from her newspaper crossword puzzle to scrutinize me as I offered her fresh coffee.

"Wait a minute," she called out to me, grabbing at my apron and peering at me over her reading glasses. "There's two of you."

"Yes," I said.

She had uttered Mrs. Snell's words, verbatim.

"Are you sisters?"

"No. I've never met her before."

"You look like sisters." She returned to her crossword, commenting to no one in particular, "Humph, Jenny's outdone herself on this one. I can't make head nor tail of it."

I attempted to soldier on with my coffeepot, but she stopped me with her inquiry.

"Can you think of a six-letter word for protective?"

"I'll give it some thought," I promised.

"I'm Nora, by the way. In case you have any bright ideas."

I wondered if she might be loony tunes, this Nora.

"What's your name?" I asked the other girl, meeting her in the kitchen. "We're both new, I guess."

"Miranda."

I smiled a tentative smile.

"I'm Molly."

She gave a brief nod. Not warm and fuzzy, this one.

"That lady thought we might be sisters," I ventured.

She laughed curtly.

"I've never been here before," she said.

"Me neither. I come from PEI."

"I'm from Kelowna."

"Wow. You're a long way from home, too."

"Yup."

Without further ado, she turned on her heel to return to work. I squared my shoulders and followed suit.

We continued at a whirlwind pace for the next couple of hours. Eventually, the crowd thinned out, enabling us to relax a little.

"Are you having any luck with your crossword, Nora?" Verna Snell inquired of the old crone, still intent on her newspaper.

She must sit here all day, I thought.

Nora looked up, shrugging her skinny, stooped shoulders.

"I'm given up on that," she admitted. "I'm on to our witch's column now."

My ears pricked up. This sounded intriguing.

"Jenny's column?"

"No, I read her stuff already. I'm on to that anti-witch one that comes out every May and October."

"Oh, yes. What's it called again?"

"Witches Among Us."

"That's it. No one's ever fessed up to writing it. It's always a real slam against Jenny."

Malcolm approached Nora, gazing over her shoulder.

"It's not really a slam against her personally. It's just against witches in general."

Verna dropped into one of the wooden chairs with a weary exhalation.

"Life isn't dull here, girls. We have our own resident witch," Malcolm said, pointing to the paper.

Miranda and I regarded each other: the two new girls, full of questions.

"She's actually our friend," Verna said in a firm voice, throwing Malcolm a warning look.

"Really?"

"Yup," Nora agreed. "I've known her forever. Still, there's more to Jenny than meets the eye. You can never be too sure what she's up to."

Somewhere, at the back of my mind, a warning bell sounded.

"And she's a witch?" Miranda ventured.

"She's a hedgewytch," Nora said, as if using a word that anyone might recognize.

"A hedgewytch," Vera nodded, then proceeded to explain. "They're different from wiccans and other witches. They work mainly with nature. You know: trees and plants and herbs. She makes all kinds of potions and herbal remedies for various things. If she doesn't have the remedy in her cottage, she'll create it for you."

"Never heard of them in my life," Miranda proclaimed.

"Well, we do a lot of business with her. You'll be making lots of trips out to Hedgewytch Way," Verna affirmed.

"Head-which-what?"

My voice collided with Miranda's in midair, eliciting a spontaneous burst of laughter.

"You should say 'jinx'," a child declared who sat waiting, none too patiently, for his mother to finish her coffee.

We should, I thought.

Miranda, however, feigned disinterest.

"It's the name of Jenny's place. Hedgewytch Way. It's just on the outside of town. I get my eggs and herbs and some vegetables from her. You girls will be heading there tomorrow."

I had no idea how I felt about this. *Visiting a witch?*

"May and October are always the most interesting months to read the *Jared Times*," Malcolm continued, "because you can read Jenny's column with all of her local bit of news and recipes and yoga stuff —"

"Yoga?'"

Miranda and I exchanged glances, quite lost now.

"Sure. She has a yoga studio there. Most of the women in Jared go at some time or another. Her column is called 'The Musings of a Hedgewytch'," he informed us.

"Very interesting it is, too," Nora declared. "Full of little bits of information and nature facts. Often a recipe or two. You'll love to read it."

"Then you can read the other witch column," Malcolm said, grimacing. "It goes on about the history of witches and Salem. I mean, it talks about Salem, Massachusetts. Where all the witches were hung. Not our little village of Salem up the road. It's none too complimentary to our local hedgewytch, though."

I felt overwhelmed by all of this information, unprepared for such an otherworldly situation.

Miranda shook her head as if she, too, had difficulty processing this data.

She looked from Nora to Malcolm, inquiring, "So really? You have your very own witch? Is she a good witch?"

"Or a bad witch?" Malcolm's eye held a teasing gleam.

"Or is she really a witch at all?" I ventured.

Verna stood up, starting to bustle again.

"You girls will find out tomorrow. In the morning, you can take an order out to her and decide for yourself."

The allure of possible witchcraft abounding in this quiet village had aroused my curiosity. I'd never known a witch or anyone who professed to be a witch.

After the café closed, and the afternoon unraveled, I took an uncertain step into the main street of Jared. I headed north towards my rooming house, one of several old war houses at the edge of the sleepy village. Mr. Crawford, my old curmudgeon of a landlord, rented some of the tired rooms out to university students. Five girls in total shared the house — it being a convenient thirty-minute drive to the university. The kitchen and living room and bathroom were shared by all five of us, but we each had our own bedroom. So far, I'd met only two of the other girls, having arrived just yesterday. I missed my home in PEI with an ache that consumed me, body and soul. But my home there no longer existed. Both of my parents were gone now; my father when I was a baby and my mother only last year. I had no siblings. The boy whom I thought would love me forever decided otherwise and so, in hurt reaction, I applied to university far away. When my acceptance letter came, I turned my back on my Maritime home, determined never to look back. So here I stood, in a strange village, isolated, alone and homesick.

Trudging my solitary way up the tree-lined street, I became aware of a presence behind me. I turned, startled, to find Miranda in my wake.

"Miranda!"

"Yup."

Still not overly friendly even after our day together. But beggars can't be choosers.

"Where are you headed?"

"Oh, just to one of those old rooming houses up on Menken Street. I'm renting a room there."

"Me too." I declared.

She said nothing further, falling into step beside me. I felt pathetically glad of her company.

We walked in silence for several minutes until I ventured, "So you're a long way from home, too?"

"Yeah. You too, eh?"

"Yes," I gulped. "I miss it."

She turned her head to scrutinize me.

"You do?"

I nodded. "Don't you?"

"Na. Not at all. Glad to be away."

"Really? I've heard it's beautiful out west. This is the farthest west I've ever been."

"This is the farthest east for me. And Kelowna is beautiful, but I was glad to leave." She looked around with indifference, shrugging, "It's nice enough here, I guess."

"Oh, it is nice here," I conceded. "But don't you miss your family?"

"Haven't got any."

"Really?"

"Nope. None to speak of. My dad and mom split up years ago. He took off with my little brother and I've never heard from them for years. There was just my mom and I."

"Well, won't she miss you?"

Miranda shook her head with resolution, replying simply, "My mom's dead."

"Oh, my God! So's mine."

"It sucks, doesn't it?"

"Yes," I agreed. "It sure does. My mom was my best friend. I know girls say that and I always thought it sounded corny but mine really was."

9

"Not me. Oh, I loved my mom and everything. But she wasn't what you'd call a friend."

She didn't elaborate, just walked a little faster. I quickened my pace to match hers.

We walked together in silence until coming to a sharp corner in the road. This landed us smack in front of my rooming house, half-hidden behind a row of budding maples.

"Well," I said, "this is where I'm staying."

"Me, too." Miranda observed.

"Really?"

"Yup. Renting from Mr. Crawford. I'm on the second floor."

"Hey, you must be right beside me," I said, my heart giving a little hopeful flutter. "Did you come last night?"

"Uh-huh. And then I had to start work right away this morning. I'm beat."

Was she trying to ward off any overtures of friendship?

Or maybe she just wanted to be left alone.

Or maybe she really was just beat.

I sighed inwardly, exhausting myself with my doubts. Mom always said I did too much overthinking.

"Me, too. And we have to work a longer day tomorrow, I think."

"Yes. And visit the witch."

"I know, eh? What do you think of that?"

"I have no idea. At first, I thought they were just kidding around. But then when that weird Nora lady pointed out both those columns in the paper, I thought they must be legitimate. She said we could take them home and read them."

For the first time, I noticed the folded newspaper under her arm.

"She also said that we're supposed to ask this Jenny about the crossword. Apparently, she sets them for the paper. I've heard that you have to be super smart to set those things."

"Oh, she sounds smart all right," I said. "Whether she's good or bad is yet to be discovered. It sounds like a hedgewytch must be a good thing, though. At least everyone seems to like her."

"I suppose," Miranda shrugged, not seeming to care either way about the temperament of a witch. "Not sure if Nora likes her quite as much as Verna Snell. I imagine there are a lot of mixed feelings about her. The witch, I mean. She sounds a bit wacky."

I couldn't disagree.

"Are you going to university in the fall?" I asked. "Mr. Crawford says that he mainly rents to university students."

"Yup. I'm taking my Bachelor of Nursing. You?"

"Bachelor of Applied Science in Early Childhood Studies."

We entered the old-fashioned hallway, turning to mount the stairs to our rooms which were, in fact, beside each other. As I turned to enter my door, Miranda called to me.

"Molly. That's your name, right? Molly?"

"Uh-huh."

"I've picked up a bottle of chardonnay, if you'd like some. It's a cheap bottle and we'll have to use paper cups, but it might suffice."

I grinned, thrilled at the prospect of pushing loneliness away a little longer.

"I'd love some."

"We can sit out on the back porch and relax a bit. Get to the bottom of these witch articles."

"Sounds good."

JARED TIMES

The Musings of a Hedgewytch in May

Well, dear readers, it's finally spring. I am not referring to that below-zero weather which has been present since the calendar said it was March 21st. It's May now, and I don't believe that May will let us down as March and April so cruelly have. (April being the cruelest month anyways, according to T.S. Eliot.)

The poor old flowers and trees have certainly taken a beating this winter with all the fierce winds and driving bouts of snow — not to mention the wear and tear on our roads. A vehicle could get buried inside some of those frost heaves on our sideroads. It's no one's fault, really. The roads in Grey County this winter were closed more days than they were open, I swear.

It was a real old-fashioned winter, methinks. The days were long and dark and the sunshine was scarce at times. It's been very hard on all of us. Sometimes days on end went by as we sat paralyzed under endless drifts of white. It seems just plain wrong to me to be cooped up for so much time. We are country folk and, when the roads are impassable, our worlds become very small indeed.

So, we should all rejoice in the light and sweetness of the very air which May has brought our way. To walk outside without a jacket and breathe deeply of that glorious spring sunshine is the best medicine ever.

But, don't worry, that won't be my only remedy for this issue — to breath in the sunshine, I mean. Always assuming that any of you dear readers were worried about such a thing.

I will talk this month about my very favourite flower ever: the lilac. I can honestly say that I have loved them since girlhood and they are among my first garden memories. As any of you know who have been up to our Hedgewytch Way, we are flanked on three sides with thick masses of them. They have rather run amuck these last few years. But right now, when they are all blooming and the air is saturated with the sweetness of them, it feels close to heaven. I am quite sure of that.

If you have any small children in your life, you should take them to visit some lilacs this spring. Allow them to marvel at the colour and perfume and purple magic that they bring to us with so little effort and so much pride. Let them observe the glory of the yellow swallowtails which abound only at this time of year and only for these lilac blooms. Let them dance with the dragonflies and baby hummingbirds and peer in awe at the little fiddleheads wrapped up like something enchanted.

Do you remember an old song called "Lilac Wine"? I love it. It was written way back in 1950 and sung by different artists over the years, but Miley Cyrus sang it just a few years back. It speaks of making wine from the lilacs and putting your heart into it so you can see what you want to see.

Listen to the song and you'll get the idea. Lilac wine is magical.

This recipe is intended to make five gallons of medium body wine.

> 20 quarts lilac flowers, petals only
> 15 lb. Sugar Shooting for 13% ABV
> Juice of 2 lemons
> Zest of 1 lemon
> 1 pound of golden raisins
> Yeast energizer
> Yeast nutrient
> 1 oz. RC212 yeast

1. Put the flowers in to a large crock or stock pan. Pour 3 quarts boiling water over the petals, cover and let sit for 2 days.
2. Pour 17 quarts boiling water over half the sugar to dissolve. Cool. Strain lilac mixture, squeezing. Return to crock with sugar water, lemon juice, and cut up raisins. Inoculate with the yeast.
3. Ferment 1 week. Strain this into your primary. Dissolve remaining sugar in a pint of boiling water,

cool and add. Fit with fermentation lock and ferment until all activity ceases.
4. Clear and bottle

I love brewing my wine in a crockpot. We almost always have one or more cooking away at any given time. If you head on down to Hedgewytch Way we will be glad to share with you. We have samples to try and bottles to buy. Who knows? Maybe you'll see what you want to see and be who you want to be, like Miley.

Lilacs bloom in seven official colours: white, violet, blue, lavender, pink, magenta, and purple, with many shades in between.

So, let's talk about the magic of the lilacs — both herbal and otherwise.

The most noticeable magical quality of the lilacs is that it can drive away ghosts instantly. The tree is linked with reincarnation and life. One of its secrets and wonders is that its flowers don't fade under hot water.

If you suffer from ghost haunting, then try this: Decorate your house with lilac flowers or even better plant some bushes in your garden. I can guarantee you will have no ghost problems once the flowers and their smell are in your house. Be aware that it will constitute a short-term solution and if you are facing serious haunting problems, I recommend a house cleansing and a home blessing. You can add lilac in these rituals for extra potency.

Lilacs have amazing protective

properties and reminds us of life — that life is a gift and not to be taken lightly. The flowers from these bushes were once used to treat fever.

Use Lilac in spells/rituals (magical properties):

- To remove ghosts
- For protection
- To bring positive energy
- To remind yourself and others the divine gift of life
- For blessing the life passage (birth and death)
- That aim to bring you the pleasures of life

Just for good measure, here is a recipe for lilac jelly:

Lilac Jelly makes 8 4-oz. jars
2 c. packed lilac flowers
2 1/2 c. boiling water

1. Pour the boiling water over the lilac flowers, cover and allow to cool. Allow the infusion to sit 8 hours, or overnight.
2. Strain the flowers from the liquid using a coffee filter, you should have about 2 1/4 c. liquid.

   2 c. lilac infusion
   4 T lemon juice
   1 box powdered pectin or Certo
   4 c. sugar

3. Place the lilac infusion, lemon juice and pectin in a large pot. Stirring constantly, bring the mixture to a rolling boil.

4. Add all the sugar at once, stirring to dissolve. Bring the jelly back up to a rolling boil for 1 minute.
5. Remove the jelly from the heat, skim the foam from the top (I got a lot of foam from this recipe) and ladle into hot, sterilized jars. Process in a water bath for 10 minutes.

After cooking the jelly and sealing it in the jar, the colour fades to a light yellow, almost clear. The flavor, however, is floral and sweet.

You can also make candied lilacs by brushing the little flowers with egg whites and sprinkling them with white sugar. They look very festive on cakes and the like.

Here's a little magic tip: Keep purple flowers by a window that faces the moonlight to draw in healing energies to the third eye and help open the window to subconscious mind.

Well, I seem to have spent most of my May column expounding on the virtues of lilacs and their by-products. I hope to see many people floating around Jared filled with the heady virtues of lilacs in one form or another.

When you do your spring cleaning, wash down your front door with a little bit of peppermint oil and warm water to refresh vibrations and welcome in luck, wealth and abundance. If you have no peppermint oil, mint tea will suffice.

As a hedgewytch, I must explain

that the "hedge" is a metaphor for the line drawn between this world and the next, between reality and dream. Why not take a deep breath and come along? Why not join us, especially now that the roads are passable again, take a yoga class, or wander around our nature trails with your children? Let them come to our story hour evenings and craft classes.

We've got lotions and potions and crystals and sachets and herbs and baked goods.

And so much more.

Remember:

Your task is not to judge or punish. Karma will take care of that. Your task is to love.

And when you can't control what's happening around you, challenge yourself to control the way your respond to what's happening. That's where your power is!

Enjoy this beautiful May with every breath you take and I hope to see you at Hedgewytch Way sometime. Just wander up that path at the edge of town that leads away into the trees and you'll find us.

Happy Spring, Jared!

WITCHES AMONG US!!

There's a witch among us! A real live witch!

She operates under the guise of a "hedgewytch". What does that even mean? Would any normal person be able to define such a creature? I say that a witch is a witch ... is a witch.

Oh, you poor benighted folk of Jared are led to believe that she is some sweet little wise woman who makes soaps and cookies and looks after children and even pets. It seems that she lulls the local women into some mental fugue. I believe that she drives them to fits of madness with homemade wine, enabling them to participate in ancient rituals, performing dances and chanting under the full moon. Mark my words, a lot of these good God-fearing women will unclothe and dance naked and without one ounce of shame.

She writes a column in this very paper and advertises her den of iniquity and promotes her business of ghastly potions, her yoga studio, and her services as a child minder. Recipes of hers appear amongst these very pages. I sure wouldn't be eager to try one. I'd be afraid for my own health and safety — maybe even my life.

How has this become acceptable to the local people?

Why has no one challenged her and her spells and herbs?

In 1692 they executed women for witchcraft. No one ever proved that these women were not witches — not definitively. Oh, sure there were theories — many theories — but nothing substantial ever came from these theories. A witch ... is a witch, I think.

Who's to say that she — Jenny — is not just as guilty as those Salem women so many years ago? After all we have our very own village of Salem just up the road. Stranger things have happened.

It would behoove us to remember the history of these witches. These 1692 witches denied their status. But this woman — this Jenny — she is so brazen that she freely admits that she is a witch. She even revels in it.

Yes, of course it was over 300 years ago, but we all know that history repeats itself. It was then that young girls began to show bizarre symptoms including convulsions, throwing themselves underneath furniture, and exhibiting weird body contortions. It was these girls that first identified that they were being bewitched and pointed out the women responsible. A total of twenty witches were hanged (not burned at the stake, as so many had been led to believe).

Jenny Smith puts to mind one of these hanged witches. Her name was

Bridget Bishop and she had made an appearance before magistrates way back in 1680. A man came forward and brought up cases of maleficium against her. (*Maleficium* means an act of witchcraft performed with the intention of causing damage or harm — even death.) He said that she had made money disappear right out of his pocket and had caused potholes in the road. She was well-known around the town, too. She was a very dubious creature. She went into taverns. She dressed in an obscene manner and she was married three times, apparently having bewitched her first husband to death. A local man testified that he and his son had gone to her house to do some repairs. They had to remove a wall and inside the wall they discovered poppets *aka* the rag dolls which are used by witches to cast spells.

Bridget was the first witch to be hanged. As she paused on the rung of the ladder at Gallows Hill, the noose around her neck, she loudly declared her innocence to the people below. Of course, no one believed her. A witch ... is a witch. People knew that then.

Even the Catholic church, at one time, confirmed the existence of such beings. It was Pope Innocent VIII in 1484 who issued a papal bull entitled "*Summis desiderantes affecttibus*" (desiring with supreme ardor) that recognized the very existence of witches, saying that many persons of both sexes have forsaken the Catholic faith and given themselves over to devils.

Belief in witchcraft is ancient. Deuteronomy 18:11–12 in the Hebrew Bible states: "Let there not be found among you anyone who immolates his son or daughter in the fire, nor a fortune-teller, soothsayer, charmer, diviner, or caster of spells, nor one who consults ghosts and spirits or seeks oracles from the dead."

Do not turn your back on this knowledge. History has shown us the way. Do not doubt that this is all true. Take a little road trip down east to New England someday. It is not that far. One can get there in a day if you keep at it. I've done it. I've seen the graves of these witches. They were real indeed. As real as they are today. As real as someone living in a cottage with a sign proclaiming to all the world that she is indeed a witch. Do not be blind, Jaredites! Open your eyes to the black magic just around the corner of your village and refuse to associate with her. Refuse to attend her yoga studio — or whatever it is that you do there, some cult or other — and refuse to buy her products of ill repute. And most important of all, refuse to leave your children in her care. God alone knows what she is filling their heads with.

I am only allowed a small space in this monthly paper, while she, it would seem, gets unlimited space.

But I urge you to think about what I've said and remember Salem. Remember that witches do exist and are right here among us.

Beware!!

2

"A purple door means a witch lives here."

Old wives' tale

I AWOKE THE NEXT DAY feeling somewhat easier in my new life. I knew the café. I knew some people. I knew Miranda, residing just on the other side of my bedroom wall.

I'd enjoyed sitting outside with her and sharing a cup of wine, being sick to death of my own company. We had read and marveled over the separate "witches" columns in the Jared Times, anticipating our visit today. Miranda had remained reserved, but not unfriendly.

I had dared to hope that in the morning we might accompany each other to the café. But when I descended the old stairs after my morning shower, Miranda had departed.

I waved a casual greeting to her at the café, as I tied my apron and picked up the eternal coffee pot.

"Are you ready to check out the witchy place?" I asked her.

"As ready as I'll ever be, I guess."

"You're going to Hedgewytch Way, are you?" a voice piped up.

I turned to behold Nora in the same booth she'd occupied yesterday.

"We are, it seems." I replied. "We have to get eggs and basil and —"

"Yes, yes," Nora brushed these details away impatiently. "Don't forget to ask Jenny for the solution to the crossword puzzle."

"I hope we didn't upset you with all the talking yesterday. She isn't really a witch, of course."

These words came from Malcolm, emerging from the kitchen, wiping his hands on his apron. "A hedgewytch is really more of a nature woman — or whatever you want to call her."

As he uttered these words, Nora of the crosswords grunted, inferring that he knew nothing.

"Oh, Nora. You know as well as I do that she just uses that for a gimmick. She's an herbalist, of sorts. That's the word I was looking for."

"Oh my," Nora clucked, shaking her head. "She is so much more than that."

"Well, yes," he conceded. "She helps run a yoga studio. And a child care centre."

"She has a dog and cat day care centre, too. And she makes all kinds of herbal potions and soaps and stuff," Nora continued.

"No shit!" and "Really!" Miranda and I exclaimed simultaneously.

Malcolm Snell shot Miranda a disapproving look, I presumed for the profanity.

"Oh, yes," Nora avowed. "She does all those things. Plus, she writes a column in the newspaper every month. And a damned crossword puzzle once a week which I cannot solve this week. Don't forget," she wagged a long bony finger at Miranda, looking not unlike a witch herself, "to take that paper with you and tell her that I can't figure twenty-two down for the life of me."

Miranda nodded with assurance.

"Oh, and tell her," Nora said, "that she needn't worry about that other column. I might have my own misgivings about Jenny, but that's between us. A person should have the courage of their convictions and sign their name if they're going to write in the paper. Anyways, I have my own suspicions who the writer is."

"You do?" I asked, my ears pricking up.

The 'Witches Among Us' had been a compelling piece of reading, albeit written from a seemingly twisted point of view. Almost the voice of a fanatic. It seemed in sharp contrast to the light and happy column composed by the hedgewytch.

Without further ado, Verna Snell emerged from the kitchen clucking (literally clucking) and bearing a set of baskets. She proceeded to stack these in our arms, a list poking out of each one.

"Off you go, now," she opened the door, gesturing for us to hasten on our way. "You have to get back before the lunch rush."

"But where is it?" I gasped, as the door closed unceremoniously behind us.

"Verna told me to follow this road and turn left when we get to the maple trees with one big oak in the middle. She said we couldn't miss it."

"I hate it when people say that," I grumped. "That's when I always miss things."

We set off together. As the road progressed it grew narrower, falling into the shadows of trees lining it on either side. We turned left, as instructed.

Suddenly, Miranda nudged my elbow, taking me off guard. I followed her gaze to behold an old woman approaching us, looking the epitome of a child's vision of a witch: her body stooped over like a question mark and deep lines lay etched into her scowling features. Her grey hair hung in lank strands around her protruding cheekbones. Her whole demeanor emitted ugliness and ill humour.

I gave an involuntary shudder. I quickly caught myself, hoping that she hadn't perceived my reaction. She glared at us with beady eyes. Involuntarily, I huddled a fraction closer to Miranda.

The sun disappeared under a big grey cloud just then. The hag pointed a gnarled finger at us, spitting out an inaudible greeting of sorts.

"Hello," I attempted, striving to keep the quaver out of my voice. "We're just on our way to the hedgewytch place."

She cackled at that, her voice an incoherent snarl. She continued to peer at us, her eyes intent slits in pockets of wrinkles and frowning creases.

Then, without a word, she turned abruptly away from us and proceeded in the direction of Jared. We both stood, stunned, watching her retreating back, bent so low that she almost completely doubled over. Occasional strands of grizzled hair caught in the spring breeze, wisping out behind her.

"Wow! Do you suppose she's the local witch?"

"Well, she sure looks the part."

"Wait though. Didn't the Snells say she was kind of sweet and did baking and looked after kids and stuff?"

"Yeah, but maybe that's just her gimmick."

"Gimmick?"

"You know — like good witch, bad witch. They were joking about that yesterday in the café."

The pit of my stomach turned over.

"Not much doubt to which one she is. Do you think that was Jenny? Really?"

"I don't know. Can't say I caught her name."

This threw us both into a nervous fit of giggles. We rounded one last corner into deeper shadows of tall pine trees and leafy maples. There, nailed to an old hemlock tree, we beheld a sign declaring "Hedgewytch Way" at the entrance of a crooked cobblestone path.

Beyond the path lay a cottage looking as if it had been plucked from the pages of a fairy tale and placed very gently in its own special spot, so exquisite it appeared. The roof seemed to be thatched; the old stone walls had green ivy tumbling along them, catching in the stonework and encircling the windows. A gold etching of a new moon with three scattered stars adorned the deep purple door. I'd never seen a door like it, rounded at the top with an ancient brass door knocker in the shape of an owl just above the door knob.

An old wooden porch hugged the entire front of the funny little cottage, scattered with wooden chairs and pots of various herbs and flowers. A large ancient hawthorn tree guarded the entrance, with dozens of herbs growing every which way. Masses of purple and white lilacs lined the cobblestone path, spilling onto the lawn and around the sides of the porch. Splashes of colour decorated the ground in the guise of early spring flowers — tulips and daffodils, and even some trilliums — interspersed with different coloured pansies, including some of the little ones my mom used to call "Johnny Jump Ups". The whole lawn murmured in the May breezes, a vision of colour and spring splendour.

Hens pecked in the grass beside the flowers while a goat grazed off to the side. I heard the "cock a doodle doo" of a rooster.

"Wow! I love it," I exclaimed.

Miranda nodded, seemingly mesmerized.

"I'm so glad. It is rather pretty, if I do say so myself."

The light airy voice floated to us on the spring breeze. It seemed to have been conjured out of nowhere. We both looked around, startled and beheld ... no one. No one at all.

Already unnerved by our previous encounter, I felt disconcerted at attending the abode of a witch. This bodiless voice did nothing to help this feeling.

"Oh, I'm sorry," the voice continued. "I didn't mean to frighten you. I'm up here. Allow me to introduce myself. I'm Jenny Smith."

As of one accord, Miranda and I tilted our heads in the direction of the voice. At first, I didn't see the owner until Miranda pointed her finger towards an apple tree on the right, a mass of fragrant pink and white blossoms. One of its branches had grown out from the trunk in the shape of a letter 'L', creating the semblance of a swing. We beheld a woman perched there, several feet in the air.

This must be the witch, I thought. *The other witch. Were there really two?*

So, this had to be the hedgewytch. I shook my head, trying to straighten it all out in my mind.

She could have been any age, any age at all, this Jenny Smith. Her face bespoke of a number of years, but her body seemed limber, her face wreathed in smiles. She looked spry enough as she surveyed us from the top of the tree, swinging her legs which were encased in khakis and running shoes. She wore a bright yellow blouse and a yellow hoodie. She resembled a little lemon drop roosting there. Her hair, a mass of grey curls, tumbled on top of her head, fastened with a bit of yellow ribbon. She could have risen straight out of the pages of a fairy tale book herself.

She surveyed us with a friendly little laugh.

"You'll have to excuse me," she lilted. "I'm all mixed up in May."

"What are you doing? Did you fly up there?"

I spoke the words without even thinking, marveling at the sight of her.

"Oh no. I haven't learned to levitate yet, much as I'd like to. I'm working on crossword solutions. Sometimes I can snatch the words out of the air."

She chuckled. I wasn't sure if she was joking or not. She stuck her hand into the air just then, but it appeared to be only to shoo away a pesky mosquito.

"Oh yes," I said, regaining some composure. "Nora wants to know the answer to twenty-two down."

Jenny Smith's laughter rang out among the apple blossoms.

"Nora King has no patience," she declared. "She thinks the crossword puzzles will improve her brain. She's right, of course, but she has to think on them awhile for those benefits."

"I think she's been working on it awhile, actually. She was studying it yesterday at the café."

Jenny peeked down through the apple branches. Two big blue eyes inspected us.

"Oh, yes, I see. You're the girls from the corner store."

We both nodded, returning her smile. And that is when I saw her eyes twinkle. They literally twinkled. I don't know how else to describe them. The flashes of light lasted only a second. I thought maybe I had imagined them until the night of her huge mysterious revelation. Then I knew for sure that they could absolutely twinkle and flash. Such a big mystery for such a little woman — witch or no.

24

But wait, I'm getting ahead of myself. This big mystery took a long time to unfold. We had barely taken a step on the path to discovering it.

I felt fascination, but I felt something else too. I discerned a stirring of unease in the pit of my stomach — a stirring first manifested at the café when I heard her name. An unfamiliar feeling ... distrust, anxiety? I observed her, knowing deep in my soul that something amiss existed between her and I — something off-key. I had no earthly idea how to describe it even to myself. But warning signals surged through my bloodstream.

Miranda seemed to have no such misgivings, appearing completely at ease.

"We heard you were a witch," she called up the apple tree.

I didn't know if this was a proper thing to say to a witch. Truth be told, I had no previous frame of reference for etiquette in this matter.

Jenny seemed not to mind in the least.

"Well, that's what they say," she agreed. "Did you see my beautiful lilacs?" She pointed towards the drifts of colour flanking the cobblestone path. "I'm very proud of them."

We turned to admire the fragrant beauty of the lilacs. When we turned back Jenny stood on the ground beside the tree.

She's just a little lady, I realized then, not much bigger that a child.

Miranda looked at me in bewilderment.

Could she fly, after all?

I seemed to almost hear her thoughts floating through mine. I shook my head a little, in an attempt to clear it.

This place is making me feel crazy, I thought.

Jenny simply wiped her hand on her pants before extending it towards us in a friendly greeting.

"Jenny Smith. Pleased to meet you. Come on inside and I'll see what I can do for you and your baskets."

Even up close, her personage glowed with a certain vibrancy. Her age remained indeterminate. Her bright blue eyes surveyed us, carefully looking from Miranda to me and back again.

"I'm Miranda."

"And I'm Molly."

Jenny Smith nodded, in approval it seemed.

"Well it's nice to see young ladies such as yourselves on this fine morning. I always long to see new faces in the spring. You get tired of the same old ones all winter long, don't you think?"

"I—I guess so," I stammered.

Jenny turned on her heel, gesturing for us to follow her.

"She might not be a witch, but she sure is weird," Miranda muttered, as we followed her down the twisted little path, through the hordes of lilacs.

"Oh, look at all of the beautiful butterflies," I cried.

Fluttering wings of sunshine filled the air on the waves of the heady perfumed lilacs.

"Those are yellow swallowtails. They're the only member of the worldwide swallowtail family to live this far north. Aren't they amazing? If you sit quietly and watch them sometimes there are a couple of dozen here at one time. They love the lilacs and so do I."

"You sure have enough of them," Miranda observed.

"Yes," Jenny laughed a little. "The place is getting a little overgrown, I guess, but I can't bear to cut any of them down. They're the oldest friends I have."

She paused, fingering one of the delicate purple blossoms. As she did, a butterfly landed right on her finger. She held it up for us to observe its intricate beauty.

"Do you know what butterflies symbolize?"

We shook our heads.

"A butterfly is proof that you can go through a dark period and emerge as something wonderful. The purpose of every butterfly's life is to set aside what was once known and embrace a whole new way of being. She's a perfect example of change, transformation and growth. Aren't you, my dear?"

Jenny lifted her finger to the sun. The butterfly remained perched there, folding and unfolding her beautiful yellow and black wings.

"If that butterfly talks back, I'm outta here," Miranda muttered in my ear.

I didn't answer. I had no wish to offend this woman — this witchy woman. She must have heard the remark, but gave no indication.

"If nothing ever changed, there would be no butterflies," she said. "She's very brave, our little butterfly."

With that, she fluttered her fingers, allowing the winged creature to glide away and alight on the purple flowers.

"Come on," she gestured. "Come on in. I'll get Verna Snell her supplies."

3

"A witch does not need to fix problems. She fixes the energy around the problems. Then the problems fix themselves."

Old World Witchcraft.com

T HE PURPLE DOOR SWUNG OPEN. We entered a kitchen chock full of magic. The worn hardwood floors and harvest table bespoke of years of living. Bunches of dried herbs — lavender and sage and rosemary — hung here, there and everywhere from the high ceiling. Bottles of wine lined the old wooden countertops. Cookies cooled on wire racks, emitting a delicious smell of cinnamon and sugar. Huge jugs of lilacs spilled over in all corners of the kitchen. Their scent mingled with the sweet aroma of the cookies and herbs, causing my olfactory senses to reel with delight.

"As if she doesn't have enough of those lilacs around."

This thought emanated from Miranda, but had she uttered the words aloud? I wasn't sure.

What was happening to me? Was I bewitched?

"I do have a lot of lilacs, it's true," Jenny said. "But I love them so much and they're here for such a short while."

Miranda looked a little startled. She nodded in deference.

"Have a cookie, my dears. They're lavender, my specialty."

She gestured to the cooling cookies. They gleamed golden brown with flecks of purple and encrusted with sugar. They looked delicious. We both reached for one.

"Very good," I declared, after taking a bite of the sugary treat.

"Oh, and please take a bottle of my dandelion wine to Verna Snell. That woman works so hard. I like to send her a bottle of my first spring batch."

I noticed then dozens of crockpots issuing a strange, sweet smell. I observed golden liquid bubbling inside of one near me, its lid partly askew. A stray bright yellow petal floated along in its midst.

"It's brewing still," Jenny said, indicating the crockpots. "But I have some already bottled. I'll just grab a bottle for Verna."

"Really? Is it just dandelion flowers? And you can make wine from them?"

We peered inside the pot, our faces full of amazement.

"Oh, well, you have to boil some water and pour it over the blossoms and strain it and stir it. Then after a few days you get the blossoms out. You add yeast and sugar and some lemon and orange and it cooks for a few days. Connie and I make it every spring. It's kind of our trademark."

I felt something soft and furry winding itself around my legs.

"Julie. Come now," Jenny shooed.

A fluffy tri-coloured cat regarded me with bright green eyes.

"Oh, it's okay. I like cats."

"How come it's not black?" Miranda demanded.

Jenny paused, considering.

"That would be too stereotyped, don't you think?" she asked with a chuckle. "Anyways, I've had Julie forever. A cat of three colours is considered extremely lucky and will keep a house from harm. Cats are known to hold the spirit of the witch they belong to."

An involuntary shiver passed through me. She had identified herself as a witch. This bold admission shouldn't have surprised me. But it made me feel ill at ease, as if something in the world was off-kilter.

"I love her a lot, but she's not very well behaved even in her old age."

As if on cue, Julie jumped up the wall to scratch at the frayed wallpaper border. It appeared to have succumbed to quite a bit of this punishment already.

"Julie!"

The cat, chastised, returned to Jenny's side and permitted her ears to be tousled. We continued our tour of this beguiling place. Jenny took us through the hall, behind the kitchen, and into a very cozy room with an ancient fireplace, big overstuffed couches and snug chairs, adorned with various blankets and quilts. Everything here looked old and worn and welcoming. It seemed to enfold you in its embrace.

She must be a good witch, I thought. *Surely only a good witch would have such a friendly home.*

A surge of warmth enveloped me, almost dispelling my earlier doubts. Almost.

"Who's this, then?" a booming voice inquired.

We turned to behold a short, squat woman. A broad grin wreathed her tanned, weathered face, which belied her gruff manner. Everything about her bespoke practicality — from her short grey haircut to her work clothes. Like Jenny, she could have been any age.

In her wake tumbled a boy of about ten years old, and a young, lithe girl with long limbs and laughing eyes. She looked to be in her twenties.

"Oh, Connie dear," Jenny turned to greet the trio. She gestured at Miranda and me.

"This is Miranda and Molly. They're here to collect supplies for Verna. They work at the Corner Café. They're both far from home, from opposite ends of the country."

Miranda visibly started. We had not volunteered this information.

Jenny continued her smooth explanation.

"This is my friend, Connie May. She helps me with my garden and making my wine and everything else. This lovely girl here is Brooke. She's my yoga instructor and she teaches dance to the little ones. And this very, very handsome young man is my grandson, Toby."

We exchanged greetings as Toby gazed from one of us to the other with undisguised interest. Bright, inquiring eyes peeked out from under a crop of brown curls.

"Are you guys sisters?" he asked.

We laughed, shaking our heads.

"Somebody at the store asked us that yesterday. I've just met Molly."

"And how did you know where we came from?" Miranda turned to Jenny. I winced at her sharp tone.

"Lucky guess. Or maybe I heard it at the store," Jenny shrugged.

Connie winked at us.

"You read the sign out front, did you?" she asked.

We nodded.

"Well …"

"Well, what?" Miranda demanded.

"Well, they say my gran is a witch because she's smart and knows lots of things," Toby piped up.

We paused as he continued, "But she's just smart and knows lots of things."

His childish logic made us all laugh.

He galloped away to help his grandma collect the "supplies".

Brooke led us outside to survey the building located a little behind the house which had been converted into a yoga/dance studio.

It, too, looked unique: a long, low building set almost into the side of a sloping hill, a wooden structure topped with a cheerful red roof. Behind it spilled an apple orchard — a beautiful thing to behold, breath-taking at this time of year with fragrant delicate blossoms. The back door of the studio opened into a clearing with a dozen or so yellow chairs. A circle of huge flat rocks formed a circle to the side where remnants of a fire lay.

We entered the red door into a spacious room with big windows and earthy decorations. Yoga mats scattered the floor and several candles adorned a fireplace grate.

"Do either of you practice yoga?" Brooke asked.

"As a matter of fact, I do," Miranda replied, much to my surprise. She didn't seem quite the Zen type to me. "I used to go every week back home."

"Where is back home?" Brooke asked her.

"Kelowna, BC."

She turned to me.

"Charlottetown, PEI."

"You really are from opposite ends of the country," she declared.

"But how did she know that?" Miranda asked, of no one in particular.

Brooke just shrugged.

"I've known her so long that I'm used to the way she is, I guess. A hedgewytch is someone who uses herbalism, healing, and a deep love for nature to practice her craft. Toby's right about one thing. She's seen a lot and knows a lot. When Toby was little, he thought she was Mother Nature."

"How old is Toby?"

"He's ten now."

"Wow, you don't look old enough to have a ten-year-old."

"I had him when I was sixteen. I loved Jenny's son so much."

Sadness filled her voice.

"Toby's dad, I mean. He was Jenny's son," she continued, by way of explanation.

"Loved? Is he gone?"

"He's dead. He died in a stupid car accident. I was pregnant with Toby."

"Oh, my. That's pretty rough."

"Yeah, it was rough all right. Especially when my folks wanted me to have an abortion and said they'd kick me out of the house if I didn't."

"Clearly, you didn't," I said.

"No, I couldn't. Buddy was dead. I couldn't kill his baby too. I came to Jenny in despair. She took me in and helped me with Toby. I owe her everything. I'm doing ok now. I finished school and I work at the bank. And my folks came around. They help me with Toby often now. But Toby loves knocking around here the best. I still come twice a week to do yoga classes, and once a week for hip hop for the little ones."

"Wow, you're busy."

"I like being busy. Why don't you come to yoga tomorrow and see what you think of it?"

"I've always wanted to try it," I admitted.

"Well then, come. The first class is free just to see if you want to continue. You don't have to sign up or anything."

We turned and strode back towards the cottage, encountering Connie and Jenny with baskets of herbs hanging from their arms. Jenny still managed to swing hands with her grandson. They looked an unlikely bunch ambling along. But their smiles beamed brightly and their laughter rang high.

Miranda turned to Brooke and inquired, "Are they always like that?"

"Like what?"

"Oh, I don't know. So loud and happy."

Brooke chuckled.

"Oh no, not always."

"Often, though," she said, reflecting. "They're often just like that."

"Here are Verna's things," Jenny said, extending the overflowing baskets to us. "I think that should do it."

A thought struck me.

"Are we meant to be paying you?"

"Oh, no, dear. I'll settle up with Verna later."

We turned to go. I surprised myself at my reluctance to leave.

"Um. It was very nice to meet you."

Miranda nodded in agreement.

"And you," they all said at once.

"You'll be back," Jenny declared.

"Well, yes, I suppose. For the store," I said.

"We're coming back in the morning," Miranda said, her voice decided. "We're coming to yoga, aren't we, Molly?"

"I guess we are," I agreed, smiling at them.

But mostly I smiled at Jenny Smith, hedgewytch extraordinaire.

And I wondered why she created this feeling of trepidation in me. Affection and trepidation, all mixed up together, like a top spinning around inside of me.

4

"There is a bit of witchcraft in all of us. That desire to heal, the love of animals and the deep-seated desire for a closeness towards the Moon and stars."

Author DJ Hinton

J ARED CORNER CAFÉ ALWAYS REMAINED CLOSED ON SUNDAY. The residents of Jared would have to brew their own coffee, I reflected, thinking of the multiple cups Miranda and I had administered the morning before. Verna and Malcolm Snell attended to their small vegetable market on their own, leaving us free to do our own bidding.

Sunday mornings can be lonely when you're far from your native town. Only the peal of a church bell broke the silence in the streets of the little village.

I felt myself becoming morose. I welcomed the sound of a staccato knock on my bedroom door. Miranda stood there, intent on attending the yoga class.

I scrambled to get ready and accompany her. I held no desire to sit in a rambling old rooming house, consumed by self-pity. Although I had some misgivings about yoga, I pushed them aside.

We trotted through the quiet street in relative silence, heading left at the lane that led to "Hedgewytch Way".

No one appeared in the lane today. No stooped, wizened figure pointing vehemence at us with her gnarled stick of a finger. We looked, though. To be sure, we looked, carefully, wordlessly for any witch- like personage.

We arrived at the yoga studio in ample time, choosing a spot and a mat with ease.

Brooke welcomed us, her smile bright and friendly. We observed Jenny on the lawn with Toby scattering hens in their wake, a basket of eggs slung between them. They had their heads together, looking like the best of pals.

"Brooke, yesterday when we were walking here, we met a very disagreeable old woman right on this road."

The memory of that unpleasant hag made me shudder still.

"She was just nasty," Miranda continued. "She looked like the wicked witch from *The Wizard of Oz*."

"She really did," I said in reflection. "Her face wasn't green, though."

"I wouldn't bet the farm on that," Miranda said. "But she was my idea of a witch. Not her."

Miranda inclined her head to the colourful Jenny, giggling with her young grandson.

"Oh, that must have been Joan Payne. She lives further down this road. She's just a very miserable, bad-tempered old woman."

"First we thought they might be like good witch-bad witch."

"You know like good cop-bad cop," I offered.

Brooke laughed.

"No, I don't think so. But they're total opposites, that's for sure. Joan's really just an old hermit, I think. She keeps to herself and always has. She has a son Roger who comes out to visit her sometimes."

"What's he like?"

Brooke shuddered.

"He's kind of creepy, too. They both have very dark anti-social personalities, giving you sideways glances when they pass you on the road. You know, just creepy." She shrugged her shoulders, unable to come up with a more satisfactory adjective.

"Well, she looks more like a witch than Jenny does," Miranda said.

"Yes. Jenny doesn't look anything like a witch."

Brooke nodded her agreement, saying, "And her place is so warm and cozy. I mean, look at this beautiful studio. It used to be just a huge old building until she installed all these big windows. It's always sunny and cheerful. You should see Joan's place. It's awful."

"How?"

"Well, I've never been inside her house — nor do I ever want to — but just check out the trail leading into her house."

"Trail?"

"Yes, it really is just a trail. She doesn't drive and never did. It's all overgrown with stinging nettles and poison ivy. Almost like she never wants anyone to go any further."

"Really? They all just grew there — those nasty plants."

"Who knows? Maybe she planted them years ago to keep people away."

How bizarre these village people seemed! I remember my mom saying that small town people were no different than city people — that life went on the same all over, love affairs and births and deaths. But Jared certainly did appear to have more than its share of eccentrics. A little old lady who was rumored to be a witch — even advertised it — but resembled more of a fairy godmother, and another one who was not supposed to be a witch, but looked the epitome of one.

We settled into our spots on the big, sun-lit floor as women started to filter through the red door. They ranged from quite young to almost elderly, from thin to heavy set — a real conglomerate of the female population. Just as the class was about to start, Jenny slipped in and took up a spot beside Brooke.

I couldn't qualm my apprehension at never attending a yoga class before. And not knowing anyone. Brooke advised me to just follow along as well as I could. I'd never been the most athletic. That had been my bestie, Moira's, forte. I couldn't stop a pang at the thought of her, far away and estranged.

They had moved on to tree pose now.

Yikes!

Brooke suggested, in her kind way, to stand near a wall for support if we needed to. I needed to, all right. Some of these unlikely-looking farmer's wives appeared to be much suppler and more grounded than me. Miranda stood very straight and tall with her foot way up above her knee. I pushed back a stab of envy (very un-Zenlike). She resembled a tree herself, I thought, tall and quiet and grounded.

Connie surprised me with her agility, perhaps because of her close proximity to the ground already. Even Verna Snell had attended. She must have left Malcolm to deal with the market by himself.

Brooke turned out to be a kind, encouraging teacher. She wanted us to do only what we were capable of, to experience no pain or discomfort.

Jenny proved to be incredible. She could fold herself up, twist all around, and do the tree pose with her foot high above her knee, seemingly with no effort at all.

The last minutes of class, *shavasana*, were spent on our backs with feet and legs extended up the wall. Apparently, this pose held many benefits hitherto unknown to me: lymph drainage and so on.

The pleasure of relaxing after all these contortions washed over me and I realized, with a start, that I had drifted off. Brooke's gentle reminder to bring us back to the present startled me awake.

My head lolled to the side to survey Jenny with her legs up the wall. Toby must have crept in beside her, because he lay on the other side of her, in a similar position. Her hand had drifted over and rested on his outstretched hand. Jenny's eyes remained closed and a soft smile curved her lips. I thought they made a beautiful sight.

She opened her eyes and, pulling him into an embrace, they both sat up. The other ladies came back to life too.

"The Light in me sees the Light in you. *Namaste.*"

"I appreciate all of you coming today," Brooke concluded.

Jenny, in turn, thanked us.

"Have a really good week, everyone," she said, "and don't forget to be happy, no matter how busy you get."

Miranda rolled her eyes at me.

No one seemed in much of a hurry to leave. On the contrary, the women appeared to be settling in.

"We usually have a bit of a chin wag before we head home," Connie leaned over to whisper to me, by way of explanation.

"Oh, I see."

"That was great, Brooke. Thanks. I needed a good old stretch today," Verna declared.

"Don't we all? Even if I don't feel like dragging my butt out of bed, I'm always glad when I do," avowed Lizzy, whom I learned was the wife of a local farmer.

She turned around and smiled at me. I found myself smiling back.

"At least it's warm weather now. That winter was so long I thought spring was just a distant dream that was never going to come true."

"Oh, I think we're all glad of that. Jenny, your garden is coming along something wonderful, isn't it now?" This from another of the women, leaning back on her mat.

Jenny smiled at the group.

"It's doing ok, isn't it?"

"I loved your recipes about the lilac jelly in your column. Those lilacs are sure something to write home about, I'd say."

"I liked the recipe for the candied lilacs," piped up one of the young girls, stretched out languidly. "My mom is going to try to make some of them for Kim's shower cake."

"That's great, Kerry," Jenny answered. "If she has any trouble tell her to give me a call. I've got a few tricks up my sleeve for that recipe."

Connie caught my eye and winked.

"Oh, by the way, thanks for the bottle of dandelion wine," Verna turned to address Jenny. "Malcolm and I had a nice glass last night after we closed up shop. It went down real smooth, I must say."

"Glad you liked it, Verna."

"I didn't know your wine was ready, Jenny. I'll have to grab a bottle before I go. Is it in the store yet?"

"Well, it sure could be, Dolores, if you want it to be. Did you want to try a little nip before you invest in it, just to make sure that it tastes okay?"

Oh my. I felt startled. It was only eleven am.

Were these yoga ladies going to start hitting the bottle?

"I'm not worried about the flavour, Jenny. Your dandelion wine's famous."

I hadn't seen Connie leave, but she appeared now at the side door with a bottle of yellow liquid and a handful of little plastic glasses.

"These are very small," she explained, passing them out. "Just enough to give you a taste, is all. You can't buy a pig in a poke."

Miranda looked askance at me, but I'd heard this expression in PEI.

"It just means that you shouldn't buy something without examining it first," I explained.

She screwed her face up. I got the feeling she thought these women were all a little weird.

I accepted a glass of the warm golden wine. It felt like summer in my mouth, almost magical. *How appropriate,* I thought. *Wine from a witch. It should taste like magic.*

The women continued to chatter and laugh, savouring their illicit treat.

They did not particularly include us in their conversation, but neither did they exclude us. They tossed their banter about like a ball — light and friendly.

Verna turned to Miranda and me, confiding, "I think this is my favourite time of the week. I don't have to hurry back for anything just yet. Mind you, I have a million things that I could be doing."

"My mom used to say that when you're busy, that was how you knew you were living," I told her.

"Well, your mom was right, I suppose. Hard work never killed anyone for sure. But it's nice to have a break and that's the truth."

The women remained in their comfortable spots, seeming in no hurry to venture forth. I suspected most of them had a busy day ahead. I, too, felt somewhat reluctant to leave this place. Even Miranda seemed to be lulled into a semblance of peace.

The side door opened, shattering the fragile peace with the appearance of a dark-haired young man. His looks resembled the surly James Dean type, his demeanor off-putting. He approached Brooke, addressing her in a brusque manner, not condescending to acknowledge the rest of us.

"Who's that?" I whispered to Verna.

"Oh, that's Eric Biggs. He lives over the east hill and he's been sweet on Brooke for as long as I can remember."

"He doesn't look too sweet to me," Miranda observed in a dry tone.

"No, I don't suppose he is," Verna agreed. "He's always been a difficult boy, that one. Never really satisfied ... you know the type. I guess she just kind of puts up with him. He does a lot for her, really."

"Not my cup of tea," Miranda affirmed in her frank manner, unconvinced.

Nor mine, I thought.

Brooke's gracious manner did not waver, as she bid us all good bye. Toby requested, and was granted, permission to stay and help his grandmother for a few hours. Thus, the little Sunday morning group broke up to separate and go their own ways into the remainder of the day.

Walking back, suddenly reluctant to leave, I let my mind wander to the unlikely couple.

All the while trying to shake the feeling at the back of my brain. The feeling telling me that nothing was quite as it seemed at this Hedgewytch Way.

JARED TIMES

THE MUSINGS OF A HEDGEWYTCH
IN THE GOOD OLD SUMMERTIME

Charge wind chimes for different purposes and hang them outside
to let the wind carry your intent into the world.

Ah, July! We Canadians wait all year for the endless sun-soaked days of July. We're so lucky here in Jared to have "ye old swimming hole" where the water is always cool and refreshing and admission is free. If you happen to have a spare loonie and a couple of quarters, you can get a lovely ice cream cone to complete your day. But if you don't, and you smile just so at the proprietor of the IC shack, you may receive one anyway. The scoops are ample and they make every day a celebration. It doesn't matter if you're one or ten or eighty, an ice cream cone is always a thing of pleasure.

My grandson Toby asked me yesterday if I'd heard about the cross-eyed teacher who lost her job because she couldn't control her pupils. Have you??

Anyways, I want to talk about summer things. One tidbit I'd like to pass on is this: if you find yourself with a sunburn, there are several things that may help. You can soak compresses in a bowl of cold milk and drape them across the burned area. The initial coolness of the milk will ease the heat and it also creates a layer of protein to protect the skin and help it heal.

Another cure that you are likely to have in your cupboard at home is cornstarch. Make a paste with cool water — not cold — and paint the sunburn. This will diminish the pain and lessen the blazing red appearance of the burn. After it has cooled, rinse it off completely.

Of course, aloe vera is very effective for any type of burns. I have it growing in my kitchen windows and usually have on hand several aloe ointments. Its relief is almost instant. You can collect the gel and freeze it in ice cube trays. This comes in handy at any time of year.

You can put together a great after-sun spray yourself. Mix together ½ cup of water, 2 tablespoons of aloe vera, 10 drops each of lavender essential oil and peppermint essential oil. Put them into a spray bottle and spray on skin that has had too much sun.

We have a wide variety of essential oils here, if so desired.

Last but not least, you can wash your sunburn gently with witch hazel — which is comprised of the leaves, bark and twigs of this plant. Witch hazel is used to help reduce swelling, repair damaged skin, and ward off bacteria. It is useful for many other ailments as well, from swollen eyes to diaper rash to varicose veins. It comes in a distilled liquid extract form, too. We just happen to have this product as well-being a Hedgewytch establishment.

I wonder how many of you fine folk remember how we became the Hedgewytch Way. Whether you do or not, I'm going to take you for a little stroll down memory lane.

I was a young woman when it all happened. A child in our village became ill — quite ill — seemingly overnight. She was a wee toddler of, I think, no more than two years of age. She became nauseated and started to vomit. She appeared to be dizzy and indicated that her poor little head was hurting her. She had been a healthy child who had never been sick a day in her young life. The local doctor was at a loss regarding her symptoms and tests were inconclusive. I was a young wife at the time, assisting my parents on our small farm and in the orchard that still surrounds my home today. My mother was among many local people who were very concerned for this little girl, the vagueness of her symptoms and her lack of any improvement.

I have always been a bit of an environmentalist, and I was most unhappy with the practice of our township for spraying pesticides along the country roads. It turned out that this little girl had been dragging her hand in the grass along the side of the road as her mom took her for a daily walk in the stroller. Her hand had brushed the grass and wild plants, and she had proceeded to suck at her fingers, as children do.

Once this was determined, the proper treatment was instituted and the child improved.

She is all grown up now and, I might add, a credit to our village, so all's well that ends well. However, because of this, some of the locals determined that I must be a little psychic. My dear mom was always interested in herbs and helping people. She had even been rumored at times to possess the *hellsehen konnen* which is akin to the "second sight" in German. Together, Mom and I researched the concept of the "hedgewytch" as opposed to other types of those maidens.

Hedgewytches focus on healing and divination magic. They work in and around the home and are generally involved in the local community. They are noted for using herbs for healing, spells and nature-oriented magic.

This suited us right down to the ground and so we developed our little enterprise bit by bit, expanding on our knowledge of herbs and country remedies and recipes. We have much to offer for anyone who cares to venture out our way.

Here are a few recipes for organic pesticides which you can make at home. If you don't wish to, you can always pay us a visit. We usually have some in stock. If not, we are quite able to whip them up for you.

Ant repellent

This is a great organic pesticide for ants. Mix 2 cups of apple cider vinegar and 2 tablespoons of dish detergent with 2 tablespoons of baking soda. It will foam up so mix it slowly and allow it to settle. Then spray it on the areas where you've had ants.

Soap, Orange Citrus Oil and Water

Mix 3 tablespoons of liquid Organic Castile soap with 1 oz. of Orange oil to one gallon of water. Shake well. This is essentially effective against slugs and can be sprayed directly on roaches and ants.

Eucalyptus Oil

A great natural pesticide for flies, bees and wasps. Simply sprinkle a few drops of eucalyptus oil where the unwanted insects are found.

And remember that there are plants you can plant in your garden to naturally repel mosquitoes. One of my personal favourites is peppermint. It, along with basil, not only repels mosquitoes, but kills their larvae. Of course, being a woman of magic, I always have sage on hand. Smudging with sage purifies your home, but you can also crush the leaves and apply the oils to your skin as insect repellent. Catnip, which is an herbal cousin of mint, repels mosquitoes as well.

So, if you include catnip, sage, basil, and peppermint in your garden or your flower pots, not only will you enjoy their beautiful scents, but you will be able to sit outside, bug-free.

How great it is to receive the hot, uncomplicated days of July. Lavender is, of course, the flower for this month. Such a fragrant soothing flower. We're so lucky to have a lavender farm close by where you can buy all things lavender. It is a vision of beauty this time of year, with a fragrance that is uplifting to the soul.

The canola fields are also lovely to behold with their unending rows of bright yellow. Did you know that canola was originally called "rape", but they changed the name as the connotation of the word became associated with that heinous act? So much nicer for such a cheerful plant.

Lavender is one of the most widely known and used of essential oils in the aromatherapy world. The yin-yang balance of lavender points to the feminine side, being very supporting of our ability to turn inward and increase our awareness. Lavender is known to promote:

- Spiritual Healing
- Tranquility
- Higher Consciousness
- Release of Energy Blockages
- Easing of Tension
- Calmness
- Purification

Lavender essential oils are gathered from the flowers of the lavender plant. You can use lavender in a bath, diffuser, or mist.

One of the most common uses of lavender essential oil is for calming and rest, promoting peaceful sleep and a feeling of happiness. Lavender may even help alleviate migraine headaches.

Lavender cookies are often found cooling on racks or on display in our kitchen. They are one of our specialties, but I am quite willing to share this delicious recipe with you.

Hedgewytch Lavender Cookies

Ingredients
1/2 cup shortening
1/2 cup butter, softened
1-1/4 cups sugar
2 eggs
1 teaspoon vanilla extract
1/2 teaspoon almond extract
2-1/4 cups all-purpose flour
4 teaspoons dried lavender flowers
1 teaspoon baking powder
1/2 teaspoon salt

1. In a large bowl, cream the shortening, butter and sugar until light and fluffy. Add eggs, one at a time, beating well after each addition. Beat in extracts. Combine the flour, lavender, baking powder and salt; gradually add to creamed mixture and mix well.
2. Drop by rounded teaspoonful onto baking sheets lightly coated with cooking spray.
3. Bake at 375° for 8–10 minutes or until golden brown. Cool for 2 minutes before removing to wire racks. Store in an airtight container.

Yield: about 7 dozen.

You may purchase dried lavender flowers from ... us, of course or any spice shop. If using lavender from a garden, make sure it hasn't been treated with chemicals. (This seems to be a recurring theme in my column this month, but it does bear repeating.)

We must love summer, we Canadians. We're obligated, really. I remember many years ago, taking a shuttle bus in Florida with my husband and son. The woman beside me asked where we were from. When I told her, she said, "Canada, really? That's too bad. You get all kinds of bad weather up there, don't you?"

I replied that we did indeed get some awful weather. But I went on to explain about the changing of our seasons, which was truly magnificent — the autumn colours, the winter purity and the beauty of spring. If you've never had a bone chilling winter, how can you ever love the sheer glory of May? It is in the changing of these that we appreciate the wonder and grace of our summer months. June, July and August are happiness to any Canadian's ears. We love these months. We live for them.

We love the long twilit evenings and the summer nights which go on and on. We drink in the fragrance of the roadside flowers and the freshly cut clover. We are glad, always, to be alive and living when the sun sets on our beautiful summer days and we love the peace of just being home in our ever-changeable Canada.

It is summer. We are happy.

5

*"The success of yoga must not be measured by how flexible
your body becomes, but rather by how much it opens your
heart."*

Millyyoga.com

"THE NURSES ARE COMING! THE NURSES ARE COMING!"
The words erupted from Toby, as he careened past Miranda and me. We had just entered the yoga studio where Sunday morning yoga class was shaping up to take place. The day shone with the sunshine of a day tumbling into the full-blown glory of summer.

"Is someone hurt?" Miranda exclaimed. We looked around us in alarm.

No one, however, appeared to be the worse for wear. Of course, you never could tell. Things seemed so different here.

The other women just laughed, shaking their heads.

"No one is hurt?"

"Oh, no." Connie assured us.

"They come in a group for yoga, when they get time off from the hospital," Verna explained. "I guess you haven't met any of them yet. When they're all together they can be quite, well, quite —"

"Colourful?" Connie offered.

"Okay." Verna conceded. "You could say that."

"Or entertaining."

"Or downright crude." Heather, one of the locals, continued.

"But never dull," Lizzy contributed, with a sly smile. "Especially when they're coming down from a night shift and are on their way home. They work twelve-hour shifts, so they're often a little punchy from lack of sleep."

"Why on earth would anyone attend yoga when they just worked all night?" I mused.

"Beats me," someone answered.

"Buggers for punishment, I'd say."

"*Sh-sh*," Toby said. "Here they come."

Verna grimaced.

"He likes listening to them because they get so tired, they don't care what they say," she confided. "And he gets an earful."

"Oh, my." Miranda looked at me. I stifled a giggle. This sounded like fun.

Four girls, of various shapes and sizes, tumbled into the studio. They toted mats and bottles of water, were clad in scrub tops and yoga pants, and looked utterly exhausted.

"Hey," they waved, encompassing the whole group in their greeting. "Sorry, Jenny, are we late?"

"No, my dears," came the cheerful reply. "Where are the rest of you?"

The nurses rolled out their mats, proceeding to take their places betwixt and between the other mats.

"Oh, Clarise and Sara are still there. Big code brown all over their end of the hall. We escaped."

They chuckled collectively.

"It'll be our turn tonight, no doubt about it," one of them said glumly, rolling her eyes heavenward.

Miranda looked at me, questioningly, but I shrugged. I had no idea what they were talking about.

Brooke began with an inspirational quote. We all proceeded to follow her gentle instructions. It pleased me to have become a yogi. After almost two months I felt quite at home in the studio. Oh, and much more bendy. I liked that part.

Jenny always attended. If she didn't start the class with us, she would join in later. Both she and Brooke came around to each of us, assisting with a stretch or to deepen a posture.

A snore erupted from the mat next to me, startling me, as I concentrated on a twist. I turned to observe one of the nurses fast asleep on her mat.

"Did she scare you?"

The nurse on my other side grinned at me.

"Oh, no. I was just a little startled."

"Poor kid. We were run off our feet all night and she was up most of yesterday at her kid's volleyball game."

"You mean she hasn't slept at all since yesterday morning? That's terrible."

"Yeah, it sure is. Night shift sucks. That's all there is to it."

This girl looked weary, as well. Dark shadows bruised underneath her pretty eyes.

"Wow. I wouldn't like that."

"Nah. Who would?"

She let out a deep sigh, abruptly closing her eyes.

Oh, my, I thought. *They're all going to be sleeping soon. What happens then?*

My eyes turned to Miranda, who seemed to be pondering along similar lines.

"They're dropping like flies," she whispered to me, with a hushed giggle.

Jenny squatted down between us and joined in our discreet chortle.

"They'll be ok," she assured us. "It's only the night shift girls that fall sound asleep and we figure they deserve it after being up all those hours."

"What do you do with them?" Miranda asked. She still spoke quietly, I assumed so as not to disturb them.

I was beginning to think a bulldozer wouldn't disturb them.

"Oh, we just let them sleep. Connie and I usually putter around on Sundays, so we're in and out of here. Eventually they'll wake up and wander home. Sometimes their husbands call and ask us to send them home, but if nobody calls, then I don't disrupt them. There is precious little time to relax when you work shift work and are trying to run a home and raise a family. Sleep is wonderful for the body, especially after a yoga class."

"I'm enrolled in nursing," Miranda said. "I'm going to start doing a couple of shifts at the Jared Manor next week."

Jenny sat down between us, interested.

'You'll be like these guys — asleep on your feet practically," I told her, gesturing at the sleeping girls in scrub tops dispersed across the floor.

Miranda and Jenny shared a smile.

"I think it's a very worthy profession," Jenny pronounced. "And I think that you'll be good at it."

"How do you know that?"

That edge had crept into Miranda's voice.

"Well, I know that because you're reliable and trustworthy. Ever since the first time Verna sent you out here, you've been punctual and she can count on you to get what she needs. You work hard in the restaurant. You're kind to my Toby. And you're a good friend, I think, to Molly."

Miranda turned a scrutinizing look to me.

"Are we good friends, do you think?" I ventured tentatively.

She shrugged.

"We're working on it, I guess," she conceded.

I smiled at her, nodding.

"I'm glad," Jenny said.

"Me too."

"Don't forget to be happy," Jenny told us. She concluded every Sunday morning with these words. Just a gentle reminder, she'd tell us.

Oh yes, Miranda heard the words every week.

But this was the first week she didn't roll her eyes.

6

"Above all, be the heroine of your life, not the victim."

Nora Ephron

"OH MY, ALICE. I HAD NO IDEA THINGS WERE THIS BAD." The yogis of Hedgewytch Way sat recuperating from their class in the wonderful yellow cushioned chairs scattered behind the studio. After yoga, the warmth of the sunshine had beckoned us outside. Around us lay the fragrant orchard, bathed in gold. We soaked the beautiful rays into our very souls as we relaxed together. Jenny had provided peppermint tea and morning glory muffins and I, for one, would have been happy never to move a muscle again. The feelings of uneasiness I held towards Jenny still prevailed, although I knew that no rational reason existed to precipitate them. She consistently treated me with courtesy and kindness. Maybe her practice of magic left me with this odd feeling. I hadn't voiced any of this to Miranda or anyone, and probably would not do so. I couldn't explain it even to myself and was sure that I would end up sounding ridiculous.

I hadn't been paying much attention to the conversation as it drifted from subject to subject. But I inclined my head at these words. They had been uttered with such emotion, directed at Alice Doane, one of the regular yogis.

Jenny's face had filled with empathy at Alice's apparent dilemma.

The nurses all seemed to be gearing up to the conversation.

I better pay attention, I thought. *Something's going on.*

Alice's head bowed in an attitude of despair.

"I thought you liked this girl he married," Verna said quizzically "I thought you set them up."

"I did. I did." Alice's words came out in a strangled cry. "I thought she was a lovely girl."

One of the nurses — Clarisse, I think — snorted.

"I know. I know." Alice shook her head, despondent. "You girls must think I'm a stupid old woman."

They hastened to assure her that this wasn't so.

"But we did try to tell you, honey."

Irene spoke the words in a gentle manner. I attempted a conscious attempt to identify these girls by their names and not just in a clump under the heading "nurses". This proved difficult, though. They seemed, at times, extensions of each other, attired in their interchangeable uniforms.

"I know," Alice repeated.

"You thought she was a nice little lonesome girl far from home."

"I did, "Alice admitted. "I was raised to believe people."

"Yes, weren't we all?" Irene sighed. "But people let you down and a lot of families are screwed right up. You know that, Alice. How long did you work with us? If you don't learn that in a hospital, I guess you never do."

"Are you a nurse, Alice?" Miranda asked.

"Yes. I worked with this bunch for years and years. Now I only work there once in a while when they're busy."

They all exchanged grins.

It's like a secret society, I thought.

"You get close in a way no one could ever believe," Sara said, confirming my thoughts. "We've spent nights together when we thought the sun would never come up again. We've seen people die and we've helped people live. We've been with each other through good and bad, Christmas, Easter, and every other holiday."

"And you don't lose that," Alice said, thoughtfully.

"No, you don't, Alice." Freddy leaned over, touching her hand. "We care about each other."

"You girls are the best. I still feel a part of your group."

"Well, you still come and help us out when we need you. You have so much experience and knowledge, Alice. We appreciate you so much."

At this, Alice's face fell into her hands and tears began to flow, silently at first, then with big gulping sobs.

I felt dismay at this naked display of raw emotion.

Jenny spoke now, her voice gentle.

"You're among friends here, Alice," she told the weeping woman.

Alice's eyes searched the circle of caring women, her face drenched. She gulped.

"I am so sorry."

"Don't be sorry," the nurses said in unison.

I tried to separate them in my mind.

There was Sara and Irene, Clarise and Freddy and several others. But these ones were present today.

Jenny sighed, shaking her head sadly.

"Unfortunately, Alice, there is nothing to be done against pure meanness. Nothing at all."

"But she has my son," Alice sobbed, the depths of her heartache evident in her tortured face.

"I know, my dear. I know."

Miranda had the nerve, which I did not possess, to ask, "What? Who has your son, Alice?"

Freddy attempted an explanation.

"Alice has a son. He's a big, handsome guy, and he'd been through a bad breakup a couple of years back. He was really bummed out, you know, moping around."

"He was sad, very sad," Alice agreed, drops of water still glistening on her cheeks.

"And there was a little chickie at work, a new nurse. Really pretty girl and she seemed nice."

"Seemed." This came from Clarisse, who clearly had her own opinion.

"Well, she did. At first, she did."

'Maybe," Clarisse admitted, her manner contrite.

"So, Alice, being the kind-hearted, motherly type that she is," continued Freddy, "introduced her to her son. He was lonely and she was lonely. They hit it off and then —"

"Bob's your uncle!" Sara cried out.

"Bob is most definitely not your uncle," Freddy replied, reproachfully.

"Okay. I just meant that they got together and got married and had a baby."

"So, what's the problem?" Miranda asked, as we attempted to follow this fragmented tale.

"The problem! The problem!"

"Yeah. What's wrong?"

"They have cut our Alice right out of their lives. That's the bloody problem."

Alice's head nodded in sad assent.

"Really?" I asked. "That's terrible."

"It's so far beyond terrible. You have no idea," Clarisse took up the thread of the story. "That girl has completely emasculated her son. Why, Alice can't even see her own grandson."

"Really?" I said again, in disbelief.

"Really," Alice agreed.

"But, why?" Miranda ventured. "I don't get it."

"None of us get it," Irene answered, contempt dripping from her voice. "There are some women like that. They can't share their husband with anyone."

"It's called 'pyscho'," Clarise said.

"Sounds like it," Miranda agreed. "But why can't you see your son?"

"I just don't see him," Alice sighed. "I don't see the baby. He'll be three this November and I've only seen him three times."

"That's terrible," I said. I meant it. "You're his grandma. Grandmas are special."

"He doesn't even know me. I offer to babysit, but they never let me. If I go over there, Adam comes outside. I never get inside the house. She doesn't even acknowledge me anymore."

"Did something happen?"

"No. I wish it had. Then I could understand all this. She's just completely cut him off from me. He's the only family I've got. I walk around on the backroads, sometimes I drive, just looking for his truck. I always look at the license plates. His last three letters are 'PRN'."

The four nurses, even Miranda, giggled a little at that.

"What's so funny?" Brooke asked.

"PRN is a medical term."

"What does it mean?"

"As required," the answer came in unison, Miranda chiming in. Jenny heard this and grinned at me.

"Oh dear," she sighed, in mock despair. "She's one of them."

"It's funny, but all of the silly abbreviations we use every day just become part of our world. It's not possible to see letters like PRN or LMP or INR without reacting to them," Sara explained.

"It's true," Alice smiled weakly. "We're an odd bunch."

"I know what INR is because my dad's on blood thinners and he has to get that done every month. It's a blood test, right?" Brooke asked.

"Yup."

"But does LRP stand for?"

"Not 'LRP.' It's 'LMP.' It stands for 'last menstrual period'."

"No way!"

"Yup. And once you've seen those initials, you can never unsee them. If I see a PRN in the end of a license plate, then I'll know that truck belongs to your boy, Alice," Miranda said.

"While the rest of us will be struggling to remember the sequence of the letters and what they stand for," I said to Brooke.

"As required," Miranda told me again. "It's usually used for medication and so on. You know like 'take two pills PRN for pain.'"

Jenny turned to Alice and, with compassion, inquired, "What can we do to make things better for you, my friend?"

Alice shrugged, utterly dejected.

"That's the hard part. That's the awful part. There's nothing anyone can do."

"What if you just went over there and told them this is just nonsense, that you can't go on and that you want to see you grandson?" Connie demanded. Apparently, all this seemed straightforward in her world.

"I've tried to go over and visit. I've tried to act as if everything's ok and keep talking. She simply refuses to acknowledge me. When I took over a gift on Ryan's third birthday, they were all sitting in the backyard. When I came, she stood up in front of everyone, saying I wasn't welcome at their house and I was never to come again."

"But what precipitated this?" Connie persisted, struggling to understand.

"Nothing. Nothing. I promise. Nothing happened. She just wants Adam all to herself."

Freddy nodded.

"She has her own agenda, no doubt, but who the hell knows what it is? She's a very calculating person."

"I've got another name for her," Irene said. "But I won't share it. She's psycho, though, that's for sure. We all kind of knew that. Sorry, Alice."

"Don't apologize. It's ok. Clarisse did try to tell me, but I thought she must be mistaken. She always seemed so sweet, you see."

"Oh. I know," Jenny nodded. "Some people are like that. They exist everywhere."

"Remember, Alice," Brooke said, her tone gentle. "Try to remember what yoga teaches: Suffering is not holding you; you are holding suffering."

"I sure am. The worst of all this is that I liked her. I really did. I kept thinking that I was being too sensitive, or that I must be imagining things. But she made it so clear on Ryan's birthday. So, I guess I wasn't imagining it."

"No, indeed, you weren't. She's a psycho, like Irene said." Clarisse said, with conviction. "And what exactly did your son say when she said this to you? Or was he there?"

"Oh yes. He was there. She said it in front of him and her friend Melissa. I wasn't really invited over, but I wanted to drop off a gift for Ryan. He's my only grandchild."

"And?"

"And Adam said nothing." Alice mumbled, misery written all over her face.

"That's disgusting," Irene declared. The others nodded in agreement.

"Well, it's hurt more than anything I've ever experienced in my life. I was heartbroken when Joe died, but it was a clean break. This is so very deliberate. Sometimes I think that if Joe were alive, it wouldn't be like this. That he would somehow make it ok."

"Maybe, Alice, but maybe not. Crazy is crazy. It's just not normal to isolate your husband so he doesn't have anyone else in his life. Her family all live out of province and he only has you here."

"Not anymore," Alice said. "I can't visit. I can't go over there when she has said so clearly that I'm not welcome."

"No. You're too nice and she knows it." Irene declared.

"Maybe he could come and visit you and bring your grandson?" I suggested.

Alice shook her head.

"I've asked and asked, but he won't go against her."

"There's more than one way to lose your son. Sorry, Jenny, but there is. You can lose him in this world just as surely as if he had died. You're just as helpless, too. I'm a sad old woman. I never wanted to be a sad old woman."

Sara muttered an obscenity, supposedly referring to Alice's spineless son.

"It's as if she has bewitched him," she mused.

"And not in a good way," Jenny piped up.

A ripple of laughter filled the studio.

Brooke looked at Alice, her face kind and said in a gentle voice, "Alice, there is only one thing that you can do."

Alice looked up, hopeful.

"Yes?"

"You have to send him love every day."

"That's hard to do," she mumbled.

"Of course, it is. But it's the best thing you can do for all of them. And for yourself."

Alice still looked doubtful. Brooke continued.

"Send him love every day, Alice. He's your son."

Alice replied in a choked voice, "I'll try, Brooke."

Several evenings later, Miranda and I were walking home from ye old swimming hole. A mantle of summer dusk had tucked the little village in for the evening. Scattered wildflowers nodded to us, little beacons in the setting sunset. In no hurry to return to the stifling boarding house, we ambled along, swinging our bags containing bathing suits and towels between us. I often wished that summer could last forever, but never more than during those fragrant hours that hung between night and day when the whole world lay hushed in peace.

I took no notice of a big old truck trudging past us. Miranda did a double take, turning to point at it. It left a cloud of dust in its wake.

"That's his truck!"

"Who's truck?"

"You know. Adam. It's his truck."

It still took me a moment to catch on.

"I saw the 'PRN'."

You would, I thought ruefully.

"Oh, sorry. Alice's son, you mean."

"Yes, that was his truck. I'm sure of it."

We paused a moment, watching the truck disappear around the corner of the crooked, country road.

"Poor Alice."

She'd been in our thoughts after the unveiling of her tale.

Then Alice stopped coming to yoga.

The nurses announced that she had resigned from her part-time position at the hospital. This upset them, as it had come so unexpectedly and without their prior knowledge.

I still thought of her from time to time.

But we never saw her again.

One Sunday after yoga, Jenny spoke of her to us.

"Her poor heart couldn't take any more," she told us.

For one morning, Alice got up and simply walked away.

7

"A bird sitting on a tree is never afraid of the branch breaking, because her trust is not on the branch but on her own wings."

Author Unknown

S UMMER CAME TO JARED LIKE AN OLD FRIEND, like a beautiful maiden who wrapped her fingers around the sweet hours and wove them into days, pulling them from sunrise to sunset with warmth and ease. The days grew languid and long. I grew to love the sunshine and the country ways and all the time measured by the trees and flowers and butterflies.

Jared was laid out, I suppose, like many of the little towns that dot the highways and byways of southwestern Ontario. It would be a typical "don't blink or you'll miss it" spot on the map.

At the junction of the two main roads intersecting the town stood the aptly named Corner Cafe, marking the towns centre. A hub of activity, as Miranda and I could well attest to, the café itself closed mid-afternoon. Malcolm and Verna did not "do" supper. They had a small vegetable market. but it, too, closed early in the day. If you wanted to go out for an evening meal, and didn't want to leave the confines of Jared's borders, you'd have to visit the "Last Stop" — named presumably for its location on the way out of town.

But local people didn't call it that. Goodness, no. They called it "Lorna's Cooking" or, more often, simply "Lorna's". I never found out why, because no one named Lorna worked or cooked there. As a matter of fact, no one could remember anyone by that name ever working there. Somehow, though, the name persisted.

I mentioned the "Last Stop" once at yoga and all the women stared at me, without comprehension.

"Where's that, now?" Connie had inquired, shooting me a quizzical look.

"You know," I said, "that restaurant on the way out of town that serves dinner."

"Oh." The women gave a collective nod. "You mean 'Lorna's.'"

So be it.

It bespoke of old-fashioned cooking — a homey kind of place where all the staff look like somebody's mom or grandma. They came out clad in crisp white aprons to recite the day's specials to you, often advising you what would be the best selection for you.

Across from Lorna's stood the feed mill — quite a big and impressive one. It's not uncommon to see these in rural towns where there still exists a substantial farming populous. They had all manner of bird seed and feeders and gardening supplies. Miranda and I had stopped there on occasion to pick something up for Jenny or Verna.

The tall magnificent trees lining the unpaved streets of Jared looked as if they might have stood guard over the town for centuries. Jared Nursing Home stood on one of the side streets. Miranda had managed to secure a part-time job there. Preparing to enter the nursing program in the fall at Guelph University, she was happy to get employment related to her studies. It consisted mainly of shift work, and sounded like drudgery to me, but she never complained. Truth be told, she seemed to enjoy it.

The General Store (called just that) served to the remainder of the town's needs. Red and white awnings adorned its windows.

Nestled into one side of it resided a small taxi company. For the life of me, I couldn't imagine anyone needing a taxi in such a small place. But you could often see the (one) yellow striped cab, carting around various citizens, either elderly or intoxicated (or both) or anyone else in need. There were only two drivers, Art and Wes, and often they would just take calls from home or wherever they happened to be. Thus, it seemed, a taxi was always available should the need arise, twenty-four hours a day.

Three churches lay scattered between the town limits — the largest being, of course, the Catholic church. Across from it stood a Petro Canada gas station with the cutest little LCBO tucked away inside of it. When we felt flush, Miranda and I would purchase some vodka to mix with whatever we had on hand for summer refreshments.

Smack dab to the east, between Jared and the next town, stood the public school. Until the end of June, you would find the school children lined up at bus stops at either end of Jared, pushing and yelling as they do. Most Fridays, Miranda and I had met some of the younger ones on their return journey, escorting them to Jenny's daycare where they stayed until their weary parents collected them after their working day. Now, of course, they spent the days there.

Behind the café and down a few streets lay, quite unexpectedly, a swimming hole. An ancient sign, proclaiming it to be, "Ye old Swimming Hole", hung by a crooked nail to a nearby oak tree. I'm not sure how it originated, probably as a pond at one time, but it had persisted as a favorite swimming spot for the locals. An air bubble that circulated the water ensured that it remained cool and deep and delicious. Summer days found it full of people from every walk of life. Beside it stood a ramshackle shed with "McAllister's Ice Cream Shack" painted on its side. They provided big heaping cones for only a dollar-fifty. Malcolm told us that "Old Mr. McAllister" had started that ice cream shack "way back when". Apparently, he'd been a bit of an eccentric with a big old heart. Before he died, he wrote into his will that the price of a cone would never go beyond a dollar-fifty no matter what the value of the dollar became. He said he wanted everyone to be able to enjoy an ice cream on a hot summer day. And if they truly did not possess the dollar and a half, then they could have a cone "on the shack". But that was strictly up to the discretion of his staff, because he did not abide "freeloaders".

Miranda and I spent many summer hours at Jenny's. I looked forward to yoga on Sundays and the outlandish conversations that followed arising, more often than not, from absolutely nothing. At least nothing concrete that I could ascertain. Fridays we helped with doggie and child care, if time permitted. We carted deliveries back and forth from the café and, thus, got to know many of the locals. Looking back, I remember feeling enchanted by the Hedgewytch Way even from that first summer. Always I held the notion at the back of my brain that magic stirred in the corners here. At least, the distinct possibility of magic. I remembered Toby's childish explanation of how Jenny just seemed to know things — things that others couldn't know and didn't see. I never shook my initial feelings of mistrust for her. Perhaps "mistrust" is too strong of a word. Yet something lay amiss between Jenny and me that could not be denied. I wanted to love her for her own sake — for her kindness and generosity of spirit. But I couldn't get past my own feelings.

Although I did admire her. I admired her forward thinking. She never put down the opinions of others — no matter how preposterous they might sound. I never heard her comment negatively on anything: tattoos, piercings, states of mind. She accepted them all, never judging.

This made conversation with her easy. You could speak of anything that might be tumbling through your mind at any given time. She didn't seem to care.

One warm summer evening, after spending hours exercising dogs and caring for children, Miranda and I lingered a little. The busy day had left us weary.

"Come," Jenny put an arm around each of us, guiding us towards those lovely yellow chairs of hers.

She poured us each a glass of her famous dandelion wine. We accepted with gratitude.

"Sometimes you need a little lift. You girls worked hard today."

Over the course of the summer, Miranda and I had evolved into members of Jenny's staff. I have no clear-cut memory of how this transpired, but we both embraced it — Jenny being more than generous with her appreciation and her wages.

Between school preparations, working at the Café and working here, the summer days flew by, jam-packed with duties. Miranda continued to work at the Jared Nursing Home, as well.

As we reclined in the comfy chairs, she spoke of an elderly woman in her care to whom she had become quite attached.

"She's really sweet. Some of them are so crusty. It's wrong to think that they're all nice little old people."

"Oh, I think old people are pretty much like any other people. Children, too. Some are nice, and some are plain awful. Most of us fall somewhere into the middle. But I don't think people change much. If you're a grouchy young person, chances are you grow into a grouchy old person."

"Some people mellow with age," I observed.

"Yes, but they don't usually change their whole personality."

"Well, we sure have a lot of grouchy ones at the nursing home. But I've looked after this little lady for a while now and she's lovely. I've never really known anyone as sweet as Esther."

"Esther?"

Jenny started at the name.

"Oh, sorry, I wasn't supposed to say her name because of confidentiality."

"We won't tell," I assured her.

"What's she like?" Jenny asked, with genuine interest.

She took a sip of wine. She nodded at Miranda, encouraging her to continue.

"Well, she's just a little wee lady really," Miranda said. "She's got Alzheimer's or a reasonable equivalent. Apparently, there are a lot of misconceptions about dementia."

"Misconceptions?"

"About Alzheimer's, you mean?"

"Yes." Miranda said, her voice earnest. "It's a big umbrella."

"Umbrella?"

"Yes. For a dementia diagnosis. All dementia isn't Alzheimer's."

"We used to call it 'having your second childhood'." Jenny observed.

"Well, Alzheimer's does account for most dementias," Miranda said. "But there's others, too. There's vascular dementia — a lot of smokers get that — or Lewy body dementia or frontotemporal dementia or just cognitive impairment."

"Listen to you, all official-sounding. You sound like a real nurse," I observed with admiration. It seemed Miranda had found her true calling.

She blushed.

Jenny smiled at her.

"Good for you. So, this wee lady, this 'Esther' ... Tell us about her."

Jenny leaned back in her chair. The July heat had flushed her face a rosy pick hue. Her ever-present topknot of grey curls sported a purple ribbon with summer daisies stuck haphazardly through it — probably the work of Toby, who liked to make his own contribution to decorating his grandma's crowning glory. I smiled at this image.

"She's so sweet. If I'd ever had a grandma, I'd have wanted one just like her."

Jenny leaned forward, clearly interested.

"Go on," she said.

"She is demented, no doubt about that. But some days she seems so lucid, it's startling."

"Startling?" I questioned.

"Well," Miranda struggled to explain. "I mean she's always pleasant, but I suspect that's her basic personality. Like you said, Jenny, people don't change much. The first few days I looked after her, she was really muddled up and couldn't answer my questions. But she's gradually gotten used to me and yesterday I had a really good shift with her. I felt as if she remembered me. We talked about things."

"Like what?"

I had no idea what you'd talk to a demented lady about, even if you liked her and she was having a good day. It seemed pointless to me.

Good thing I'm not the one training to be a nurse, I thought.

Of course, I didn't say this. Miranda seemed so happy with Esther's progress.

"She asked me about my life, but we're always supposed to reflect the conversation back to the patient. So, I asked her about herself, about what she remembered when she was young. She was born in Germany and she and her husband immigrated to Canada in 1950 after the war. She was so serious when she told me that not all Germans were Nazis. Of course, I knew that."

"I'm glad you told her that," Jenny observed.

"It's like saying all Muslims are terrorists. I told her that. But she didn't understand what I meant. I guess it was harder in her time. People were against German people because of the war and she had to put up with a lot of prejudice."

"She told you that?"

"Uh-huh," Miranda nodded earnestly.

"She doesn't sound very demented to me," I observed.

"No, I know. She can remember long ago stuff really well: the war and coming to Canada. But she can't remember she has to go to activity centre at ten o'clock in the morning."

"I think that's fairly typical," Jenny said.

"Yes. It's the short-term memory that people lose first. She told me about coming to Canada and how she and her husband were admitted with the help of the Canadian Christian Council for the Resettlement of Refugees. I guess that was a government-authorized agency created by some of the churches for the admission of ethnic German refugees."

"Wow," I said, impressed. "That's a lot to remember."

"I know. She told me how the world was so different then."

"Did she have kids?"

"She and her husband had a little boy who died when he was little — only two years old. Then they had a girl. Esther says that she was the best girl in the whole world. She has such a nice voice, soft and sweet. I've heard German accents that sound really harsh, but hers is lovely."

"I know," Jenny nodded, her smile sweet and sad.

We both turned, looking at her with curiosity.

"I know," she repeated. "I'm the girl."

Miranda and I regarded her, baffled. I could almost see the unspoken thought hanging in the air between us.

What girl??

"The best girl," she said.

Miranda caught on before I did.

"Esther's your mom?"

"Yes."

"Really?"

"Yes."

"Oh, wow. I should have guessed. She always has such a beautiful bouquet of flowers and baked goods. Well, she sure is sweet, your mom."

"Your assessment is right on. She is sweet. She always was. I go and see her every Sunday afternoon and, if I'm in Jared through the week, I pop in."

"Does she know who you are?"

"Most of the time. Other times she just knows that she knows me. Sometimes she remembers my name, but she always smiles when she sees me and calls me her girl. So, she remembers that she loves me anyways. Who can ask for more than that?"

"Is your dad dead?"

"Yes, he died when he was just 62. My husband and I lived in the little house out back. The one that's the yoga studio now. We lived there with Buddy, our little boy. We always intended on getting another place, but could never really afford it. Then Papa died so young. Julian and I just moved in with my mom, helping her on the land and with the orchards. It turned out to be a good arrangement, overall. We were happy together."

Miranda's face still registered amazement.

"I never would've made that connection. Of course, now I can see the resemblance. But I never saw it before."

Jenny nodded, her face unreadable.

"Yes, like a lot of things in life, I think. I hated to put her in that home. I really did. I mean, it's a lovely place and I know she gets treated well."

Miranda nodded.

"It's just that she loved it here so much. I take after her in that way. This place is my heart and soul. I know every tree and bush and turn of the path in the orchard. I love the plants and flowers and so did my mom. I learned that love right at her knee, the love of nature and the earth."

She smiled at the memory. I'd never heard Jenny talk about her own life.

"It's so hard when a person starts forgetting things. Dr. Jenkins said that as you get older your brain shrinks and that's what causes Alzheimer's."

"I think that it's diagnosed mainly by symptoms. It's really hard to understand," Miranda sighed. "There's a lot to learn."

"You'll learn it all," Jenny said, with conviction. "I think dementia's tough because some people get it so early and others live a long time and never get it. I guess the longer you live, the greater your chances are of getting it."

"That's true," agreed Miranda. "The number one cause is aging."

"My papa would have been so sad to see my mom like this. He was a very stern man, hard at times, but he loved her so much."

"That's nice," I ventured. "That he loved her, I mean."

"Yes. Oh yes."

"Please, Jenny, would you tell me about how she used to be?" Miranda queried. "I feel so close to her. She makes me feel good every time I see her even when she's having a forgetful day. Like I said, I never had a grandma."

These feelings did not come easily to Miranda. Jenny and I both knew this by now.

Jenny smiled softly.

"I didn't either," she said. "It seemed like all the girls at school had grandmas they could bake with or go places with. I used to imagine a sweet little lady who loved me no matter what I did. I suppose, technically, I did have grandparents, but both sets lived in Germany and spoke only a little English. Nowadays, there's Skype and Facetime, but we didn't have those when I was a kid. Only a telephone, and even making a short phone call was expensive. My parents were always very frugal. Anyways, I'm making up for it because I sure love being a grandma. My life is so good with Toby in it."

She smiled, laying back against the chair. The humidity had caused her topknot to curl even more. Locks of grey escaped the ribbon, wisping around her quaint little face. She gazed into the velvet dusk of summer sky.

"As for how Mama used to be, well, she was great. She worked hard, really hard, right beside my dad. But she never lost her sweetness no matter how tired she was. She always had time for me — time to listen to me and ask me how my day was. I used to feel bad for some of my friends at school who came from big families. They'd complain that their moms never had any time for them and their siblings always got more attention than they did. I was lucky. I always had my mom's undivided attention. My dad was strict, with her and with me. It was hard for them to immigrate and scrape out a living on the land. My dad was a good man and I knew he loved me. But there was no softness in him. When he made up his mind about something, that was it. There was no chance he'd ever change it. And Mom would go along with him because that's just the way it was then. Most of the time I didn't mind. There was only one time when I minded terribly. One time when I would have turned myself inside out to make him see my point of view."

She sighed deeply. I felt one of those funny feelings towards her, as she said these words. Something lay hidden inside of her, something unknown to the outside world. I could feel this without having any comprehension of it.

She didn't elaborate, but continued with her story, gazing into the orchard.

"See that line of trees along the cobblestone path, at the end there? See how they're all bent the same way from the wind blowing them that way for years and years? They're fixed in that position, unyielding. They always remind me of a person who has firmly implanted ideas and can think only one way. They're simply incapable of opening their minds to any other way of thinking. It's more comfortable, no doubt. It's easier for those trees to bow their heads down and stay put. It's always hard to straighten ourselves and think a new way. But it's so much better. My poor dad couldn't ever quite manage it."

She looked away from the gnarled old trees to smile at us.

"But that was a long time ago now. Anyways, Miranda, I'm so glad that you've taken a shine to my mom. She's such a great person."

Jenny lifted her glass. The sun hovered just above the horizon, the evening air lay sweet and warm around us, like a summer blanket. A breeze lingered in the apple trees, whispering among the leaves.

"I always wanted to live where the wind talked to the trees and, if you listened hard enough, you could make out the words." Jenny said, apropos to nothing I could fathom.

"So, this has been your home always," Miranda marveled.

Jenny nodded.

"Oh yes. I love it here."

We lingered in a companionable silence, drinking in the beautiful summer evening. An owl hooted, awakening the orchard, sounding surprisingly nearby.

"We all love it here," I observed softly.

Miranda nodded.

8

"People are oceans, she said, you cannot know them simply by looking at the surface."

Beau Taplin

"I HONESTLY DON'T KNOW HOW PEOPLE MANAGE to have affairs nowadays. It was so much easier in my day."

The statement permeated the yoga studio, filling an unexpected lull that had fallen into the rambling Sunday morning conversation.

Miranda's eye caught mine. I giggled.

I caught myself, looking around for the speaker. It happened to be Dolores. Dolores, reserved and middle-aged, always ready with a friendly greeting and smile for us. This seemed out of character for her.

Her blushing countenance confirmed my thoughts as she realized her observation had been overheard in the ensuing silence.

"Sorry," she mumbled.

Jenny waved her apologies away.

"Don't be silly, Dolores," she assured her. "There's no need to apologize. There are no taboo subjects here," adding with a wicked little chuckle, "I've never actually had an affair myself."

"Oh Jenny," Dolores protested. "It's not like that. No one's having an affair."

Brooke lifted her hand up, stating, "We don't judge."

But Dolores shook her head, insisting they had only been talking in general.

"It's true," Lizzy confirmed. "We were just yakking."

"I only meant," Dolores explained, "that in my day you only had to be discreet. There was no call display on your home phone, which is all we had. There was no history inside the phone saying who had called or when. There were no cell phones, so people couldn't get inside your texts and see who said what. Also, you had a little time between communications. Everything is so instant now. You get a text and often reply in anger or hurt before you really have time to think things through properly."

"That's true, I think, Dolores," Jenny agreed. "It's not a bad idea to take an extra moment before you reply rather than repenting later. Although, I think that's true of communication between anyone, not just illicit lovers."

Dolores smiled, shaking her head at Jenny's teasing rejoinder.

"It's a much more open world now, that's for sure. I guess that's good in some ways, but maybe not in others," she replied.

"Yup. Just like everything," Verna Snell said. "We always hear how good progress is. Some of it is, I suppose. But I can't help but thinking some of it's detrimental. Like the poor farmers. It used to be a good life, farming. Now it's becoming harder and harder to make a decent living on a farm. Unless you have a family farm that's been handed down through the generations, the cost to start up is astronomical."

"So much of our beautiful farmland is being sold to developers," Lizzy agreed. She was married to one of the local farmers. "Pete's people are from down around Georgetown and we were there a few weeks ago. Pete said when he was growing up there were farms everywhere. Now there's rows and rows of townhouses. All the beautiful orchards and farms have been torn down for developments. I think it's heartbreaking. One of the old strawberry farmers that Pete knew since he was a kid was offered over two million for his property. Imagine! He met Pete's dad at the store and he told him that 'you have to pick a hell of a lot of strawberries to make a couple million bucks.'"

We all laughed in appreciation of this sentiment.

"You know what, though?" Lizzy continued, her face serious. "He only enjoyed that money for about six months. Then he had a stroke and died."

"Money isn't everything, that's for sure," Verna sighed. "What a shame. After working so hard all his life."

"Well, I'll tell you one thing that's better now, a lot better," Freddy piped up. "Health care."

Everyone nodded in agreement.

"My grandma died of kidney failure when my mom was only eleven. It was awful for Mom." Heather said. "She had to go and live with her grandma who was a real witch. No offense, Jenny."

"None taken, my dear," Jenny replied, with a smile.

"Now we would have just dialyzed her three times a week and you'd still have a grandma," Freddy told her.

"Not likely, Freddy. I'm fifty years old. But my mom would have been raised with love instead of resentment and that would have made a big difference to her. My mom was really bitter about her life."

"Dialysis is common now," Irene agreed. "People don't die from kidney failure anymore. And cancer research is progressing by leaps and bounds. But the most amazing progress is in cardiac research. One of the older nurses was telling me that when she started working, if someone had a heart attack, they just sustained damage to their heart. That was only twenty-five years ago. These people would end up in heart failure and became cardiac cripples. Now we just send them to the city, they get a stent or a balloon and bingo, they're fixed. Even bypass surgery isn't a big deal anymore. They do it every day."

"True," Dolores said. "My brother-in-law had a heart attack one night. Frank brought him in to emergency and they shipped him to the city. They did an angiogram and angioplasty and he was discharged the next evening. Did I get those words right?"

Freddy and Irene nodded at her.

"Sure did. So, you see, Dolores, a lot of things are good now."

"Oh, I do know that, dear. All I'm saying is that everyone's reaction to things today is instantaneous. Sometimes it's not a bad idea to take a moment before offering an opinion, kind of like counting to ten before you respond when you're angry."

"Or having an affair?"

Dolores blushed again, shaking her head at Freddy.

"If you must know, I wasn't the one having the affair."

"Who then?"

It came in a single breath of a question, the combination of mingled whispers from the yoga ladies, leaning forward in interest.

Oh, women do love to gossip, don't they?

This thought filled my mind, even as I felt it escape from Miranda and float past me on the air. She turned and grinned at me.

Dolores shook her grey bob, answering with rueful resignation, "You guys are awful, you know."

"Aren't we, though?" Freddy agreed, rubbing her hands in glee.

"Nurses are the worst gossips ever," Miranda leaned over to whisper this in my ear.

"Well I suppose it doesn't matter now because she's long dead, but I was thinking about my mother," Dolores said, her voice a little sad.

"Your mother?"

"Yes. My beautiful, kind mother. I wasn't raised around here, so there's no chance that anyone knew her. If there was, I'd never tell her story. But I grew up down around Kingston. I only moved here when I married Frank. I had wonderful parents and I loved them both with all my heart. I knew girls at school who had mean dads or dads who were drunks, but not me. My dad was sweet. He and Mom always held hands and did things together. I thought we had the perfect family. So, I was shocked and horrified when I was fourteen and I discovered that my mom was in love with our neighbour. He ran the store down the street where we always got our groceries. I think it might have been going on for years and years, but I didn't notice it until I was going through puberty myself."

"Maybe it was just a flirtation," Brooke suggested.

"Well, that's what I thought at first," Dolores said. "But then one day I caught them together."

"In bed?"

Dolores hesitated, casting her eyes down. An expectant silence filled the room.

"I've never told anyone this before, not ever. I was too embarrassed at first. Then I was too frightened."

"Frightened?"

Jenny asked the question gently.

Dolores lifted her downcast face, nodding.

"Yes, I was terrified that my mom wouldn't love me and my dad anymore. I thought she'd leave with Mr. Goodall and I'd never see her again. We were a family. I didn't want anything to change. And I've never mentioned it out loud, not ever. You must have bewitched it out of me, Jenny Smith."

"Well, it is my specialty," Jenny said. "Sometimes we need to tell our story. This is a safe place to do that."

"So, did any of those things ever happen?" Verna asked, clearly racked with curiosity. "Did your mom leave with the store keeper? Or did she stay? And did she know that you knew?"

"In other words, tell us the rest of the bloody story!" Freddy exclaimed.

Everyone laughed, even Dolores.

"Well, it's really not much of a story," she conceded. "I realize now that most of it took place inside my teen-aged head. And I didn't actually find them in bed, but I did catch them in an embrace and a long steamy kiss one day. I just backed away. I don't think they heard me or knew I was there."

"That could have been innocent, though. Just a kiss."

"Oh yes. That's what I told myself. Then another day I came home from school early with menstrual cramps. Mom heard me and she came down the stairs straightening her clothes and looking sheepish. At least I thought she looked sheepish. She tucked me into bed lovingly with a hot water bottle and hot chocolate. But after she'd left my room, I sneaked down the hall and looked out the end window. And I saw Mr. Goodall leaving ever so sneakily out the back door. I knew for certain sure then. My whole world felt as if it were kind of shifting underneath my feet."

"I guess that'd be pretty tough. Your mom is ... well, your mom." Irene said.

"How very astute you are," Freddy teased.

Irene gave her a playful jab in the arm.

"You know what I mean."

"I do know what you mean," Dolores said. "Even though I was a teenager, my mom was still my whole world. I'd lie awake at night and worry that she might leave us and I'd never see her again. It consumed me for most of my high school years. Then I'd worry that she was just waiting for me to graduate so she could leave. I was like a tormented soul. Mom was the one I talked to about all my problems, but I just couldn't bring myself to approach her with this one."

"You were being very mature for a teenaged girl. That must have been difficult," Jenny observed.

Dolores sighed.

"I wish I could take credit for being mature. I really do. But the truth of the matter is that I was just scared stiff. I thought if I said it all out loud that would make it real. But I still worried about it all the time."

"Whatever happened? Did your mom and dad stay together? Did your dad ever find out?"

"I don't think Dad ever knew. At least, if he did, he never showed it. He always just adored my mom, and me too. The knowledge would have killed him, I'm sure. He was one of the gentlest people I've ever known. They stayed together till they died."

"And you never spoke of it with your mom?"

"Ah, my poor little mom. She developed Alzheimer's at quite an early age. They didn't call it that then. It was known as 'senile dementia'. She was only seventy, poor soul. Dad looked after her at home as long as he could, but eventually we had to put her in a nursing home for her own safety. It broke his heart. He still walked down and saw her every day even when she didn't know who he was."

"Did the other guy ever visit?"

Dolores looked vague for a moment, then gave her head a tiny shake.

"Oh, you mean Mr. Goodall. No, he moved away when I was in my last year of high school."

"So, you never found out the gory details," Freddy said, rubbing her hands together fiendishly. The other women laughed.

"You are incorrigible, Freddy."

She was, of course. But it was impossible not to like her.

Dolores smiled.

"I never did, Freddy. Sometimes I wish I knew the whole story so I could understand it better. Then other times I'm glad I don't know. Once when I was visiting her in the nursing home, she asked me where Abe was."

"Abe?"

"Mr. Goodall. That was his first name."

These last words hung suspended in the warmth of the summer air, as Dolores's little story concluded. In that first year I spent in Jared, I realized that everyone has their own story. Every single one of us has a tale to tell. These women, these ordinary-looking women who were so much older than I, each had some tale of life woven throughout the days and years of their youth.

My mind reached back, searching for the quotation Brooke had offered to us at the beginning of yoga today.

"Be the one who nurtures and builds. Be the one who has an understanding and forgiving heart, one who looks for the best in people. Leave people better than you found them."

I loved the words of inspiration Brooke read to us. She, herself, had become my inspiration, so kind and gentle and encouraging.

We basked in the soothing spell of the summer sun. I thought I should muster up the energy to meander home, but it seemed a shame to leave this pleasant place.

A shadow descended on our little group. A dark shadow. An unfriendly shadow. A shadow in the shape of Eric Biggs, coming to collect Brooke.

That ended the confidences for the day. No more laughter and comradery.

Eric Biggs certainly knew how to dampen a day.

9

To me being spiritual means ...
Whispering to trees,
laughing with flowers,
falling in love with sunsets,
consulting the water and
worshipping the stars.
One hand to my heart.
One hand to the earth.
And sparkles.
Tons of them.

Tanya Markul

"TODAY," Brooke announced in her soothing yogi voice, "today, we are going to breathe in patience."

"If only it were that bloody easy," Nora, stretched out beside me, snorted in a loud aside.

Usually I disregarded Nora's eternal cynicism, but today I felt inclined to agree with her.

Patience. Ah, patience. It eluded me in its finer form. I could force it onto myself by sheer willpower, but that's different from possessing an inherent supply. My mother had been ever patient, thus making her a source of constant solace. Patience remained a virtue that I aspired to and admired. But not something I could breathe in at will.

Oh dear. I must stop my mind from wandering. Yoga supposedly controlled the wandering mind — the "monkey mind" — that yattered at you without ceasing. My monkey mind had decided to go ahead a mile a minute today.

I breathed in deeply, as advised, attempting to inhale with patience and full concentration on Brooke's words.

Brooke always included meditation with her yoga, some days more than others. Today the focus was balancing *chakras*. Oh, dear. I should have been paying attention. Because I didn't have a clue what constituted a "chakra".

I turned my head discreetly in Miranda's direction, but she appeared to be off in the zone. No doubt she knew all about chakras and how the hell you went about balancing them.

I determined to pay closer attention to Brooke.

"The seven *chakras* are the centres in our body which energy flows through. '*Chakra*' is a Sanskrit word meaning 'wheel'. A chakra is like a whirling, vortex-like powerhouse of energy. Whenever emotions are out of balance, they become blocked, and this can cause illness or aches and pains in your body. So, it's very important to know where they are and how to balance them.

"You need to struggle to bring balance to the stream of energy that flows through your body. This energy stream has the *chakras* which spiral inside our bodies. They can get messy because life can get messy. That's when they get blocked.

"Opening the *chakras* is intense. But we should try to keep them unblocked."

Wow, this sounded serious. It also sounded like a lot of effort. I must listen carefully if I was going to get these darned things unblocked. Who knew I'd been walking around with blocked *chakras* all these years?

I felt some of Nora's skepticism despite myself. It all seemed a little obscure. You couldn't see energy with the naked eye, so how are you supposed to know if it's coming or going or what it's doing?

I snuck a look around the studio at the various women sprawled about. They appeared to be deep in concentration — every one of them. I closed my eyes in turn, waiting for an intense bolt to hit me anytime soon.

"We'll start with a grounding meditation. Remember that one conscious breath, in and out, is a meditation."

Well, I thought. Even I could stay focused for one breath. Couldn't I?

It's harder than you think. The mind wants to go where it wants to go. At least mine does.

"Get comfortable on your backs. Turn your palms upwards to receive energy. Breathe in deeply to the count of five. Then exhale to the count of five. Try to empty your mind. As you do this, imagine the earth's energy flowing through your body."

I lay still, breathing deeply. It did feel good to have this total abandon of anything save breathing. My days had become so busy.

"The goal of meditation is not to control your thoughts, but to stop letting them control you."

I heard these words and attempted to comply. The total abandon of the first few breaths didn't last. Try it sometime. Try to lie still and think of nothing except your pattern of breathing. I could do it for about five breath rounds and then that incessant chatterbox of my brain started again. Monkey brain.

'I better do that paper when I get home. I won't have time tomorrow and it's due on Tuesday. Oh, I should pick up some herbs for Verna today too. She couldn't make it because she's going somewhere with Malcolm. I think Miranda has the basket. But if not, Jenny has lots of extra ones. I'd like to just stay here and chill, providing I get my chakras cleaned out or however it goes. I wonder what kind of treat Jenny made for afterwards. Oh, dear, I'm really wandering now. I better listen up. This sounds important.'

On and on went my mind. Over and over thoughts tumbled amongst each other. I wondered if everyone had these thought problems. The others appeared pretty darned focused to me. Who knew, though? Their heads could be fraught with just as many odds and ends as mine.

Brooke's voice filled the room, beautiful and soothing.

"Use the white light energy that you've pulled up from the earth during grounding to run through your *chakras*. Start with the root *chakra* and open them, one by one. Imagine them opening — red, orange, yellow, green, blue, purple, and lastly the wonderful white of your crown *chakra* — connecting you to higher spirituality.

"The first *chakra* is the root *chakra*, located at the base of the spine. Its colour is red and it represents the feeling of being rooted or grounded — our foundation and our stability. It deals with survival issues like security and financial independence. It connects us to our tribe, to each other. It is blocked by fear.

If it's blocked you can feel exhausted, like you have the weight of the world on your shoulders."

I thought about this. My dad had died when I was only six. That hadn't done much for my sense of security. My world had been turned completely upside-down.

I could remember my dad's funeral and putting my hand up to stroke his face. Such a beloved face to me but so white and cold that it seemed to sting my fingertips. A neighbour had gasped in horror at my gesture, but my sweet mom only said, "Let her touch him. He is her dad. She loves him."

Even at age six, I knew what dead meant. I knew he was gone and never coming back. My security had been rocked forever, my world off-balance.

Methinks that it might take more than some deep breathing to balance me and root me to the earth. However, I determined to make an honest effort.

I took a deep breath, attempting to be rooted.

Brooke continued, saying that walking in nature would help our root *chakra*, using essential oils like cedar and clove and even just wearing red (the colour of the root chakra) to enhance our connection to the earth.

"And remember, ladies, you are safe in this world. You belong here and have a right to be here. You can stand up for yourselves. The earth nourishes you. You are rooted and grounded in life.

Feel that white energy light opening your root chakra, keeping you centered and grounded to the earth. Let go of fear and know that you are eternally safe right here where you are meant to be."

I attempted to open my mind and think outside the box.

"Now pull that white energy light up and through the sacral *chakra*. It's right here," Brooke indicated her lower abdomen with her long slim fingers. "It's about two inches below the navel. The sacral *chakra* — or *svadisthana* — means one's sweetest abode.

Your inner child lives here. It's the colour of orange and represents creativity, pleasure and your sexuality. It affects your ability to accept new relationships or situations into your life. It can become blocked by guilt. This can cause you to take a long time to relax and make it hard to feel any emotional connection during sex. You have to figure out what you're blaming yourself for and forgive yourself if you wish to be positive to the world."

Well, at least I didn't have to worry about sex right now. That ship had sailed from my harbour, metaphorically speaking, over six months ago. At that time, I'd sworn up and down and all around that I would never be hurt by another male as long as I lived.

I was a normal red-blooded Canadian girl. I'd enjoyed sexual relations with my boyfriend, believing him to be loving and faithful. I thought I'd love him forever and he would love me right back for just that long. I had envisioned my future with Tod, setting down roots close to my mom on Prince Edward Island, producing beautiful babies and living the dream.

But Tod's future visions had not coincided with mine. This sacral *chakra* of mine might take quite a lot of work before it could be balanced.

No prospects of sexual enjoyment loomed on my horizon anytime soon. Nor was I seeking any. Once bitten, twice shy, as they say.

I took a deep breath in an attempt to open my *chakra*, even if it was just for Brooke's sake. She went on to elaborate about the sacral *chakra*. It could be boosted by wearing orange.

Apparently, you could clear it by reflecting and increasing your awareness of the emotional drivers in your life. You could do creative things like painting and dancing and designing new ideas, any kind of creativeness it seemed. Of course, Brooke observed, the ultimate creation was procreation.

Well, that wouldn't be in my cards any time soon. Still, I thought about all the art and activities that Miranda and I did with the kids at the studio, paints and glitter glue and clay, helping them with dance moves and yoga postures. Maybe these could help with that raw sexual anguish that tore into my body sometimes when I let my guard down in the wee hours of the night. Get my *chakra* balanced, anyways. I didn't know about the rest of me.

Brooke continued to guide us through the healing of the sacral *chakra*.

"I am a sensory being full of creative potential. I embrace life with passion and enjoy plunging into joy. My senses are alive, aware and connected. I am kind, radiant, creative and passionate and in control. This is the second *chakra*."

Only the second *chakra*.

Oh, my! How many were there again?

The solar plexus *chakra,* located between the navel and the bottom of the sternum, came next, associated with our confidence, self-esteem and success in life, helping us accomplish all our dreams. The yellow colour represents that confidence and is linked with positive mental attitudes. It is our personal power *chakra*. We open it by empowering ourselves. It deals with self-esteem and self-respect and is blocked by what shames us.

Whoa! I sighed from the depths of my soul, my mind tumbling back in time.

Moira Anderson had been my BFF. She and I became fast friends on the first day of kindergarten. Our friendship never faltered. We did everything together: graduating from playing with dolls to baseball to biking. Gradually we became interested in makeup and boys. But our friendship always came first and foremost.

Then in our last year of high school, I fell in love with Tod Williams. First love is such a cliché probably because everything said about it is so darned true. I fell for Tod like a ton of bricks. Moira had a boyfriend as well, a nice boy from up the east point. We used to go out as couples quite often. I couldn't imagine Moira loving Jake as much as I loved Tod, but the four of us had a lot of fun together.

I guess she couldn't imagine loving Jake that much either, because after the songs and celebrations of New Year's settled, and January rose to greet us, Moira and Tod announced that they were 'oh so very sorry', but they had fallen in love with each other.

In love? But we were in love, I thought. I loved Tod with every fiber of my being.

The whole situation totally blindsided me.

By then, Mom had been diagnosed with stage 4 cancer. I felt alone in the world and utterly devastated.

The horrible betrayal from Tod paled in comparison to Moira's betrayal. That had been unsurmountable.

"The saddest thing about betrayal is that it never comes from your enemies."

How true rang those words to me. How shattered I had been at the disloyalty from my beloved boyfriend and my dearest friend.

Impossible not to feel like a victim. Unfeasible to gather together shards of self-esteem and self-worth.

"To heal the solar plexus," Brooke continued, "stop seeing yourself as a victim and start seeing yourself as empowered. Just tell yourself, 'I got this. I can do this.' Take charge of your free will and set goals. Challenge yourself to step outside of your comfort zone. Remember that you are connected to the source of all power and it flows through you to encourage the power in others. Get out in the sun more. Wear the solar colour yellow to brighten your mood, raise your vibrations, and increase your confidence."

Nora muttered about the slim possibility of her wearing any such colours.

Brooke commented with a half-smile, "I am nowhere near done yet, my dear yogis."

Nora harrumphed.

"The heart *chakra* is located right in the centre of your chest," Brooke went on smoothly, "represented by the colour green. It's where our spirit lives. It's all about our ability to have loving relationships and to love unconditionally. Sounds easy, right?"

Several murmurs of "uh-uh" slipped through the room.

"You're right. It's not. It just never is. And it gets blocked by grief."

Ah, my poor heart. Just when I thought it couldn't withstand another thing, the cancer eating away at my mom took its final toll on her. She died one short month after Tod left me.

I'd tried to keep up a good front, but Mom knew me well. She'd been mother and father to me for so long that she could see right inside of me and she recognized how broken I had become. Moira had been running in and out of our house for so many years that her absence was acute, Mom feeling this as much as I.

She tried to stay strong for me, but nothing could arrest the cursed disease that held her in its tight grip. It ravaged her body, stealing her bit by bit, gnawing away at her until she was little more than a shell.

She stayed at home with me in our little brick house. With the help of our family doctor and the home nurses we kept her comfortable. Then one bitter cold February morning, her eyes fluttered open, she gripped my hand to look past me into a world I could not see. She called my father's name with her last ragged breath. And just like that, I found myself completely alone in a cruel world.

If ever there was a heart *chakra* blocked by grief, it dwelt within my chest.

"To unblock the heart *chakra*, you must make a conscious effort to receive love that is directed to you. Accept compliments, hugs and smiles. Allow the loving energy that you receive to recharge you with love and fill your heart *chakra* back up. Fill it with compassion, self-love and peace. Release your grief to the skies and let love, which is the biggest and best energy of all, swirl around you."

I sighed deeply. This sounded like a lot of work.

"Because the heart chakra is green," Brooke continued, "you should try to get out in nature and let the green vibration fill you and heal you. Visualize a bright green light filling your heart chakra. We are lucky to live in Jared, so close to nature and beauty."

The thought flitted through my mind that Brooke's own heart *chakra* may well need a bit of work, if the evidence of Eric's behaviour was anything to go on. He certainly did not seem to be serving her very well. I shook the thought away. I had enough to worry about on my own. And maybe he was nicer than he appeared to be.

"The heart *chakra* flows with love for ourselves, others, and for our world. It is the most important *chakra* to keep clear and flowing with ease."

What if your heart had been broken apart? What then?

My thoughts soared unbidden through my mind.

I thought of the various stories that had unfolded here, making me realize that lots of women had experienced heartache in one form or another. I knew in some uncanny way that many more stories would be told here in this yoga haven.

"Next —"

"Oh, God, there's more," groaned Nora.

Brooke chose to ignore this.

"Next is the throat *chakra* located right here." She tapped her slim throat with her three middle fingers. "It deals with truth and is blocked by lies ... the lies we tell ourselves. It's the colour blue and represents our ability to communicate clearly and speak our truth. When it's out of alignment, we can't express our thoughts properly or with honesty. Just remember that deep inside, you know who you really are."

As a child, I had felt believed and loved in our ocean city, in my cozy home. I spoke freely to my mom and my best friend, never thinking twice about being believed for my own sake. When this had all been taken, through death and betrayal, I felt my truth had been taken as well. I had no words to express the extent of my loss and heartache.

I realized that this had slowly changed since my arrival in Jared. But never again would I be the naïve trusting girl I'd been a year ago. And thank God for that.

Who knew? Maybe this chakra *clearing wasn't all bullshit after all.*

"Our throat *chakra* flows with freedom and acceptance of ourselves and others. To unblock it you must speak up for yourself and express yourself with clarity and confidence. When you speak never back away from what is true. And don't forget to always express gratitude towards life. Even when it's difficult, life is a wonderful thing."

Brooke smiled around the room.

"We're getting there, Nora. We have two more *chakras*. Think of how balanced you're going to be."

Nora, wisely, remained silent.

"The third eye is located on our forehead right between our eyes. Our third eye is the source of our inner magic — our sixth sense, if you will. It is the centre of our wisdom and our intuition dealing with our sense of purpose and direction in life. It is the colour indigo which represents our ability to see the big picture and our insight. The yogis tell us to close both eyes to see with the third eye.

"If it's hard for you to trust someone and you have trouble making decisions, or you don't have a clear understanding of your future, your third eye may be blocked. Be aware that your intuition is your ability to know and recognize all that you need for a fulfilled life. It's blocked by illusions usually ones created by ourselves. So, trust your intuition and your decisions and, most of all, trust yourself. Again, it sounds easy, but it's harder than you think."

The note that had crept into Brooke's voice made me think, once again, that she had her own hurdles to surmount in life. Someday I might gain the courage to ask her why she tolerated Eric's obvious contempt and rude manners. Her love for Toby shone so brightly from her. It didn't seem natural to expose him to such a boor of a man.

"I always kiss Toby there, right between his eyes," Brooke continued. "If you kiss the centre of the forehead between the eyebrows with a thought of compassion for that person, it activates the pineal and pituitary gland, bringing a sense of security and wellbeing to them. This can be very healing."

I realized, almost with a start, that my mom had often kissed me right there — whether by chance or design I didn't know. Either way, she certainly did make me feel secure. Sometimes, I remembered a simple thing like that and her memory washed over me in a flood of sorrow. I still missed her so much. I felt engulfed in longing for her.

"Listen to your own deepest wisdom," Brookes words flowed through the room. "Open your third eye to yourself. Forgive yourself your past but keep only the lessons from it. No judgement, just learning. Be connected to the wisdom of the universe. Love and accept yourself. Be at peace with yourself and the world around you. See the world with your third eye."

A general shifting could be heard around the room. We were not accustomed to such a long meditation.

Were we done yet?

"Finally, there is the crown *chakra* located right here," Brooke patted the top of her glossy brown curls. "At the very top of your head. It is violet representing our ability to connect fully with our own spirituality and our divine wisdom. It is pure cosmic energy and governs our consciousness and our connection to our higher selves. This is the hardest one because this cosmic energy is blocked by earthly attachment. Think about what binds you to this earth. It requires that you connect to your perfect self so that you can bring the balance back.

"This space governs your consciousness. We all feel lonely and alone at times. We're only human. Attempt to bring your awareness up to this chakra and remind yourself that you are always guided by love. Visualize a cord of light streaming into the crown of your head and filling you up with its beautiful white life force energy. It can be opened by daily meditation."

And, as I lay there, the thought filled my mind of how lovely it would be to have that energy force inside me instead of doubt, to have peace instead of anxiety. I felt my body melt into the worn old hardwood floor. I thought that maybe — just maybe — I could achieve this wonderful peace someday, opening up instead of turning inward.

"Good work, ladies. It's not easy, not any of this. But for our bodies to function properly every one of the *chakras* need to be balanced. Then energy can flow effectively through us. Say to yourself every day, 'I am pure energy. I am my very own healer.' Everything that you need — courage, strength, love — everything is already inside of you. It's right there. You don't have to look anywhere else."

Silence prevailed in the studio. No one said a word. Not even Nora.

I guess because we were all so completely balanced.

10

"The most effective spell ever cast did not come from a book, it came straight from the heart."

"Jenny, Jenny — I need a spell!"

The last dredges of sunshine for the day glistened through the apple trees that rustled above our heads. Miranda and whirled around to see "the nurses" rounding the corner of the orchard, advancing with breathless excitement.

My goodness, I thought. *They're always in a bunch and all tangled up with each other. I've known them for months now and it's still hard to keep them straight in my head.*

I must, I thought with deliberate effort, *I must start thinking of them by their proper names and not just the nurses. The blonde ones are Clarisse and Chris. Sara is the redhead who speaks her mind. Well, that's not much help. They all speak their minds. And they finish each other's sentences and laugh at inappropriate things and have their own abbreviations which I'll never understand. I like them though. I can't help it. They're just so real, so human. Irene is the beauty of the group, that's for sure, and Freddy is the clown. And that's not her real name. A patient dubbed her Freddy years ago, and it stuck. Ok, I think I've got it. Clarisse, Chris, Sara, Irene and Freddy. I'm not going to try to remember the names of the others who just come whenever. These five are regulars and I'll try to keep them straight.*

It was these five who had regaled upon Jenny today, but Sara was requesting the spell. I could feel my curiosity growing. I'd been aware of various murmurings and rumblings about magic and herbs and so on. I'd never witnessed an outright demand for an actual spell.

Hmm ... might be interesting. I turned to Miranda feeling, in that uncanny way, the identical thought floating from her. I caught it in my mind.

She nodded at me, declaring, "Maybe we'll see some real magic."

Jenny turned to the girl to ask gently, "Are you sure?"

Red curly locks bobbed up and down vigorously.

"Do you remember the number one rule of any witch's spell?"

"Yes, yes. Of course I do, Jenny." Sara's tone held an edge of impatience. "Do no harm. Am I right?"

"Harm none." Jenny affirmed, her expression serious. "The most important tradition of all witches is to 'harm none'. Because, of course, whatever you send out will return to you three-fold."

Jenny held up three fingers. She regarded the young nurse earnestly.

"Three-fold, Sara. Three times ill or three times good. That means that if you wish someone ill, that it will come back to you three times worse than whatever you intended."

A sheepish look crept over Sara's face.

"It's never, ever worth it, my dear, to wish misfortune on anyone.

Aside from the three-fold rule. It's just not good for your own soul."

"So, the stereotyped wicked witch is just a myth?" Miranda asked. "They really don't send out evil spells."

Miranda never minded rushing in where others feared to tread.

"I suppose evil witches do exist just as some evil people live among us. But any authentic witch or magician — or whatever you feel inclined to call us — will never send out into the world a desire to harm any person or animal. Never."

I felt intrigued. An open request for a real magic spell. A thrill of excitement and anticipation shivered down my spine, mixing with the other feelings that lurked at the back of my mind towards Jenny. I wanted to believe totally that she existed as an innocent magician — a witch person interested in doing good. But I couldn't. Part of me knew without a doubt that there was more to Jenny than what met the eye. Much more.

"Magic is really just energy like everything else. Everything is made up of energy. We can create magic with our thoughts and deeds. Magic spells can take many forms from words to candles to oils. It's the focus of our energy and intent that allows these actions and words to become magic. So, magic is actually just energy with intent. But we must only use magic to do good. Magic can be done if it harms no one. Not a soul."

Sara plunked herself into a yellow chair, composing herself with a visible effort.

"I'm sorry, Jenny. I wasn't really wishing anyone harm. Not really. It's just that there's this girl at work —"

Jenny waved these concerns away.

"It's all right, Sara. I wasn't criticizing you. I always make it clear that I don't want any negative thoughts or feelings associated with my little abode. It's more difficult than you might imagine keeping them at bay. But it's something I strive for. I reiterate this to anyone who wants a bit of magic thrown their way."

Two of the nurses and one of the village ladies nodded at Jenny's words. Clearly there had been no shortage of magic spells available in Jared.

I took a moment to wonder if this would be something I might even experience myself someday. It seemed incredible that magic might exist in such a blatant manner.

"I know, Jenny. I wish no harm either."

"Good girl. And always remember that the best magic is inside you already. It's already there, Sara. You just have to look for it."

Sara looked unconvinced.

Clarisse and Irene, caught up in the moment, gathered behind Sara.

"Now then," Jenny proceeded. "What are you looking for this fine day? I wonder if I can guess."

Her smile fell kindly on Sara's flushed face.

"Am I that transparent?"

"No. Not at all. But believe it or not I do remember what it feels like to be young."

I did believe it. Jenny seemed like a young girl at times, like a garden sprite.

"There's only one thing in the world that makes your heart trip on its own beat and fills you with longing from the tips of your toes to the top of your head."

"That's it, Jenny," Sara cried. "That's exactly it."

"A man!"

The cries erupted from the nurses simultaneously. A palpable wave of excitement rippled through the group.

Sara's red head bobbed up and down in eagerness.

"Ready to go?"

A harsh male voice rang into the orchard, causing everyone to start, so out of sync did it sound in our circle of feminine warmth. Eric Biggs emerged from among the shadows, wearing his perpetual expression of annoyance.

Brooke turned. She summoned Toby from among the sweet summer grass where he had been cajoling happily with Julie and some other cats. Mother and son appeared subdued as they murmured good bye, turning to trudge down the path. At the corner of the orchard, Toby turned and raised his hand in a dejected gesture of goodbye.

The rest of us had received no acknowledgement from Eric, leaving us feeling rebuffed.

"He's a bad apple, that one," Verna Snell observed, her eyes following his retreating back. "Not a nice young man."

"You're right, of course, Verna." Jenny agreed. "But it will sort itself out before too long. Never fear."

"Oh, you and your magic," Nora snorted at the innuendo.

"Just wait and see," Jenny replied airily.

She turned to Sara, sensing that the young redhead might burst with contained excitement.

"And as for you, Sara dear. Is the object of your affection worthy of it? I'd like to know."

"Oh yes, Jenny. He's nothing like that Eric Biggs. I don't know why Brooke puts up with him. She is beautiful and smart and sweet."

"That she is," Jenny agreed. "But what about your beau, missy?"

"He's not my beau, Jenny."

"That's the problem," Irene explained. "She wants him to be."

"Ah," Jenny nodded. "How far have you proceeded in all this? Have you spoken to him?"

"Oh yes," Sara's eyes sparkled now, her words tumbling over each other, eager to be understood. "He's very sweet. He comes from Alberta, so he doesn't know many people around here yet. He just started at the hospital two months ago."

"He's a nurse," Clarisse interjected.

"A nurse. So, he must be compassionate and caring, like you girls."

"Like us!" They all laughed together.

I'd never known a male nurse before. It made me curious. Maybe Sara could bring him to yoga.

I spoke these words aloud without thinking. Several of the woman grunted with laughter, much to my chagrin.

But Jenny seemed to consider it.

"You could, you know. Lots of men practice yoga. It promotes flexibility and muscle strength and keeps you balanced too. Men need that as well as women. You could bring him here on a Sunday morning."

Sara eyed Jenny with skepticism.

"I could see about that, Jenny. It might be an idea," she replied slowly.

"Brooke and I have been tossing the idea around of a men's yoga class, actually," Jenny continued.

"But she wants a real spell!" Freddy burst out. Sara nodded vigorously.

"I do! I do!"

Jenny chuckled, making me wonder if she'd been pulling Sara's chain all along.

"Does this paragon of virtue have a name, pray tell?"

"Jamie."

"Ah. Jamie. All right, my dear. I'll see what I can do."

Jenny turned, the others following her through the orchard and into the back door of the kitchen. We'd been inside her kitchen dozens of times of course, but never had I noticed this door standing behind the big counter. An abundance of hanging herbs and, it must be admitted, cobwebs obscured it from easy view of the kitchen.

Miranda and I hesitated, but Connie told us that we were welcome to follow if we so desired.

"Really?" I asked, excitement welling in me.

"Sure. Most of the girls have been down there at one time or another. It's interesting to see all of the oils and herbs and so on."

Did that mean that lots of these women had received a magic spell? Wow.

Miranda and I carefully picked our way down the rickety stairs, creaking in the wake of the nurse's steps.

An amazing room unfolded before us, as we made our descent. The scent of rosemary and lavender hung in fragrant clouds above our heads. Row upon row of jars filled with dried flowers-stalks and petals adorned a huge wooden table that seemed to stretch across the entire basement. Smaller tables lay scattered about, covered with assorted oils and crystals. Wicker baskets heaped to overflowing with herbs and berries and pebbles stood at every angle. The counter held an old-fashioned sickle and two separate mortar and pestle sets. A baking rack stretched with cheesecloth served as a large drying rack for bundles of various herbs sitting atop it. Dozens and dozens of rolls of ribbons in every colour of the rainbow interspaced with scraps of fabric of all shapes and sizes lay strewn everywhere.

A sign hung amongst this hodgepodge, looking as if it had been there since time began. Old-fashioned letters bore the message: "I gather this herb for a magic spell, bringing harm to none — may it turn out well."

Hundreds of different coloured candles, tapers, and votives and mini tealights adorned another crooked shelf. A frayed chart, nailed above the shelf, proclaimed wisdom about the variety of colours and candles.

I could only decipher some of it:

Blue – Peace, hope, healing, the element of water.
Green – prosperity, health, gardening, faery magic, the element of earth.
Pink – Affection, friendship, children's magic.
Yellow – creativity, communication, knowledge, the element of air.

An old wooden sign beheld the message: "Add sugar to a spell for stopping gossip. Put the name of someone bothering you in a baggie of water in the freezer to freeze their actions."

Another said, "A witch lives here and Magic is afoot!"

Sprawled across the actual wall written in black sharpie with a firm hand read, "I don't believe in magic, darling. I am magic."

There were other messages written hither, thither, and yon, but many lay obscured behind bits of posters or messages on paper. I marveled at the literature arrayed on these walls. You could sit here for days and just read them.

The women gathered around this paraphernalia, milling about as women do. It could have been any old meeting of a book club or sewing group, so ordinary did it appear. Even Jenny herself looked like a sweet little lady with grey curls and flowers swinging about on top of her head. Not a witch!

Jenny remained calm and unhurried even as Sara's excitement escalated.

"I must go over the rules of magic, Sara. I know some of you have had spells at different times in your lives, but nonetheless I am going to go over the mainstays so there's no confusion. And to ground us all a little bit."

Sara nodded.

Jenny continued, her hands passing amongst the flower heads and oils, lingering for moments at a time.

"The art of magic is really just manipulating psychic forces to cause some change. Sometimes small ones, but sometimes quite big ones. Magic can tap into the hidden powers of herbs and plants to produce differences in our lives. Of course, most paramount of all is that we must always believe. And we must want any change for the powers of goodness, never for evil."

Jenny eyes fell on Sara, then searched over the intent, concentrated group of women. The air fairly crackled with energy.

She continued, her fingers ever moving.

"Magic is a conscious manipulation of the energies that already exist in our world. It's a lot like cooking really. You just follow the directions as you would a recipe. Magic is a very old-fashioned art and it requires all our attention. No multi-tasking. We can't rush a spell. It's not instantaneous. It requires effort and patience. We have to linger a little so we can feel it right through us."

Jenny nodded towards a picture of Einstein on the wall, bearing the quotation:

> *Everything is energy and that's all there is to it. Match the frequency of the reality you want and you cannot help but get that reality. It can be no other way. This is not philosophy. This is physics.*

"You can think of it like the late, great Einstein, if you want. Think of your energy and your intention. That's what makes or breaks the spell."

Sara listened intently, her eyes glued to Jenny's face.

"Magic should never be performed for pay," Jenny continued.

"Or you'd be rich, right, Jenny?" Freddy piped up in her usual cavalier manner.

Jenny chuckled.

"Pay would tempt the magician to use the art for evil or frivolous means," she explained. "It's against the rules. By the same token, magic should never be used to play up one's vanity or pride. Magic is meant to be a divine art, so you have to try and keep your thoughts pure and true to our purpose. You have to have faith or we won't get positive results."

"I do, Jenny, I do!"

"And most important, of course, is to harm none. No magic ever requires you to harm another creature."

Sara nodded, her face solemn.

Jenny dragged a book out from underneath the cupboard. It appeared to weigh at least as much as she did. The dusty ancient cover bore dabs of various coloured marks and scraps of old calligraphy.

Jenny pulled her reading glasses from — where exactly? From thin air? Or had they been hiding amongst her hair ribbon and flowers? If so, I'd not previously observed them. Nonetheless, they now adorned her dainty nose. Her brow furrowed in concentration.

"Love, hmm. Love." She shook her head from side to side as she murmured, "Romance. Love. Make him love me. Is that it?"

Her eyes flew to Sara, questioning.

"Yes, Jenny. Oh, yes. That's it, all right."

"Here we go, then. Now remember, you must do this at home alone. You must pour all your heart and faith into the magic of this spell. Choose a spot that's all yours and yours alone, a spot happy and peaceful and sacred to your magic. This spell is most powerful on a New Moon Friday."

I had my doubts that Sara would be able to wait until one of those came along.

"First, blend honey, jasmine flower water, orange flower water, and rose water in a shallow dish."

Jenny drew these items onto the counter in front of her, as she named them.

"Place a pink votive candle in the centre of the saucer. Then, using a pin or a rose thorn scratch his name and yours, enclosed with a heart on each of five sugar cubes."

She was even producing the sugar cubes. *My goodness, was there nothing she didn't have down here in her witch's lair?*

"Arrange the sugar cubes around the candle in the saucer. Then strongly visualize the fulfillment of your heart's desire. Then you're ready to light the candle."

Jenny laid down a box of odd little matches.

Are they magic matches? I wondered.

Miranda shrugged, catching my eye.

"Before you strike the match, you must meditate on your purpose and set your intention. Focus all your energy on your spell as you light the flame. Believe in the magic of the flame. Never blow out a candle that has been used in a spell. Always use a candle snuffer or wet your thumb and forefinger and pinch the wick quickly. When you do extinguish the candle, extinguish it with gratitude, and allow the smoke to carry your intention."

Jenny looked up finally, spreading her hands out and smiling at Sara.

"For even more intense results, repeat this every night for five consecutive nights. And remember, Sara dear, it's your intention that creates the magic. The magic doesn't exist in these things. It exists inside of you."

Jenny arranged the articles with great care inside a woven basket, presenting them to the young redhead with a smile of encouragement.

"Oh, I will, Jenny, I will. Thank you so much."

She threw her arms around Jenny's neck, unwittingly knocking her topknot askew. Clutching the precious basket in her hands, she turned, erupting up the stairs and out the dusty door.

"If patience was something I could collect and sell in a bottle, I'd be one very important magician, wouldn't I?" Jenny asked, smiling at Sara's hasty departure. Her words held no sting.

She turned to contemplate the conglomeration of items scattered across the table.

Connie, explaining that Jenny liked to tidy her "magic bits and bobs" in solitude, ushered us out of the extraordinary room.

"Wow, I hope it works," Irene said, as we all blinked, emerging into the sunlight. "She's been pining after that guy for weeks now."

"Oh, it'll work," Connie assured her. "If it's meant to, it will work."

"But how will you know if it's meant to?" I asked.

"We won't know. But Jenny will."

All very dark and mysterious indeed. I made a mental note to inquire about Sara and her young man at a later date.

"She'll bring Jenny something next time she comes to yoga," Irene observed.

"As payment?" Miranda ventured then, correcting herself. "Oh no. There's no payment, right?"

"That's right. But we usually give some token of thanks to show appreciation. Jenny never asks for anything, but people bring her things anyways."

Connie nodded, explaining, "That's why she gets such good service. She always gets her snow ploughed in the winter. She's never stranded. That young Jed McClure ploughs her driveway first thing in the morning and his father did before him. She always offers to pay, but Jed never accepts. He just asks her to keep him and his family safe."

"That's just one example," Clarisse agreed. "Lots of people do extra things for her."

"Is that true? I mean the part about her keeping the McClures safe? And the other people? Is that really true?"

I directed my question at Connie. Always I looked to unravel the part of Jenny I didn't understand. The part that niggled at me, elusive, even a little sinister at times.

Connie shrugged.

"The thing is they think it's true, you see. And that's what matters. If you were to ask Jed, he'd give Jenny all the credit for keeping his family safe. And he's happy to plough her driveway. She always makes him a cup of coffee, — her black magic she calls it, — and something she's baked for him to eat on the fly. He says it doesn't matter what time he comes — even if it's the middle of the night — she's always up and brings him out his coffee and treat."

"Have you never wondered why her chairs are so comfortable? Way more than any other lawn chairs anywhere."

"Or why you always look so good in her bathroom mirror?"

I reflected with astonishment that I had indeed noticed these things. I just hadn't thought they held any particular significance, certainly not magic.

I didn't know if I believed everything I'd seen and heard this evening. But it did give a person food for thought.

Miranda and I mulled it over amongst ourselves as we meandered down the crooked little cobblestone path, heading for the rooming house.

As of one accord, we paused at the end of the path to look back at Hedgewytch Way cottage. The velvety dusk had settled around it, tucking it in for the night. It lay peaceful and serene in its fairy book setting.

Jenny stood at the purple door, her arm lifted in farewell to us. As if there'd been no doubt that we would turn and wave back at her. As if she had been standing there, waiting only for that very thing.

11

"The day that I decided my life was magical, there was suddenly magic all around me."

HOOT! HOOT!

I jumped a little from my slumped position in the yellow chair.

The days were getting shorter, dusk descending earlier, although I tried to keep this thought at bay. Summer days are so precious. Nonetheless we could feel the longer, cooler days marching relentlessly across the calendar, heading our way.

"What was that?" I asked.

Toby lay in the grass between his mom and his grandma. He turned over to consider the gnarled branches of the lordly oak tree that guarded the entrance to our orchard.

"Oh, it's just Hoot," he told me.

"I know it's a hoot. Is it an owl?"

"It really is Hoot," the boy assured me, his young face solemn. "And it really is an owl. It's Grandma's pet owl."

"How come I've never heard it before?"

"You have to be here at just the exact time. He's very particular about when he's seen and heard."

I turned to Jenny with questioning eyes. I didn't want to appear skeptical, but I thought Toby might be having me on.

"You're right, dear. He is very particular. He's not exactly my pet, though. You're not really supposed to have owls for pets in Ontario. He is quite wild and free. I just kind of look after him. He lives in our old abandoned shed."

"Well, isn't that what a pet is?" Toby's expression feigned gravity, his brown eyes round and inquiring. "You give it a home and you look after it."

Jenny laughed and tousled his hair. Then she started to tickle him and the two of them ended up in a heap together in the soft summer grass.

Brooke looked on, a tolerant smile on her face.

"One's as bad as the other," she observed.

Miranda leaned towards Brooke to ask about the authenticity of the hooter.

"Oh, he does exist and that is his name. At least that's what Jenny calls him. She's had him a few years now."

"We had owls out west," Miranda said. "but they were really wild. I never saw one up close, only in a zoo. I always heard they could be vicious if you got too close to them. This hoot fellow sounds like he's pretty close."

Jenny gave Toby's head one final rubbing with grass then settled herself back in her chair. Toby crawled over and laid his head in her lap, hugging her around the knees. Jenny stroked his brown curls and bent to deposit a kiss on his sunburnt forehead.

If someone were to draw a picture of them just then, it would be entitled "Love".

"Oh, they certainly can be vicious. No doubt about that."

"But not Hoot, right, Grandma? He's not vicious."

Toby lifted his head to make this inquiry. I watched his eyes shift to the orchard path and saw the light fade from them. I didn't have to look. I knew who could wipe the joy out of this boy's face without a single spoken word.

Eric's features seemed to glower as they fell on Toby and his grandma. The picture of love, so beautiful to my eyes, seemed lost on Eric Biggs.

"Ready to go?"

He directed these brusque words at Brooke, ignoring the rest of us.

Brooke gestured to Toby. He scrambled to his feet.

Jenny said nothing. She remained calm and unruffled, her eyes following the departure of Brooke and Toby with the taciturn young man.

At the edge of the orchard, Toby looked back and blew her a kiss. She responded in kind, smiling at him.

He turned to trudge reluctantly behind his mom and Eric.

Jenny directed her attention to the rest of us.

At this point, I must mention something about the other ladies who had crept into our Jared lives — the "yogis" — as Brooke fondly referred to them. I've already described the bunch of nurses. They had to be sorted out first, being such a colourful group.

But others attended regularly. There was, of course, Connie, Jenny's indispensable assistant. Her thick set body stood low to the ground, but I'd seen her move at a high rate of speed when necessary. Her salt and pepper hair lay thick against her head, cut in a short no-nonsense fashion. Her words came outspoken and blunt, but never unkind.

Verna Snell always seemed an unlikely candidate for yoga, being such a brusque businesswoman, but she came almost every Sunday morning. I liked her. As a boss, Miranda and I found her to be fair and straightforward, appreciative of hard work. She belonged to those women who are never uplifted, but never melancholy-middling, my uncle used to say.

Dolores, whom I supposed to be sixty or more, moved with a grace and fitness that belied her age. Her grey bob shone in sleek lines. She was always well groomed, her clothes colour-coordinated. Since she had shared her story with us, I'd felt curiously closer to her. The concept of a person that age having a whole other life intrigued me. It had taken my mind beyond the innate selfish outlook of my youth.

Kerry and Dora were easily the youngest of the regulars. Both had small children and had opted to be stay-at-home moms. That's where their similarities ended, however. Kerry was bright and cheerful, whereas Dora appeared always to be fretting about one thing or another. She did not often stay, as many of the others did, for tea and companionship. Always, it seemed she had a pressing task or errand of some sort to attend to.

Lizzy, Heather, and Faye, the remaining of the regulars, were all farm wives of about the same age. Sometimes I wondered if their busy lives held little in the way of social outings and this might be the reason they embraced the yoga community. Lizzy portrayed a serious countenance most of the time, occasionally emitting a caustic remark. Heather's demeanor was always quiet, always a little unsure, a little apologetic, offending easily. Sometimes she could be exhausting.

Faye was a beauty, inside and out. Well into her fifties, she still glowed with health and cheerfulness. Her gentleness and friendly kindness endeared her to me, especially in the first few weeks when I was unfamiliar with all things yoga. I never heard her say an unkind word in all the time that I knew her.

That just left Nora, definitely the oldest yogi, probably well into her seventies and the crustiest one by far. We'd first encountered her at the café, poring over a crossword puzzle, and she continued to ask us for answers to various clues. She never thought it fair, she said, for Jenny to just "pluck words from the atmosphere" when she herself had to struggle so hard for answers. Although she seemed to perpetually find life unfair, she was colourful. You never knew what she might say next.

"Hoot! Hoot!"

"Hoot is being unusually sociable tonight," Jenny observed.

"Not like some people I could name," muttered Lizzy.

"Who cooks for you? Who cooks for you all?"

These words sang out from Jenny in a voice that had a remarkable resemblance to the great hooting calls bounding through the orchard. The sound came in a series of eight accented hoots ending in an *oo-aw* with a downward pitch.

"Who cooks for you? Who cooks for you all?"

I felt rather than heard a slight rustling sound. My breath caught in my throat at the unbelievable sight of an immense owl soaring noiselessly into view. His movement resembled coasting more than flying, and he landed with infinite grace in the crook of a nearby apple tree. Then he lifted his regal brown and white striped head, looking around with complete disdain. He had to be at least twenty inches long and his wingspan spread across the evening in magnificence. Dark rings covered Hoot's pale face from which materialized a yellow beak and enormous brown eyes. Rows of brown barred his chest horizontally and his belly vertically.

Jenny stood up and drew a little away from the rest of us. She plucked an old sweater from the back of one of the orchard chairs. She wrapped it deftly around her hand and forearm. Then she extended her arm out towards the owl offering him a perch. She continued with her eight-count call, her voice lower now and softer. In between these calls she clucked and cooed gently, her whole being fixed on the owl's presence.

Hoot seemed to be observing us from the safety of his position in the apple branch. He now turned his head and looked straight at Jenny with deep soulful eyes. Then, with an air of nonchalance, he drifted down and alighted on the sweater encasing her arm.

Miranda and I gasped at this unprecedented sight. It boggled my mind to witness a creature of such grandeur and stature displaying this degree of casual familiarity.

Jenny continued to croon in a low voice. He cocked his head at her. She reached out her free hand and ever so softly caressed his beautiful feathers. His huge, unblinking eyes stared straight into hers. He looked as if he had perched thus hundreds of times. Perhaps he had.

The sight seemed unreal — Jenny being such a tiny woman, the owl so huge and regal perched atop her forearm. Her grey topknot, fastened with a green striped ribbon, tumbled a little as she nodded her head at the wise creature in accordance with her whispered words.

"He's quite a fine fellow, isn't he now?" Jenny asked, still in that melodious soft voice. "Very fine indeed."

Miranda and I nodded in fascinated agreement, keeping a wary eye on this mysterious being.

"They're very smart, very wise, you know," Jenny continued. "Doesn't our Hoot look ever so wise?"

We agreed, in hushed voices, that he did indeed look wise.

"Did you know that a group of owls is actually called a wisdom or a study of owls? It can be called a parliament too. They all show how intelligent these fellows are."

I dared to take a closer look and observed his large talons with two toes facing backwards and two toes facing forwards. He appeared strong and mighty as he clung to the slender arm.

He turned his beautiful brown head away from Jenny directing it to Miranda and me. I held my breath as he turned around to the rest of our circle of women.

"My God," Miranda breathed, "Does his head go all the way around?"

"No, not quite. Only about two hundred and seventy degrees. He can't turn his eyes so he must turn his head when he is looking around. He has three eyelids. One is for blinking, one for sleeping and one for keeping his eye clean and healthy."

Her voice remained low and monotone.

She began to address the owl again, with a series of croons and murmurs. He gazed solemnly into her face. Then, giving an enormous blink, he spread his substantial wings for our admiration. He hooted and, displaying great majesty and grace, slipped away without a sound into the dark shadows of the trees.

Jenny removed the sweater from her arm and hung it back on the chair. I had seen that sweater slung across the yellow chair numerous times, never attaching any specific meaning to it. Which proved that you just never knew what might prove to be of significance at this beguiled place.

Jenny sighed, slumping back into her chair.

"He's getting so big. He must be eating a lot of mice lately. Or squirrels. Or birds. He has a little perch up there in the old oak tree past all the apple trees. That's where he stalks his prey. He's a great hunter."

"He is just wonderful," I breathed. "I've never been so close to an owl in my life."

"He is wonderful," Jenny agreed. "We saved him, Toby and me. He was just a baby when we found him after a torrential thunderstorm three years ago. He was all wet and tattered and shivering out in the lower field. He let me pick him up, although he clicked his beak with a lot of force and tried to scare me. But he was too little to be very scary. Toby took off his windbreaker and we managed to wrap him up in it. We didn't try to take him inside, but we brought him back to the orchard where there was a bit more shelter. Owls like eating meat the best, but they'll eat insects and worms if they're hungry enough. We were able to keep him going until he got stronger. I don't know what ever happened to his mother, but I guess he was young enough to bond with us. We found out that he is a barred owl. They're called a striped owl, too — or sometimes an eight hooter, because of their funny call. Anyways they don't migrate. They don't even move around very much. Hoot has stayed close to us since we found him."

Dolores gazed into the evening sky, her voice amazed as she observed, "I've sat in this orchard for years after yoga. I've never seen him or even heard him hoot. Mind you, I've heard Toby speak of him. But I wondered if he was just a figment of his imagination."

"Oh no," Jenny declared. "Hoot is real all right."

"He sure is," Miranda said. "I just can't believe how big and powerful looking he was."

"My grandmother used to say that when an owl landed on your roof that it was an omen of death. And that the constant hooting of an owl near your house foretells death. She said that my grandpa heard an owl hoot one evening and he died in his sleep that very night," Lizzy said, her voice tentative.

"Well, my mom said that if an owl nests in an abandoned building then it must be haunted. Apparently, owls are the only creatures who can abide a ghost," Dolores added.

Jenny remained nonplussed.

"There may be a few ghosts out there. I don't know. But I'm quite sure that they would be friendly ones."

"I always thought they were sacred to the Greek goddess of learning, Athena," Miranda said. "They're supposed to be really smart. Probably because of those big eyes. Wow, I can't believe how huge his eyes were. They look like they can see right through you. No wonder they spook people out."

"They're meant to be rulers of the night and seers of the soul," Jenny declared. "I think that's why they got a bad rap for foretelling death. But death, symbolically, can mean transition. So, an owl is simply guiding the spirit from one energy plane to the next. Transition can also be of the spirit or emotion — like a change of heart. It doesn't necessarily mean physical death. Owls live in the world of shadows, so they are well equipped to help us with these transitions."

Dolores grinned at Jenny.

"Methinks that you love that old hooter, Jenny Smith."

Jenny laughed.

"I do indeed, Dolores. Every single time he lands on me, I feel a thrill right through me, even after all this time. During medieval times, it was fabled that owls were witches and wizards in disguise. Even nowadays, some people believe that an owl is a witch's familiar — an animal soul linked to a spiritual person with a unique bond."

"Really? That's handy for you," Freddy observed with a twinkle in her eye.

Jenny shook her head. She replied, her voice serious, "Oh no, Freddy. Hoot isn't my familiar. That's what Julie thinks she's here for."

On cue, that fuzzy calico popped up from among the orchard grasses, green eyes gleaming in the half light. She sprang onto Jenny's lap and began to purr with great abandon.

"Julie just wants you to know that she is very special to me as well," Jenny remarked, affectionately scratching that feline's stubby ears. "But you already know how much I adore my dear kitty, now don't you?"

Observing the hedgewytch and her beloved familiar, we all nodded.

Of course, we did.

JARED TIMES

THE MUSINGS OF A HEDGEWYTCH IN OCTOBER

"We are all one child-spinning through Mother Sky." Shawnee Indian saying.

October! Now there's a month with magic encrusted right into its name. Its days are filled to brimming with excitement and anticipation of its grand finale — Halloween!

Here's a witchy tip: Put a glass of water with salt and vinegar in any part of your home to remove negative energy.

And to keep an unwanted visitor from returning, sweep the room or rooms they were in as soon as they leave your home.

Everyone loves a little tip from a witch, but witches are, of course, given a bad name at Halloween. We think of the stereotypical green-faced witch with her high-pitched cackle and her evil spells. But, just as there are many different types of mortals, there are many different types of witches.

Why don't you decide for yourself? Why don't you come out and join us in our annual witches walk on the last eve of October? Everyone is welcome, but you must dress up. It is amazing to see the wonderful women of Jared coming together and walking through the town. If you've never been, then come at dusk to the Hedgewytch Way and we will swoop onto the village. If you didn't believe in magic before, you will then — let me assure you.

A note to all the tried and true, dyed-in-the-wool witches: don't forget that the veil between worlds is the thinnest at Halloween. You may want to take advantage of this to cast extra powerful spells, read the future, and communicate with spirits who have passed on.

But we are not actually going to do any of those things. I'm a hedgewytch, after all, and our main claim to fame is a deep connection to the earth and all that it stands for. The witches walk is just for fun. Please bring some non-perishable food items and we will pack them up and send them into Guelph to the food bank.

And, to all of you knitters out there, it's time to start knitting scarves and hats and mitts for people who need them. If you've never knit and want to try it, we are going to be holding some "how-to" classes on Friday evenings after the children have departed from our care. Or if you just want to come with your knitting to click needles in the company of others, that's great too. I have a whole big box of odds and ends of wool left over from last year, so please come and use it up. Let's keep everyone warm this winter.

Even if you just knit in a square and go around and around it may be enough to keep someone warm. People can be down on their luck at any time and need an extra boost.

You can feel the ever-growing chill in the air as the days tumble closer to darkness in the afternoon hours. The leaves blaze in their autumn glory only to fall inexorably to the earth leaving us a carpet to rustle through and crunch beneath our feet. We must gather ourselves in readiness for the cold ahead — light our fires, brew our tea. We are moving in closer to hearth and home.

October means the eighth month. October was the eighth month in the year according to the old Roman calendar until January and February were added to the start of the year.

The Old English name for October is *Winterfylleth*, which is said to refer to the Winter full moon. I just love the very sound of that word: Winterfylleth. It sounds like magic to my ears.

October has two birth flowers: the cosmos and the marigold.

The marigold stands for fierce undying love, while the cosmos signifies order, peace and serenity.

Both flowers are annuals who thrive in full sunshine and are incidentally dying in this month as the summer sun is overpowered by the cool sting of autumn.

Individuals born in October get to choose between two birthstones: tourmaline and opal. Each gem unveils nearly limitless possibilities, as each one comes in a rainbow of shades and colour combinations.

In fact, both of October's birthstones came to earth through a journey involving rainbows, according to legend.

Long known as the Wish Stone, opal is supposed to promote love and romance and to grant wishes and personal happiness. However, many believe that it is unlucky to wear an opal if it is not your birthstone. It is quite amazing to note that this belief comes not from ancient beliefs, but in fact from a fictional book. This book by Sir Walter Scott written in the 1800s depicts a heroine who wore an opal which reflected her changing fortunes. After the publishing of this novel, the value of the opal was greatly reduced. So, ladies, if you wish to, just go ahead and wear those opals. They are beautiful gems.

As millions of people prepare to participate in the fun of Halloween on the night of October 31st, we should note that it stems from the ancient Celtic roots of the Samhain Festival. Two thousand years ago, Samhain was the division of the year between the lighter half (summer) and the darker half (winter). Samhain quite literally means "summer's end" — as the Celts only had two seasons. It was a great period of transition between the fullness of summer and the fallow of winter.

At Samhain, it was believed that the division of our world and the other world was at its thinnest allowing spirits to pass through — that this time of year is thought to be one in which the natural and the supernatural were particularly permeable. The traditional dressing up — also known as guising — as ghosts and witches was meant to be an attempt to frighten away evil spirits by looking scarier that we really are.

In more traditional witchery, Samhain is celebrated as a festival of the dead and a time to remember those who have passed away and honour their ancestors.

Whatever you choose to believe is, of course, entirely up to you. I'm just sharing some of the different sentiments.

> *There is something in October*
> *sets the gypsy blood astir*
> *We must rise and follow her*
> *When from every hill of flame*
> *She calls and calls each vagabond*
> *by name.*

William Bliss, the acclaimed New Brunswick poet, wrote this poem many years ago. And oh, how I love its musical lines that I learned by rote as a girl. It strikes a chord deep inside of me every year.

I love the glory of these autumn days. We're lucky to live in a land where the colours afford such a beautiful backdrop to the days of our lives. The village of Jared is vibrating with the magnificence of so many different coloured mums and asters. They dance in the breezes and comfort us with their rich hues. I love the wildness of the purple asters rambling idly in the fields and byways. I even love the yellow of the goldenrods. The pumpkins and apples are now glowing as they ripen to perfection. Nature tries so very hard to make our world bright and cheery as the days shorten relentlessly.

The apple is said to be associated with peace and earth magic. Some have been known to bury apples in the garden on Halloween to nourish the souls of those who have died in the past year.

And don't forget that nothing ever makes your house smell as wonderful as apples bubbling away in the oven or on your stovetop.

Brooke told me of an apple pie recipe wherein you cut up slices of Pillsbury cinnamon rolls and place them together to cover the bottom of a greased pie plate, topping it with sliced apples and a little brown sugar with flour and cinnamon. Toby and I tried it and it was indeed delicious. It did not survive even one evening at our children's centre. What did not get eaten by the kids was enjoyed by their parents. Very simple, but very nice.

Here is another recipe for Apple Sweets:

1. Steam about 2 to 3 cups of peeled sliced apples until they are soft

2. Cool them and then puree them in your blender or food processor if you have one

3. Pour them into a saucepan

117

and stir in 2/3 cup of sugar

4. Simmer this until it is thickened about 45 minutes
5. Remove it from the heat and stir in 1/3 cup finely chopped almonds a teaspoon of lemon rind and 1/2 teaspoon cinnamon
6. Pour this concoction out onto a greased cookie sheet and spread it out to about a half of an inch and chill it.

When it's chilled, you can cut out any shapes you desire — pumpkins and witches for this time of year

If you are in need of romance, you can replace the almonds with pistachios. Just a little tip.

These are lovely snacks and quite healthy. Sometimes I hang them on the trees as a treat for our little birdie friends.

So, enjoy October, everyone. Enjoy every single day of this vibrant month while it lingers here.

And join us on our witches walk if you're able.

Don't let witches get a bad name this year. Let's give them a good name and make Halloween (Samhain) a night of fellowship and laughter and fun.

You need not bring a broom. I have plenty of traditional witch's besoms.

Let's try them out and have some October fun.

And remember don't ever take life too seriously.

Nobody gets out alive anyways.

JARED TIMES

WITCHES AMONG US!!

Oh yes! There are witches among us. Never forget that, my good people of Jared. And October is when they are abounding — drawn as they are to the black magic and sorcery of this month.

Halloween is a Christian term meaning literally All Saints' Evening, but to these hellish beings it is known as "Samhain", which is a Gaelic word pronounced SOW-EEN. Witches have special ways of celebrating this and, even though they do not believe in Satan, it is Satan himself who gives them the experiences they have and deceives them into thinking that they are tapping into forces of nature. They believe that on this night the barrier between this world and the next becomes very thin, thus allowing the spirits of departed ones to travel freely back and forth between our world and the world of spirits.

So, it is quite a day in their evil practice. They have wild parties into the deep dark hours of the night and play silly games. They read from their personal diaries of spells known as their "Book of Shadows". Here in our own Jared, they partake in a witches walk — a walk of evil and black magic. I understand that some benighted local folk even allow their children to participate. Ignorant fools.

Beware in this month of bewitchment! Beware these creatures who can fascinate with a glance — these fascinatrix *aka* bewitchers — and induce fatal disease merely by gazing at their victim. This casting of the evil eye is equivalent to casting a spell, but without all their rituals. It is the witch's own ability to do harm which is no doubt heightened in October.

Belladonna — have you heard of it? — nasty, nasty stuff. It is also known as the deadly nightshade and it is a perennial plant. It produces purple bell-shaped flowers and purplish black berries. It is only one of the most toxic plants in existence and a highly poisonous alkaloid with hallucinogenic properties. Do these witches even understand all of this — what is therapeutic and what is not?? They have no medical training. Atropine can be extracted from this deadly nightshade (and other plants) and its effects are potentially deadly.

And what about Mandrake? The very word makes me shudder at its evil properties. *Atropa Mandragora* — that's what it's called — and it is related to the dreaded nightshade. The pharmacologically active ingredient is also atropine. As well as inducing the aforementioned hallucinations, it can make your heart rate drop to a dangerously low rate.

Read your history books, my dear

people! Tradition has it that the very mandrake root has magical powers. The roots shriek — they shriek — when anyone tries to uproot them because it has grown from the seed of a dead person executed for murder. To prevent demons rising from the roots, three circles must be drawn around the plant with a double-edged sword. Why, in some parts of Europe, to be caught with a mandrake root used to be punishable by death. And yet these witches have been known to harvest this despicable mandrake at night, wash it in wine, and wrap it in silk and velvet. The crushed root would cause hallucinations followed by a death-like trance. They sold these mandrake potions to individuals who desired to discover the secrets of others and to those seeking superior knowledge. They would use the root in love potions and of course flying potions.

All the October ritualistic potions involving mandrake call for the witches to rub an ointment containing this stuff on their foreheads and wrists and hands and feet as well as on their broomsticks or whatever they choose to ride upon. These potions are often applied in the nude. The friction of their stick as they straddle it and the ointment applied there caused it to be absorbed into their systems. They had a floating sensation and think they are riding in the sky on their broomsticks.

Despite concerted efforts each year by Christians to ban it and thus cleanse the world, Hallowe'en continues to grow.

In the early days in England, there was another kind of witchcraft known as Druidism. The Druids were called "men of the oaks" and were a strange clan of men who dressed in white robes. The Druids worshipped Cernuous, the "horned hunter of the night". Halloween was sacred to the Druids because their sun-god receded to the underworld on October 31st, which is why darkness increased and light decreased.

As darkness set in on October 31st, the clan of Druids would put on their white robes and hoods. They would carry sickles and Celtic crosses as they began a torchlight procession. At the beginning of the procession, a male slave was killed and dragged by a rope fastened to his left ankle. The Druids would walk until they came to a house or a village where they shouted the equivalent of "trick or treat." The treat was a slave girl or any female to be given to the Druids. If the people refused to a girl as a "treat", blood was taken from the dead slave and used to draw a hexagram or six-pointed star on the door or wall of the village. Spirits of the "horned hunter of the night" were invoked by the Druids to kill someone in that house or village by fear that night.

If the house or village gave a girl as a "treat", the Druids put a pumpkin with a face carved in it in front of the door or gate of that place. Inside the pumpkin was a candle made of human tallow to keep evil spirits away. Thus, the Jack-O-Lantern was and is a sign that you have cooperated with Satan.

The treats or female victims were taken to Stonehenge where they were raped and killed and then sacrificed on the sacred bonefire until only glowing embers were left. The "bonefire" is the origin of the modern-day bonfire. As a matter of luck for winter survival, all villagers were expected to use the glowing embers of the bonefire to light their hearths.

As we can clearly see, Halloween is not harmless. Satan has people in our modern era mimicking the witches and Druids of old. All of this is cursed of God. We live in a time when witchcraft is being revived. Movies are filled with witchcraft and vampires. Present-day books are likewise furthering the cause of Satan.

Halloween is no joke and is not harmless fun! This evil holiday has no part in the life of a Christian. May God help you as you read this. May you do your best to avoid Halloween and warn others that it is strictly the invention of Satan and can never be anything but evil of the first magnitude.

In most — if not all — of these accounts, Samhain is immersed in blood and sacrifice. Often in the earliest of times, those sacrifices were human.

So please, please, Jaredites consider these facts that I have laid before you today. And they are facts, let me assure you. You may look them up anywhere.

Beware of this vicious form of witchcraft rolling through our village and consuming it. Do not partake in an asinine "witches walk".

It is not for fun! It is not for amusement! It is only for evil.

Remember — pure evil. It exists today just as it ever did before. Maybe even more.

Open your eyes. Be not blind to the danger at hand.

Jenny Smith is evil incarnate!!!

12

"October is known for its sly, haunted feel. Every day, the air feels more and more alive with energy. Too often we sense a presence. Just behind us … It's not your imagination; spirit activity is more prevalent now."

"Warning: witch property!! Trespassers will be used as ingredients in the brew."

"I DON'T EVEN KNOW WHAT A WITCH'S WALK IS. I've never heard of such a thing."

Miranda's words held a cross note as we rummaged around in our rooms, attempting to piecemeal together a costume with little to no success. The sun hung low in the late afternoon sky, nudging us gently, reminding us of the lateness of the hour.

"I've heard of them. They're becoming popular," I told her, trying to keep her mood up. "And it sounds like fun. Lots of girls are going — even two of the others from here."

Miranda shrugged.

"How are we going to resemble anything like a witch?" she asked. We regarded the mess of our rooms which had yielded, truth be told, no joy in the costume department.

"Well, Jenny says she has brooms —" I began.

"How does she know how many brooms she needs when she's asked the whole town to come?" Miranda demanded, determined to be negative.

I dragged out a pair of black tights and a black t-shirt. Miranda held similar attire in her arms.

"Let's just go," she said.

And without further ado, we went.

A few young children spilled onto the tree-lined streets, running ahead of their parents, their excitement at fever pitch. I loved the rustle of the leaves crunching under my feet. I loved the clear sky ever darkening, making the trees stand out like glorious silhouettes. I loved the tinkle of laughter emitting from trolls and minions and princesses as they scampered with unadulterated glee on their quest for treats.

We walked together to the end of Jared proper, turning left towards the cottage. Barely had we set a foot onto that road, when we practically stumbled onto Joan Payne. I stifled a gasp.

"I'd almost forgotten about her," Miranda whispered.

"That would've been nice," I whispered back, bracing myself. "Well, she would be out on Halloween, wouldn't she?"

"Of course, she would."

We drew closer together, almost holding hands, although neither of us would have admitted this.

"Oh hello," I croaked, making a valiant attempt to keep my voice steady.

At this salutation, Joan stood stock still, surveying us with bright beady eyes. Her hooked nose and pointed chin came close to meeting in the middle of her face.

A shiver passed straight through me and into Miranda.

Only a high-pitched cackle escaped from Joan's withered mouth. Then she turned her back on us and headed towards the village.

"It's funny," I mused when we had recovered sufficiently to converse. "That's the second time we've met her on her way to the village, but I've never actually seen her in the village."

"That's ok with me. Shit, she's horrible, isn't she?"

"She sure is. She's just nasty."

A sharp contrast met us as we approached the Hedgewytch Way.

Strings of fairy lights illuminated the yard. They twinkled and peeked through the almost naked branches of lilac bushes and the hawthorn that guarded the purple door. An assortment of little pumpkins adorned the cobblestone path. Their carved faces peeked out into the gloaming — some smiling, some frowning, and some quite frightful. Ghosts made from white sheets and tied under their heads floated amongst the branches of the shrubs. The whole place teemed with mystery and allure.

It amazed me how many "witches" had actually turned out for this event. It seemed the local women took this event quite seriously.

I recognized some of the yogis, but it was difficult to ascertain who was who under the guise of costume. Some had masks and wigs. Most had black skirts and black hats although there were a couple of hats of other hues, purple and green and silver.

"We forgot hats!" I turned to Miranda, who had just realized this.

At precisely that moment, Brooke opened the door, a beautiful witch with a pert black hat and form-fitting black dress. Her brown curls tumbled onto her shoulders, catching in the sequins and buttons of the material. Her smile beamed large and contagious.

"Jenny sent these out for you," she said, passing us each an elaborate black hat embroidered throughout with feathers and ribbons and stars, the like of which I have never seen.

"Oh my!"

"Put them on and come in. Freddy and Irene have some spooky make-up and they are trying their hand at it."

She ushered us inside amongst the dozens of milling witches. It would have been impossible to say how many there were in total. They seemed to be everywhere, all shapes and sizes.

The whole night reverberated magic and mystery. Even the moon seemed in cahoots with the spirit of the season displaying a beaming orange globe, making the night sky very mysterious.

I fairly shivered with excitement as I regarded my mirrored self after the makeup and hat had been donned. I almost didn't recognize myself. I resembled an ethereal being.

Miranda peered over my shoulder, regarding our reflections. I started at the uncanny image of our likeness, in costumes and painted disguise.

Once everyone had been suitably attired, we poured out the door, congregating on the porch as Jenny and Toby handed out brooms — or *besoms,* as they are more aptly named. Besoms are the traditional witch's brooms composed of twigs tied in a bunch around a thick stick.

Toby wore a wizard costume not unlike Harry Potter, with a tall hat fashioned from material gleaming with stars. He looked as cute as a button, although I would never say that to him. I remember what it felt like to be his age. I'm quite sure that he considered himself a force to be reckoned with.

Jenny was so small that she could have been mistaken for a child if you didn't look too closely at the crinkles and creases of her face where laughter and love lines defined her features. She wore a long black dress with a satin red sash.

A big black pail painted with moons and stars stood ready for food donations to the local food bank. I'd had no idea what a big fundraiser this walk was, unprepared for the great number of cans and boxes displayed in the pail. It made me happy that we'd remembered our contribution.

As it happened, Miranda and I were the last two to join the crowd congregating on the lawn.

"Ah, there," Jenny declared, handing us the last two besoms from the pile on the porch. "Everyone has one now."

"How did she know how many of us there would be?" Miranda murmured.

"She just does," a passing witch answered. "She always does."

"Does everyone have a besom?" Jenny turned and asked. "They're just for effect really. We don't actually fly on them. Although, witches can use them symbolically to sweep the ground and clear out negative energy."

She shrugged a little, adding, "It never hurts."

"Are we going to play any games this year, Miss Jenny?" asked a very cute little witch of about eight years old with a turned-up nose and sparkling blue eyes.

"We could, you know, Maddie dear. We sure could."

I looked around and realized that the front yard had been set up into a play area.

A witch hat ring toss game stood where the children could toss a ring to land on the point of a witch's hat. A huge web carefully constructed from cardboard strips lay on the side of the cottage with a sign to "Pin the spider on the web", A game of bowling sported besoms and gourds. And a huge galvanized pail sat on an old table, sloshing over the sides with water and apples floating about in its midst.

"Remember that old Agatha Christie novel about Halloween when a child is killed bobbing for apples? Her head is held down and she drowns."

I had no clue who had uttered these words due to the masterful disguise of their painted face.

"That's terrible," said someone next to her.

"Well, she was the Queen of Mystery, so she was. She could spin a yarn of gore and murder about anything."

"Well, they'll be no such goings on here tonight." I recognized the brisk voice and bulky body of Connie. "This is a very civilized Halloween party."

I grinned a little, as if this might be a possibility.

"If you want to find out who your future partner in life is going to be, we could try a little divination spell," Jenny announced, from the apple bobbing table.

"We could?"

"Oh, indeed. That's quite an easy one. The apple love spell. Brooke," she caught that girl's arm as she rounded the table.

Brooke halted, observing her, a wary expression on her pretty features.

"Jenny, I did not request a spell."

"Oh, I know. I know. But no harm will come from this one, I promise. Here," she thrust an apple and a paring knife into the young girl's hands.

Brooke accepted the apple, still looking uncertain.

"Just peel it, my dear. Just peel it in one long piece."

Brooke obliged, beginning to peel the apple. Jenny recited the words to the spell, line by line, so Brooke could repeat them as such.

"I pare this apple round and again

My sweetheart's name to flourish plain

I fling the pairing o'er my head

My sweetheart's letter on the ground be read."

"Ah, just so," Jenny said, with encouragement. "Good job there, Brooke."

The peel had come off in one strip to Jenny's clear delight. Brooke obediently flung the apple strip over her head.

Jenny rubbed her hands in glee and anticipation, approaching the peel.

"It will be in the shape of your true loves initial."

"Oh, honestly," Brooke scoffed.

The rest of us, though, felt quite intrigued and eager to investigate the letter, if indeed it had formed a letter.

"It's a Z!" Toby yelled. "It's a Z!"

"A Z?" cried Brooke. "How can it be a Z? "

Several other witches had ventured forward, confirming that yes, it was indeed a letter Z.

"What nonsense, "Brooke said. "There aren't even any names starting with Z for heaven's sake."

"Zachary!" Miranda offered, starting an outcry of names.

"Zachariah!"

"Zane!"

"Zander!"

"Zeke!"

"Well, ok. But I don't know anyone by any of those names and I —"

Jenny's voice permeated the dusky air, as she observed the letter from a different angle.

"Actually, Brooke dear, I think it's an 'N'."

We advanced a little closer to the offending apple peel, peering at its formation. It could have been either an N or a Z, I supposed.

"If you look at it from where it stands facing Brooke, then I think it may well be an N," Connie mused.

"Exactly," Jenny agreed. She winked broadly at the witches, unseen by Brooke.

"N is a very respectable letter for a first name. And now," she continued, before Brooke could say that she knew no one with a name starting with N, "we should start to walk."

Everyone raised their besoms and Jenny, with the assistance of a very fine wizard, lined up the children to proceed in the walk.

I saw him turn to his grandma and heard his clear childish voice say, "At least it wasn't an E."

Jenny hugged him quickly. We all set forth on our way towards the village.

"In Ireland, there's a belief that if you hear footsteps behind you on this night — on Halloween, I mean — that you shouldn't turn around," one of the witches observed. "They believe that the footsteps are those of one of the dead. If you turn and see them then you'll be next."

Someone shushed her, reminding her of the presence of children. She shrugged in her black apparel, impossible to say who she was.

"I can't help it, can I? I'm Irish and that's what they believe."

No sooner had we rounded the corner than we met Joan Payne, apparently on her way back home.

Jenny raised her besom in greeting, calling a good evening to the miserable crone.

Joan looked back at her, pointed her bony finger and cried "YOU! YOU!" in that horrible high-pitched voice.

"I've never heard her speak before," Miranda whispered to me.

"I could have gone my whole life without hearing it," I told her.

Jenny remained calm and unperturbed.

"Yes, Joan, it's me. Happy Halloween to you."

Joan screeched, continuing on her way.

She had visibly upset some of the children.

"Don't worry, guys," Jenny said in a matter of fact voice. "She has no power."

"I don't like her," Maddie replied. "She's awful, Jenny."

That's an understatement, I thought.

"I know, honey. Come, let's get into the village."

We ascended on the village. The stores and homes were mainly comprised of men, most of the women being with us. The little Ontario village had participated in a big way towards this Halloween festival. Malcolm had opened the Corner Café, serving peppermint hot chocolate to the children and mulled wine to the women. I'd never had mulled wine before, but I highly recommend it — especially when your bones are chilled from witchy ventures. Baked goods and treats stood on display on every available counter space.

"Did you get some wine, Miranda?" Malcolm inquired of me.

He took a second look, realizing his mistake.

"Sorry, Molly. You witches all look alike tonight."

We spilled back out into the streets. The entire main street had been closed to accommodate stalls, set up with homemade crafts, more games and huge amounts of candies and treats. Pumpkins illuminated the darkness and fairy lights twinkled everywhere.

"Wow, this sure beats Halloween when I was a kid," I told Miranda.

We'd just finished laughing our way through a game of glow in the dark bowling, consisting of knocking over ghost figures set up in front of the general store. The night air glowed with electricity from the energy of the kids, and it must be admitted some of the women.

"Yeah. This is something," she agreed.

I surveyed the whole scene with amazement and the thought filled my being that maybe this was where I was meant to be. Right here, right now, here with these witches and all this magic.

Maybe I had a little bit of witch in me, too!

13

"If you want to attract something into your life, start giving that area of your life or the object you seek praise, as if it is already where or how you want it to be."

THE DAYS WERE GETTING SHORTER AND DREARIER. November is a dark month — not winter, not autumn, little sunshine.

Miranda and I trudged our way down the path to the yoga studio on one such grey Sunday morning.

"Toby! Where is my broom, love? How do you expect me to get to town for my groceries?"

Jenny looked up to greet us, her face wreathed in smiles.

Here, I thought, *is the sunshine for today. Right here in her face.*

Toby rounded the corner at his usual high speed, the sought-after broom in his hands.

"I was just sweeping off the floor for you, Grandma."

"Oh, you are a dear boy. Thank you. You know that I can't be without my broom."

Toby's face twisted with laughter.

"One of these days I want to see you fly, Gran. Just so I can tell the kids at school. They're always asking."

"Oh, they are, are they?"

It hadn't occurred to me that it might be tricky to have the local witch for your grandmother.

Many of the locals tumbled in, seeking solace in the sanctuary of the yoga studio. The drabness outside made the day feel oppressive.

We lingered, after the echo of the last "*namaste*" drifted off, reluctant to leave the comfort of the studio. Little lay ahead for Miranda and me in the damp, grey afternoon, save preparing for class tomorrow.

Jenny and Toby rolled the tea cart in as we sat trying to muster up the get up and go to –well, get up and go. Mugs and a pot of honey, a pitcher of milk, and the lovely blue tea pot adorned the cart. This week it was lemon balm tea. Jenny said this tea was good for lifting the spirits in these sun-less days. There were lavender shortbread cookies as well, with a hint of mint and lemon to them. The air filled with the mingling smells.

I gazed around me, thinking how fond I'd become of the odd assortment of women lolling on their yoga mats. This place represented a haven on such a bleak day.

"A day like this always makes me feel a little homesick," Verna observed, gazing out the window with hooded eyes. "It makes me think about what might have been."

The remark took me by surprise. Verna seemed to be such a down-to-earth person, not given to flights of fancy.

Silence ensued for several moments. I, for one, had no idea how to react to such a statement.

"It's funny to think about your girlhood looking back at it now, isn't it, Verna?"

Jenny asked the question in a gentle voice.

I wondered if the revelations that came to light in the afterglow of yoga were just part and parcel of the magic of Hedgewytch Way. It seemed that this was Verna's time to tell her story. Just like that.

"Yes. It seems a long time ago that I was a girl. Yet in some ways, it seems like yesterday. Sometimes I look in the mirror and wonder where Verna McIntosh went. That was my name when I was young: McIntosh. Nowadays girls often keep their names, but when I married Malcolm it wasn't an option. You took your husband's name. No wonder so many of us got lost along the way. You know what I mean, Jenny?"

Jenny nodded, her topknot bobbing in silent affirmation.

"I used to lie awake at night and watch the big darkness outside when I was young. I hated to go to sleep and close out the stars and the moon. I grew up in the sticks and there was a huge apple tree outside my window. You could climb out onto it and escape into the whole, big world."

My mind boggled at the vision of Verna Snell, middle aged and stout, crawling out of her bedroom to explore the night. I couldn't even picture her as a young girl. She seemed so very well-established in her present life.

Jenny continued to nod at her in encouragement.

"I didn't really do that — climb out the window at night, I mean. I just dreamed about it. I was the second child. I always did what I was told," her tone matter-of-fact as she recounted this. "Not my older sister though. She was the rebel. She was the one who broke the rules and pushed the limits. I guess that's why I tried to be good. Because Ruth just wasn't. She used to sneak across my bedroom floor and crawl out my window."

"Wow. Did she know that you knew?"

"No. I always pretended to be asleep. I don't know why. She was six years older than me and very beautiful. I thought she was exciting, in spite of her bad behaviour. And she always was just sweet to me. So, I never wanted to give her away and get her into more trouble. I used to wonder if things would have been different if I had."

"What do you mean?"

"Well, I knew she was going out to meet a boy, but I never said anything. Partly, like I said, I didn't want to get her into trouble. But partly because it was neat to be in on the secret, even if Ruth didn't know I was in on it. Sometimes they'd talk and I could hear what they said. I didn't understand half of it, but still it was exciting. I'd try to stay awake and wait till she came back in to sneak back to her own bedroom. Sometimes I would, but mostly I just fell asleep. When I think back to those nights, all I remember is lying in my bed waiting for Ruth to either come back in through my bedroom window or escape by it."

"That sounds cool," Clarisse observed. "Like something in a story: climbing out onto an apple tree."

"Yes, I thought it was pretty cool too," Verna said in a flat tone of voice.

It was clear that there was more to this story than happily ever after. I wondered if we would hear it all today. But the story had begun and, so it seemed, must be finished.

"When I was ten, Ruth started going steady with a boy. That's what we used to call it — going steady. His name was Wayne and my parents didn't like him. His family were poor. Not that we were much better off, but we were more respectable, I guess. Dad was a farmer and worked hard. Wayne's father had been disabled in the Korean War, so his mom went out and cleaned houses. Not very many women worked when I was a kid. It was sort of frowned on. Wayne was a nice enough guy, I guess, and I'm sure if Mom and Dad had held their tongues, it would have all just blown over. That's usually how it goes. But as soon as they raised objections about him, Ruth decided that Wayne was the only boy in the whole world that she would ever love. They forbade her to see him, which just added fuel to the fire. She used to climb out the apple tree and meet him all the time. The whole summer I was ten, she spent almost every night with him. I wish now that I'd told my mom about it."

Verna looked out the window and sighed. It amazed me to see her eyes alight with unshed tears. Silence fell over our little room as she pulled herself together. Even I could anticipate the outcome of this story. There were only a few endings to such a tale. A simple, broken relationship did not procure a lifetime of regret in a younger sister.

"I'd listen to them talking. They talked about their love and how they would run away together as soon as they were done school. Wayne was older, so he would graduate first. Sometimes it almost seemed like they were talking in my dreams. It was so nice to hear how tender and sweet they were to each other.

"Until they weren't."

Here it comes!

I caught the thought as it came through the air at me via Miranda.

"One night it woke me up, the arguing. I knew I wasn't dreaming this time. It startled me enough to make me sit up in my bed. They were angry and their voices hurt me to hear them. I crept to the window and listened. I was a child really, and didn't understand, but I will remember always the words because of the vehemence of them."

"She was pregnant, wasn't she?" Brooke's voice was almost a whisper.

"Yes, love. She was pregnant. Like I said, I didn't really understand. I could tell she was really upset. He was yelling. It's a wonder they didn't wake my folks up. I was crying myself as she crawled back up the tree. She cried out loud when she saw me there at the foot of the window. She told me to go back to bed. Then she lied down beside me, holding me until I went to sleep. She was weeping as if her heart was broken clean in two. I kept saying 'It's ok, Ruthie, it's ok.' But I was only ten and I was powerless."

"What happened to her?"

"That's just the thing. I don't know."

"You don't know?"

"No. I really don't. It was never mentioned in front of me. If I hadn't heard things that night, I wouldn't have known anything."

"They never told you?"

"No. Not a word. Ruth was sent away to my aunt who lived in Toronto to go to school in the fall. I missed her like crazy, but I was never allowed to visit her. In those days, people didn't phone like they do now — especially long distance. She would write me letters, though. But they were just letters asking how I was and telling me about the city. There was never any mention of a baby."

"Maybe there was no baby."

"Oh, I'm very sure there was a baby. In those days it wasn't easy to get an abortion. Mom and Dad were always very strict and worried about public opinion. When I tried to ask why Ruth had to go away, they just said that my Aunt Mary needed help. I was shut right down. Children never questioned these things."

Silence reigned amongst the women. Verna's sadness filled the room, a tangible thing.

You never know about people, I thought. I marveled at the wells of memories that these women dragged around in their hearts. It made me feel young and green, even with all of my own heartache.

"What happened to Ruth?"

"She graduated from high school at Aunt Mary's and she stayed down there and got a job. She never lived at home again. I missed her like I'd miss my arm if it got chopped off. I used to cry and cry at night. She only came home for one summer when I was in high school myself. But she wasn't the same Ruth. It was like the spark had gone out of her, as if a light in her had been extinguished."

"From giving up her child. It was the light of her child inside of her that was gone," Brooke said very softly.

She got up and put her arms around Jenny.

"I was luckier than your Ruth, Verna. I had Jenny to save me."

Verna's words were strangled as she said, "I would have given anything — anything at all — if I could have saved her."

"I was lucky too," Jenny said. "I got a beautiful grandson to love."

She turned to Verna and said, "You were only a child yourself, Verna. You were powerless."

"I know that in my head, but my heart still wishes I could have done something."

It was an old, old story I suppose, — one of the oldest. Boy and girl fall in love. Girl gets pregnant. How the story plays out from there is anybody's guess.

"Did you ever find out about the baby?"

"No, I never did."

Verna's voice held a lifetime of regret.

136

"Ruth worked in Toronto as a secretary in a law firm and eventually married one of the junior partners. Very respectable for a girl who used to climb out apple limbs and ride the summer wind and kiss boys in the grass. That Ruth died when they took her baby away from her. She had a beautiful home in the Bluffs, very prestigious, but she never had children. I would sometimes go and visit her as I got older, and she'd take me on the subway to Ontario Place and the Exhibition. She always treated me with love. One evening, when we were sitting on her porch swing and Dan was away on business, I got together all my courage and asked her about the baby. She told me that everything happened for the best and I was not to worry. I reminded her of the night that we cried in each other's arms until dawn and she told me that I must have imagined that night. I told her that she would have been a wonderful mother and she told me that without a doubt she would never have a child because she didn't deserve one. That's what happens when you're raised with a regimented religion. You always feel unworthy."

"That's a very old-fashioned way of looking at things," Dolores said, her voice soft and kind.

"Yes, but we were old-fashioned, you see. We believed if we didn't follow the rules then we'd be punished. Ruth believed that her punishment for premarital sex was to never have another baby. She would have been a great mom, too. She sure was a wonderful sister. I loved her more than anyone in the whole world."

Her voice caught on these words. I realized what an enormous effort it had been for Verna to share this part of her life with us.

"Did she die?" Jenny asked gently.

Verna nodded.

"When she was forty. She got breast cancer that went undetected for too long. She probably thought she deserved that too. It's hard to break the bonds of childhood beliefs. I had the boys by then, but Malcolm was good, and I managed to get down to care for her — especially towards the end. She was sedated with morphine and I'd just sit with her. Lots of times she wanted me to talk and so I'd talk about the boys and the store. I'd tell her little snippets about Jared life. Once, she opened her eyes and said to me, as clear as a bell, 'My boy would be twenty-four now, Sissy — just imagine.' That's the only thing she ever said to me about the baby. I didn't even know it was a boy until then. I hope he got a nice mom, but I can't think that anybody in the world would have been better than Ruthie."

We sipped our tea together. I felt the unity of these beautiful women.

Verna put her mug down and said, "It doesn't do to look back. I know that. As you always say Jenny, 'Don't look back, you're not going that way'. I don't usually. There was just something about today. November. It would have been her birthday."

"I'm glad you still remember her with such a lot of love," Brooke said.

"I do. I really do. It's what we can do for people isn't it? Remember them with love."

"It's the best thing we can do," Jenny agreed.

14

"Nature is calling your name on the breeze, LISTEN, to the witch inside."

Author DJ Hinton

T HEY SEEM TO START WITH ALL THE CHRISTMAS MUSIC and celebrations much earlier than they used to. Have you ever noticed that? It's mid-November and the stores start belting out carols. Festive lights can be seen everywhere in our little village, even without any snow. That hurt me somehow. It's hard to get into the spirit of the season without snow — and without being home.

Ah yes — that is the big hurt. I am not home. As much as I have come to love Jared and so many of the people in it over the last seven months, there are times when my heart just aches for my native PEI. I love it with my whole being. The thought of not being there for Christmas is almost more than I can bear.

But bear it I must. The idea of Tod and Moira as a couple has altered my perception of my whole life. And losing my beloved mother has made the thought of visiting the Island intolerable. None of this stops me from missing home, though.

Still, I remained in Jared. And with every twinkle of Christmas lights, and every merry note of carols, the burden of my heart became a little heavier. I longed for the holiday seasons of yester years.

I kept busy. I worked hard and studied hard and helped at Jenny's. The days slipped by easily into December and we got some snow. All the while, I tried with quiet desperation not to think about that central day — that one big day when I would be completely alone: Christmas Day. Every time the day and events surrounding it were mentioned, I kept silent, daring not to open my mouth lest I blubbered like a baby on the subject of loneliness and loss.

I tried to be determined to look ahead at my life, to take Jenny's advice and 'not look back'. Things, however, always seem more difficult at this time of year. So many memories hovered close, waiting right inside of me, as the beautiful bells and the old familiar words of the well-worn songs filled the air. Memories flooded back to me, coming with a will of their own.

Just by virtue of our classes and living arrangements and jobs, Miranda and I spent some of each day together. We both loved the snow and how the world becomes magical and clean after it falls, covering the sins of the dead leaves and debris of autumn. We threw snowballs at each other, and made snow angels with Toby and some of the children that came for child care. We read the Christmas stories which are new every year to childish ears and made Grinchy noises and Scrooge-like voices and lit candles smelling of pine and cinnamon. We made gingerbread men and snowman cookies, helping small fingers with festive shapes. But we never talked about our own Christmas Day plans.

Miranda gathered some of the girls we knew from school — including, of course, yours truly — to carol at the Jared Nursing Home. This was meant to be specifically for Esther, Jenny's mom, of whom Miranda remained very fond. Only a meager group of five had been willing to brave the cold and set out on the uninspiring trip to the nursing home.

Jenny's mom was petite like her daughter, with white curls and a very sweet face. Her countenance lit up when she saw Miranda. I knew that even though Miranda's stint at the nursing home had ended, she still went to visit Esther. The elderly woman seemed delighted at the rest of us, as well. She even joined in some of the old songs and clapped with great enthusiasm as the notes died away. I could certainly see why Miranda maintained such an affection for her. She kissed Miranda as we left and blew kisses to the rest of us, thanking us for sharing our songs with her and all her friends.

"She doesn't seem very confused," I observed, as we shivered along in the darkness of the chilly street. "She seems fine actually."

Miranda sighed.

"I know. That's what makes it so hard. She was great tonight. Thanks for coming with me, Molly. It meant so much to her. But it's a crapshoot, really. Some days she is very vague and barely knows her own name."

"Well, she sure is fond of you."

"I quite love her, Molly. I really do. I got attached to her, hearing about her coming to Canada after the war and her new life here and losing her little son. I admire people who go through shit in their lives and don't get all bitter and miserable."

There was a pause and then a sigh.

"Maybe it's because I never had a grandma and she is just how I always imagined a grandma would be."

"She's pretty sweet," I agreed. "It's a shame that she has no other family, isn't it?"

"Jenny is good to her, but I know what you mean. Too bad Jenny's boy didn't live. What was his name again?"

"Buddy. She talks about him sometimes."

"Who does?"

"Esther. I've never heard Jenny talk about him. Not really."

"Maybe she'll tell us about him someday."

"She will, I'm sure when she's ready."

The lights from the village glowed brilliant and beautiful. The snow drifted around us like a snow globe, transforming the world to soft, shimmering white.

But still we hadn't spoken of Christmas Day. And I was glad.

Of course, no other subject was in evidence by the women after our Sunday yoga session — what they had to bake and cook and what they had to shop for. Many of them, it seemed, felt not so much the joy of the season as the insurmountable amount of work that came with it. They did it, though. They did everything that was expected of them — and more. I marveled at the tasks piled on their agendas. It was no wonder that they seemed reluctant to leave their rest positions — their *Shavasana* poses — and tread wearily back to the demands made on them by children and spouses and work. As I listened to them, I seriously doubted if I would ever be able to accomplish half of the things that these women did in a day. Some days I could barely tend to myself and my own needs.

"Well, I don't have to cook Christmas Day dinner this year," Kerry said. "That's one thing."

"Where are you going? To Jamie's' folks?"

"Yup. It's his mom's turn to cook dinner and she wants all of her family together."

"That sounds nice," I observed tentatively, pushing away the thought that I had nowhere to go for Christmas dinner. And no family to spend it with. If I had a loonie for every time that I'd made a conscious effort to push that thought away in the last week alone, I would be a wealthy girl.

Kerry shrugged.

"I guess so," she conceded.

Jenny laughed.

"You don't seem too enthusiastic, my dear."

Another shrug. Then Kerry spilled out her feelings, as people were wont to do in this odd, little place.

"Oh, I know I should be grateful to her for doing all of the work. And I am really. But I would gladly contribute something — anything at all. She absolutely refuses to let you help, but then she complains about being exhausted from cooking all day. One time I brought a sweet potato casserole, and she 'forgot' to produce it. When I mentioned it, she wondered out loud why on earth I would have brought such a thing and that no one in their family had ever cared for sweet potatoes."

"You can't win then."

"Exactly!" Kerry rolled her eyes. "That is exactly right. I can't win. And they all bicker at each other. Even Jamie is different when he's there. It's like he reverts to being a kid, arsing around with his brothers. I have two kids. I don't need another one."

"Have you tried discussing it with Jamie? He's usually pretty good, isn't he?"

"He is. He really is a good guy, but I don't know, he seems to just get sucked into it all when they're together. And his mom thrives on it. She stirs the pot of discontent and then sits back and listens. I despise bickering, but she seems to love it. I want to tear my hair out by the end of the meal. I tell you there is no peace to be found in that house. It's a two-hour drive there and a two-hour drive back and we are all exhausted by the time we get home."

"Maybe you could bring it."

This came from Brooke in the very gentlest of voices.

Kerry wrinkled her forehead and turned to her.

"Bring what, pray tell?"

"Peace. Maybe you could bring some peace to her house this year. "

Kerry gave a short chuckle.

"Brooke, you are an amazing person, but I don't think that you quite get it this time. That woman doesn't know the meaning of the word peace. Discord would be more to her liking."

Brooke nodded.

"I know. She sounds awful. Really. But that doesn't have anything to do with your inner peace. You can bring that with you. Wayne Dyer said that peace is the result of retraining your mind to process life as it is, rather than as you think it should be." Brooke often came out with these little gems of wisdom. "Sometimes just forgiving her for being awful will give you peace in yourself and that is a good reason to do it. Even if she doesn't deserve the forgiveness you, my friend, deserve the peace in your own soul."

Kerry remained skeptical.

"Well, that all sounds well and good," she said, "but it's easier said than done. When I get there and it's all bedlam and arguing, it's hard to remember such idealistic words."

"Just bring a little bit of peace then," Brooke persisted. "What you can manage. You have it in you, Kerry. You do or you wouldn't be here."

Jenny nodded.

"It's like I tell Toby when he says someone was mean to him or said something unkind. It would be worse to be that person, wouldn't it? I ask him. It would be awful to be an unkind person."

"I guess," Kerry's conceded, her tone doubtful. "I guess I could try."

"Of course, you could," Brooke looked around at the kind, amused faces of the country women surrounding her.

"And you, Lizzy, you could bring hope and Verna here could bring joy. Try it. See how it goes."

The women were all laughing now and shaking their heads.

Brooke remained unperturbed, her smile serene.

"Well," declared Connie, amongst the laughter. "Aren't I the lucky one? All I have to bring is plum pudding. That's a lot easier than what some of you girls have to produce."

15

"If you want to change the world, go home and love your family."

Mother Theresa.

D ECEMBER DAYS SEEM TO MOVE FORWARD with a life force of
their own.

On the last day of classes, Miranda and I went out and had drinks
with some of the other students. We giggled and joked and roared
with laughter as only young girls do. Some flirting and dancing with
local fellows occurred. There were no serious outcomes, though. I, for
one, was not ready for any kind of a relationship just yet. My days
were much too busy already, and the wounds in my heart too fresh.
As the night grew old, we split our money on a cab and parted with
hugs and good wishes for a wonderful Christmas and promises to
have the best year ever ahead of us.

Miranda and I walked the length of our quiet street, guided
by the Christmas glow of lights and decorations along the way.
Still, we did not speak of the big day looming ahead.

It was only as I lay alone in my room, classes done and the semester behind me, that I allowed my mind to drift back to my beloved Prince Edward Island. I thought of the Christmases which comprised my childhood. I thought of my parents —my mom mainly, as my dad was just a distant memory — and how I always felt completely encircled in her love.

My mom's hair had been a beautiful shade of auburn. It never really turned grey, only grew paler year after year. She had kind blue eyes and a sweet smile. If I was going somewhere, even to school, she would say to me, "I'll just be here loving you until you come home, Molly girl."

Sometimes I would come in the house and yell to her, "What are you doing?"

"I'm just over here loving you," she would reply.

That was my mom and the way she talked. It wasn't until I was much older that I realized how lucky I was to have a mother who did just that. I had no siblings. She loved me totally.

Memories flooded over me: of beautiful red sands and winds sweeping over the ocean, bearing that distinctive salt spray and smell. I thought of our warm cozy house which had always been home.

I allowed the reminiscences to enter me at last. They broke me. I lay on my bed and wept as I had not wept in forever. The tears poured from me as yearning swept through me and consumed my soul.

And lying there, looking out at the glowing lights on the street, I cried myself to sleep.

The next morning, I rose with a resolution to deal with this whole Christmas dilemma.

The café was closed on the twenty-fifth and so I would not be required to work. I had nowhere to go. I must face this head on. I would do it today. There were only three more days until Christmas Day.

On my morning trek to our shared bathroom, I encountered Miranda.

"Hey," she called. "When you're done washing up come over and have a coffee with me. I was just going to make one."

"Sure."

I did not meet her eyes since I felt quite sure that mine were a little the worse for wear. I hoped with all my heart that she hadn't heard me crying last night.

We sat cross-legged on her braided rug and sipped coffee with appreciation after our late night. We mulled over the night's events, as girls do. It felt great to be getting a break from our studies.

Then Miranda stretched out her flannel clad legs and said with a nonchalant air, "So have you any plans for Christmas Day?"

The dreaded question spoken out loud. The elephant in the room addressed.

I shook my head.

"No. What about you?"

"I don't either. I'm not flying back to BC. It costs way too much and there's no one there now."

Sadness and shame filled me. I had been so consumed with my own self-pity that I had spared no concern for Miranda.

"Did you read Jenny's column in the paper last week?" Miranda asked.

"No. Not really."

Wow, I thought, *talk about changing the subject.*

Miranda seemed to sense my thoughts. She grinned.

"I'm only asking," she continued, "Because, well, because she invited us to her house for Christmas dinner."

"She invited us?"

I felt incredulity cross my face.

Miranda nodded.

"Well, she wrote that she's having her usual Christmas spread and that she hopes all her friends will head down and keep her company. Apparently, she does this every year and lots of people go. I think we should go — you and I."

I considered.

"Do you think it'll be all right?"

"I guess so. It's better than sitting here by ourselves, isn't it?"

"I suppose." I tried, without success, to keep a grudging note out of my voice.

"Well, think about it. It might be nice. I even thought maybe if Esther was having a good day I could go and get her."

I could feel my spirits starting to lift at the possibility of an actual plan.

"That's a nice idea. I could help you."

"If she is well enough, it would be great. And I would definitely need your help, Molly. Like I said, think about it."

We finished our coffee and went to prepare for the day. We both had to work, so we parted and met again at the café.

We donned our aprons in the kitchen and attended to the usual milling Saturday crowd, catching our breath only as the last customer departed for the day.

Verna entered the kitchen and said, "So I suppose you girls will be heading over to Jenny's on Fri?"

I had to stop and think, but Miranda was ahead of me (as usual).

"For Christmas, you mean?"

"Yes. Jenny loves it when lots of people come for her Christmas dinner. You know what she's like."

"Well, we were just talking about that and wondering if it would be ok."

"Ok? Of course, it would be ok. Where on earth else would you go, if you're not going home? You can't just sit in that little boarding house. It will be next thing to empty over the holidays."

Verna's brisk manner always seemed to get to the heart of the matter.

"I've got a couple of baskets for you to take to her on Christmas Day, if you don't mind. Just some things I threw together for her. I like to send her an appreciation from the café. You girls can take them now. We're closed tomorrow on account of Malcolm and I are driving down to Goderich to spend Christmas with our eldest boy."

She produced two huge baskets from underneath the counter filled to the brim with baked goods and bread and candy and topped with cellophane and holly leaves and berries. They smelled delectable.

"Oh my! These are a work of art," I breathed. "Jenny will love them."

Verna smiled her thanks.

"Well, even if you bake yourself, it's nice to get something that you didn't have to slave over. That's what I think. It always tastes better when someone else makes it."

She gave us each a Christmas card containing a nice bonus and told us how happy she was with both of us.

"You work well together," she beamed at us. "You really complement each other. Have a nice rest and a Merry Christmas. I guarantee that you will be glad you went to Jenny's. I know she's expecting you."

"You do?"

"Oh yes. You know how she is. She always seems to know who's coming often before they know it themselves."

She bustled around, thrusting the baskets into our arms and ushering us out the door.

"Merry Christmas, girls!"

"Merry Christmas, Verna!" we called in return and proceeded down the street, laden with our beautiful Christmas baskets.

Miranda laughed.

"Well, now I guess we have no choice."

"Yes, it seems to be settled, doesn't it? With not much input from us, I might add."

I laughed too. I felt my heart settle into the sheer comfort of knowing that there were no more worries about spending a lonely Christmas day.

We were going to Jenny's for dinner.

I'd never spent Christmas with a witch before.

16

The pagan origins of the Christmas tree: The tree was taken into the house, so the wood spirits would be kept warm during the coldness of winter. Food and treats were hung on the branches for the spirits to eat. Bells were hung so they could ring when an appreciative spirit was present. A five-pointed star aka a pentagon was placed on the top of the tree to represent the five elements.

And that, according to the witches, is how this all began, this Christmas. Before the Christians got hold of it.

THE THOUGHT OF WAKING in the old boarding house on Christmas morning dwelt heavily on my mind.

Even so, the hours marched on and that morning arrived with inevitability.

Miranda and I had spent Christmas Eve sipping wine and watching *Home Alone* #1 and #2. Just try to watch those movies without laughing. I'm telling you: it's impossible.

My mom and I had always watched *It's a Wonderful Life*. I loved that movie so much. I could practically recite it line for line.

The thought of watching it without my mom felt unbearable. Miranda, as well, wanted something that would be entertaining and not too deep.

So *Home Alone* it was.

We giggled and drank and ate treats not usually indulged in. For once, we did not have to get up at a certain time.

I was afraid my inherent sense of timing would awaken me anyways. Not so. I groaned awake on Christmas morning only to turn over with great pleasure, returning to sleep in my lovely warm bed.

At length, I awoke and drifted towards Miranda's room to welcome the day. We were two broke girls with no notion of exchanging gifts. I had bought some Tim Horton pods and Miranda produced some cinnamon rolls, all of which we consumed with great gusto.

If not for the fear that Miranda would roll her eyes and accuse me of being corny, I would have declared what a wonderful gift her friendship had been to me since my arrival in Jared. I satisfied myself by raising my coffee mug and declaring simply, "To us!"

Miranda responded in kind.

Miranda had decided to take Esther out for the day. We arrived in the early afternoon to find that beautiful lady bedecked in a soft red blouse and a big smile.

"Merry Christmas, girls!" she sang out. "How very, very lovely of you both to come for me."

The white fairy lights adorning the trees up and down the streets made the world wonderful, despite the dull dreariness of the weather. I felt happy. I didn't want to delve too deeply into my feelings, not wanting to examine what lay beneath the surface of them. So, I just decided to stay happy in this moment. Brooke, I reflected, would be proud of me.

After the short cab ride, we arrived at Hedgewytch Way. Miranda held out the fare to the driver. He shook his head at this.

"Oh dear, no," he declared. "It's my pleasure to drive Miss Esther here for her Christmas meal. I would never accept money for it — not ever. She is very precious cargo indeed. I've taken her before, but she's never had such lovely young ladies accompany her, I'll say. Restores my faith in the youth of today so it does."

We both felt a little hesitant, as if we should make some monetary offering at least for our own passage. He brushed our concerns aside.

"You just go and enjoy yourselves and don't worry about a thing. Jenny is right good to me and all."

We thanked him and he assisted Esther out of the taxi.

"Besides," he boomed, with a wink, "I have to stay in the good graces of our local witch, don't you know."

We led Esther along the frozen cobblestones. She overflowed with Christmas cheer and joy. What a lovely gift Miranda had bestowed on her.

Jenny swung open the door with a smile that matched her mother's. They embraced warmly. The cottage rang with delighted squeals and Christmas greetings, as Connie, Brooke, and Toby appeared behind Jenny. The delectable smells that only Christmas could produce permeated the air: turkey and apples and cinnamon and the haunting aroma of evergreen that no artificial tree ever created.

Mrs. Snell's baskets were flung over our arms. They were received with exclamations of joy. I felt absolutely enveloped in the welcome of the little cottage. Any stray thought floating about in my head that maybe we had not been properly invited faded away.

I look back on that Christmas with such fondness, even now. I had been so young and newly on my own, far from my home and without any family of my own. I had been dreading this day for weeks. Now it had arrived, and I received it with joy and wonder.

Several long tables had been unearthed and swathed in Christmas fabrics and boughs of holly and mistletoe. Candles adorned the Christmas tree. Mulled wine in several huge crockpots smelled heavenly and tasted it, too. We might have stepped into someplace else. Someplace magic.

People lolled everywhere — on the chairs and the floor and by the fire. I recognized many of them, but some I'd never seen. A few of them looked as if they had been living on the streets, which I was to discover was not far from the truth. Jenny had been supplying a Christmas dinner to anyone who needed one for years now. Brooke told me that she and her husband started the tradition years ago when Buddy was little. Jenny had kept up with it after his death and now it was quite an occasion. She never knows exactly how many people are coming, but she always has enough food. (Imagine that.)

Jenny alighted beside Esther and pressed her cheek gently into the older woman's. Jenny's topknot bobbed about, fastened with a scrap of bright red fabric. She wore an apron covered with holly. Pink roses bloomed in her cheeks. She looked like a Christmas doll.

"How wonderful to have our girls here, Jenny."

Jenny lifted her head and gave her mother a quizzical look.

"Our girls." Esther nodded her head towards Miranda and I, who were seated across from her.

"Oh yes, Mama. That is Molly and Miranda. They've been helping me with supplies and with the kids."

Esther's head shook in a gesture of impatience.

"Miranda. Molly. I don't care what you call them. Jenny. They're our girls."

"Yes, yes, Mama."

Esther's frustration seemed to grow despite Jenny's quiet, soothing words.

"Uh-oh," Miranda said in the barest of whispers. "I hope that she doesn't get riled up and have to go back early."

"I don't get it," I whispered back. "What is she talking about?"

"It's the dementia. Sometimes she gets upset about things that have no bearing on reality."

Poor thing. She did seem to be agitated. I had no comprehension as to why.

I tried to ignore the fingers of doubt winding around my heart — that doubt that never totally trusted Jenny Smith. Despite the affection that I felt for her, a part of me held back from her. There was so much more to her than met the naked eye.

Or why would Esther — her own mother — be acting like this? She seemed to mistrust Jenny too.

"It's the dementia," Miranda repeated. But I wasn't so sure.

Esther stood up and came over to Miranda and me, pointing her finger at us. I made a huge effort not to shrink back.

"These girls, Jenny. They're our girls."

Jenny put an arm around her little mother, pulling her into an embrace, showing no sign of provocation.

"Yes, indeed, Mama. They are our girls for sure. I'm so proud of them."

Esther visibly relaxed and allowed herself to be guided back to her chair.

"I'm glad, Jenny. I'm so glad that you have them here now. And I'm glad that I got to spend a Christmas with them. This is my last one, you know."

"Is it, Mama?"

"Yes. I can feel it. But it's ok."

"Aw, Mama."

Jenny's voice quivered. She held her mother's frail frame in her arms. With great tenderness, her lips touched the top of her white head.

"I know that you're the one with the magic in you, but I know things, too," Esther pronounced.

"Of course, you do. Where do you think I get it from?"

"Not from your father, that's for sure."

Her tone sounded uneasy.

"My father was a good man," Jenny said.

She turned to us and added, "But he didn't have an ounce of imagination in him, let alone magic."

"He was a good man," Esther agreed. "He worked hard and he provided for us, but there was no give in that man. If he made up his mind that was it, there was no changing it."

"That's for sure," Jenny agreed.

Her words fell on the air, light as a feather.

"He was determined. But that's not always a bad thing, Mama."

Esther's face crumpled like a little flower. Her emotions seemed somewhat unstable and close to the surface.

"Except that one time, Jenny. Except that one time."

Her words escalated feverishly and in the blink of an eye she was almost shrieking.

"I'm so sorry, Jenny, about our girls. I'm so sorry. He wouldn't give in. So stubborn. German man."

She almost spat these last words out.

Jenny smiled and took her hands. She answered in her calm clear voice, not missing a beat.

"You're German too, Mama, as am I. Lots of people are stubborn. It can be a good thing."

"Not that, Jenny, oh no, not that."

"I've never seen her like this," Miranda whispered to me. "Never."

Jenny made no apology for her mother's behaviour. She simply sat beside her and rocked her gently, murmuring softly to her, like a small child. Slowly the elderly woman returned to a state of calmness.

Connie came into the room and commanded everyone to take seats and ushered "Miss Esther" up to the head of the table.

Esther followed her dutifully with her face wreathed in smiles and just a few remnants of tears clinging to her faded cheeks, like little sparkles. She said she felt like a queen at the head of the table.

Jenny assisted all the others to various spots at the long tables. Eventually everyone found a seat. Every single person had a chair, with none to spare. Miranda and I exchanged a glance, impressed.

What an odd assortment of folk perched up and down those tables passing bowls and platters to each other with shy smiles and mumbled greetings.

Some of these people I had never laid eyes on before. Several middle-aged men looked as if they might have crawled out from under a log somewhere. One elderly man in a three-piece suit seemed to be hovering on just the other side of tipsy. Three women appeared to be somewhere in the vicinity of ninety or a hundred. Four boys, who looked about my age, clumped together at one corner and ate as if they hadn't had a meal in weeks. A teen-aged girl resembled a ragged little matchgirl. She barely uttered a word. Two of the nurses attended as well, because they had to work — and had worked — all night and couldn't get home to their families. They greeted us warmly and told Miranda to reconsider her career choice because look at them half asleep, desperate for a meal, and far from their loved ones. Miranda, too, was far from home, but she laughed good-naturedly and inquired about their shift.

When there was no doubt that anyone could eat another morsel, Connie came and deposited a huge plum pudding on the table.

"I made the plum pudding, as promised," she grinned.

"I wonder how Kerry's doing with the peace she was going to try to produce for her mother in law," Brooke mused.

We grinned, recalling the conversation after yoga.

As we finished up our dessert, the music of a piano floated through the air.

I cocked my head and wrinkled my nose at Miranda.

"What is that song?"

"I don't know." She, too, inclined her head, her words thoughtful. "I feel as if I should know it, though."

The conversation faded to nothing as the sweetness of the music filled the kitchen.

We tumbled from the groaning table to behold Jenny at the piano.

"'Somewhere in my Memory'," she spoke in response to my question. "That's the name of the song. Do you know it? It's lovely."

I had heard her singing and fooling around with Toby, but I'd never heard her sing in earnest. Her voice sounded like springtime. And magic (of course).

Candles in the window
Shadows painting the ceiling.

I let the music and beautiful lyrics embrace me.

Memories of my childhood
When I was 5, 6 and 7
I would wake when dawn would
Living in Christmas Day Heaven.

My beautiful childhood memories washed over me then, as the words engulfed my very soul. Music can do this as nothing else on earth can. Music can transport you to another time and place. Even against your own will.

All of the music, all of the magic
All of the family, home here with me.

It was one of those moments that come like a little blessing slipped into your life. We sat in the afterglow of the song, full of good food and Christmas joy.

Suddenly I knew where I'd heard that music.

"*Home Alone*!" I cried out at the precise moment as Miranda. Everyone laughed.

"Jinx!" Toby called out. "You have to link fingers and make a wish."

"Yes, it's from *Home Alone*," Jenny confirmed. "They don't really sing the words though. I think they just play the music. Bette Midler sang it back in the early nineties. I love the lyrics."

"They make me sad," Miranda said.

Her face looked as if she'd surprised herself, saying the words aloud. She'd certainly surprised me.

"Yes," Jenny sighed. "Yes, a lot of songs do that, especially at this time of year. Songs can have great power over the memory. Music is a form of magic all by itself, methinks."

She turned back to the piano then and allowed the rollicking notes of "Grandma got run over by a reindeer" to fill the room. Many voices merged together in the mirth of the song's absurdity. Toby and Brooke laughed with easy abandon. Toby pointed at his grandma and cracked himself up as the lyrics spilled from him.

"The Twelve Days of Christmas" came next with most people messing up the words or the order of the gifts. Or both. More laughter.

"I Saw Mommy Kissing Santa Claus." "I Want a Hippopotamus for Christmas." "The Chipmunk Song – Christmas Don't Be Late." "Nuttin' for Christmas."

I'd forgotten these silly tunes. Miranda and I stumbled along with the lyrics as best we could, consumed with glee.

I had not previously noticed a waif of a small girl child who sang "All I want for Christmas is my two front teeth". She stood up on the piano bench beside Jenny, her grin literally spreading from ear to ear as she pointed to her mouth which showed the lack of the two teeth in question. She laughed so hard that I feared she might fall off the bench. Toby gallantly came to the rescue, assisting her down as he chuckled at her antics and sang along with her lisping lyrics.

The afternoon flew by. The day that I had dreaded had become a day that I didn't want to end. It got dark so early in December. By late afternoon, it seemed as if it had been night for hours.

Everyone seemed satiated after partaking in tea and hot chocolate and mulled wine. Some of the people had gathered themselves together and departed. Others were making verbal rumblings about leaving. The old taxi guy had arrived for Esther and Jenny had handed him a big plate covered in aluminum foil and a bone in a plastic bag to boil for soup and then pass on to Max. His dog, presumably.

He again expressed his thanks to Miranda and me for the assistance at the nursing home. We offered to accompany her back, but he assured us that he would be just fine. Those fine gals at the home would come out and help him at the other end.

Esther gave Miranda and I both a huge embrace. Her upset from earlier in the day had disappeared, dissipated like mist in the sunshine. She had remained calm and contented, albeit a little more confused.

"So glad that I got to see you both," she said with warmth, taking our faces in her little wrinkled hands one by one. "It's my last Christmas, you know, and you have made it the best one of my whole life."

We hugged her back and declared our pleasure at spending the day with her and her family. Jenny stood beside us and we all waved and blew kisses as the cab rounded the corner. Even the driver blew a kiss.

"She says it's her last Christmas," Miranda turned to Jenny as we shut the door against the damp cold night. The warmth of the country kitchen embraced us.

"Yes. I know," a little sigh escaped Jenny's lips.

She smiled with a sweet sadness. "It can be a curse knowing these things. It can be tough on you. My sweet little mama."

I looked at Jenny with doubt.

"So, you think it's true — that this really is her last Christmas?"

Jenny looked from Miranda to myself with a curious unreadable look on her face. Again, I felt the something inside of her that I could not fathom. Therefore, I mistrusted it.

She seemed on the verge of speaking. But she hesitated and the words disappeared.

A brief pause transpired. Then she spoke.

"I think it might be true," she conceded. "It's been a green Christmas for the first time in years."

Miranda and I exchanged glances, not understanding the connection between these two statements. Jenny answered, like she could hear our thoughts in that strange way that she sometimes had. I found it a little unnerving.

"A green Christmas means a full graveyard," she explained. And that was that.

Toby tumbled out to the doorway just then. He encircled his grandmother's legs in his arms, giggling.

"Grandma, Grandma."

"Toby, Toby."

We accompanied them back to the big room. There remained some stragglers sprawled out, seemingly too exhausted or contented (or both) to move.

"It's a full moon tonight," observed the well-dressed older man lingering by the fire.

"Yes. It is a full moon," Brooke said. "It's called a 'cold moon', I think, or a 'Christmas moon'. There hasn't been one since 1977, and there won't be another one until 2034."

"Look at you, all full of information," Connie teased her.

"Actually, I saw it on Facebook," Brooke admitted. "But it's still interesting."

"I agree," Jenny said, as if, being a witch, she did not already have this information at the snap of her fingertips.

Brooke beamed at her. She was so beautiful when she smiled. I realized then why she seemed so happy and unencumbered. Eric Biggs was nowhere in sight.

My grandma used to say that some people gave pleasure by their presence and some by their absence. Eric definitely fit into the latter category.

"Full moons are full of magic," Jenny went on. "That's why some people go a little crazy under their influence. It's called the lunar effect. There are many magic spells which can only be performed by the light of a full moon."

"Scientists," Connie, always the devil's advocate, observed, "are now saying that there is absolutely no correlation between a full moon and any abnormal human behaviour. That it's all just an old myth."

Irene and Clarisse, lolling on the rug sipping from ceramic mugs, sat up with cries of outrage. Trust the nurses to react to this.

"Oh yeah. Right. These guys have never worked a night shift in a hospital or any kind of institution. They should spend a half of a shift there and they'd soon change their tune."

Even Miranda nodded in agreement.

"Of course, it's true," Jenny said. "Not everything can be proved by science. There are an awful lot of things in this world with no such explanation."

The little girl with the missing front teeth was just leaving, accompanied by the young girl who I had likened to the match girl. I realized with a shock that this scruffy being was in fact her mother. Jenny had laden them down with bags of food. Connie had nonchalantly thrown an old-fashioned knitted purse over her shoulder. The little match girl looked at her with a question in her eyes, but Connie had observed, in her matter of fact way, that she needed a purse for her things. Brooke told me later that the purse was crammed full of essential items and snacks. Connie, who could be quite gruff at times, appeared to have a heart of gold beating inside her thick solid chest.

They waited at the door for the cab, who apparently let people ride for free on this festive day. Art — or was it Wes? They looked like Pete and Re-Pete to me — ushered them into the ancient vehicle. His voice boomed with affection at the young ladies.

No wonder he was so cheerful. Every time he made an appearance, Jenny presented him with some sort of treat or another.

"A full moon does seem just like magic, doesn't it, Mama?"

The child gazed upwards, mesmerized and basking in the luminous glow of the moonlit sky.

The tired young woman nodded and clutched at her newly gained possessions.

She smiled with love at her pretty little daughter. I felt glad that she'd had this magic day. Life is hard as a single mom.

Christmas Day had ended for another year.

As Jenny would say, "So mote it be."

JARED TIMES

THE MUSINGS OF A HEDGEWYTCH IN JANUARY

I release all things from the past year that have caused any negative attachment.
I prepare and welcome new change, new lessons, and new adventures.
I welcome new opportunities to grow emotionally, mentally and spiritually.
BLESSED BE!

Well, it's January. We knew it had to come and here it is.

The festivities of Christmas have been laid aside for another year. The chill of below zero Canadian winter is upon us.

Before I talk about January, I would like to share an old recipe with my readers that is typically indulged in on New Year's Eve. Our lovely and talented Brooke has made them for us for many years now, and it dawned on me this year that I have never shared them — the recipe that is. I've shared the finished product with lots of folk that happen to wander by on our little cobblestone path as they bid farewell to the shadows of the old year and welcome the new one with open arms (we hope).

Before we ate this delectable treat, we enjoyed a huge shepherd's pie made with love from all the Christmas turkey leftovers. And do not worry, no shepherds were harmed in the making of this pie.

And then — this deep-fried treat!

The recipe is called "oli bolen" and it is pronounced "olly bolly" (both of the 'o's are long ones). It is a Dutch treat that is typically made on New Year's. I keep a deep fryer tucked away in my kitchen just so that Brooke can treat us to them every January. She had a Dutch maternal grandmother who made them every New Year's Eve and Brooke has carried on the tradition. They are time consuming, but oh so tasty.

Here is the recipe:

3 cups of flour
3 tsp. baking powder
2 eggs
A dash of salt
2 tbsp. sugar
Currants and wee bits of apple cut up

Mix all of this with enough beer to make everything a proper consistency for deep frying.

You may use milk, but the beer gives it a lighter yeastier feel and better for deep frying.

It takes time and patience to fry these up.

Serve with icing sugar for dipping.

They remind me of the *raderkuchen*, which is a German dish that my mother used to make. I brought some in to the nursing home for her, but her appetite is not so good anymore. However, the nurses and PSW's enjoyed them. A small treat for working so hard over the holidays. I am going to talk a little bit in my column this month about gratitude. Those of us who have family members at the Jared Home owe a huge debt of gratitude to the staff working there.

So, January, we are in the cold grasp of your icy winter fingers. We head fearlessly into a whole new year. Let's release all thing negative from the old year. Let's prepare and welcome new changes, new lessons and new adventures. Even if it's tough, let's try to welcome new opportunities to grow emotionally, mentally, and spiritually.

When things are the toughest, that's when we need to embrace new things the most. Brooke says the same thing about yoga poses. She says that the ones which give you the most trouble are the ones that you need to practice more. It figures, eh?

We should try to be kind and have patience with everyone. We need specially to have patience with ourselves. Get yourself up from the ashes and dredges of last year whatever they might be, dust yourself off and get started again. It's a new year. It's a new chance.

Toby says to me, if I am dragging my heels about something or other, "You're someone, Grandma. You deserve to be happy and have a good time too."

What a wise boy. Wise words for all of us. We are all someone. We all deserve to be happy. Have a good time.

This year, or maybe just this month, try very hard to be responsible for your own happiness. Let everyone else in your life off the hook. No matter how they behave, don't let it affect your core being. You are the keeper of your own happiness.

Don't start this year with broken pieces and bad memories of last year. Let the new calendar page open on a whole new chapter of your life story.

One of our lovely yoga girls told us some time ago to get a mason jar or the like and write down when something makes us happy throughout the year. Then, at the end of the year, you can read through the scraps of paper and remember all those happy moments.

I've done it now for a few years. What a wonderful feeling to look back at those moments. And forget the bad ones.

Another simple trick is to be grateful for something every day. Even if it's only for a fleeting second, and even if there's no bright spot in the day, try to find something or someone that you are glad is in your life. Gratitude is a powerful thing. And just by practicing it, you are enhancing the very thing that you are grateful for with your intention. Every time you think fondly of another person, you are enhancing them even if you never tell them.

Intentions are powerful things and so much better for the vessel {YOU} to send out positive thoughts into the world. It has an overabundance of negative ones already. It doesn't need any more.

As if that isn't enough reason to practice gratitude regularly it is a scientific fact that gratitude releases the neurotransmitter serotonin which makes us feel better. It can even help in the battle against depression — which is a big deal in these sunless days.

Try it. Start with little things that you're grateful for. Even if it's just a warm fire on a cold winter evening or the laughter of a friend to keep you company when the sun isn't shining.

After all, people can either inspire you or just drain you. Think about this before choosing your company. It's a good reason to attend yoga classes with Brooke. She is a most inspiring young lady.

We always feed the birds at this time of year. They get hungry too, wee things. It also keeps life interesting — seeing who's who at the feeders. We have a pair of beautiful cardinals this year and they are very gracious. However, some of the jays can get aggressive, squawking and chasing the littler ones away. I love them too though with their brilliant blues and harsh cries. After all, they get hungry as well.

My favorites, though, are the little black capped chickadees. The next time that you're out at the Hedgewytch Way, stroll down to the back past our yoga studio. You'll see quite the bird meeting place there. Toby and I have a big pail of sunflower seeds and if we gather a handful and call out softly "*chick a dee-dee-dee-dee*" those little ones will come and eat right out of our hands. It's such a thrill when they alight on your mitten. They are so tiny that they are almost no weight at all, and they are very swift just pausing long enough to snatch a single seed. At least once a day I go out to offer them seeds. They are very friendly now. Nice to help our little feathered friends in these dark days. It only takes a little seed and time but quite a bit of patience.

In these cold winter months, it can get very dry inside as so many of we country folk heat with some type of wood stove. Why don't you try hanging eucalyptus in your shower? The steam will release loads of beneficial oils from it. Eucalyptus is great as an antiseptic, good for the respiratory system, and is also an anti-inflammatory. Plus, it smells lovely.

If you have a sore throat: mix together 2 tablespoons each of honey, vinegar, and lemon juice with a dash of cinnamon in hot water. It will fix you right up.

But if you're feeling all right, then pull on your winter duds and get out for some of that invigorating winter air. Try and find the beauty in our Canadian winter, harsh as it may be at times. We are blessed to have a little village that does not hibernate at this time of year, but embraces it.

The last weekend of January — which is rapidly approaching — they are going to freeze the whole hill on the main street as it goes west out of town and make a slide. Take the kids out. Better yet, try it yourself. There is nothing like the feeling of sailing down a hill on a sled to make us all feel young again. And, of course, there is always delicious hot chocolate and coffee at the Corner Café.

Also, there will be the annual snow man building contest in Jared Park. Try your hand at some snow art. Think outside of the snowman box.

We, here at Hedgewytch Way, continue to plod along through the winter days.

Brooke has her yoga studio schedule up until March, so check it out. It's posted at the post office and also at the Corner Café. It's always good to give your body a good stretch when you can't get out as much as you'd like. It's good for your mind as well. Brooke always has pearls of wisdom to share about getting the most out of yourself and each day.

Remember Helen Keller, that wise young girl, said, "What I'm looking for is not out there. It is in me."

Yoga will help you find that.

This winter, we have also introduced a dance class for kids every other Friday night. They can be any age from six to thirteen, although most of them seem to average around ten to twelve. It's just for fun. Between Brooke and Molly and Miranda the kids have been taught any number of dances — some old like the YMCA and the Macarena, but mostly modern ones. You should see those kids do the Whip song. There is some hip hop in there as well, so we have decided to dub the music used for the classes "mish mash".

Our mish mash classes are five dollars for the whole evening that includes popcorn made in our big cast iron pot and a bottle of water. Any donations are welcome and, if any of you adults out there have a dance move that they would like to share with these kids, come on out this Friday. Nothing like music to get the body going.

If you have little ones, we have story time on Saturday afternoons. There are two groups. One is for the smaller kids which includes a little puppet show. And for the bigger kids, we are reading two chapters of a book, continuing each week. Right now, we are on *The Land of Stories*. It is a very popular series. I love it myself and find myself wondering what those Bailey twins will be up to next.

So, no need to be bored just because it's January.

January's birth flower is the carnation. I love carnations. They smell so beautiful. When I was a girl, I once visited a friends' uncle who had a greenhouse in Dixie (which doesn't exist anymore being swallowed up by Mississauga). It was full of carnations and the perfume of them was just wonderful. It has stayed a pleasant memory for me. A scent can take you careening down memory lane, just with one little sniff.

Carnations can be used in tea to relieve stress, fatigue, depression, and insomnia. I am going to try my hand at producing some at Hedgewytch Way.

They can also be used in massage oils to treat skin irritations and reduce the appearance of wrinkles. I'm going to have to manufacture some of that, as well. I have accumulated quite a collection of wrinkles in my life thus far. As befits any self-respecting witch, I might add. I do feel that a proper witch should have at least a certain number of wrinkles to appear authentic. What do you think?

Anyways, getting away from my wrinkle aggregation, I wanted to say that the different colours of carnations portray different messages.

For instance,

Red means deep love and admiration

White means pure love and good luck

Pink means a mothers' love

Yellow means disappointment or rejection

Purple means capriciousness

Striped means rejection or regret

According to a Christian legend, Mary began to cry when she saw Jesus carrying the cross. Where her tears fell, carnations grew — which may have been why the pink carnation was chosen as a symbol of motherly love.

This connection between the carnation and Mary was immortalized in the 1475 painting *The Madonna with the Carnation* by Leonardo da Vinci. It is housed in Munich, Germany as part of a collection of famous works and is also called the *Munich Madonna*.

Carnations have been used in many countries and many cultures. They were used to tell fortunes in Korea. Young girls would place three carnations in their hair. It signified that her last years would be difficult if the top flower died first. The earlier years would be difficult and hard if the centre flower died first, and superstition held that her entire life would be miserable if the bottom flower died first.

Just some January lore for you to file under "useless information".

So, remember for the new year — Come out and dance with us!

Forgive others but most of all yourself.

Be grateful for something every day and watch your serotonin rise.

Hang eucalyptus in your shower.

And try to find joy in these January days of winter.

17

"The world is full of magic things, patiently waiting for our senses to sharpen."

W.B. Yeats

I T SEEMED THAT MIRANDA AND I always ended up at the heart of the community activities offered by Jared. And for such a small place, they have a lot of activities.

A snowman building contest, which no self-respecting college student would willingly participate in, seemed to be a foregone conclusion for Miranda and me. The children whom we helped care for at Jenny's had a lot to do with that arrangement.

Toby accompanied us, industrious in his efforts to produce an outstanding specimen. He wanted us all to work together and enter the snowman under "Brooke's Yoga".

The little girls from dance class worked their hearts out, rolling snowballs, almost engulfing themselves into the balls as they flipped right over to form them. Toby lifted their concoctions as they were produced, sculpting them into the shape of a man with his mitts.

A huge bonfire dominated the centre of the village, crackling and roaring. Hot chocolate and roasted chestnuts in little aluminum foil jackets adorned its edges, just waiting to be consumed.

Our mish mash dance class had been practicing for weeks. They performed a dance amid swirling snowflakes complete with snow pants, hats, and mitts, as everyone waited for the snowmen to be judged. What they lacked in raw talent, they made up for in enthusiasm. Not to mention their utter adorability.

We didn't win the snowman contest, but we did get Honorable Mention. Malcolm Snell took a photo which appeared in the next issue of The Jared Times, right beside Jenny's' column. This made her as pleased as punch.

Usually Jenny attended the village festivities, but today she'd felt it necessary to stay at the cottage and finish up a batch of herbal balms and sachets.

In the last light of the winter evening, Miranda and I herded the girls down the road to the cobblestone path to regale that hedgewytch with tales of our day.

She had just finished with her work, she declared, and was glad of an opportunity to sit and hear about the events of the day.

She passed us each a cranberry oatmeal cookie fresh from the oven and set out the blue tea pot with some mugs. No herbal tea today, she said, just good old Tetley.

Her kitchen labors had flushed her cheeks a pretty pink, the heat from the stove curling her topknot more than ever. Little wisps had escaped her hair ribbon and brushed against her cheeks. Her blue eyes gleamed with pleasure as she listened avidly to the animated stories of her charges.

The little girls tumbled over one another, each trying to be heard above the other. They related with glee the story of their snow creation, including the other snowmen, the roasted chestnuts, and the huge ice slide which had replaced the village main street.

Then they performed their dance for Jenny, with very little persuasion, sans winter gear, their reward being much applause and cheers. So full of joy and winter spirit were they, that their enthusiasm seemed to fill the cottage.

"I love winter!"

"I don't want the snow to ever go away."

"Snowmen are magic, don't you think, Miss Jenny?"

Miranda and I exchanged a smile, sitting and enjoying the comfort of the tea and cookies. It had been a fun day, to be sure. However, the older I got, the more dreams of spring and warm weather allured me, as opposed to images of ice and snow.

"Yes, there certainly is magic in the snow," Jenny beamed at them. "Imagine living where the weather was always the same."

"Boring!"

"Yes, it probably would be boring," Jenny agreed. "And there wouldn't be any snow days."

The girls groaned. They adored snow days — unexpected days when the school board deemed the roads too dangerous for the school buses to run. Of course, the children who walked could still attend, but they would move heaven and earth not to go on these allotted days. And who could blame them? When Grey County issued a snow day, it seemed only sensible to take full advantage of the situation. Toby often collected a dozen or more children to come to Jenny's on any given snow day. Just because buses didn't run, parents were afforded no such break from work. Jenny's seemed to be the destination of choice for local parents when child care was necessitated.

Such a snow day presented itself the following week. It happened to be a study day for Miranda and me. We studied in the morning, but after lunch we plodded through the snow to Jenny's, knowing that she would have her hands full.

Indeed, she welcomed us gladly as Brooke had to work at the bank and Connie had taken to her bed with a case of strep throat. We beheld Toby busy organizing some games.

"I knew it was going to be a snow day," Paige, one of the dancing tribe, announced, her voice full of triumph. "I knew it even before Mom told me."

"You did? How did you know that?

"Because I remembered to wear my pajamas inside out."

She spoke with great conviction.

"Your pajamas?"

I couldn't fathom the connection.

The others, though, nodded solemnly.

"Oh, yes. Everybody knows that," declared Maddie.

Miranda and I looked at each other, our expressions blank.

"If you wear your pjs inside out, then it will be a snow day for sure."

"I've never heard that," I said, trying to keep the dubious note out of my voice.

"Well, maybe not where you come from, but around here everybody knows it's true. And see," Paige's voice rang with jubilation, "it worked."

There is absolutely no use arguing with the logic of children. Because, of course, it had worked, requiring no further proof of its authenticity.

Miranda and I tramped them all outside, despite the cold biting winds.

They created a field full of snow angels.

"Do you think that people in heaven can look down and see snow angels?" a little boy inquired, his tone wistful.

Miranda squatted beside him. She regarded him quizzically and, when she spoke, her voice held an unexpectedly gentle tone to it.

"I'm quite sure they can. Do you have someone in heaven, Jacob?"

He nodded, his big boyish eyes spilling over with huge drops of tears.

"My Papa. He went to heaven before Christmas and everybody cried all through the Christmas holidays. I wish that I could jump up high enough into them clouds and pull him back down."

I looked at Miranda, at an utter loss for words.

"So, he could see my snow angel, I mean," Jacob went on to explain.

"Oh, I see. "

Miranda nodded, a thoughtful look on her face.

"Just wait here a minute with Molly, Jacob."

With that she turned and ran into the cottage, reappearing with a bag full of squirt bottles sporting various colours.

"I got these at Canadian Tire."

She reached inside and handed Jacob a bottle.

"I thought that we'd make some designs in the snow with all the kids, but I think we can spare some to outline Jacob's snow angel. Don't you, Molly?"

"I do." I agreed, entering the spirit of the moment.

"What was your Papa's favorite colour, Jacob?" I asked him.

"Blue," he said, without hesitation. "He liked blue because my eyes are blue."

They certainly were. Jacob's eyes shone a deep clear blue. He grinned from ear to ear as Miranda handed him the squirt bottle containing blue paint. With painstaking effort, he outlined his little snow angel, with amazing effect.

The other children pounced upon the remaining bottles. They squirted flower shapes all along the banks of snow leading up to Jenny's cottage, dousing them in vibrant colours, even giving them stems and leaves.

Jenny emerged an hour later, in her boots and red shawl, to announce the presence of fresh caramel popcorn and hot chocolate. She stopped short at the beautiful sight leading up the path to the Hedgewytch cottage.

"These are just amazing. I never knew such a thing as snow paint existed. It looks like spring has come already."

She hugged the children, all of them clearly delighted in their finished project.

Jacob came forward and, taking her hand, led her to where his snow angel lay in the orchard.

"Oh my, Jacob. That is so beautiful. Did you outline it in blue so that your Papa Henry can see it in heaven?"

Jacob did not seem surprised that Jenny knew this. Children accept so much on blind faith.

"Yes."

"Well, he'll sure love that. He'll be able to tell which one is yours for sure."

"Do you really think so, Jenny?"

"I really think so, Jacob. I do."

"Because —"

A shadow fell across the pure blue of those beautiful young eyes. He cast them down towards the snow angel.

"Because —"

"Because what, my love?"

"Because Dillon says there's no such thing as heaven."

"Ah."

Jenny sank to her knees beside the small figure in the snow, holding open her arms. He stepped inside the shelter of her red shawl.

"Jacob, I want you to listen to me, ok?"

He nodded.

"Dillon is mistaken. Very mistaken. There is a heaven. There really is and your Papa Henry is there."

"For certain sure?"

"For certain sure."

Jacob regarded Jenny with grave eyes.

"Tonight, when you're in bed you think about how happy you made him today with your snow angel."

The little boy smiled and hugged her. Jenny stood up and brushed snow from her knees. We accompanied her and the scampering children back through the banks of white.

"Do you really think there's a heaven, Jenny?" Miranda inquired.

Jenny turned to smile at us.

"Yes, I do."

She gave a wry little laugh.

"I don't advertise that in my column. I must keep my integrity as a witch. But I believe in heaven. Maybe not the conventional idea of heaven. But I am certain sure that there is an afterlife."

She took our hands, proceeding to swing our arms as we approached the beautiful warmth of her little cottage.

"Because if there is no heaven, then what would be the point?"

"The point?"

"Yes, you know, the point of all this."

She swept her arms up, lifting ours in the process.

"The point of all this," she repeated.

She gave her head a little shake.

"I just like to have faith in things — even if they are little things. Like Papa Henry seeing that blue angel. You know?"

Not so long ago, Miranda may well have rolled her eyes at such a notion. But Miranda, it seemed, had evolved in a subtle way since our arrival in Jared, her harsh edges softening. I, on the other hand, only seemed to feel more skeptical and unsure of things as time passed. Once I'd been so rooted in my beliefs of the world and life, my vantage point safe and sure. But I feared now that my outlook had sharpened too much, largely due to the ever-present feeling of wariness which pulled me both to and away from Jenny. I railed against this even as part of me felt affection, even love, towards her. Yet, always inside me, dwelt a feeling of distrust directed at her. I seemed unable to shake this.

Miranda and I, in some strange way, seemed to be growing more like the other.

An unsettling thought to say the least. I shook myself out of my reverie.

A wreath of smiles beamed on Jenny's face, as she held open the funny purple door. Despite my qualms, I entered the warmth of her bewitching kitchen with eagerness. I smiled back at that hedgewytch, determined to keep an open mind.

The following Sunday, we all gathered inside the yoga studio, observing Brooke as she smudged the studio with sweet grass and sage.

"I try to do this on New Year's," she explained. "But things got away from me this year. It's still January though so I'm going to say the smudge prayer for a new year."

She rose and wafted the smoke to every corner of the room, encircling each of us, in turn, with the sweet-smelling smoke.

Into this smoke, I release
All energies that did not serve me,
All negativity that surrounded me,
All fears that limited me from the last year.
I walk into the new year
With light in my heart

And hope for better things to come.
So, it is.

As the prayer ended, she put aside her smudge pot and owl feather, assuming the lotus position at the front of the studio. She smiled at us, her yogis, her friends.

"It's January. There's a whole new year ahead," said Brooke, "and I'm going to try to have lots of faith this year. Faith in all things, but especially in my lovely circle of yogi ladies."

She raised her hand to us in her customary gesture of inviting us to join in.

"I'm going to have faith that spring will come," Nora spoke up, her tone denouncing that this may well be futile.

"I have faith in terminally ill people who have not lost their spark of kindness." Irene's voice was, by contrast, gentle and caring. "Or their sense of humor, for that matter."

"I'll try to have faith in the sun even on dark snowy days — or worse, freezing rain days," Kerry declared.

"I have faith in autistic children," Freddy piped up.

An unexpected idea, I thought.

"I have faith in Toby," Jenny said, a simple and sincere choice.

Silence fell then.

I surprised myself by speaking at the last possible second.

"I have faith that Papa Henry can see Jacob's lovely blue angel."

I paused and gulped.

"And that my mom can see me."

18

"You can't go back and change the beginning, but you can start where you are and change the ending."

C.S. Lewis

“**D**ID YOU THINK I WAS GOING TO HURT YOU?”
“I think everybody's going to hurt me.”

I regarded Heather with curiosity, as she uttered these words. The Sunday morning itself seemed quite ordinary, the sharpness of Heather's tone out of sync with the peaceful atmosphere which regularly followed our yoga practice.

“Sorry. I didn't hear the cart behind me. I was looking at that wild snow coming down out there.”

Miranda and I turned to witness the exchange taking place between Heather and Connie. Connie had, it appeared, been wheeling the usual cart of refreshments around the corner. The ensuing noise had startled Heather.

The relentless winds of winter had unleashed their energies out in the orchard, banging at the confines of the studio window.

We instinctively drew closer to each other against the force of these elements, witnessing their ravaging path across the stark fields and barren trees.

"Why ever would you think that, my dear?" Jenny asked.

"Think what? That everyone is going to hurt me?"

"Yes. That."

Heather shrugged.

Jenny poured her a cup of raspberry tea, handing her a ginger snap as well. The rest of us settled around the yoga mats with tea and cookies. Heather continued to struggle for an answer of sorts.

So, this is Heather's day to tell her story.

Miranda and I exchanged glances as the thought bounced between us.

The day seemed ripe for someone's story to be told. Yoga had relaxed us, and the prospect of tea and a cookie loomed ahead, infinitely more appealing than walking home against the bitter, mind-numbing wind that whistled and roared amongst the naked limbs of the apple trees.

"Oh, I guess it's just the way I was raised, Jenny."

"People hurt you?"

"Well, you know."

Heather's sigh seemed to come from the tips of her toes.

"The world was different then."

"Yes, it certainly was," Jenny agreed, "very different indeed."

"How so?"

This question came from Clarisse. It appeared necessary for the nurses to get all the facts straight before a conversation could continue. I would have just accepted Jenny's statement at face value.

"Everything was different. You can't imagine it now. Teachers gave the strap. Spare the rod and spoil the child and all that stuff."

"There's something to be said for that."

Nora's pursed lips emitted this remark.

"There was no lack of discipline back then that's for sure. Not like some of the stuff that passes for discipline nowadays. Reasoning and talking things over and time out. Sometimes it's just a good old-fashioned boot in the backside that is needed, let me tell you."

"Well there should be moderation in all things, I believe," Jenny said, ever the diplomat. "I'm not sure that there's any real merit to physically punishing a child."

"There isn't," Heather said, with conviction. "Let me tell you. None at all."

Nora looked unconvinced, but she fell silent, deferring to Heather.

"My very first memory was of my father lifting me up in the kitchen almost to the ceiling. I remember specifically because it wasn't something that he usually did, lift me up, I mean. He was very aloof as a rule. It was early in the morning and I had been awake for a while already. I always woke up early, before anyone else. I couldn't help it. I tried to sleep longer because I knew it annoyed my mother when I got up so early. But I was always wide awake first. Well my mother must have complained to my father about it because this particular morning that I mentioned when he held me up, I thought he was going to hug me. What he actually did was pull down my pants and spank my little butt until I screamed. I think I was as hurt with the disappointment as the physical pain."

"I don't get it." Freddy looked quizzical. "Your mom was annoyed that you got up early, so she told your dad on you and he spanked your butt."

"Pretty much. Yup."

"Wow, that does seem a little harsh."

"Oh, it wasn't so bad really." Heather shrugged. "But I can still picture the exact moment when I thought that I was getting affection and received punishment instead. It was just an incident, but it seemed to set a precedent for my life somehow."

She laughed wryly. "I seem to be quite melodramatic today."

"Here at the yoga studio you can be however you desire," Brooke said, her voice kind.

"Indeed," Jenny agreed. "And it's funny how much of our lives do seem to shape around patterns of behaviour no matter how hard we try to change them. That's one of the difficult tasks of self-growth: breaking patterns that are ingrained inside of us."

"It's true," Heather nodded. "Did you ever notice in marriages that one person is always the punisher and one receives the punishment?"

"What do you mean, 'punishment'?"

Clarisse, again, asked, "You mean physical punishment?"

"Oh, no, not necessarily. There's lots of ways to punish someone."

Heather shook her head in a frustrated manner, as she continued, "You're young. You might not know this yet."

"I'm a nurse," Clarisse's voice took on a defensive note. "I know how a patient can punish you. How you can bend over backwards all day and then have them complain to their doctor about some little thing you forgot."

"Yes, more like that. But in a marriage, it's more personal. You say something off hand or maybe you ask him to do something and it doesn't seem like a big deal but he doesn't like it, so he punishes you for saying it or asking for it in the first place."

"He hits you?"

"No, not that. But his manner is cold and distant for a few days, maybe a week, until you wished with all your heart that you had never opened your mouth in the first place."

Brooke nodded her head in understanding, thinking, no doubt, of the loathsome Eric Biggs.

"Yes, my dear," Jenny said, her voice soft. "But that's not the way it's meant to be."

"No, of course it's not," Heather agreed, with a tinge of impatience. "I know that. Everybody knows that. But it so often is that way, isn't it? You see women who have men that treat them like queens and they are just awful. And men who have wives that are bloody saints and they treat them like slaves. And that's just the part that the world sees. Who knows what goes on behind closed doors? Do you women know any couple that are good to each other and treat each other in a perfectly equal way?"

She warmed to her topic as her tale unwound. I munched my cookie and silently wondered if it would appear impolite to eat another one. I'd heard other stories since arriving in Jared, but this one seemed uninteresting. I guess I thought Heather herself was not very exciting.

I gave myself a mental shake. If I were to succeed in my Bachelor of Science pertaining to Early Childhood Education, then I'd better pay attention to what made people tick and how their early years influenced this. Even women appearing as dull to me as Heather had a tale to tell.

"Did something happen this morning?" Jenny posed the question softly.

"Oh, I took the front mirror off the side of the van when I came back from the store. I hit a hydro pole."

"My goodness," Brooke exclaimed. "Thank God you're ok."

Heather turned to Brooke, an odd expression on her worn features.

"Indeed, Brooke. That should have been my first reaction no doubt. Being thankful that I'm ok, I mean."

"It wasn't?"

"No. I got out of the van, looked at the shattered mirror and thought that Ted was going to kill me."

"Really?"

"Well, not kill me exactly, but you know get mad and huff and puff and make my life miserable for a while."

"Punish you." Jenny acknowledged.

Heather nodded, peering at our faces.

"There's many uneven marriages as you say," Clarisse admitted. "I've seen that but," she held up a finger to Heather, "don't say that I'm young. That's not fair. I've seen a lot of life. How many marriages do you think we deal with every day as nurses?"

"I know," Heather admitted, her tone grudging. "But when you're young, you do look at things differently. The older you get, the more you learn what people are capable of."

"You said that incident was your first ever memory," Clarisse pointed out. "How old were you? Three? Four? How far back do children remember?"

"You're right. About three or four," Jenny nodded. "And I think that it's a very individual thing. Children's brains are not developed enough until at least then to retain a memory."

"I can't remember how old I was." Heather said, shaking her head in frustration. "I've never been able to remember too much of my childhood. But that memory for me is vivid. My father walks into the kitchen. I am in my red flannel pajamas. He takes me in his arms, lifts me up and whacks my ass."

"Do you have any other clear memories like that of him?" Brooke ventured. "Some nice ones?"

"Probably. None as clear as that one, though. He wasn't an overly affectionate man. He was mainly a disciplinarian. But that was considered normal back then."

It's interesting to reflect on what makes a life "normal" to others. I couldn't remember my father, and had no personal knowledge or experience of living in a two-parent home. The ideal family portrayed in tv shows and books is still our default image, but so very few people have experienced that life. The older I got the more I realized that it truly was just an image having no basis in reality. Some older people would lead one to believe that the "good old days" were far superior to the world today, but hearing these women I didn't believe it. Visions of strict fathers bestowing blows on tender unsuspecting bottoms sounded horrible. I'd keep my memories of my dear mom and her unconditional loving tenderness to me.

I glanced at Miranda, but she did not reveal any emotion. Someday I would hear the story of her childhood. The fact that she talked so little of it spoke volumes.

"Yes. I think that men were very much in that role when we were growing up, Heather," Jenny said. "My father was German, as you know. He was a good man. He was God-fearing and hard-working all his life. But, oh, he was stern. I was lucky though. My mom was sweet and loving."

"I know I wasn't the worst treated girl ever," Heather conceded. "I know a lot of that was par for the course growing up in the sixties. I just think that all of it formed who I am. I always expect to be punished."

She likes that word, doesn't she?

I caught Miranda's thought hovering on the edge of my mind.

"That is only a belief because you keep thinking it, Heather."

"You can't love who you are if you hate the experiences that shaped you," Brooke interjected.

Heather looked at her with saturnine eyes.

"That's just it, Brooke. I don't love who I am. I hate that I flinch every time someone raises their voice or that I always expect the worst of people."

She turned to Jenny and concluded in a half whisper, "I can't help it."

An unaccustomed silence prevailed on the studio today, punctuated by the occasional howls of the wind. I thought of the children whom I worked with now and wondered what they would be revealing about their early years down the road. Because, of course, Heather was once a small girl. A small girl with an unassuming bottom. It's sad to think of how a single act can change things for us, rocking our foundation.

"The thing is that girls of our generation weren't taught to love who they were," Jenny said. "We had to adhere to rules and stereotypes of behaviour. It was expected of us. There was no middle ground — just black and white. When I first entered high school, girls weren't even allowed to wear pants."

"Really?" Miranda and I giggled the word together.

Even Brooke appeared incredulous, but Nora and Lizzy nodded.

"Absolutely." Jenny affirmed. "Things were very regimented. And that wasn't so very long ago, at least I like to think so. I went to school in the late fifties, early sixties."

"It was a different world for sure," Nora said. "Children should be seen and not heard," she quoted.

"Do as I say, not as I do," Lizzy piped up.

"Oh yes, all of those," Heather agreed. "I'll never forget the first time I learned that it was inappropriate to say, 'bad girl' or 'bad boy'. They said that you should identify the deed and not label the child."

I couldn't ascertain if Heather agreed with this or not.

"That's right." Brooke agreed. "When you say, 'bad boy', you are insinuating that the boy is bad when in fact it's just his behaviour that's bad."

"What if he really is a rotten kid?" Verna asked, grinning.

Everyone chuckled, happy for some comic relief.

Verna could afford to be the devil's advocate, with her two boys already raised and doing well.

Brooke said, "I know. There's that too. Some kids are just bad kids, I guess."

"I think that most kids are a lot like adults," Jenny mused. "Some of them are lovely and some aren't. Some are obnoxious and mean and some are sweet. We don't grow up so very different than how we started off. You can tell just from observing our kids' circles."

She turned to Miranda and me. We nodded in affirmation.

"I was raised on those words," Heather said.

"Which ones?" Jenny asked.

"You know — bad girl and how could you be so stupid and get in there and change because you look like a slut." She shrugged. "All that stuff."

"That in itself is a form of punishment," Jenny observed. "It's setting you up to feel insecure and unsure. It's fine to say sticks and stones can break my bones, but the reality is that words can hurt a great deal. Someday, Heather you must forgive that little girl inside you that got so hurt. Just forgive her. Then she will be free to go."

"Words sure can hurt," Heather agreed with vehemence. "They stick right with you. It's hard to get away from the echoes of them in your brain. I think that I'd rather have a belt across the face and just be done with it."

I stifled a gasp. I felt sad for any of these women who thought that either one of these types of punishments could be deemed justifiable.

"Aw, Heather," Jenny's voice held only kindness, her words echoing my thoughts, "I wish you hadn't had either one of those things: no belt across your face and no unkind words. When a person is punished, then they feel like they could have avoided the punishment by being good. Our brain tries to have reasons why bad things happen to us. If we believe the bad thing is our own fault, then that must mean we could have avoided it if we'd behaved better. But sometimes it's not our fault. Sometimes bad things happen to good people. To all of us."

Heather hung her head.

"Now I just feel foolish." She said. "I don't know what got into me today."

"Please don't," Jenny said. "Please don't feel foolish. We're all here together, trying to get through this life as best we can, trying to find some inner peace."

"Amen to that," Freddy spoke up. "You've got just as much right as anyone else to speak about your life, Heather."

"I just don't feel that way," Heather murmured.

I wondered about her husband. She certainly seemed very subservient.

Brooke moved towards her and said softly "Sometimes the reason that good things are not happening to you is because you are the good thing that must happen to someone else."

Heather gazed downwards.

"I don't see how that could be."

"Why not for heaven's sake?"

Verna contributed this, in her usual brusque manner. You could just tell that she'd had enough of this talk.

"Don't let anybody make you feel less than you are, Heather. We're all so glad that you're a part of our lives and this group. My God, girl, how many times have you saved our necks by helping with the local kids and driving the cancer patients? These aren't little things, you know."

"Indeed," Jenny agreed. "Please believe us, Heather, when we tell you that you're a big part of our lives. We all value your friendship."

I realized, with a sort of wonder, that it remained immaterial whether Jenny was, in fact, an actual "witch" or not. Because she possessed her own brand of magic — something quite unique. It consisted of kindness and empathy. She sprinkled it on everything, it being as much a part of her as the little knot of curls which bobbed away on the top of her grey head.

This seemed like a huge revelation to me and it felt like a pleasant change.

I wished I could keep this feeling and push aside the other one — that weird feeling of unease, almost dread, that Jenny still invoked in me.

I realized, too, that Jenny tended to everyone's needs and hurts with that kindness. But no one tended to her. Perhaps she, too, needed something more, something else, to help her become whole. For it was dawning on me that we, none of us, are whole. I knew for sure that I wasn't. There seemed to be no particular age when this might occur.

Heather appeared abashed at Jenny's last words.

"I'm sorry. I'm really sorry for acting this way."

"First of all, don't be sorry." Jenny said, smiling at Heather. ""Just simply don't be. You have nothing to be sorry about. We all appreciate you. There's no magic required there."

Her eyes moved amongst the circle of women.

"Try not to remember the ones that broke you down, just the ones that made you smile again." Brooke's words took up the thread of this sentiment, her smile gentle and kind.

"Well, that's easy," Heather smiled back. "That would be you girls."

The women, as of one, rose to embrace their friend.

"Hey, nobody said 'group hug'!"

I caught the words as they came, unbelievably, from Miranda's lips, curved into a grin.

Group hug at Jenny's on a winter day before slipping out into the icy world.

A beautiful thing.

19

"Death is not the end, it is simply walking out of the physical form and into the spirit realm, which is our true home. It's going back home."

Stephen Christopher

"MOLLY! MOLLY!" I heard my name in some faraway part of my mind at the back of my subconscious. The initial thought whispering through my mind was that I might be dreaming. I blinked my eyes and sat up in bed. The winter wind savaged the trees outside. Gusts of snow danced past my window like shadows of ghosts.

The red numbers of my clock glowed 2:35.

Was I dreaming?

"Molly! Are you awake?"

The words drifted in and floated around my bedroom. I sprang out of bed, fumbling through the darkness to the ancient wooden door. My heart hammered in my chest. A summons in the middle of the night could never be good news.

I opened the door to find Miranda huddled outside of it, the light of her cell phone illuminating her face.

"Oh Molly! You're up!"

She sounded so relieved that I bit back any obvious sarcastic reply.

Instead I whispered, "What's up?"

"It's Esther. She's had another stroke. A bad one. I talked to Kendra. She's a PSW at the home and she doesn't think she'll last the night. I'm going down to sit with her. Jenny's already there."

The unspoken question hung in the air.

Did I want to accompany her?

Well, of course I didn't. It was minus 20 degrees outside with a wind that whipped right through you, body and soul. What I wanted, what I really wanted, was to burrow back down into my warm bed. I wanted to stay there till morning, maybe even spring.

But how would I ever summon sleep back now, knowing that Miranda braved the elements on a mission of mercy?

"Are you sure it's ok if we go? We might be in the way," I ventured, the thought hopeful.

I despised the whole idea of death and dying — and even of the nursing home, for that matter.

"Yes. Yes. Jenny called me. She wouldn't have called if she hadn't wanted us to come."

I stifled a sigh and led her into my room.

"Give me a minute to dress and brush my teeth."

I pulled on yesterday's clothes and grabbed my parka and mitts and toque. We crept out together into the winter night. The stars shone with stark crystal beauty, even as the piercing winds howled around us.

We left the shelter of the porch and rounded the corner just as Jared's taxi approached us, its window rolled down. It was an unexpected sight to see Jared's only taxi cruising up to us at this hour. Wes — or was it Art? — that pleasant man who had taken us to Jenny's on Christmas Day, leaned out of the window and told us to hurry up and get in.

Despite the lateness of the hour, he appeared keen and alert, his manner cheerful.

Barb Bissonette

"Come on, girls. It's as cold as a witch's heart out tonight."

He chuckled at his own words.

"Some exceptions apply, of course. Our friend Jenny's heart is very warm. She left me a lovely baked apple fritter and a cup of hot chocolate. There's one for each of you as well. Get in. Get in. Here. Drink up and eat up. Very good they are."

I felt as if we should protest.

"It's really not that far," I started to say.

He waved my words away, as Miranda already started to climb into the back seat.

"Well, of course it's not. Nothing's too far in Jared now, is it? But it's late and cold and Miss Jenny sent me to fetch you, so here I am."

"How did she know we would come and when we would be ready?" I pondered, unable to keep the wonder from my voice.

"How indeed?" Wes's shoulders gave a matter of fact shrug.

He turned the wheel, heading towards the Jared Nursing Home. The fritters and chocolate tasted warm and wonderful.

"I am real sorry about Miss Esther, I must say. She's a sweet old thing, even if she is a bit loopy now. This'll be hard on Jenny. It's hard to lose your mom. It sure as hell is. I used to tell my brothers when they acted up, you only get one mom.'"

He kept up his monologue until we reached the nursing home.

I felt more than a little nervous about entering the nursing home at this ungodly hour. Miranda, however, had no such compunctions.

It's that nursie thing, I thought to myself. *They're on a whole different level than the rest of us. They can't help it. They just are.*

Miranda smiled at me with encouragement. She tucked her arm in mine and I felt her pleasure in my company.

I squared my shoulders. I could do this.

A tall brunette met us at the entrance and ushered us out of the frigid night air. She spoke to me.

"Hi, I'm Kendra. Thanks for coming."

She looked exhausted right to the marrow of her bones. Yet she still smiled, albeit wearily, as she guided us down the hall towards Esther's room.

189

I had imagined that a nursing home would be quiet at three o'clock in the morning. This appeared to be quite the contrary. The halls resounded with patients snoring and calling out. Some seemed to be almost screaming.

One woman yelled, "Martin! Martin!" over and over again. I thought I might lose my mind if I had to spend any time at all here. Miranda, though, seemed unfazed.

"Mira's having a bad night again? I thought she was doing a little better," Miranda observed.

"Aw, you know how it is," Kendra shrugged. "Nothing really helps. Some nights are just better than others. Old Duncan started up tonight, too. We had to call his daughter in to sit with him he got so riled up."

"That's a shame. He's such a sweet old guy."

Miranda seemed to know them all.

"He is," Kendra agreed. "He really is, but boy, when he gets going, there's no reasoning with him. I hated to call her because I know that she has to get up and go to work in the morning, but it's her choice. She wants to be called. She's told us over and over that she doesn't want him restrained. She always comes in no matter what time it is. And, of course, she came tonight. She's sitting with him. He's fine now, quiet as a mouse."

She gestured at Duncan's room as we passed by. An elderly man lay in the bed with a chair pulled up beside it. A young woman sat there, holding his hand, both sound asleep.

A lump rose in my throat.

This is what love looks like, I thought.

"How's Esther now?" Miranda whispered.

Kendra stopped and placed a hand on her shoulder. Compassion shone through her tired features.

"I know you've gotten really fond of her, Miranda, and I'm sorry, but she's on her way out. It won't be long now. Jenny knows."

The three of us crept into Esther's room. She lay like a waxen statue, her eyes closed, her breathing labored. Jenny sat beside her stroking her hand. She smiled as we entered the room.

"Aw, you wonderful girls. Thank you for coming."

I felt instant shame at my earlier reluctance. Kendra left the room, returning with two chairs which she placed on the other side of the bed. We each took a chair, murmuring our thanks.

"It won't be long now," Kendra repeated. "She's starting to Cheynes-Stoke."

Miranda nodded, turning to face the tiny figure in the bed.

"I don't know what that means," I whispered.

"Nor do I," Jenny admitted. "But I feel sure that Miranda will fill us in."

Miranda nodded, her face grave.

"It's just a pattern of breathing that people develop when death is eminent. Their breathing gets deeper and faster until they start to have periods of apnea."

I almost glared at her in frustration.

I sent the thought to her in my mind, so affronted that I almost threw it at her.

We are not all nursing students!

Miranda shook her head, mumbling an apology.

"Apnea is when you stop breathing, absence of breath. So, if you start having periods of apnea typically what happens is that they get longer and longer until ... until ..."

"Until you stop breathing altogether." Jenny said. "It's ok, Miranda. Don't feel badly. Esther would not want you to feel badly. She was one of the most realistic people I've ever known. Death is a part of life — the final part."

"I know," Miranda said. "I know. But it's hard not to feel sad. She's so sweet."

"Yes, she is pretty sweet, that's for sure."

I don't know how long we sat together in the shadows of Esther's little room. A great sense of stillness, almost peace, had filled the room. I think Miranda and I may have dozed off a couple of times. But every time I dragged my eyes open, Jenny sat wide awake, quietly holding Esther's hand and stroking her brow, murmuring words of comfort and love to her.

What a lovely way to leave this earth, I thought.

The last grey shadows of night crept across the sky to greet the morning sun when I realized that no more ragged breaths filled the room. Esther's face lay on her pillow, still and white as marble.

"She's gone!" Miranda caught back a sob.

"Yes. My dear Mama is gone. Gone into the dawn of this new day to meet my father."

I recalled Jenny's assurances to Jacob that she believed in heaven.

"I really did love her," Miranda said, almost to herself. Her tone held a tinge of disbelief. Love, I think, did not come easily to Miranda.

"Oh yes, Miranda dear. And she loved you too."

"Do you think so?"

"Yes indeed. I know so."

I did not, as yet, understand the significance of this exchange. But I felt certain that it was important.

I wondered anew, as I had so many times before, what the question was that I wanted to ask Jenny? Because I knew with certainty that there was a question hovering between us, something that would make things clearer. Sometimes I felt it so close I could almost reach out and touch it. Almost. More often, though, it eluded me. Maybe I could find it in my brain now if it wasn't so fuzzy with exhaustion.

That would be nice, I thought with weariness.

It would be nice to clarify things with Jenny and break the barriers I sensed between us. I could never fathom if she felt this way towards me, or if it was all one-sided.

Miranda seemed to feel no such dubious feelings towards Jenny. She had never voiced so much as a single doubt about her. For this reason, I had never mentioned my own misgivings to her.

Even so, my heart ached for Jenny. Nobody ever loves you like your mother does. Even as young as I was, I had learned that.

When we emerged into the steel grey morning, it felt immense and empty. The loss of a single soul can make the whole world feel like a desolate place.

"How lucky I've been to have someone that makes saying good bye so hard."

"Is that a quote, Jenny? Who said that?"

A weary smile hovered on Jenny's sad eyes.

"Some wise old bear."

"Bear?"

Miranda's mind, as usual, jumped several steps ahead of mine.

"Winnie the Pooh."

We shared a chuckle that floated away into the clutches of the winter morning.

"He did say some very profound things," Jenny declared.

JARED TIMES

The Musings of a Hedgewytch in February

"No matter how kind you are; German children are kinder."

Well, my dear friends, it is February. We made it through the cold days of January — such a long month I always think. February is short and sweet by contrast, with Valentine's Day and Family Day marking it as special.

February the first is St Brigid's Day (also known as Imbolc), which is the start of the Celtic spring. It is the halfway point between the winter solstice and spring equinox. Typically, this celebrates the arrival of warmer longer days and early signs of spring, celebrating the return of the light after the dark winter. You can make this day special by lighting a candle to welcome back the sun and set your intentions ahead to the seeds and plants you will nurture in the spring.

Brooke and I made Brigid's Crosses with the children. They are a four-ended cross made from straw with a knotted pattern in the middle. You set them over doorways to protect your home from harm.

I made a cross for each room of my cottage. Then I lit a red candle and as I opened the door I said, "I welcome in the Goddess and seek the turning of the wheel away from winter and into spring."

I like to keep my wee cottage safe and protected, my haven in this big old world.

Of course, the legend of Brigid is an old one, stemming back many centuries. Now we have much more accurate and up-to-date ways to calculate the arrival of spring. We have our Wiarton Willy, who, I am told, this year did see his shadow and thus we have six more weeks of winter ahead of us.

It has been a pretty open winter on the roads this year though. Last year, the local children enjoyed a total of six snow days, while this year they have only had two so far. And this despite the persistence of our local young who wear their pajamas to bed inside out and rest their heads on pillows with spoons nestled under them. I quite like snow days at Hedgewytch Way. The village children gather here, and we have the whole day to indulge in crafts and games that we may not otherwise have time for. They can stay in their pajamas all day long if they wish. We don't mind. Lots of memories have been made here on snow days.

I don't mind the winter myself as long as the roads do not become too treacherous. I remember my dear mother looking out the window at the orchards and fields here on our beloved homestead and remarking that winter was a very peaceful time of year. Indeed, she was right. The snow gives the world a semblance of tranquility and purity.

She is uppermost in my mind and heart these days, my little mom. As many of you, know she died two weeks ago and is now at peace. I want to thank each and every one of you who came to pay your respects to her.

"Your life was a blessing, your memory a treasure, you are loved beyond words and missed beyond measure." Author unknown for this beautiful quote. So many great authors are unknown, it seems.

Any of you who have lived in Jared for any length of time knew my mom. Esther Shafer.

She was born in Berlin Germany in 1923. She was sixteen years old when the war broke out. Like everyone who lived through those terrible years, it took a toll on her. But it never made her cynical or hardened; it simply made her grateful for everything in her life. I didn't know my grandparents, but, by all accounts, they were stern and unyielding. My mother was nothing like that. She was kind and generous of spirit.

She married my father and came to Canada in 1950. My parents had a baby boy when they first moved here — in fact I believe that my mother was pregnant before they even left Germany. In those days it was a two-week journey on a ship. It's hard to picture being tossed around on the ocean when you are pregnant and no doubt, feeling unwell. Not to mention the worry of what may await you in a strange new country. I can scarcely imagine how brave they were. They came on complete and utter blind faith with high hopes for a bright new future. At that time, it was the Canadian Christian Council for the Resettlement of Refuges who assisted people like my parents to find a better life in the new world.

I remember Mom saying that when the ship pulled into Quebec City, they couldn't believe how beautiful Canada was. They never wavered in this belief. They both loved Canada and were grateful to live and raise me in a country that was at peace and free.

My brother died at the age of two from scarlet fever. His name was Thomas. My mother always spoke of him with great love. She must have been pregnant with me when Thomas died. I look back on the hardships that befell my parents and I don't know where they got the strength to bear them. But they did. It never made them bitter. It made them grateful, ever grateful. They appreciated their freedom and their life here. And me. I felt loved and appreciated always. What a rare, precious gift that is.

They bought the piece of land and orchard where I still live today. My dad worked the land tirelessly. He also worked at the paper mill. Esther didn't work outside the home, but she was busy every second. She had a vast garden and she knew all about herbs and plants. She taught me many things — many cures for everyday maladies that could be obtained right in our own back yard. A lot of the products that I sell in my store are derived from her old recipes.

My father died when he was only sixty-two. I was thankful that he'd had a chance to hold his grandson and get to know him before he died. Now they are all together.

My husband and I moved in with my mom shortly after my fathers' demise. We soldiered on together.

She was everything that I could have asked for in a mom. She was sweet and kind and totally loving.

When I first began to dapple in magic, that is herbs and potions and spells, she was deeply interested. Her friends would shake their heads and ask was it not humiliating to have a daughter who got herself up to be a witch?

But Mom was not humiliated, not in the least. Truth be told, she was known to have the "second sight" herself. Or "*hellsehen konnen*", as they say in German. She would often know or perceive things before they happened. She was open minded about everything. She helped me endlessly with potions and candles, making soaps and potpourri.

How very lucky I was to have had such a mom.

We were talking about heaven on the last snow day with some of the children. One of them asked me if I believed in heaven. I replied in the affirmative.

I do believe in heaven. Perhaps not the conventional one recorded in the Bible, but I certainly believe that a wonderful place exists where loving souls commune. I expect my little mom is there right now, keeping an extra eye on me.

I'll feel her in the stars and the gentle breezes blowing around the orchard. I'll see her in the glory of the flowers in her old garden that she loved so much.

As many of you know, she was suffering from Alzheimer's in her last years. I'm glad that she is free from that terrible burden now.

Thank you to every one of the beautiful caring staff at the home. Esther loved all of you. Thank you for your kindness and patience with her. Thank you to Miranda and Molly who stayed with me as her spirit slipped away into the dawn. Thank you to my dear friends, Wes and Art, who always have their taxi ready for me when I am most in need of it. Thanks to all of you who have acknowledged her passing.

And please never hesitate to mention her to me. It will make me happy to hear her name on your lips.

She is a wonderful memory here at Hedgewytch Way. I feel closer to her now than ever.

I'd like the memory of me
To be a happy one,
I'd like to leave an afterglow
Of smiles when life is done.
I'd like to leave an echo
Whispering softly down the ways
Of happy times and laughing
Times and bright and sunny days.
I'd like the tears of those
Who grieve, to dry before the sun.
Of happy memories that I leave
When life is done.

Good bye, my dear, dear Mama. I
will love you always.

20

"This is a wonderful day. I've never seen this one before."

Maya Angelou

M ARCH CAME IN LIKE A LION, roaring along at terrific speed. The days started to lengthen in earnest. The sun attempted to eke out more warmth. The roads improved, muddy and terribly rutted, but free of ice and snow. The world released itself, slowly but surely, from the clutches of winter.

Miranda and I remained so busy with our respective schedules that only on our treks to Jenny's did we perceive spring's grand entry. We beheld the blades of grass poking ever so gently out of their winter entrapment, coaxed by the increased sunshine. Buds crept onto tree branches reaching overhead towards the azure sky.

"I've got spring fever, Molly! I could throw back my head and howl with it."

Miranda's words soared into the throes of the atmosphere with uncharacteristic abandon.

"Spring fever, is it, Miranda?"

"Oh yes. You know, Molly. You know."

"Do I?"

We laughed, running through the bare patches of road more like a couple of kids than two college students. Heavy parkas, toques, and mitts had been strewn aside for spring jackets making us feel free and untethered.

"Yep. You do. You want something."

"What do I want?"

"You don't know what you want exactly, but you want it so bad your heart can hardly stand it."

"That's spring fever, all right," I declared with glee.

We chased each other down the cobblestone path just for the sheer joy of the season.

Spring fever seemed to be in the very air around us. The children reacted with near delirium at the prospect of being relieved of heavy winter gear.

The first day we sighted a robin, I clutched Miranda's arm with joy. It signified such a solid sign of spring, such a reassuring emblem of days to come. We witnessed it hopping in the new grass as we headed out to give our Friday help to Jenny and the afterschool gang. The chance meeting with that little bird filled us with heartfelt gladness.

Quite different from our next encounter that very day. Although this personage embarking towards us on the road could very well be likened to a big black menacing bird. No bearer of springtime gladness this one.

Miranda and I instinctively drew closer to each other, as seemed to be only right in the presence of Joan Payne.

The birds stopped their melodies, clouds covered the sun, and the world stilled as she approached us.

I had no knowledge at that time as to her actual age, but she looked like the oldest person to have ever walked the earth. I say "person", because anyone appearing less feminine would be hard to imagine. I often wished now that I'd taken a picture of her not, of course, to remember her with any fondness, but to have literal proof that she did look as repugnant in reality as she does in my memory. Even so, it would have been unthinkable to produce a phone and take a photo. One might have been turned to stone for doing so. Still, if you picture in your mind any hideous stereotype of a cackling witch with beady eyes and a chin that came very close to a beaked nose, then you'd have a pretty fair image of Joan Payne.

I'd not seen her often on my travels — perhaps four times over the course of my life in Jared thus far — but every time I viewed her with renewed horror. One tends to think that someone can't really be as gruesome as we remember them, that our mind is exaggerating.

Well, Joan really was that bad.

Miranda and I shuddered together as she stormed by us, glaring our way. We knew better than to speak now. We each gave a curt nod which only served to incur more glaring.

Then the world commenced again. The sun burst forth from the grey clouds. Our little robin warbled in a weak attempt to be heard and herald his glad tidings of spring.

"There he is, poor little guy," Miranda pointed to the bird's red breast. "See him, Molly. He was bloody mesmerized by that old crone."

"Weren't we all?" I laughed.

Then, daring to look back, I saw Joan had turned around to look at us, pointing a bony finger in the air.

We ran down the cobblestone path to tell everyone about the robin.

We assisted Jenny getting all the kids into their spring coats and rubber boots. We accompanied them outside to search for the little red breasted fellow, but to no avail. His appearance had been fleeting. Finally, the cool drops of early springtime rain forced us back into the studio. We had to be content with the fact that Miranda and I had witnessed him and hope that he would come again soon.

Brooke and Toby burst into the studio, studded with rain sparkles everywhere. When they heard of the robin sighting, Toby promptly led the children in a resounding round of "Robin in the Rain".

I didn't realize that I even remembered this old tune until the melody took over my memory.

Music can trigger old memories like that — like a gate unleashed by a torrent of water. Miranda explained to me later, when I mentioned this, that listening to music engages large scale neural networks across the entire brain. This, in turn, fills us with emotional memories.

Fortunately, "Robin in the Rain" filled me only with the vague memory of my school days, nothing too nostalgic.

We all yelled the end of the song out of the open window.

"Don't get your feet wet!

Robin on a rainy day."

When the kids had all been picked up, Jenny produced a bottle of her dandelion wine. Miranda, Brooke, Toby and I accompanied her to the protected confines of the porch. We could still smell the fresh earthy odor of the spring rain but remain dry. Here she poured us a glass of that liquid sunshine. Toby had a plastic wine glass which he used on such occasions. His grandma filled it with apple juice and a splash of carbonated lemon water.

We all held our glasses up and clinked them together.

"To spring!"

"You can smell it today. You really can," Jenny observed. "I forget every year how absolutely wonderful that first breath of spring is. It's by far better magic than anything I could ever conjure up in my basement."

We laughed in unison.

My gaze wandered out and into the whispers of grey collecting around the corners of the March evening. Shadows lengthened in a world which had not yet succumbed to darkness. It hovered in the half light of dusk — 'cats light', my mom used to call it, although I never knew what that meant.

"My mom used to say that the first whiff of spring air on the Island made her feel like living again after the long winter," I said. She seemed close to me tonight, somehow. I recalled the joy she'd always derived from the return of spring following the harsh PEI winters.

"I know just how she felt," Connie avowed, stepping out onto the porch. She settled her substantial behind into an aged wicker porch chair, accepting a glass of wine from Jenny with gratitude.

"I know just how she felt," she repeated. "Every year as the snow piles higher and higher, I wonder if I'll survive until spring."

She took an appreciative gulp of her wine. Julie had scampered outside with her, curling in and around the legs of the chairs, her mottled tail twitching behind her. Maybe cats could catch spring fever, too.

"I might just move to Florida in a few years."

Toby looked up in alarm. Jenny remained serene.

"Aw, but Connie dear, what would we ever do without you?"

"I have no idea, I'm sure," was the blunt reply. "Probably burn the place down with your candles or let the house be overrun by stray cats and dogs and children. It's bad enough as it is."

Toby's eyes filled with concern.

"Oh heavens, Toby. I don't mean you, and well you know it."

Connie reached forward, patting his knee with affection, planting a wayward kiss on his beautiful boyish curls.

"Besides," Jenny said, with a sly wink, "you're ours, Toby, not a stray."

Toby grinned, his peace of mind restored.

The smile died quickly with the appearance of Eric Biggs rounding the last corner of the crooked little cobblestone path. He strode in a determined manner. His face wore its habitual scowl.

Brooke stood up and gestured to Toby.

"Drink up, love. Eric's here to walk us home."

Toby uttered no words, but every movement portrayed his reluctance to depart. He shuffled over to his grandma, hugging her tightly, then turned to say his good byes to the rest of us. Brooke ushered him hurriedly off the porch not wishing, I supposed, to incur the ill temper of Eric Biggs.

Why on earth does she keep on with him?

I caught Miranda's reflections as they lingered in the spring air. They mimicked my own thoughts. I had no idea why a loving person like Brooke would consider spending time with such a vile man.

Little did we know that before the onset of summer, these things would be made clear to us.

For now, we watched as they retreated down the path. Toby stopped at the corner and waved to us. We, as of one, waved back. Jenny and Connie blew him a kiss.

Jenny pulled her weathered red shawl closer around her shoulders.

"We'll be able to sit out on the porch more and more now that March is bowing out," she remarked with satisfaction.

"It still gets cool as the sun goes down," Connie observed.

"Oh, I know. But once you feel and smell that spring air, then it's just a matter of time. You know the warmer weather is on its way. I agree with Molly's mom. It does make you feel like living again."

A wave of sadness and longing washed over me. A deep sigh escaped from my lips.

"What is it, Molly?" Jenny asked.

"I miss her sometimes so much that it just comes over me and I feel like I'm drowning in it. I remember her saying that year after year about the spring. And then when she got cancer, she fought so hard. She said that she wanted to live for me. She didn't want to leave me. My dad had died when I was little, and she said she'd always prayed that she'd live long enough to raise me. But then she got cancer when I was just done high school. She said that just wasn't long enough. That she was not ready to leave me yet. She tried so hard, my poor mom," my voice broke a little, despite my best intentions.

I paused, gazing at the other three women sitting with me. I had surprised myself with my outpourings of sentiment, not usually given to sharing these intimate thoughts. Especially when I still felt very much wary of Jenny and all that she stood for. But their faces seemed open with kindness and caring at my revelations. I continued.

"That last winter, she fought so hard to keep going. She said that it would be a cruel twist of fate to make it through a cold Canadian winter and not get to enjoy at least the first breath of spring that brings so much joy."

"And did she? Did she get to smell that first whiff of joy?" Jenny asked gently.

"No. She died in February. Somehow it just didn't seem long enough to have my mom."

"I don't think it's ever long enough to have your mom," Jenny observed.

I felt a pang as I realized that it was only a couple of months since Esther had died.

"Well spring is well on its way now. I do love May," she went on. "Not just because I was born in it."

"So was my mom," I said.

"And mine," Miranda chimed in.

We all laughed.

"See, it's a special month," Jenny smiled at us. "I just love how everything becomes alive again: the trees and the birds, and even the insects. I love to sit up in my apple tree perch after a long winter and get all mixed up in May."

I remembered the first time ever we saw Jenny. She had been perched in the apple tree swing dressed in yellow and declaring this very thing, that she was "all mixed up in May". I nudged Miranda. We both chuckled. Miranda reminded her of this meeting. It seemed impossible that we had known her less than a year. We felt as if we had known her forever — that this little hedgewytch world had always been a part of our life.

"Oh yes," Jenny laughed too. "It does seem to be an annual occurrence. May is just my month to get muddled up in."

She looked from Miranda to me with affection.

"I suppose everyone has a certain time of year that is specific to them — a favorite time when they feel special. May has always been that month for me. But also, things become clearer to me then."

"After the muddle?" Connie asked, in her usual dry manner.

She rose and started straightening up the porch. The light had faded now; a mantle of dusk had enveloped the trees. Only the croaking of frogs sounded through the hush of evening.

Miranda and I rose as well. The time had come to wend our way home through the shadows of the old country path.

"Oh yes." Jenny's reply came late but clear and concise. "After the muddle. It's then that things become clear to me, just like crystal."

I remembered these words much later, when I was the one requiring clarification.

21

"She was a witch all the time, not just in the season of pumpkins and crisp leaves, but always and forever to the depths of her soul."

MickieMuellerStudio

ASTER LOOMED AHEAD OF US NOW, bringing with it the promise of spring and beautiful sunny days that we had waited so long for.

Jenny, it seemed, provided a meal for local people in need at Easter as well. She actively prepared for any number and assortment of humanity that might wander out her way. Miranda and I, it appeared, would be busy on this holiday too, and that suited me fine. I didn't want extra time on my hands to think about Easters gone by. Holidays could be brutal if you had no family.

Although Jenny did not, to my knowledge, attend any church services, she was certainly the most generous person I'd ever known. Despite the misgivings I personally felt towards her, she made me rethink my whole idea of religion and good works. For, of course, it's one thing to go to church and pray for mankind, but it's quite another to open your home to strangers (who may or may not be a little sketchy to say the least) and produce a vast meal for such people. I knew folk from our church back home who'd have looked right down their noses at some of the people who came to Jenny's for a meal.

Jenny just welcomed them.

The days grew warmer. Doors and windows were flung open and the sweet fresh air embraced us in the fragrance of spring. Jenny had a habit of "strewing flowers" — a practice which I was unfamiliar with. Seemingly, it involved placing blossoms under door mats which then erupted into a beautiful aroma when stepped upon. The whole cottage and studio smelled delectable and, I must admit, quite magical. The first flowers of spring hold a sweetness all their own, such a joy to behold as they free themselves from the icy grasp of winter.

The breezes that wandered through the open windows of the cottage caught their perfume as they swirled in and out of its nooks and crannies. Lavender and thyme spread their beautiful aroma everywhere, transforming each breath into a delight.

Jenny told us to go outside and stand amongst the sweet winds of springtime. She told us to visualize the wind passing through us, letting it carry away any last bit of negative energy that clung to us from the grey winter months.

She got out her trusty besom and swept the floors chanting, "With this broom I sweep away all negativity that comes my way."

Spring had brought a whole new feeling of splendor to the world at large and, in particular, to our little Hedgewytch corner of it.

Another extraordinary thing happened that spring. I'd written a little story about chickadees, strictly for the purpose of amusing the children at the Friday circle. One of the moms knew someone employed at a local press and asked my permission to send it to them. This press was a small enterprise, just starting out. But I felt absurdly honored when the editor liked my story and wished to publish it.

Brooke announced this one Sunday morning as we indulged in our after-yoga treats.

"I only wrote it to amuse the children at the circle," I laughed as the ladies congratulated me. "It's not much more than a little jingle I put together. I never intended it to go anywhere."

"And that's why it's so good," Brooke commented. "Because it came from your heart pure and simple. I love it myself."

"I do too," Jenny agreed. "I especially love the last few lines of it. I'll sell it in our little shop. It certainly is in keeping with our mission statement. Or it would be, if we had one."

Laughter erupted amongst the yogis.

"What are those last few lines, Molly? I didn't hear the ending the other day when Jenny was reading it," Freddy said. "I had to leave for my shift. But I loved the part that I heard."

"Thanks, Freddy," I mumbled. "I can't remember it word for word, though."

"I can." Jenny piped up. "Those last lines go like this:

There is magic in these little black capped fellows.
Having them light on your hand, even for a heartbeat, brings
*   that magic right into you.*
It's wonderful to have this magic in your life.
You don't need much to get by.
Just the tiny beat of a chickadee in your hand.
Just a bit of magic."

Everyone clapped. I felt myself blushing right into the roots of my hair.

"It's ok, Molly. It's wonderful. We're all very proud of you," Freddy told me, acknowledging my embarrassment.

"You've made a story that the children can read and walk right into. They know it happens. They've seen Toby with chickadees in his hand. Good job. I'm definitely going to buy it for my grandchildren," Dolores said.

"Me too," Faye joined in, beaming her kind smile at me.

"I'll buy it as well," Kerry said. "I love children's books that the kids can relate to."

Lauren nodded in agreement. I felt pleased at the outpouring of support from these women.

Maybe someday I'll write a story about them, this hodgepodge of women, I thought.

Someday … when I was finished my Bachelor of Applied Science in Early Education. Not much time for writing with that hanging over my head — not to mention the added burden of trying to support myself.

But, wow, I'd be loaded with ammunition if I ever wanted to compose a story about this odd assortment of lives. And I haven't even heard the half of them yet.

"When it comes out in all its glory, we'll have an official book signing right here at the Hedgewytch Way," Jenny declared. "That will be great publicity for us."

"As if we need any more publicity," Connie moaned. "We've already got more than we can handle every day."

"I know. I know," Jenny agreed. "How right you are, Connie. It's always busy this time of year. There's no getting around it."

"What crafts have you girls got lined up for the Friday crew? Anything special for Easter?" Brooke asked, turning to Miranda and me.

"We're thinking of a few things," I answered, relieved at the switch in topics.

"We're going to make tussie mussies." Miranda said.

Jenny and Brooke nodded in approval.

"What the heck is a 'tussie mussie'?" Lauren asked.

Miranda hastened to explain, as some of the other women were murmuring that they "had no clue" what it was either.

"It's actually just a fancy name for a nosegay of flowers. You're supposed to gather fresh flowers and fragrant herbs. We're limited in that, because of the time of year. But Jenny has quite a few things we'll be able to use in her herb garden and little greenhouses. We can get lavender and thyme, and they both smell wonderful. Molly and I will go to the dollar store and get some scraps of coloured material to brighten them up. The kids select what they want for theirs, then Molly and I help tie them into a close little bunch. Then we'll cut a white lace doily down one side, wrap it around the base of the bouquet and tie it up with a ribbon."

"That sounds great," Heather exclaimed. "I almost wish that I had a child in your day care circle so I could get one of those."

"I can make you one, Mrs. Winton." Toby declared solemnly.

"Oh no, no. I was just kidding," Heather waved the suggestion away.

She looked at the sincere expression on Toby's face and her faded face broke into a smile. Maybe Heather was learning too.

"Do you know something, Toby? I would love that."

Toby beamed.

"I never cease to be proud of that boy," Jenny leaned over, whispering these words to Miranda and me.

"You should be," Miranda replied. "He's a great kid."

"We also got a few pots of washable yellow paint," I continued, "We're going to get the kids to put their hands in the paint and then put their hand print on a piece of paper. If they keep doing that, but rotate their hands around in a circle, they'll make the shape of the sun. Their fingers are the sun beams. It's just a nice spring idea. Then we'll draw a happy face in the middle part and have the kids sign their names to make an Easter card."

"I don't know how you girls think up all of these things."

"Mostly we get them from Pinterest. They have great ideas for kid's activities and crafts."

"I don't know what we ever did before these two came to work for us," Jenny declared.

"Me neither," agreed Brooke.

After the execution of all these crafts on Friday, though, I felt exhausted. When the last parents approached along the crooked little path to collect their respective urchins, relief flooded through me. Miranda and I both sported different shades and degrees of yellow paint, smelled delicious from the various herbs, and felt quite fatigued after our combined day of classes and leading the craft circle.

We sprawled onto the wonderful orchard chairs, full of gratitude to be able to use them again after the long winter. The rays of the sun warmed our very souls.

"We'll go back and clean up the studio a bit, Jenny," Miranda told her. "There's quite a bit of yellow paint everywhere."

Jenny chuckled.

"Don't worry about it. We can get it later on. At least yellow's a cheerful colour. Those sun faces look so good I might ask the kids to paint some on the walls at the kids end of the studio."

"Or my end," Brooke laughed, "because they are pretty cheerful."

If anyone else had said this, I might have thought they were teasing. But I knew that Jenny and Brooke were quite capable of getting the children to create bright yellow suns fashioned from their handprints all over the walls. And they would appreciate the end result.

Easter Sunday morning dawned bright, sunny, and warm. Miranda and I arrived at Jenny's quite early in the day to assist in the arranging of flowers and herbs and baked goods. Her huge harvest table groaned with its burden of food, a sight to behold.

We assisted Connie and Brooke and Jenny in hiding approximately five hundred little foil wrapped Easter eggs amongst the budding orchard grasses.

In the early afternoon, the village children started to arrive. Many I knew, of course, but some were totally unfamiliar. They seemed to come in droves around the corner and up the cobblestone path.

Strains of "Here comes Peter Cottontail" sounded in various off-key voices.

"Oh, they come from far and wide for the Easter egg hunt to be sure," Connie had declared that morning. At the time, I thought she might have been exaggerating.

She had not. There had to be at least fifty children scampering and tumbling into the orchard. I looked askance at a group of several teenagers, but Jenny didn't seem to mind. She welcomed them all. The air came alive with laughter and giggles. Children rolled without abandon in the sweet spring grass, gathering leaves in their hair and sunshine in their eyes.

Jenny had provided wicker baskets in which to gather the eggs. The orchard flowed like a brilliant sea of vibrant colour. At the location of a single egg, cries of triumph rang out.

Jenny beamed.

"I love my home like this," she declared. "I feel like this is exactly the way that it's meant to be."

Most of the children wandered their way home as the afternoon hours started to stretch into evening. Some lingered and stayed for the Easter meal.

As at Christmas time, people situated themselves everywhere partaking in the feast. But instead of being confined to the rooms inside, they spilled out onto the porch, balancing their plates on their laps, gulping in the warm weather.

I pondered all of this anew as I went around, collecting plates and cutlery from the grateful beings scattered about. I'd been raised with religion as a big part of my life. We attended mass regularly, and would never have missed it at Christmas or Easter. No religious element existed in this hedgewytch cottage. In fact, the whole premise of magic and supposed witchcraft would have been deeply frowned upon by the church. I shuddered to think of what my mom would have opined about the whole concept.

But if she'd lived, I never would have made my way to Ontario, let alone Jared and the crooked little cobblestone path leading to this cottage. I couldn't imagine such a thing now. I felt as if I completely belonged in this village. I'd created a whole life here, at the university, at the café, and most of all here, at this funny little cottage with these kind quirky people.

I gazed about the cottage. I loved the purple door with its rounded top. A wreath adorned it now, made from scores of Easter eggs previously dyed by the children, fashioned with love and endless patience by Jenny and Connie. I loved the stone walls that looked as if they had stood there since time began and the thatched roof the likes of which I'd never seen before, save in fairy tale pictures. The cottage itself deceived you because it appeared quite minimalistic on the outside. Only upon entering the purple door did you realize the full depth and breadth of it. It sprawled in all directions. It seemed to expand inexplicably as you walked from the front hall into the kitchen and then the huge adjoining room, encompassing a stone fireplace and long harvest table. Above this, tucked into gables, stood several bedrooms facing out to the east. And, of course, if you exited out of the back door the majesty of row upon row of apple trees welcomed you.

I picked up the last cup, chuckling to see Julie making her way in between bushes and plants, her calico fur spangled with an assortment of Easter egg shell remnants and foil wrappers.

Miranda joined me on the porch, her arms laden with dishes.

"The days are getting longer. Look, Molly. It's almost seven and it's still light out."

"You're right. We survived the Ontario winter," I agreed, as we proceeded into the kitchen to dump our arms into soapy dishwater. "The days will just keep getting longer and warmer now."

Jenny came and linked arms with us.

"Leave those for now," she said. "Come and sit by the fire. We'll have an Easter toast."

She gestured us into the large room where the fire glowed a warm welcome.

Only Connie, Brooke, and Toby remained. I felt tired and happy.

The wariness that I felt for Jenny seemed to be easing — some days more than others. Today, I could feel my heart softening towards her as she lifted her glass in a toast to Easter and all good things to come in the summer ahead.

22

"The circles of women around us weave invisible nets of love that carry us when we're weak and sing with us when we are strong."

Sark

THE ONSET OF WARMER DAYS HAD INSPIRED JENNY, she announced to us one beautiful spring morning. We had remained in our post yoga circle reluctant to disperse, eager to linger. She, the queen of so many varieties of tea, had decided to serve a totally diverse beverage.

Lavender honey iced coffee.

Apparently, it involved something like soaking raw almonds in water overnight, then placing the almonds and water in a blender. Lavender being Jenny's perpetual favorite, she always had dried stalks on hand. She'd mixed these in, along with some honey, blending it, straining it and adding shots of expresso. This concoction got poured over ice, the ensuing result quite delicious. Herbal teas tended to be warm and comforting. Today's drink seemed much more exotic, calling for a different kind of a morning.

Toby observed as much as he dispensed mugs from the refreshment cart.

"This is different. Iced coffee. We should do something exciting, Gran, to go with it."

"I have some pumpkin muffins," Jenny replied, deliberately misunderstanding. "They're pretty exciting."

Toby guffawed.

"You know what I mean. Let's do something we don't usually do. Something witchy."

"Witchy?"

"Something magical. I know! You've got tarot cards right, Gran?"

Jenny's lips crinkled into a smile.

"What kind of a witch would I be if I didn't, Toby dear?"

"I can get them. I remember where they are."

Eagerness spread over his young face as his eyes pleaded with Jenny. She nodded her assent.

"I won't touch them," he added, hastening from the studio.

He returned with the tarot cards, wrapped in silk and nestled inside a pine box.

"Only Gran can touch them," Toby explained, his manner cautious. "Unless she's doing a reading and then only that person can touch them. It's so the cards can feel their energy."

Jenny nodded her approval.

I bristled with curiosity. I knew exactly nothing about tarot cards.

Eight yogis surrounded the mat holding that mysterious box on this particular day, Lauren, Brooke, Miranda, Faye, myself, Freddy, Verna, and Connie.

Anticipation rose in the air, like a tangible thing.

Jenny took the cards from the box, her hands caressing them as she unfolded them from a worn bit of green silk.

"Green for a hedgewytch," Miranda murmured.

Jenny glanced around, surveying our eager faces.

"I can't do a full reading for everyone," she said. "That would take forever."

She picked the cards up, turning them over in her slender fingers. Fingers that seemed to spark little shards of light from them. Or had I just imagined that?

"There are seventy-eight cards in a tarot deck. Fifty-six of these cards are called minor arcana cards and they represent your free will — the lessons you need to learn in your daily life. The remaining twenty-two cards are major arcana cards. They represent your soul's progression on your life's journey toward enlightenment. Each card has its own meaning. For instance: the fool means awareness, the magician means attention, the moon means deception, and so on."

We listened with interest, this being uncharted territory for all of us.

Jenny continued. "You should always try to ask open-ended questions of the tarot cards. For instance, don't ask 'Will I win the lottery?' or 'When will I die?'. Instead, you should ask something like 'What do I need to do to achieve financial success?" or 'What can I do to improve the quality of my life?'.

"Another little thing is that you can think of a goal or a desire. Then you can give the deck a good shuffle and, when you feel like the time is right, you can split the deck in your hands, holding up the cards on either side. The card revealed in your left hand represents what will hinder you, while the one facing up in your right hand represents what will help you."

She looked up from the cards and smiled at us.

"A whole tarot reading usually lasts at least an hour. It would simply take up too much time. I'm just telling you some really basic things about them."

"What if you let everybody pull one card and read that card? Would that work?" Freddy inquired.

Jenny considered this possibility, then nodded her concession.

"We could do that, if you want to. As long as you ladies remember that it's just for fun, especially if you're only pulling just one card. I can tell you about the card you pulled and how it pertains to you, but we can't take ourselves too seriously.

Particularly when there are no other cards to give it sustenance or back up."

We all nodded in agreement, eagerness rampant in the air.

She shrugged.

"Ok then. Who's going first?"

"I will," Lauren said, her voice fervent and excited.

"All right. Lauren, you must shuffle the cards at your own pace, in your own way. When you're done shuffling, just hold the cards in your hands and feel the transference of your energy into them. When you feel ready, pull a card and lay it face up on the mat."

Lauren took the proffered cards.

"And remember," Jenny repeated, "It's just for fun. Don't take it too seriously."

Lauren shuffled with much ado.

Finally, she turned up a card and laid it on the mat. Jenny picked it up and studied it.

"The Chariot," she announced.

"Is that good or bad?" Lauren asked.

"Neither. It's just a card. Hm-m. The chariot. This is the card most often associated with victory and control. Remember that it's hard for a card to stand alone in a tarot reading. When you have a full spread of cards, you can see how this card fares in relation to the ones around it. But right now, we've got only the Chariot. The main thing that it represents is victory. It is about decision-making, focus, and determination. It's a willingness to take the reins. Control, will power, assertion, determination. These are the words the chariot speaks of. The chariot indicates a lot of energy, but not free-for-all energy. Its energy is directed and controlled with a definite goal in mind. See here on the card, Lauren, the triumphant chariot and the armed warrior and the canopy of stars. It's a victory card."

Lauren nodded as Jenny relayed this information. I couldn't help thinking that the card suited her, at least what I knew about her. Despite her age — which was closer to mine and Miranda's than some of the other yogis — we had not grown especially close to her. She always seemed so pressed for time, always on a mission, often making the rest of us seem less important by comparison.

She handed the cards with reluctance to the person on her right, which happened to be Brooke.

Brooke shuffled, stating that she really didn't believe in tarot cards.

"I know," Jenny said. "We're just being a little silly today. See what turns up for you, my love."

Brooke presented a card with a young man standing in front of the ocean, wearing old fashioned clothes and holding a golden cup in his right hand. A fish poked his head out of the cup and looked at the young man.

"Ah! The Page of Cups. Imagine that."

"Imagine what, Gran?" Toby interjected.

"It's very interesting, that's all. The Page of Cups is a dreamer — a young man with an old soul and the heart of a poet. This is a fine uplifting sign to receive in a tarot reading. It's a signal to allow your child-like side to come forward and have some fun, to play and dream, and be a little less serious. Someone is on their way with a message for you."

"A message?"

"The page of cups is Cupid," Jenny went on, her manner nonchalant. "He is bringing you opportunities for love. It could be there's a chance that love will blossom soon."

Brooke muttered something unintelligible and, looking daggers at Jenny, passed the cards to Miranda beside her. Clearly, she had no desire for any romance or message of such in her life anytime soon.

Miranda proceeded in kind, picking out her card.

We all gasped at the sight of her card. Miranda seemed frozen.

There could be no doubt about this one. The card depicted the grim reaper.

Only Jenny appeared calm and collected.

"The grim reaper, Miranda, does not mean that he is coming for you, my dear girl. Everyone gives a little start when they see this card, but there's no need for alarm. This card is the thirteenth trump card in most traditional tarot decks. But in spite of that, it's not a bad omen or a foreshadowing of doom. It almost never refers to actual physical death. It's about releasing old habits, ending old relationships, Miranda, closing one door to open another, going through transition and moving from the known into the unknown. This card is about rebirth and transformation. It represents the passing of the old, the natural end of a situation, and the dawn of a new opportunity."

Miranda remained silent, her expression unreadable.

"Does this sound a little familiar to you, dear?"

Miranda continued to stare at the grim reaper wielding his scythe above his skeleton head.

"This is a card about being in the path of sweeping change and being caught in the unescapable, then accepting the inevitable."

As close as Miranda and I had grown, I sometimes felt a distance between us still. I longed to know more about her life story and what this card might mean to her. Her face, however, remained indecipherable and I was left wondering.

Without a word, Miranda passed the cards to Faye, on her right.

Faye shuffled the cards in her gentle manner, turning up a card with a queen sporting yellow hair, holding a gold chalice and sitting on a throne decorated with cherubs.

"The Queen of Cups," exclaimed Jenny. "What a perfect card for you, Faye. So far, the cards have been accurate, I must say."

Brooke and Miranda muttered comments to the contrary.

Jenny chose not to listen and proceeded with Faye's reading.

"The Queen of Cups is among the most loving archetypes in the tarot deck. She indicates compassion, love and concern for her fellow man. She is quite enlightened, this queen. She has learned life's lessons."

"You don't get to be this age without learning a few lessons along the way, I guess," Faye conceded.

"She has learned to be kind, this queen." Jenny continued. "See the lid on the chalice she holds? That lid holds deep love inside it. In tarot, cups represent energy and queens represent female energy. She has a kind word for everyone and never reacts with anger. She is admired for her warm heart and honesty. Does this not sound like our Faye?"

We all nodded. It did indeed sound like her. But I couldn't help reflecting that it wasn't as interesting as some of the other cards. We're all intrigued a little more by the extraordinary. Everyday kindness is wonderful, but not necessarily magical. Or exciting.

Faye handed the cards to me and I thought that I might live to regret these last thoughts. God knows, I didn't want to see the grim reaper staring up at me. I wouldn't have minded Brooke's card though. I felt ripe for some romance.

I squeezed my eyes and concentrated, attempting to impart my energy into the cards. Then I cut them and produced my chosen one.

I peered at it with interest. It depicted a clear blue sky with old fashioned buildings in the foreground. It looked like a village square. A boy and a girl stood there, the boy holding a golden cup with flowers in it. He is handing it to the girl and they're both sniffing the flowers.

"The Six of Cups," Jenny pronounced. "If you were to seek guidance from just this card, Molly, it would be difficult. The card standing alone has less meaning than if it were pulled in the middle of a spread. It's a card focusing on childhood and nostalgia. You want to return to the happy memories of your past, your childhood. You long for the happiness of days gone by and your childhood innocence. That, I think, is quite true for you, is it not, Molly?"

I felt inexplicable anger and resentment rise inside of me.

Who was she to speak of my childhood like that? What did she really know about me?

Nothing.

I looked down at the card and felt astonished at the stabs of saltwater pricking my eyes. Was I that fragile and transparent that I could be hurt at a stupid card reading?

Apparently so.

I passed the cards to Freddy without even lifting my head. I didn't care if I appeared rude and childish. I didn't feel so polite just then.

Freddy, ever tactful, disregarded my hurt demeanor and took her turn.

I expected her to turn up some sort of brilliant card to match her bright funny personality.

But her card looked awful. It pictured a man lying face down on the ground with a bunch of swords stuck into his body and a black sky above.

I shuddered. *Yuck.*

Freddy portrayed no alarm. Her face wore an odd expression, almost as if she had expected a horrible card.

"Ten of Swords," Jenny said. "The Ten of Swords is about hitting rock bottom, being burned out. You can feel like a doormat, like a total victim, always putting your own interests last. This card is symbolic of despair, of lack, of the metaphorical death of some aspect of your life."

Freddy visibly flinched at these last words.

I wondered why the hell we thought this would be entertaining.

"But see this golden sky in the distance, Freddy? Underneath the black part, closer to the horizon?"

Freddy peered at the card and nodded.

"That golden sky represents hope in the situation. By coming to terms with a bitter realization, you are learning that moving forward is the most important way to heal."

"That's good," Freddy said, her voice non-committal.

She turned to Verna and passed her the cards, her old grin restored to her mouth, even if it didn't quite reach her eyes.

Verna shuffled with speed and efficiency, as she did everything. She turned her card up and placed it firmly on the mat. It showed a naked lady dancing over the earth surrounded by a green wreath.

My eyes met Miranda's and I stifled a grin.

"The world," Jenny said. "Very fitting for you, Verna Snell, I must say."

"How so? All I see is a naked lady dancing around." She sniffed. "Doesn't seem much like me."

"See the four elements in each corner of the card, Verna? Water, air, earth, and fire. The world. There are different meanings for this card especially when it comes up in a full reading of cards. The common theme, though, is one of satisfaction. Satisfaction for achieving goals which are important to you. Completion or fulfillment of an important task. And just to stay on the path you've chosen and keep going. In other words, do what you're doing."

"As if I have much choice," Verna scoffed.

She seemed pleased with her card, though.

She passed the cards along to Connie with a grin.

"Last, but not least," she declared.

Connie turned up the weirdest-looking card yet. It pictured a stone tower set against a black sky. Flames shot out the top of it and two men fell from it: one backwards, one forwards. Clouds of grey smoke billowed everywhere. I shuddered to myself. This couldn't be good.

"Come on, Jenny. Tell me the worst."

Connie did not seem to be taking any of this seriously, which made me a little embarrassed at my earlier hurt reaction. I had not yet learned the art of self-awareness. I needed to view myself with a touch of humor.

"The Tower. See these two men falling from the tower. Neither of them has done anything to cause the destruction and chaos they are enveloped in, but still they are caught in it. It is a card about going through sudden change, breaking through pretense and letting go, falling and having a revelation. You know, like having a burst of insight and realizing the truth."

Connie chuckled and tossed the cards into a pile again.

"Really, Jenny? I couldn't have turned up a nice rainbow or something? I have to turn up that monstrosity."

"A rainbow?"

Connie nodded.

"Sure, isn't that the accepted symbol for the gay community these days?"

"You're gay?" Miranda asked, seemingly too surprised to mind her manners.

Connie didn't seem to care.

"Yes, my dear. I guess that's what the card stands for. I did have a terrible time when I was younger. I even got married, because that's what you did in my day. But I knew for a long time that I was simply not attracted to men. If Jenny hadn't taken me in and helped me along, who knows where I would have ended up."

Miranda and I gasped, as in one breath.

"You and Jenny?"

Connie laughed, shaking her head.

"Oh no dear. We're just very good friends."

"The best," Jenny declared.

"I was lost and alone with nowhere to go when I met Jenny. I'd wandered into the post office in Guelph, wondering if there was any kind of work that I could find. You know how they post ads and stuff on the board there? Well, I was reading some of the postings and not feeling very hopeful when Jenny came up behind me with a piece of paper in her hand. She said she was just about to post it on the board."

"Were you really?" Freddy asked.

"Oh yes." Jenny replied.

"She needed help, you see," Connie continued. "Her husband had died, and she needed help to keep her business going. And she told me," Connie's voice cracked.

She seemed unable to go on.

"I told her that she was just the person I was looking for," Jenny finished for her. "And she was. She still is."

"She told me she was a hedgewytch and she hoped that wouldn't put me off. Well, let me tell you something, ladies: when you've been thrown out of your home by your husband and your only sibling is disgusted and chooses not to know you because of your sexual orientation, you're not put off by very darned much."

"Do you live here all the time now?" I asked, surprised that the thought had never occurred to me before.

"I have an apartment in Guelph, just a little one that I share with someone when she can get away to be with me. But I have a room here too and I spend a lot of my days here."

A funny image came into my mind of Connie's bedroom at Hedgewytch Way, of her folding it up and tucking it away underneath the stairs when she went to Guelph and reassembling it again on her return.

I gave my head a shake. The fancy had been so real that it left me feeling startled.

Was the magic getting inside of me now?

"Imagine you being there right at that moment, Jenny," Freddy mused.

"Just imagine," Jenny replied.

"It changed my life, so it did," Connie said.

"It's almost enough to make you believe in magic," Freddy went on.

"Never doubt it, Freddy. Never doubt it."

I thought of the sparks emitting from Jenny's fingers, of Connie's story and of my cryptic image of her little room tucked inside of Hedgewytch Way.

Could magic be a thing that you caught? Like a virus?

Jared had certainly changed the way I perceived things.

I looked at the oh-so-different women around me and realized that I had now heard several of their stories.

And I knew, with a rush of certainty, that others were yet to be told. Stories that would change my own life story.

Somehow. I just didn't know how.

Not yet.

23

"Each time women gather in circles with one another, the world heals a little more."

I T STARTED AS ANY ANOTHER BRIGHT SPRING DAY.
I marveled as I reflected that I'd lived in Jared for an entire year. A year like no other. A year in which Jenny continued to hold a mystery for me. I didn't feel the degree of uneasiness towards her that I once had. Still the feeling never left me that the image she portrayed to the world had little to do with her in her entirety. I felt warmth and affection towards her but never trust.

We'd finished our Sunday morning yoga. The breathtaking clarity of the blue sky cut at my heart with its splendor. The fresh air brimmed to overflowing with the sweetness of spring's fulfillment. We had opted to have our tea outside in the orchard. The new grass gleamed fragrant and verdant underneath us as we arranged our mats for refreshments. I'd never cared much for herbal teas before, but enjoying Jenny's different concoctions each week kept life interesting.

Some of the nurses lolled on their mats, not sleeping, as none had worked the dreaded night shift, but lolling just the same. Miranda and I relaxed amidst the other yogis.

Toby assisted Jenny, passing out mugs and milk and sugar from the cart, along with little cinnamon donut holes.

Sporadic bursts of laughter rang into the air, as we enjoyed comradeship and the pleasure of soaking up the glorious May day. It seemed that we had finally turned the corner into warmer weather. Our long Canadian winter had departed, leaving us with the joy that only spring can bestow with her kisses of sunshine.

Then, abruptly, a cloud fell across the sun.

We all looked up. No, it wasn't a cloud at all. Well, not exactly. It was Eric Biggs.

Remember that old nursery rhyme? Goes like this:

I do not like you, Dr. Fell
The reason why I cannot tell
But this I know and know full well
I do not like you, Dr. Fell.

It was like that with Eric Biggs. In fact, I could have substituted his name and I thought, inconsequentially, that the syllables would have fit perfectly even if they didn't rhyme.

Although my dislike for him I could identify readily enough.

Eric's behaviour towards Brooke seemed to be invariably threatening. Or something like that. You couldn't put your finger on it with any degree of precision. He seemed to treat her with disdain and intimidate her. Her beautiful spirit dimmed when he appeared. And he appeared a lot. She always said she was grateful to him when he came to accompany her. But those were just words.

Now he cocked his head at Brooke and asked shortly, "Ready to go?"

Brooke looked lovely reposing on her yoga mat, her chestnut hair shining in the beacons of sunlight.

"Just finishing my lemon rosehip tea," she replied.

"Oh, you are, are you?"

He sneered the words at her.

Sneering is his specialty, I thought.

The chatter ceased, bit by bit, as women turned to watch this exchange. Toby and Jenny, too, paused in their tea distribution. A worried frown had developed on Toby's beautiful face. I hated Eric for making that happen.

He seemed ripe to pick a fight today, his demeanor more sullen than usual.

"Yes, Eric," Brooke said serenely, but her words held a slight quiver. "I'm going to hang around a little longer today and help Jenny out. I appreciate you coming for us, but no need to wait. Really."

Brooke always addressed him like this, careful and polite.

"No need, eh?" Another sneer. "No need?"

"That's right, Eric. You might as well go."

"I'll go when I'm bloody well ready to go. I don't need you to tell me anything."

I felt a little shiver, knowing in my heart that this wouldn't end well.

Brooke scrambled to her feet, eyes downcast, as she proceeded to rearrange her mat on the orchard grass. I never knew if she intended to depart with him or not. Because other things happened then.

A subtle change seemed to take place in the little group. No one pretended not to notice the sheer hatefulness of Eric Biggs. One by one, we stood and, without a word, approached our beloved yoga teacher. Toby had crept in beside her and was holding her hand, gazing up at Eric with stricken eyes.

"Isn't that right, Toby?" he snarled, his tone causing the boy to cringe against his mother. "What the hell are you cowering about?"

Jenny, in that funny way she had of appearing soundlessly like a small shadow, stood beside Brooke now. One arm crept around Brooke's shoulder. The other embraced Toby.

She stood very sure and straight, presenting an imposing figure despite her diminutive stature.

"Eric Biggs."

Her voice rang clear, her words clipped.

"You are not welcome here. Please go."

The scene shifted, as we advanced to surround the three, Brooke and Toby and Jenny, in a silent show of support. If an aerial view could have been afforded, it would have shown the dark figure of a menacing young man facing a tight little group of women, all shapes and sizes, and a topknot of grey curls bobbing in its midst.

"Oh, you all think you know so much, you old cows. Well, I could tell you a thing or two about your precious Brooke."

Brooke looked as if she was going to faint or vomit. Or both.

Toby gasped in horror.

"Tell us whatever you want," Freddy took a small step forward, hands on hips, head thrust high. "Do you think any of us care what you think?"

The other nurses nodded in unison, murmuring in agreement.

Wow, these nurses are ready for a fight.

None of this appeared to have any effect on Brooke, save to heighten her misery. She seemed to be shrinking inside of herself. Jenny took another step. She now stood a mere few inches from the dark young man.

But she did not direct her next words to him.

Without moving a muscle, she said simply, "Connie."

Connie came forward then, her squat figure bristling with indignation. She required no instruction. She reached her arms out for Toby.

"Come with me, Toby dear," she instructed, her voice calm and measured.

Toby looked askance at his mother who seemed incapable of speech. He turned to Jenny.

"Go with Connie," she told him. "Go with Connie now, Toby."

"I don't want to," the child protested, his voice choked. "I want to stay here with my mommy."

"Your mommy," Eric sneered again.

Jenny gave him a withering look. He did not wither, but he did fall silent for the moment.

Jenny turned and knelt beside the distraught child. She held him until he became calmer.

Then she stood and repeated, "Go with Connie now, Toby. I will explain everything to you later on."

"Really?"

"There are things which you won't understand today, but I promise you that when you are old enough to understand, I will explain it all to you."

"I want you to tell me now." Toby started to whine.

Jenny remained unperturbed.

"Toby," her voice spoke true and definite. "You know that I won't break a promise to you; you know that. I can't explain it all to you today. You'll just have to have faith in me."

"Then when?"

"I don't know that for sure, but I do promise that everything will be all right. I promise that right this minute."

I felt completely baffled. Looking around, it seemed the others felt the same way.

Brooke's eyes bore into Jenny, engulfed with doubt and misery.

"Promise?" Toby pleaded.

"I promise and cross my heart," Jenny said, making the appropriate gesture. "Now go with Connie like a good boy."

Toby allowed himself to be led away.

Jenny turned again to face Eric, drawing herself up to her full height.

"This, Eric, is our day of reckoning."

"Day of reckoning?"

Miranda and I looked at each other, full of angst and unease.

The whole scene felt utterly foreign. Our usual haven of cheerfulness and goodwill had been turned topsy-turvy. Worry and displeasure filled our yogi circle, but I felt something else too. I felt courage and friendship, even love, between us as we stood side by side in our silent support of Brooke.

Jenny's stance relaxed somewhat now that Toby had been removed from the orchard. She linked her arm under Brooke's. The look of fear had left Brooke's face and been replaced by something else. Resignation? Defeat? Sadness?

"Now," Jenny addressed Eric, her gaze steady and sure, "Now, Eric, that we are all adults let us proceed, shall we?"

He looked at her warily. He didn't seem so tough now, confronted as he was by the female population of Jared.

Jenny's eyes never left his face. I got the distinct feeling that she knew exactly how this scenario would play out.

An uncanny silence prevailed. Only the sweet song of a lark rang across the bright spring air.

Then Eric came to life, attitude and all.

"You guys think you're all so great."

"And? "Jenny prodded him.

"And you think you're all so much better than everybody else."

"And?"

"Well you're not that great, any of you. That's all."

These words seemed an anti-climax.

Jenny remained self-composed, her voice steady and sure.

"Eric, if you have anything to say, anything at all, I implore you that this is the time to say it."

"It is, is it?"

Another sneer.

"Speak now or forever hold your peace. I think that's what's happening here."

This from Freddy, with Clarisse and Irene nodding beside her. Eric turned to them, happy to have a new focus for his contempt.

Jenny stood rooted in her spot. She needed no back up, being a force unto herself. She took another small step forward, indicating that this battle belonged to her alone.

"Eric?"

"I could tell you things that would rock your world, Jenny Smith."

Brooke cowered visibly now, looking as if the wind might well knock her over. Her face had paled as white as the hearts of the apple blossoms blowing above us.

Miranda looked at me. I shrugged. Neither one of us had a clue what was going on. The air hushed inside the fragrant orchard walls.

"Go ahead then, Eric."

"You won't like them."

"There is nothing you could tell me that would rock my world, Eric Biggs. You may rest assured of that. Nothing."

I've never forgotten how she looked that day, like a warrior. The sun illuminated her in a warm encasing glow and her eyes flashed with blue fire.

Everyone held their breath. We all felt that the next words spoken would change everything.

As they did.

"Toby is not Buddy's son."

Eric's sharp words cut through the crisp spring air.

Jenny's gaze did not falter.

"I know," she declared calmly.

"You know?"

Eric dropped his façade of contempt in his astonishment.

"Of course, I know, Eric Biggs. Do you seriously think that they call me the local witch for nothing? Do you think that I've done nothing at all to earn my reputation?"

Eric Biggs, rendered speechless, gaped at her.

Then he laughed shortly.

"Well, you could have fooled me with all the fuss you make over that kid, and her."

He jerked his thumb in the direction of Brooke whose jaw had dropped open in incredulity.

"That has absolutely nothing to do with anything. I don't need you to tell me how to feel about anyone. By the way, Brooke will be fine without your company from now on. If that was the only thing you had to hold over her head, that is."

"But — but —" Eric sputtered now. "Don't you get it? Toby isn't your grandson."

"I get it."

"Well, what do you think about that?" Eric's voice held some of the old defiance now.

"I think that I love Toby and Brooke. They're my family and always will be. And I think that if that's the extent of the damage you think you can do for today, then perhaps it's time for you to leave."

Eric stared.

"I think that you should go now," Jenny repeated.

She turned to the rest of us, the ghost of a smile hovering on her lips.

"Go now. Before somebody drops a house on you."

A giggle rang across the yard, breaking the tension. Eric turned and with a final glare at Brooke disappeared down the path.

"Oh, Jenny," Brooke moaned.

Jenny turned and pulled the broken girl into her arms, allowing sobs to consume her young body.

"Everybody knows," she breathed in abject misery.

"Yes," Jenny agreed, her voice gentle.

"And nobody cares," Faye spoke up.

"Really?"

"Really," several voices answered at once.

Brooke raised her head, daring to confront her beloved yogis.

"I was so young," she said. "I was so young and so foolish."

"I know," Jenny said. "It's ok now. He's gone for good, I hope."

"Good riddance," Verna called out.

"He's made me so scared all these years," Brooke observed in wonder. "And now he's gone. Just like that."

"Why didn't you just speak up years ago?" Clarise asked.

"I couldn't. I just couldn't."

"You weren't ready." Jenny told her. "It wasn't time yet."

"I guess so. But mainly I was just scared."

Miranda looked at me and I could feel the question inside of her. *What was going on?* There was more to this than met the eye.

"Scared of what?" I dared to ask.

Brooke looked down at the new grass fluttering in the soft breeze. She plucked a stray apple blossom between her trembling fingers.

"Scared —" she began, her voice trailing off.

"Scared of the truth," Jenny ventured.

"Yes," her words barely audible, her tone flat and miserable.

"The truth is that — that —"

She lifted a face full of despair.

"The truth is that Eric is Toby's biological father."

Her words came out in a painful rush.

Jenny nodded her head slightly.

"You know that, too?" she asked, astonished.

"I suspected it for years."

"Really?" Even Verna spoke with shock in her voice. "How on earth did you deduce that, Jenny Smith? And how did you know that Buddy wasn't Toby's father?"

Sobs overtook Brooke once again.

"Oh, Jenny, I'm sorry that this all had to come out and everybody knows now."

"Ach, it doesn't matter to me, Brooke dear. These women are our friends. They all love you."

Brooke's eyes traveled around the circle to witness those kind women nodding their assent. Every one of them.

"The people that mind don't matter and the ones that matter don't mind," Faye said in her beautiful way.

"And isn't it better to have it out in the open so there's no more secrets? There's nothing Eric can say or do now," Freddy said in her cheery way. "I'm glad to see the ass end of him, let me tell you."

"I was so young. I was so young and scared. And I did love Buddy. You know I did, Jenny."

"Of course, I know that. He loved you too. But I always knew that Buddy wasn't anything more than a special friend to you, as you were to him. I knew there would never be anything romantic between you."

"You did?" Brooke gasped her disbelief.

"Of course, I did. Buddy told me and his dad that he was gay when he was fourteen years old. We'd suspected it already, though."

"Did you mind?"

"Heavens, why would we mind? He was a wonderful boy and we loved him with all our hearts. I know that if he'd lived, he would have kept Toby in his life and helped you with him, every step of the way. I just knew that it wasn't likely he'd fathered Toby."

"Jenny, you are amazing!"

Brooke threw her arms around Jenny. Tears flowed unchecked down her cheeks.

"Of course, I'm amazing," was her matter-of-fact reply. "I have a reputation to uphold."

I could feel my brain groaning as it attempted to process all this information. Poor Brooke had been living with it for ten years. I remembered her telling us that when she first became pregnant, her parents had kicked her out and it had been Jenny who had taken her and her baby in. What a burden she'd endured all these years, wondering and worrying about the truth coming to light.

Little snatches of sentences drifted through the orchard.

"Did you really know all this, Jenny?"

"Why didn't you ever let on?"

"I never had an inkling that Buddy was gay."

"I hope Eric stays away from them both now."

"Well, Toby is lucky to have you, Brooke."

Brooke smiled at this, her smile shining sweetly through her tears, like the sun after rain.

"I'm lucky to have him too. And I'm lucky to have Jenny. I'm the lucky one."

"Seriously, Jenny," Verna couldn't help being who she was. She required an answer. "Seriously, how could you just go on pretending, for ten whole years that Toby was your grandson? Wasn't it hard?"

"No, not really. "

Jenny looked up as Toby now appeared at the door with Connie. His face shone in a wreath of smiles. Eric had disappeared, and everything seemed back to normal in his small world.

"Not really." Jenny repeated. "Sometimes —"

Toby ran, beaming, straight into the circle of love created by his mom and his grandma.

Jenny's face radiated love back to him. She inclined her head towards the circle, finishing her sentence.

"Sometimes you just need a child to love."

24

"Somewhere deep in your memory, you know the ancient ways of the witches. This is why you find yourself drawn by a deep-seated urge. An urge so powerful that you don't even question it or fight for it. You long for it."

I HAD NO IDEA THAT 'BELTANE' had such a huge impact on the Hedgewytch world. Mayday. The first of May. A day of great festivity.

Miranda and I did a bit of research, since we'd never heard of this celebration. Beltane is the Gaelic May Day Festival held halfway between the spring equinox and the summer solstice. It welcomes abundance to the earth after April showers have passed. It's celebrated from sunset April 30th until sunset May first. Samhain, its opposite, celebrates the beloved dead by dividing summer and winter. Beltane, on the other hand, celebrates the living world — dividing winter and summer and marking the return of vitality and passion.

Jenny informed us that Beltane can be called Walpurgis Night — a German word. Over there, they believe that witches fly on their brooms to the mountains, where they gather around bonfires all night and dance.

Miranda chuckled at these words, causing Jenny to say that she would have her broom in order just in case this might be required of her.

Then she proceeded with one of the tidbits of information she sometimes dispersed into her conversation for no apparent reason. She told us to always make sure, when visiting a witch, to check which way her broom stood at the entrance of her house. If her broom stood upside down, then she did not desire company. And woe to those who paid an unwanted visit to any witch. Jenny uttered this in a voice of foreboding that brought my misgivings, never too far away, rushing back.

Then, with a smile, she continued to speak of Beltane.

"It used to be feared that the earth would continue to slumber and remain fallow if not awakened by the fire festival of Beltane. So, people began the tradition of lighting bonfires and dancing around Maypoles to celebrate the awakening of the earth. The cares and fears of winter could then be sloughed off to give way to youthful exuberance. It's a time to rejoice and give thanks for the gift of life. We're having our own Beltane party on May first," she informed us with glee. "Outside in the orchard."

The first day of May dawned sunny and radiant. Jenny had suggested, with that inexplicable twinkle in her eyes, that we should hasten outside on Mayday and wash our faces in the early morning dew. This would reputedly keep us beautiful both inside and outside. I'd paid little regard to this sentiment, but Miranda greeted me at my door that morning, nudging me into the hall and down the worn steps, with her blue and white checkered hand towel slung over her shoulder.

"Oh," I groaned. "You're not taking all this literally, surely."

Miranda didn't reply, but pointed to a metal bowl standing at the corner of the rickety porch. Dredges of milk clung to the inside of its bottom.

"Tell me you didn't leave that out for the Mayday fairies. There's no kids here."

"I filled it with milk and left it there last night," she grinned, "Don't laugh, Molly. I know what you're thinking."

I did laugh, giving my head a rueful shake.

"You really don't want to know what I'm thinking. I know she said they'd come on Beltane eve, but give your head a shake, girl. Those cats up the street that spend half the night outside our windows howling probably licked up that milk. I hope you saved enough for coffee, Miranda. I'm low."

I felt and sounded grumpy, I knew.

"Oh, yeah," Miranda replied in a voice as airy as the Beltane day.

"She's making witches out of us, Miranda. It's kinda scary. I don't quite trust her, you know."

The words escaped my lips before I could catch them back. I'd had so many doubts about Jenny over the past year. But I'd never once verbalized them and it had not been my intention to do so now.

Because, of course, everyone loved Jenny. Definitely the yogi circle anyways. On the other hand, there did exist a newspaper columnist who had no love of her, believing that she represented all evil things personified by the word 'witch'. And who knew how many others?

I suppose I was somewhere betwixt these two opinions. The words that had slipped from my unwitting lips probably said it best. I didn't trust her, plain and simple. Still I wished I hadn't said them.

Miranda looked incredulous, increasing my feeling of regret.

"Really, Molly? You don't trust her?"

"Well, just look at us down here in our pajama bottoms and t-shirts washing our faces in the grass. What next?"

"C'mon. Let's go get coffee and then maybe you won't be so grumpy," Miranda observed, collecting her bowl and steering me inside the porch door. It must be admitted that her features looked radiant after dousing them in the fresh May dew. But I didn't care. My bare feet felt freezing cold and I felt tousled, disheveled, not ready to be outside in the world yet.

"I'm not grumpy," I grumped as we ascended the creaking stairs. I followed her inside, plunking myself on her threadbare burgundy couch. She handed me a mug full of coffee.

I carefully inspected it to ascertain that she'd indeed saved enough milk, but it appeared to be just the way I liked it. We'd shared the rhythm of our morning ritual for a year now. It felt familiar and comfortable.

"Ah. Lovely," I pronounced with the first gulp, my good humor restored. Morning coffee will do that.

"I just want to try and explain something to you, Molly. How I feel about all this. Being a witch isn't what I used to think it was," Miranda said, her eyes intent, her expression thoughtful. "There's a whole new movement of witches around today."

"Wiccans, you mean? I've heard of them."

"No, not really. Although the word 'witch' comes from the Saxon word *wicca* which means 'wise one'."

"Wiccans are a religion or something. Pagans, I think."

"But, Molly, a pagan is just a person who feels a strong connection to nature and holds the earth and its creatures sacred. A natural witch can sense the inner spirit in things and people. I've started to look into it a bit. There are women all over who feel the power of the sun and moon, especially the full moon. They have empathy for others — more than most and they can sense the energy around people. They feel deeply connected to the earth, drawing power from it. They can perform healing from herbs and plants. I read this, Molly, and it stuck with me. The living energy that runs through our bodies is just more intense in witches. Energy is like a form of magic. A natural witch can focus on their life energy and heal or enchant someone."

"Wow, you have been reading up," I observed. "I just think it's something Jenny uses for a gimmick or something. I never thought she was a real witch. She even says herself that a hedgewytch isn't a real witch."

"But that's what I'm saying, Molly. There's a stereotype of a 'real witch', but it's passé now. Magic spells can be spoken words, candle burning, mixing oils, throwing crystals, using your own words and gestures into magic spells. But real magic is inside you. It's part of you. Even that chick who wrote Harry Potter, you know?"

"J.K. Rowling."

"Yes, her."

"She's a witch?"

"No, I mean I don't know, but even she says that it's important to remember we all have magic inside us. And Roald Dahl says that if you don't believe in magic, you'll never find it."

"He wrote *Matilda*, right?"

"And *BFG* and *Charlie and the Chocolate Factory*."

"And *The Witches*. Maybe they're just trying to sell their books."

"Maybe. But look at you. You wrote your kids book about the magic of chickadees."

"That was about the magic of nature. Not witchcraft."

"But that's what I'm saying, Moll. They're not different. Not really."

"So, you're a witch now?" I asked her, unable to keep the skepticism from my voice or face.

I observed her over the rim of my coffee mug, her face earnest as she struggled to explain. I balked at her revelations from the depths of my soul. Because if I accepted them, what did I become? *A witch, too?*

"I've always loved magic, Molly. And witches and spells. All the best stories have witches in them. Think about that. But they're just stereotypes of witches.

"Didn't you feel something the very first time we went downstairs at Jenny's and saw all the crystals and smelled the herbs and oils? Didn't you feel part of you respond to all that?"

I didn't answer. I didn't know how I felt. I hadn't seen this coming. Maybe some sort of Beltane magic was bewitching Miranda. So, where the hell did that leave me?

"A witch goes to nature to be soothed and healed and have her senses restored. A green witch helps heal children by bringing them back to nature. Don't we do that at Jenny's every blessed Friday?"

Miranda pleaded with me for my understanding. I found it difficult to muster up.

"I suppose so. When you put it like that. Anyways, we'll have to hurry if we want to get into town and back and have time to help with the big party. It's a busy day ahead."

I rinsed my mug and slipped down the hall to my own room. The whole conversation had left me uneasy and wary, the way

Jenny herself so often left me feeling. I didn't want to reflect on the possible reality of all this — not now anyways.

Late afternoon found Miranda and I hastening down the path, eager to participate in activities we'd never experienced before.

Most of the village children had arrived at the orchard, scampering with glee among the sweet spring grasses. Floral crowns adorned the heads of the children. Toby ran forward and greeted us with wild abandon, the fluff of dandelion flowers straggling down around his ears. The girls wore violets and May drops and buttercups, looking so sweet they might have walked straight out of the pages of an old fairy tale.

Jenny sported a flower wreath of sorts perched on her topknot that, I suspected, the children had all had a hand in creating. She wore a frilly pink blouse, resembling a fairy queen herself. Somewhere she'd procured little glitters of light strands which she'd woven throughout the straws of her broom. Or *besom*, as Miranda corrected me. It brought to mind the witchy fact about the upside-down broom. I couldn't imagine that Jenny would ever turn her broom like that. Little did I know.

The air had come alive with the beautiful scents of spring, the sweet apple blossoms, the fresh new grass, and so many colours. Children scampered with ribbon sticks, waving all the colours of the rainbow. There stood a big basin of soapy water and rods with hooks which many dunked in and created bubbles of all shapes and hues. And at the centre of the orchard, inside that ancient circle of stones burned a bonfire, emitting sparks up, up and away into the velvet sky.

Coloured ribbons hung from the limbs of apple trees with childish writing on them. I learned that blessings or wishes had been written on each one. The intention was for the wind to carry them away, sending them into the world, so they could achieve fulfillment. Red ones stood for love and passion, white for peace and harmony, green for good fortune and wealth, while purple ones stood for spiritual growth, yellow for joy, and blue for wisdom and healing.

Jenny handed us a ribbon with a Sharpie, urging us to write on it as an offering to Mayday. Miranda chose a purple one, but I opted for red. I didn't know if I could stand any more spiritual growth just now.

A ten-foot pole had been erected in the open area behind the studio with a wooden disc on top of it from which sprang a multitude of ribbons.

"That's the Maypole," Brooke told us, gliding through the orchard, greeting us with her brilliant smile. She appeared full of light and happiness, a beautiful Mayday sight to behold. No more Eric Biggs to worry about for her. He had apparently left town not wanting, as Freddy surmised, to get nabbed for any child support.

"I've never seen one," I admitted, gazing up at the impressive pole.

"Well, there's one ribbon for each child — or person, really. It doesn't have to be a child. Anyways the ribbons are about one and a half times the length of the maypole and they're all different colours, as you can see. So, you divide the dancers into groups and get them to take their positions holding their ribbon in their hand. Then they skip in opposite directions going under one dancer's ribbon and over the next one, chanting as they go so they don't get mixed up. It's all about teamwork and creation. It teaches the kids that when we all dance together it produces a beautiful result. You'll have to join in, you two. Come on, they're about to start."

She guided us towards the colourful concoction as the children and some adults gathered around, each holding the end of a ribbon.

It sounded simple, just dancing around a Maypole, but I soon discovered that it required a certain degree of skill and coordination. Jenny put on background music which sound uncannily familiar. I couldn't place it until everyone started singing to the tune of "Here we go 'round the mulberry bush".

Here we go 'round the maypole, the maypole, the maypole,
Here we go 'round the maypole, to celebrate May Day.

The completed Maypole was a thing of absolute beauty with much antics and laughter erupting in the creation of it.

And so, I attended my first Beltane, my first Maypole dance, my first magical bonfire. Sometimes when I thought about my life here in Jared, I wondered if I'd stumbled into a nether world — a place with no connection to the life I'd known before.

Although, it must be confessed, there did exist an element of 'May wine'. This, I discovered, is a wine traditionally drunk for May Day celebrations. It consists of pouring a bottle of chilled German (what else?) Riesling wine over a handful of fresh sweet woodruff and sliced strawberries. To me it tasted like spring itself — if spring had a flavor — all sunlight and joviality. And it makes you feel wonderful. I could feel myself positively shining.

This May wine flowed freely, many jugs of it adorning the table. After a while, I began to feel completely untethered. I looked around for Miranda, but she seemed to have drifted off into a Mayday world of her own.

The glittering besom and gossamer apple blossoms grew more beguiling as the afternoon waned into evening. Dusk settled its velvety mantle over the world, creeping in with stealth and softness to cover the earth, like a gentle blanket.

I thought I might be ready to slip away myself like some liquid creature. Some creature who'd indulged in too much of the fruity beverage gleaming in the ewers. Jenny appeared at my side just then, with a plate of pansy shortbread cookies and a lovely slice of honey Beltane cake. Miranda materialized, too. She somehow grounded me, bringing me to rest in one of the yellow chairs, anchoring me.

The world came into focus and I beheld the scene before me with amazement. At the sparks ascending from the fire to mingle with the brilliance of the first glowing stars. At the gleaming shreds of ribbon, hanging everywhere now and twinkling in the firelight. At the wishes whispered by the children in drooping flower crowns winding their way home on the arms of family members full of honey cake and Beltane wine. At the glittering *besom* ready to sweep or fly or do anything required of it.

And, of course, front and centre, at the shimmering enchantress in the frilly pink blouse who appeared to somehow grow at twilight time and shine like one of the stars. I saw her throw back her head and send a smile soaring upwards into the night, landing on an owl hovering in the orchard who hooted in return. This made the tortoise shell cat pouncing in the orchard grass pause and take notice before prowling along on her way.

A wave of affection rushed over me for my yogi friends, my tribe, who stood clustered under the boughs of the apple trees. Crusty Nora; dull, but kindly Faye; fretful Heather; the ordinary farmer's wives — Lizzy and Dolores — and then Kerry and Lauren, so caught up in that busy world reserved for young mothers. And the nurses: Clarisse, so forthright and straightforward; Freddy, with her cheerful personality and good humor, and Sara, standing hand in hand with her tall handsome nurse counterpart obtained by virtue of the first magic spell I'd ever witnessed. The first, but not the last.

Several other young guys mingled with the nurses. A couple of them, Keith and Brandon, became friends with Miranda and me. We hung out off and on for a while. I knew it would be forever and ever before I would give my heart to anyone as completely as I had to Tod. The first time your heart is broken, it is never the same vessel to bestow — always cracked and imperfect thereafter. Still, it proved quite pleasant to have some male companionship.

Jenny and Toby pulled the old cart into the orchard and I welcomed it like an old friend. It held that blue teapot which never ran dry and a dish of purple coloured sugar. For a moment, I thought the wine had come back to haunt my perception, but Jenny explained that it was lavender sugar, especially created for tonight. She said that Beltane can be a powerful time for magic and lavender is associated with calming energies and dreams. If we stirred a little lavender sugar into our evening tea, we might have a psychic dream or two.

Wow, just what I need tonight!

I sank into the chair, the mug nestled in my hands, the tea warm and sweet.

Shadows lengthened as the sun sank behind the apple trees. I watched them dreamily, sipping my mystical tea. One of the shadows shaped into a distinctive figure and emerged ever so slightly into the dusk.

I stifled a gasp as I recognized, or thought I did, the figure of Joan Payne. The black swooping figure of that repellant woman who always made my blood turn cold and my heart beat faster. Jenny lifted her hand in a greeting, which caused the figure to shrink away and merge with the inky shadows again.

I turned to Toby and inquired if that had been Joan Payne.

"Yeah," Toby asserted. "She comes sometimes when we have a party and watches from the trees. She never joins in though."

I felt grateful for that fact.

"She freaks me out, Toby. I can't help it. She gives me the creeps."

"I know," he replied. "I don't like her either, but Gran says I should always be polite and at least wave at her."

"Do you think she's evil, Toby?"

Toby shrugged.

"Probably. But I don't care."

"You don't?"

"Na, 'cause Gran is the good witch, and good always wins over evil."

I wished I could feel the conviction that his words held, but I dropped the subject, not wanting to upset him.

Jenny announced that she planned to use the ashes from the Beltane flames to spread around the perimeter of Hedgewytch cottage to bring protection and abundance throughout the coming summer and spring. She added that couples could jump over the residue of the fire to bless their union now, if desired.

The night had settled, the darkness almost impenetrable. Sara and her man grabbed hands and ran through the orchard, leaping over the ashes, tumbling, giggling to the other side.

Then the world tilted on its Beltane axis again at the sight of Connie, hand in hand with a woman I'd never seen before, springing into the air to jump too, gasping and dissolving into laughter. Squat, middle-aged, and breathless with mirth.

I sat in silence as I beheld the last sparks of the Beltane fire receding into the night. Imbolc and Beltane and Litha and Samhain, all representing a unique calendar, so different from the one I'd inhabited before. There existed a world studded with magic just hovering on the fringe of life, hitherto unknown to me.

And here I stood, teetering on the edge of it, here at Hedgewytch Way.

25

"They say when a witch lets her hair loose, she unleashes tornadoes and hurricanes, and causes comets to fly through the sky and volcanos to erupt."

Katarina Silva

"JENNY, MOLLY AND I THINK YOU SHOULD GET A WEBSITE."

"A website? Me?"

"Yeah, you know. To advertise everything you do."

"But people know everything we do already."

"Well sure, but look at the things you make here — all the soap and lotions and stuff. Not to mention your baking. Why, your lavender cookies alone deserve their own website," I declared.

Jenny chuckled.

"They're pretty good, aren't they? But I put the recipe right in my column a couple months ago. Anyone could get the recipe from there and make them."

Miranda and I snorted in unison.

"Sure they can, but they don't taste like yours and you know it."

"Do I?" Jenny's eyes grew round with innocence.

"No. Nothing tastes the same as when you make it."

"I'm glad you think so," Jenny agreed, looking pleased. "Anyways recipes are only guidelines."

"What?"

"Guidelines, you know. Suggestions. But I don't need a website. I have all the business I need around here. Not to mention my newspaper column. I have lots of publicity, for a witch."

She chuckled again. Something seemed to be going on inside that witchy head of hers today. It made me wonder. A scarlet ribbon encircled her topknot. When Jenny wore red, she always seemed to be up to something, I'd noticed.

"Brooke could use the publicity too," Miranda ventured.

"Brooke has her own website already. I don't even own a cell phone to Twitter and Google on."

Jenny giggled now. I exchanged looks with Miranda who clearly had no more idea what was going on than I did. We'd have to bide our time.

Jenny's telephone in her kitchen had only recently been upgraded to a touch tone. When I first came to the cottage, it had been an old rotary style. Jenny seldom missed out on any news, though. She just seemed to know things by osmosis. Or something.

Perhaps this had tickled her fancy today — the knowledge that to her the ways of social media seemed redundant. But we aren't all Jenny. Some of us must rely on them.

"Did Brooke set up her own website?" I queried.

"No. I think someone from the bank helped her out."

"Should we ask that person? Molly and I know a little something about it. We could help too. What do you think, Jenny? About the whole website idea."

Jenny's eyes crinkled into a smile of confirmation. She nodded.

"Why not? I guess I better get with the times. Toby has an iPod. He knows more about this stuff than I do. I suppose you girls are right about getting the internet hooked up. Ruin my reputation completely."

"It won't ruin anything. Just think how much easier it will make things for you. If you want to have a little dandelion wine get-together you could just put the word out to everyone at once."

"Very true. Although, I've never noticed a shortage of women gathering here for dandelion wine."

It was our turn to giggle now at this home truth.

"It's not a bad idea though," Jenny went on. "It's been suggested to me before. But I wasn't ready. It wasn't the right time."

"Do you want me to ask Brooke for that person's name?" I offered.

"No thanks, dear." Jenny's eyes held that twinkle denoting mischief at its finest. "I've got someone in mind. I want him to come when Brooke is here though, and you girls too. We may well need your input. He'll come Sunday morning after yoga."

I gaped at Miranda. *How had that just happened? Had we been played?*

Like a fiddle!

Miranda sent the words flying through the air to me.

Sunday morning yoga always seemed to keep us grounded in life as we swept along its busy path. It represented a time of guaranteed pleasure, an oasis in the week.

We speculated with curiosity on the mysterious person coming to set up things while we ambled down the path on Sunday, soaking in the warm sunshine. It filtered through the canopy of brilliant green overhead, as the trees sprang back to life. Jenny's beloved lilacs perfumed the air with their sweet, cloying aroma. Swallowtails flitted from branch to branch, yellow creatures of beauty and grace.

We heard Freddy's laughter, never too far from her lips, as she and Clarisse and Sara hastened to catch up with us. Verna and Lizzy and Faye and Dolores already had their mats out and were stretching accordingly. Kerry and Lauren joined us making the yoga studio almost full. Sunday mornings tended to have a good turnout.

No one mentioned anyone else coming, so Miranda and I kept quiet. We would just have to wait and see.

Brooke had opened several of the windows. A gentle breeze rustled the apple tree branches sending a wonderful scent wafting inside. Honey bees droned in their unique, somnolent way.

Brooke seemed lighter somehow since the 'day of reckoning'. Five weeks had elapsed since then. No one had realized the shadow she had been living under. Now that it had lifted, the brightness of her spirit shone like a beautiful beacon.

I surveyed the mish mash of shapes and sizes and ages of women all striving for better balance of body, spirit, and inner peace. Affection had developed in me for each one of them, in spite of — or maybe because of — our differences. Our energy extended and encircled Brooke. She had seemed hesitant towards us after her revelation, but none of it made any difference to us. We loved her for what she brought to us through her practice. We were loyal yogis.

After the class, Jenny and Tobey entered the studio with the customary cart filled with herbal tea and a beautiful apple cake adorned with brown sugar and walnuts.

Wow, Jenny had outdone herself this morning!

Miranda and I exchanged a knowing grin.

Jenny cocked an ear towards the door. I heard a knock through the laughter and conversation of the women. For the life of me, I couldn't say if the knock came first or if Jenny heard it before it happened.

"Oh, that must be Neil," she indicated the door. "Brooke, would you open it for me please. My hands are sticky from cutting the cake."

Brooke obliged. Miranda and I turned our curious gaze towards the broad masculine figure filling the entrance to the studio door.

I seemed to see Brooke through his eyes then, her lithe supple body, her beautiful chestnut tresses, and her eyes that beamed with kindness and compassion.

Easily a full twelve inches divided their heights. He had to stoop to speak to her over the feminine din.

She nodded and smiled at him, gesturing over to where Jenny stood, handing out slabs of delicious apple cake. Jenny lifted her face, waving a greeting to him.

"I bet she'd give you a slice, if you smiled sweetly at her," I heard Brooke say, her voice full of laughter.

"I could do that," he agreed. He proceeded to do just that, crossing the studio with long strides. Not to mention a very sweet smile, indeed.

A hush fell over the chattering women. Such a fine specimen of maleness did not visit every day, that's for sure. Swarthy complexion, jet black wavy hair, clear brilliant eyes that crinkled at the corners when he smiled, exposing one lopsided dimple. Miranda and I exchanged nods of approval.

Jenny cut him a lovely corner piece of apple cake. Toby handed it to him with a napkin and fork.

"Thank you, my good fellow," he nodded to the boy.

"This is my son, Toby," Brooke told him.

She placed a hand on Toby's shoulder, her voice full of love and pride.

"And you are —?"

"Neil. Neil Laidlaw. I'm very pleased to meet you, mate."

Neil did some juggling with his cake and proffered a big hand to Toby. Then he leaned forward and observed, in a stage whisper, "You've got quite a nice mom there, don't you think?"

Toby grinned, nodding his agreement, while Brooke blushed a brilliant pink.

I realized then that Jenny had engineered Neil Laidlaw's arrival for Brooke. And for Toby.

The situation seemed crystal clear. Jenny gave me just the barest glimmer of a wink and I knew I was right.

"Your mom," Neil continued, "is an 'oenomel', I think."

"A what? What's my mom?"

"It's a word you can look up, Toby. It means something combining strength with sweetness. I'm a logophile. That means a lover of words. I'm always on the lookout for unusual words."

"I like them too, Neil," Jenny remarked. "I forgot about you and your words. The word for today would be 'kairos', I think."

Neil flashed her a smile. I felt a little at sea myself.

"Anyways I'm glad you could come," Jenny said, her manner the epitome of an innocent little old lady. "Sit down and eat your cake before we get down to business."

"Business?" Brooke asked.

"Well, Miranda and Molly are trying to modernize me. They think I should have a website and a Facebook page and all that stuff."

"Way to go, Grandma," Toby said. "I can help you."

"I'm quite sure you can, my dear. Neil is going to set it all up for me. Maybe he can take a look at yours too, Brooke."

"Jenny I've been trying to get you to do that for years, literally years," Brooke said, growing suspicious.

"I know you have. But it wasn't the right time."

"And now is the right time?"

Jenny's eyes turned towards Neil, who sat attacking his apple cake with gusto and replied simply, "Yes, I think so."

"You don't even have the internet, Jenny." Brooke pointed out.

"Oh, but I do. I'm all prepared. I knew Neil was coming today."

Many sideways glances passed between the yogis.

Jenny remained nonchalant.

Brooke looked a little blindsided.

"It'll be great for the business, Jenny. I've been telling you that for years."

"Would you mind taking Neil over to the cottage and showing him where everything is, Brooke? I need to just get this cart looked after."

"I'll look after the cart, Jenny, and you take Neil to the cottage. You're the one who needs to learn about the internet and tell him what you'd like on your website page."

Brooke clearly wanted no part in Jenny's matchmaking scheme. She, however, proved to be no match for Jenny, already bustling about the cart.

"Maybe you could show him the website that girl set up for your yoga sessions. And don't you have a Facebook page too, Brooke? Toby, cut Neil a big piece of cake and wrap it up in a napkin for him so he can eat it while he's deciphering things on my computer. It'll help him think. Glucose feeds the brain, you know," she chirped away.

"That is true," Clarisse said solemnly. "That's why people with too many low blood sugars can sustain brain damage."

Jenny nodded, as if this settled everything.

Things could just happen at Jenny's, unexpected things. All that magic roving around untethered in the air must be responsible. Brooke knew it too. She led Neil out the studio door. Every woman's eye followed them as they disappeared around the corner of the orchard.

"Well, that's that," Jenny said, making no attempt to disguise her delight.

"What's that, Grandma?" Toby looked up with questioning eyes. "What just happened?"

Jenny smiled at him, tousling his glossy brown hair.

"Oh, nothing in particular, Toby. Maybe your mom just met a new friend."

Toby shrugged.

"Maybe. I hope he's nicer that Eric was."

"He is so much nicer than Eric. Nicer in every single way."

"Promise?"

"I promise." Jenny said, crossing her heart with grave assurance.

"I'm glad Eric isn't around anymore since that day you guys had the fight in the orchard."

"Me too. Your mom's happier, I think."

Toby nodded and grinned.

Eric's departure had been good for both of them. My mom used to say that the truth sets people free — that's from the Bible, I think — and it certainly had for Brooke.

Toby gave Jenny's topknot a gentle pull, as he often did, then dashed out the door and towards the house.

"Should we call him back?" Dolores asked, looking concerned.

"Why?" Jenny wondered.

"Well, did you just set something into motion, Jenny Smith?"

Jenny regarded her, wide- eyed.

"Did you?" Dolores demanded.

Jenny laughed.

"Oh Dolores, everything is fine. I've known Neil for years. I know his family. He's a lovely young man."

"How come we never heard of him then?" Verna inquired.

"He's lovely all right," Freddy interjected, giggling.

"You ladies don't know everyone I know," Jenny observed. "After all, I've lived here all my life. It just wasn't time to produce him before."

A collective gasp consumed the studio, then everyone spoke at once.

"Produce him?"

"What are you up to now?"

"Jenny, is this one of your spells?"

"Jenny, are you matchmaking?"

To me, it appeared blatantly obvious.

But that lady remained completely unruffled.

"You ladies know fine well that I can't be giving out all this vital information. I have a reputation to uphold."

Then, with a grin spreading from ear to ear, she picked up her cake knife and asked, "Now does anybody want another piece of cake?"

JARED TIMES

THE MUSINGS OF A HEDGEWYTCH IN JUNE

Witchy tip: If you want to invoke things or bring them to you stir your drinks, food or potions clockwise. If you want to banish things or drive them away stir them counterclockwise.

Oh my. It's June again. It seems like I just turned around and the calendar did a full rotation. I believe that is a sign of growing old. The years are tripping me up. I am spinning with the speed of time.

Did you lose your joy over the long grey days of the winter months? You didn't really lose it. Take a closer look and you'll see. Here it is right here in the beauty of June. It's been here all along, just waiting for you to come and reclaim it.

What is so rare as a day in June? What indeed?

We should all be like my dear Toby, who tells me that he is going to stand outside and be OUTSTANDING. I think he already is, but I may be the tiniest bit prejudiced.

We have big news here at Hedgewytch Way. We have been transported into the modern world via social media.

We have a website. We have a Facebook page. We have a Twitter account and an email address.

I know that I was dragging my heels before. I know that I was reluctant to change. But these lovely young girls who assist me here at Hedgewytch Way, not to mention my very technical grandson, have made me see the error of my ways and have hurled me headlong into the media world. I survived and am actually enjoying certain aspects of it.

Although, when all is said and done it is hard to teach an old dog new tricks. It really is.

So, there you have it. We have all of our schedule posted for the month on our website — our boutique hours, our child circle times, our dog minding days and, last but very definitely not least, our yoga schedule in the orchard studio with our very own lovely Brooke Flurry.

Never fear, I will still uphold my obligation to this column and continue to expound every season in our local rag. That is especially for all the old-timers, like myself, to stay on the up and up of all the local news. As for all you modern folk here in Jared, you can log onto *countrywitchjared.com* and we will do our utmost to keep it up to date for you and not let it become a 'gallimaufry'. This is a word meaning 'a confused jumble'. I recently talked with a young man who is a 'logophile' — which is a Greek word meaning a word buff or simply a lover of words. I used to know lots of unusual words like this, but somehow I've gotten away from them. Now that I'm so connected, I plan to look up all sorts of neat words like these ones. And use them too, as they were meant to be used.

We are very pleased to announce that our very own Molly Beacon has had her book published. It is entitled *The Magic of the Chickadee*. It was recently accepted by a local press and we are bursting with pride over this. We will be holding an official book signing here in the orchard studio at the Hedgewytch Way next Saturday. There will be tea and coffee and baked treats supplied. There will also be dandelion wine available for purchase by the glass, if desired.

It is an endearing book for children and would make a wonderful gift. Some of the apple blossoms are lingering and the scent in the orchard is heavenly. If it's a fine day, we will host the book signing outside.

Ralph Emerson Waldo said that "A weed is a plant whose virtues have not yet been discovered."

I always think of dandelions when I hear this quote. I love dandelions; they are so bright and cheery, bringing some of the first colour to the world after the snow melts. It is said that burying dandelion flowers at the north east corner of your house will bring favorable winds. Blow the seeds off and make a wish. This shows how long you'll live, a year

per seed remaining on the head. So don't blow too hard.

It's possible to make the loveliest lotion from dandelions. Here's how:

Gather dandelion flowers by plucking them off the stem. Put them in a bowl, making sure there's no ants or bugs in them and no pesticides were sprayed near them. Stagger where you pick them. You don't want to pick one area bare because they're a food source for some of nature's creatures. Let them completely dry. This will take a few days because they have a high water content. Then fill a jar half full of the dandelions, covering them with about half as much oil sunflower or olive then cover the jar and let it sit in a windowsill for a week or two.

The result: dandelion oil.

If you can't wait that long take one cup of the dandelion blossoms, allowing them to dry overnight. Then take one and a half cups of olive oil or other oil and gently simmer for a few hours. Strain out the flowers.

Put 16 oz of the dandelion infused oil and 2 oz of beeswax in a container, sit it in a pan with water and gently bring it to a boil. When the wax is melted, remove it from the heat. It's nice to stir in a few drops of lavender oil. [But that's just me, I'm partial to lavender]. Pour it into little jars and store it. It's great for dry chapped skin.

It's nice to have something that is created right from nature, I always think.

Nature is what makes the world go around after all. Long before any of us were born, nature protected the world in her endless cycle of life.

Now the honey bees are endangered and this makes me very sad. Not only that, they are a vital part of our very existence. One third of the food we eat comes because of bees and other pollinators. More than 130 fruits and vegetables that make up a nutritious diet are cross-pollinated by honey bees. Think about that, if you will, we would have no apples, blueberries, tomatoes, zucchini, to name a few, if we had no bees. Many, many species of flowering plants depend on the bees to help them pollinate. Without bees hundreds of wild flowers and other plants would struggle to survive.

We're all connected in this old world. We all are part of each other. Nature helps us dance to the rhythm of the world, helps us remember to keep our feet planted in the beautiful earth and our head in the starry skies.

So don't forget about the bees. We can all do our bit and together that is a big bit.

First and foremost:

AVOID USING PESTICIDES!

There are natural solutions to pest control and none of them involve anything with neonicotinoids in them. This is a relatively new class of insecticides that affect the nervous system of insects resulting in paralysis and death. The name literally means "new nicotine-like insecticides". These chemicals affect bees physically and mentally causing loss of flower recognition and hive disorientation.

Anyone who knows me, knows how I detest pesticides anyways. When I was a young girl, I read Rachel Carson's book entitled *Silent Spring.* It depicted the adverse effects on the environment of the indiscriminate use of pesticides. It had a profound effect on me. I have tried always to investigate a more natural solution.

Another very important thing you can do is plant bee-friendly plants. It doesn't matter if you have a big garden or just a small space, everyone has an option.

Here is a list of bee-friendly plants. Some of my very favorites are among them:

Sunflower, lavender, sage, wild garlic, thyme, mint, catnip, honeysuckle, bee balm, rosemary and my favorite of all, lilac. There are more, this is just a few of them.

And leave some of those dandelions in your lawn. And clover. These are a haven for bees.

Try to always buy local, raw honey. It's the healthiest option anyways. It's anti-bacterial and full of calcium and magnesium. Verna Snell always has a supply at the Corner Café from two of our local farmers. What can be better than using honey made here in our own town of Jared? I always keep a bottle on hand for the kids because nothing really goes better with peanut butter sandwiches than fresh honey.

And try to give the bees some water. They get thirsty too and they need a special place to land and get a drink. Get a shallow bowl or plate, line it with rocks and then add water. Place it somewhere near your garden so they can stop for a drink after pollinating your plants.

Think of what a huge service you are providing for our world.

Just a little recipe for 'herb infused honey' before we let the bee subject buzz away.

Infused honey is wonderful to have on hand. Depending on the herbs you use, you can get a lot of medicinal benefits from it. The best thing is to use fresh herbs, chop them into fine pieces and place in a re-usable tea bag. Some herbs to use are: chamomile, lavender, mint, ginger, cinnamon, rosemary or lemon grass. Use two to five tablespoons, depending on how strong you want the flavor.

Fill your mason jars with local, organic honey and immerse the tea bag completely in the honey.

Close the jar and sit it in a windowsill for a couple of weeks.

Dandelions, honey, bees. Can't you just smell and taste and hear them?

June is an easy month to fall in love with. The flower for June is the rose. Roses are, of course, available in a variety of colours from red to pink to white and yellow. Each colour has its own special meaning but the underlying message of the rose is one of love and passion.

June is named after Juno, the Roman Goddess who presides over the family household. It is therefore considered lucky to get married in the month of June.

Married in the month of June
Life will be one long honeymoon!

It's worth thinking about, you young people out there, if any of you are dragging your heels.

And it's the month with the longest daylight hours of the year.

In Latin, "summer solstice" means "the sun standing still". We must enjoy the first day of summer, the longest day and shortest night. This is the day when the sun reaches the apex of its power, summitting to its highest point in the sky. The warmth stretches to the farthest reaches of the North Pole, bringing light to the darkness. It is the divine midpoint of our year, the tipping point between light and dark, fire and water, past and future. The sun will begin its journey south, ever so slowly, shortening the days.

Summer solstice, aka *Litha*, is a celebration of life and growth. It's a time to strike a balance between fire and water in order to sustain you as you journey through the remaining half of the year.

Of course, we will have our annual Litha celebration here at Hedgewytch Way on June 21st.

Try to attend. Everyone is welcome. And remember to tell your children that during this day fairies bestow good luck upon those who respect nature and the old ways. And of course, it's the very best day to see a fairy. So keep your eyes open. Fairies are known for their brilliant disguises. Take a second look at those dragonflies as they soar past you. Thins aren't always as they seem. Especially on nights of heightened magic.

I will close this column with a lovely old recipe for Fairy Cakes. My mom always made these for Litha.

Esther's Fairy Cakes
Makes a dozen

1 cup heavy cream
1/3 cup milk
3 eggs
4 cups lady finger cookie crumbs
1 teaspoon of rosewater
1/4 cup of flower petals chopped up
Fresh flowers for decorating

(you may use any flowers you wish, but make sure they're edible. Pansies, violas, rose petals, gardenia, nasturtiums are among this list. If you're unsure, look them up first to check).

Break up the ladyfingers into fine crumbs. A food processor would work very well. I just put the cookies in a plastic bag and hammer away at them. This is good for any pent-up frustration, as well.

Mix the cookie crumbs with the cream, milk, eggs rose water and the cut-up flower petals. Spoon them into cupcake liners and bake at 365 for 30 minutes.

Let them cool at little then drizzle them with icing, beaten from ½ cup icing sugar and1 tablespoon of fruit juice and a sprinkling of lemon or orange zest.

Top them off with edible flowers or petals.

They are a wonderful treat for our Litha celebration.

I will leave you with another new word: VERNALAGNIA, which means 'an increase in sexual desire or romantic mood which occurs in the spring as the days lengthen and become warmer'.

You see, the month of June is good for each and every one of us.

26

"Witches spend time alone in nature to listen to the whispers of the earth."

Old world witchcraft.com

"WITH OPEN ARMS I EMBRACE WARMTH AND LIGHT. May the magic of Litha shine bright tonight."

Miranda and I stepped into the orchard just in time to hear Jenny hurling these words into the evening sky. She made an impressive sight, standing in the stone circle with her arms open to embrace the summer, grey curls flung back. Little sparks glimmered from the tips of her fingers.

The whole clearing seemed fairly buzzing with the energy exuding from the women gathered there.

No, I corrected myself, scanning the stone circle and surrounding area. *Not just women.*

"There's Neil," Miranda hissed to me, nudging me with her elbow. "Over there."

I observed several other males too. Sara had her friend Jamie in tow, again, as well as Brandon and Keith. We smiled and waved. Irene, Freddy and Clarisse made up the rest of the group, seemingly in high spirits and ready for fun. Hopefully the hospital did not require any additional assistance tonight. These girls clearly had their feet planted firmly in the midsummer night celebration.

Scatterings of children chased each other throughout the apple branches, while the adults stood or lounged on the grass and chairs. Even Malcolm had come with Verna. They appeared different and relaxed, away from the cares of their business day, as they conversed with Nora, Lizzy, Heather and Dolores. Two older men with grey hair stood beside them. I assumed the taller, more elegant-looking one to be Dolores's husband. It shocked me to learn later that he was Heather's, while the dumpy bald man belonged to Dolores. Kerry and Lauren pursued children darting between apple trees, chasing bigger kids. Connie and Jenny had organized herb candles and bunches of flowers everywhere. The evening resembled Beltane, minus the Maypole, by way of the long table with all manner of food dishes. At regular intervals stood ewers brimming with 'witches sangria'.

Miranda and I had assisted in the stirring up of several batches, so I knew what it consisted of and why it shone such a brilliant orange. It contained brown sugar, red wine, orange juice, orange liqueur, club soda and orange segments, mint leaves and various berries. It looked and smelled delicious. Freddy informed us with her usual high spirits that we'd be making popsicles out of the left-over sangria. Always assuming there would be left over. I, however, had no desire to go careening off the ledge of sobriety as I had on Mayday. I wished to stay perfectly grounded in the here and now. Who knew what on earth would happen if I let my guard down, with so much mystery abounding?

I redoubled my resolve to stay sober as I observed the huge cauldron bubbling away on the firepit. I didn't want to miss anything tonight. Magic crackled everywhere, floating in the orchard air. One of these times I just knew that it would land on me. The stone circle alone portrayed witchcraft at its finest, not to mention the cauldron boiling away in its midst.

"'Double, double, toil and trouble,'" Freddy quoted Shakespeare, her voice full of mock witchery. "Eye of newt and toe of frog, wool of bat and tongue of dog, Adder's fork and blind worm's sting, lizard's leg and howlet's wing, for a charm of powerful trouble, like a hell-broth boil and bubble!'

"It's funny what I remember from high school Shakespeare," she observed. "I remember those three witches so well. They used to fascinate me. Wish I could remember facts from my nursing books that well."

"I don't even remember that," Irene said. "Is that from a *Midsummer Night Dream*?"

"No. *Macbeth*. The three witches chant in unison to predict Macbeth's future. They're saying that twice the amount of trouble will now be brought on him."

"Who knew you were so clever, Freddy?" Jamie asked. I recalled that he worked with these girls who could be so silly and tease each other with relentless abandon.

"I know. I hide it well."

"'You have witchcraft in your lips','" he quoted. "I remember that one. There seems to be no shortage of that around here."

His tone made it impossible to ascertain if he was in jest or not.

"That's from *A Midsummers Night Dream*," Sara said.

"I looked up that potion," Miranda said, gesturing to the cauldron. "None of its ingredients are anything like what they actually are. 'Eye of newt' is just mustard seed."

"Really?" I asked, intrigued. Only Miranda would think to look that up.

She'll be her own version of a hedgewytch before I know it, I thought.

"Oh, yes," she nodded, eager to impart her newfound knowledge. "And toe of frog is buttercup. Wool of bat is holly leaves, and tongue of dog is hound's tongue."

"We had to come just to hear what you girls talk about on these occasions," Keith said. "And now we know."

"Yup. You decipher witches brews," Brandon said.

"And *Macbeth* quotes," Keith added.

"I only came for the mead. I heard midsummer is the time for homemade mead. I think it's one of the oldest alcoholic drinks known to man."

I turned to observe the speaker who had drifted over and seemed to be addressing Keith and Brandon. He turned out to be Heather's husband, Ted, and surprisingly pleasant, I thought, not forgetting Heather's tale of his difficult temperament.

I felt a little at sea actually (without consuming one sip of alcohol), having no idea of any Shakespeare quotes or meanings and no idea what mead consisted of.

But the other guys knew, and they started conversing about it, drifting into a separate group in the peculiar way that males have, as if by osmosis or something.

Apparently 'mead' is a drink produced by fermenting honey with water and sometimes different spices. Jenny did, indeed, have a supply on the table because of its significance for Litha — which lead to more male discussion, eventually landing on the honey bee crisis. Apropos to Jenny's discussion in her column.

The other women came to join us as the men procured the mead, sampling it with eagerness.

"Children, children don't forget
There are elves and fairies yet," quoted Faye.

I turned to observe her smiling with fondness at the children scampering and tumbling through the growing shadows of the orchard.

"Did you make that up?" I asked her.

"Oh, no. It's an old poem we used to say many years ago. That's all I remember of it, the first two lines."

"It talks about fairy toes and grassy rings and moonlight dances," Dolores contributed. "But I don't recall any of the actual rhyming lines. Just the gist of it."

"It's a good old poem," Jenny said, joining us in her sudden manner of materializing, "If dragonflies were to turn into fairies it would be tonight."

Dolores stepped back a little to make room for her. Brooke slipped into the circle beside me. Neil stood a little awkwardly beside Jenny, seeming a trifle overwhelmed at the magnitude of the festivities. I recalled feeling this way myself, once upon a time.

"I like it," Brooke said. "I've never heard it before."

"Dora Owen is the poet's name," Jenny informed us.

I had the distinct feeling that Jenny could well have recited the poem in its entirety had she chosen to.

"I hope this bunch knows that," was all she said.

"Knows what?" Neil asked.

"That 'there are elves and fairies yet'. I hope they don't lose the magic they find along their way," Jenny continued, smiling indulgently at the careening children.

"Ah, yes," Neil replied. "Their sense of the orphic."

"Exactly," Jenny said, while the rest of us gaped. "I love how you love these special words, Neil."

"What on earth does it mean though?" Verna demanded. "And what's the use of using words that no one knows the meaning of, I'm asking you?"

"It means beyond ordinary understanding," Neil clarified. "Like something mysterious. I think I'll join the men over there. Is that mead, Jenny?"

"Indeed, it is. Connie and I made it from some of our own local honey. Enjoy."

"Show off," Nora muttered. Jenny just laughed.

"It's good to know different words, my friend. It would help you with your crossword solutions."

Nora sniffed.

"He seems like a nice young fellow," Verna said, seeming to regret her hasty words. "I'm just not used to someone like that."

Julie and several other cats pounced from behind the trees pawing at the shadows lengthening in the grasses. Black-eyed susans and daisies gleamed into the dusk like tiny beacons lighting the path. The first stars came to glimmer in the darkening sky. Children began to weary from their antics and flopped to the ground, laughing and screeching at each other.

I knew all the kids present tonight. I used my hours at Jenny's day care towards the volunteer hours necessary for my university course. But my attachment towards them exceeded a mere professional one. I knew Miranda's special affinity she felt towards her patients mimicked the feeling I had towards these kids.

Toby had rounded them up together so they could proceed to the table and obtain something to eat, assisted by the oldest girl who attended daycare, Kat. They called her 'Kat' because her name was Katherine. She hated her full name and she loved cats. She was almost twelve and told us at regular intervals that there was no reason she couldn't stay home alone if her parents would let her. She had an older brother at home. Jenny suspected, for whatever reason, that her folks did not want her home after school with a sixteen-year-old boy and his friends, although this had never been stated aloud. Jenny always made everyone aware of Kat's role as a helper. I suspected that she paid her a little, as well.

Anyways, Kat helped us with the younger ones at the day care and we appreciated everything she did. So much of caring for children involves mundane tasks, the constant assisting with hygiene, shoes and sunscreen.

Our eyes followed the children now herding towards the laden table under the direction of Kat and Toby.

"They're a nice bunch," Jenny said. Then adding to Brooke, "When they're running around in the orchard like that, they put me in mind of you and Buddy."

"Oh, Jenny, were we ever that young and carefree?" Brooke asked, her voice wistful.

"Yes, Brooke. You were. I remember those days very well. Julian and I were young and happy and Buddy was our whole world. He was happiest when he was outside in nature. Toby reminds me of him in a lot of ways."

Brooke's breath caught in her throat.

"Oh, Jenny."

"He does, you know," Jenny continued, seeming to deliberately misunderstand, "I've always thought that children who are closest to nature find the most happiness right at their fingertips."

"What was your Buddy like?" Miranda asked rushing in where angels, or fellow yogis, feared to tread.

"Buddy? He was my only child and I loved him with my whole heart. When I see him in my mind, he is spun from summer sunshine. He is shining and smiling and ever in motion."

"Sounds lovely," Faye murmured.

Everyone's ears pricked up now. Jenny did not usually speak of her personal life.

I glanced at Miranda, excited to be hearing a story about a woman whom I felt so ambivalent towards. Freddy's face caught my eye and I noticed, with astonishment, the naked sadness displayed there. Most unusual for Freddy.

Jenny continued.

"Oh, yes, Faye, he was lovely," Jenny continued. "He was the friendliest little guy. When he was small, he used to talk to everyone and wave at them whether he knew them or not. Oh, I know, Lauren," catching that young mother's eye, "I know all about stranger danger. I know how careful you must be with young children. You're not wrong. Of course, you're not. But Buddy somehow was different. He lived in a world of light."

"He did, didn't he?" Brooke said softly, allowing herself to remember. She and Jenny exchanged a look of deep affection.

"He was such a happy boy. I think sometimes that happiness is meted out at birth and some people quite simply receive more than others. Look at all the different kids we get here. Some are happy all the time, while others complain constantly. I don't think it has too much to do with their circumstances either. I think they all have an inner quota. Buddy's quota was filled right up, I think. It went hand in hand with how friendly he was. Often when Julian and I were out, even when travelling, and he waved at people they would say 'Hi Buddy.' Of course, it's just a figure of speech, but he thought for a long time that everyone he met along the way was his friend."

"That's a nice thought," I mused. "Everyone along the way was his friend, his buddy."

"Exactly. I like that thought too, Molly. It comforts me."

"His given name was actually Julian, like his dad, wasn't it?" Brooke asked, "He told me that once. But I never heard one single soul ever call him anything except Buddy."

Jenny nodded.

"That's right. His given name was Julian. I always liked that name. I thought it was very distinguished. But Julian thought that it was too big of a mouthful for a little boy. He called him Buddy the very first day he was born and it just stuck. It suited him."

"It did suit him," Brooke agreed. "He was a great guy. And he really never changed. Even as we grew older and got to be in our teens, he was never moody or short-tempered like some stupid teenaged boys get. He was always lovely to me. He was my best friend."

Her voice broke a little over the last words. I wondered if Jenny, in bringing up the subject of Buddy tonight, was allowing Brooke freedom from her tangled-up emotions, allowing her to remember her friend with purity and love.

"Oh, he could be stubborn and strong-minded. Of course, he could. But he was a wonderful person. You're right, Brooke. He filled our lives. He just filled them right up to the brim with love and joy. When he died and my Julian died, I didn't think I could go on. My sadness was so big it seemed to overflow from my heart and into my veins and fill every part of me. And my poor, poor little mom. She would try to comfort me, but her heart was broken in two. Buddy was her only grandchild."

"It was a car accident, right, Jenny?" I asked.

"Yes. An elderly man was driving from Sarnia and decided to take the scenic back roads. He had a massive heart attack and didn't even have time to pull over. He collapsed at the wheel and drove right into oncoming traffic. Julian and Buddy died instantly. That was the summer Buddy had his G1, and Julian took him out almost every evening to practice, thinking that the backroads were deserted enough to be safe."

"So, Buddy was actually driving?"

"Yes, but the police officer didn't think that it would have made much difference. The poor man lost complete control of the vehicle. A head-on crash is often fatal."

Silence fell on our little group as Jenny concluded her sad story.

Her story seemed so short compared to those told by the other women — surprising in a hedgewytch. One might suppose that her story would be more detailed and longer than those of ordinary country women. Little did I know how much more made up the entirety of Jenny's story, how much deeper her story line ran than this section of tragedy.

"Time really is the best healer of all. That's such a cliché, mainly because it's so true. My mama and I clung to each other day and night for months. We survived bit by bit until gradually our hearts eased a little. And then we received the gift of Toby. That lifted us up and never let us down. The gift of a child is the best gift that anyone can ever receive."

Brooke cast her face down, sobbing, "Oh, Jenny."

"It's true, Brooke. It's so true. I love Toby with all my heart and so did Mama. You know that."

"Jenny, Jenny," another sob escaped. "I'm ashamed."

"Never, my dear. Never. Buddy would never want you to be ashamed."

"But —"

Jenny held up her hand.

"No, dear. No need. Buddy was your best friend, just like you said. He would have been right here along every step of Toby's life if he could. I love that you remember him so fondly. Believe in his kindness and love. Never waver in that belief. I don't and I never will."

A tear spilled from Brookes clear brown eyes, sliding down her cheeks. Then she nodded and forced a smile to her pretty lips.

"When someone you love so much dies, it's the worst thing that can happen," Jenny continued, "It's the ultimate loss. But now I realize that I never have to worry about Buddy or Julian anymore. I don't have to worry about them getting sick or suffering. That's all over for them. I can think of them at peace and there's a huge comfort in that. It makes my heart warm to see these children frolicking about and remembering you two doing the same thing. The older I get the more these memories comfort me."

"I'm not sure I'd feel that way if something happened to my husband or kid," Lauren said.

"I hope nothing like that ever happens to you, Lauren. Just remember to count your blessings. People don't do that much anymore, but I always advise it. And mark my words, my dear, when you count your blessings, it's never things you count. It's always people. It's always your loved ones. I've always tried to count my blessings. Julian always said I had rose-coloured glasses, but I prefer to see things that way."

"I don't think it's very practical," Miranda said.

"Oh, I'm quite sure it's not," Jenny agreed cheerfully. "But it's my way. It's the way I can survive. You know I remember how I used to see a little bluebird. Some people thought it was an indigo bunting, but I always felt that he was the little bluebird of happiness. You've heard of him?"

We nodded.

"There have been long periods in my life when I haven't seen him, but I never gave up believing in him. I knew that happiness was just around the corner, that it was within my grasp, that it was a possibility, you know?"

Miranda shrugged, appearing unconvinced. But I thought I understood. Once you've had real happiness, you know it exists.

"You know, Miranda dear, those happy days end eventually just like the sad ones. There's always a new one ahead."

"Well I don't understand how you always stay so darned happy especially after what you told us today," Miranda said, a sideways smile taking some of the sting from her words.

"It's a choice, dear. Brooke offers us that choice every day in her yoga practice. The choice for inner peace and enlightenment."

"It does help," Kerry agreed. "Even if you have to persevere with it. At least we have a lovely teacher to guide us."

"We do. That's for sure," Lizzy nodded. "I was talking to a friend when I was in town the other day and she told me she went to yoga classes with her daughter-in-law. She was down in Toronto visiting and her son thought it would be nice bonding for them. I always speak highly of our yoga classes so she thought it would be great."

"Did she enjoy it?"

"No. Not all. I guess it was kind of a high-class yoga studio and all the ladies had on flashy outfits. Not like us," she said, glancing around at the plain black tights and capris most of us sported. "Then I guess she had some gas."

Everyone giggled.

"It happens," Brooke said, shrugging her shoulders.

"And then," Lizzy went on, "During *Savasana*, she fell asleep and started to snore. Her daughter-in-law told her she was a huge embarrassment to her and she'd never take her again."

"Well that doesn't go along with the whole meaning of the practice, does it?" Verna asked.

"It certainly doesn't," Brooke agreed. "Tell your friend to come here next time you see her, Lizzy."

"Yeah, we don't care if she snores," Clarisse opined.

"Or farts," Freddy put in.

All the nurses began to giggle like a bunch of schoolgirls. Previously I might have thought that this may well be due to sangria, but I knew this bunch better now. Fits of unrestrained giggling could manifest at any given time and for no apparent reason.

We all wandered over towards the table now that the men and children had dispersed. Despite the number of previous visits, it still held ample food and drink for the ladies.

I sampled the honey mead, finding it to be light and sweet. Miranda lifted her cup to mine, clinking it and declaring, "Happy Midsummers Night, Molly."

She seemed to glow beside me in the twilight. A rush of unexpected affection engulfed me for this girl whom I'd spent so much time with over the past year. Yet, still I knew so little about her. In her own way, she remained as mysterious as Jenny.

I turned on impulse to hug her. She returned the embrace with awkwardness.

"To you, too, my friend," I replied and was rewarded with a warm grin.

When Moira betrayed me with Tod, I never wanted to have a close friend again. Miranda remained so different from anyone I ever knew. And yet something about her called to me. That's the only way I could describe it.

The others held up their cups now. The golden mead glowed as the cups made contact, seeming to set off a spark of fire. Jenny had strayed into our midst, smiling at us with that curious knowing smile of hers. I gazed at her intently.

I thought that if I'd had one more sip of that sweet summer mead, one more taste of witches sangria, my tongue might well loosen enough to ask her about the tension that ebbed and flowed between us.

'Why don't I trust you?' I would ask her. 'Why can't I trust you?' Why? Why?

But the moment passed. I had missed it.

"'By the pricking of my thumbs, something wicked this way comes,'" quoted Neil, moving in amongst the ladies.

The groups had broken apart now. The hush of dusk had fallen on the orchard, the celebrations winding down.

"That's from *Macbeth*, as well," Freddy asserted.

We all turned to see where Neil pointed into the darkening contours of the west corner of the orchard. My eyes strained to adjust for a minute before I could make out the shadow-*cum*-witch shape of Joan Payne. We'd spotted her in that very spot on Beltane night. I wondered why she lingered there when clearly she had no intention of joining us. Her contempt of us emanated from her like a tangible thing.

This time I thought I discerned two silhouettes among the shadows. I blinked my eyes, unsure.

"It's Roger!" Verna hissed in a whisper filled with shock and horror.

Miranda and I looked to her, without comprehension.

"It's her son."

Curiosity overcame me. I'd never seen her son. If he resembled his mother in any way, I preferred to observe him with others present.

Even as we scrutinized them, they dissolved into the darkness, becoming imperceptible.

"Wow," Neil breathed. "That was a pretty scary sight. Who are they?"

Even Jenny appeared disconcerted. Clearly the combination of these two had a profound effect on her.

However, she steadied herself with a deep breath, replying simply, "Neighbours."

"She looked more like a witch than you do, Jenny," he observed.

"Well, Neil, we all have magic in us. It's just plain energy after all. How we choose to use it, that's what defines us."

A definite chill had descended onto the circle. The previous gaiety had disappeared.

Midsummer Night had ended for another year.

I'd have to wait for another time to get my questions answered, my doubts assuaged.

27

"And if you are to love, love like the moon loves. It doesn't steal the night. It only unveils the beauty of the dark."

Isra Al-Thibeh

SUMMER BLEW OVER JARED AGAIN with its winds of sunny warmth and long unfettered days. I sometimes couldn't believe that this was my second summer here — that my life of yogis and children and classes was flying by at such record speed. I'd always known that the four years of my university course would be fleeting, that I wouldn't inhabit this village for more that my allotted time. Yet I had been unprepared for the strong connection I felt towards the café, towards Hedgewytch Way, and even my rickety old boarding house room.

Hadn't I always known Miranda and Verna and Jenny and Brooke and the other yogis? Hadn't they existed somewhere in the back of my mind waiting for me to bring them into my life? Sometimes I couldn't imagine that there existed anywhere else for me to exist. I seemed so totally here.

And now we had a Neil. A connoisseur of words. A logophile. A delightful addition to life at Hedgewytch Way.

Neil had arranged Jenny's website in a wonderful manner. At the top corner, he'd positioned a photo of Jenny, attired in lemon yellow, her hair fastened atop her head with a yellow ribbon, eyes crinkled up into a beaming smile. Gleams of blue shone from them. She looked just like she was — a sage woman full of old lore and wisdom. Below her photo Neil had arranged a calendar with the events of every day outlined: all the yoga classes, children circle times, dance classes, dog walking hours, plus any special events upcoming. Opposite this information were the store hours and the products that resided there — from soaps and sachets to baked goods, homemade salves and bottles of dandelion wine.

"See how much more convenient it is for you?" Miranda asked her, as we surveyed the website in its entirety.

"You're right, of course. It is convenient. Neil did a wonderful job as I knew he would. I quite love it."

"Why were you so opposed to it then?" I asked.

My curiosity had been piqued. She seemed to have embraced the whole social media world so completely.

"It just wasn't the right time before," Jenny declared.

"The right time?"

But Jenny never ever gave away her secrets. She knew all about timing.

And Neil became a part of life at Hedgewytch Way.

He would visit ostentatiously to check out the website and see if there were any problems. Which there weren't. Jenny took to the social media world like a duck to water.

She posted on her Facebook page daily to keep people up to date. She tweeted regularly. She lavished praise on Neil for his work on her website.

Neil arrived at the studio one Sunday after yoga, apparently invited by the hedgewytch herself. We had scattered ourselves out in the orchard, indulging in tea and lavender cookies.

"These are your specialty, aren't they?" Neil inquired, taking a bite from one as he folded his lengthy form into a vacant yellow chair which stood, by happenstance, beside the dainty figure of Brooke. "I remember from the specialties that we set up on your website. Lavender cookies. Dandelion wine. All different herbal teas."

"Oh yes," Jenny laughed. "We've usually got all of those on hand."

We soaked up the beautiful sun, happy to partake of tea and cookies and friendly easy conversation. A delicious quality of peace and contentment prevailed over the day.

Toby lay on the grass between his mom and grandma, languidly waving mosquitos on their way.

"Toby?"

Toby sat up as Neil called his name. He turned his eager boyish face to meet Neil's questioning gaze.

"Yes."

"Do you want to go fishing next Saturday?"

"Fishing? Really?"

"Well I was gonna ask your mom if she wanted to go for a picnic with me, and I thought if you liked to fish — do you?"

Toby nodded his head vigorously.

"Well then we could all have a picnic and you and I could maybe try our luck at some trout. What do you think?"

"I think that'd be great," Toby beamed.

Neil nodded his approval. Then he turned to Brooke who had watched this exchange with an amused smile playing on her lips.

How clever he is, to include Toby, I thought.

"Brooke?"

"Yes, Neil."

"Would you like to go for a picnic with Toby and me next Saturday, maybe over at the river. Toby and I were thinking that we might like to throw our lines in and try our luck at some trout."

"Well, I do have to work at the bank that day, Neil."

"Until when?"

"Three o'clock."

"I have often thought," Neil said, speculating gravely, "That three o'clock is a perfect time to go for a Saturday picnic."

"Really?" Toby asked.

"Really. Three o'clock. Perfect time for a picnic. The fish will be thinking about a nice juicy worm to munch into right around three o'clock."

Toby looked at his mother, his eyes full of eager questions.

Jenny's eyes flashed with that unique sparkle all their own.

Brooke looked from Neil to Toby, then nodded slowly. Toby flung his arms around her legs and howled in delight.

Neil's face creased with pleasure. He stood up and departed, waving a cheerful good bye. His long khaki-clad legs strode through the orchard grass, his chin held high as he whistled his pleasure with each step.

We turned to Brooke with a collective smile as he traipsed out of sight, the tones of his whistling fading into the summer afternoon.

She refused to be caught up in our general air of excitement.

Toby, on the other hand, somersaulted in the grass, his curls popping up covered with grass, his face split open with a wide grin.

"I love fishing," he declared. "And I never get to go."

"That's not true, Toby." Brooked admonished him. "Grandpa's taken you fishing before."

"Not this year. And only once all last summer. And I had to sit and be quiet and not eat —"

Brooke laughed, brushing aside these complaints.

"Maybe Neil will make you sit and be quiet and not eat," she laughed.

"He won't, Mom. I know he won't. I can tell. And anyways it's a picnic. There's bound to be good food."

Everyone laughed at that.

"Oh yes," Jenny pronounced, getting to her feet.

Her tone sounded conclusive as if someone had asked a question. Though no one had.

"Oh yes." She repeated

"'Oh yes, what, Jenny?" Lizzy demanded.

Jenny grinned.

"Oh yes. It's time."

"You always say that it's time for this or time for that. What is it time for now? Time for romance?"

"We-e-ell." The syllables drew out slowly.

Toby flipped over again, landing at Jenny's feet. Jenny reached down, pulling him into an embrace. They held hands, circling around in some crazy summer dance, their laughing faces flung back, drinking in the sweetness and light of the sun.

They tumbled down, falling on top of each other, landing in front of Brooke. She attempted a stern attitude, but did not resist as they reached for her, pulling her into their bear hug. Her laughter came then unbridled, mingling with theirs and echoing through the apple trees.

Summer held her own brand of magic, warm and infectious, full of delight and sunshine and maybe even romance.

Jenny sat up, her pants stained with grass and little apple blossoms clinging to her topknot. She resembled a garden nymph more than a country witch.

"Let's just say that it's time for a change!"

28

"Change knelt down beside me in the wilderness and in the gentlest voice I've ever heard, she said: I love being the reason for all of Your beginnings. Then She kissed the tears from my eyes, stood up and reached for my hand."

Heather O'Hara

A CHILD, UNKNOWN TO ME, came to Hedgewytch Way as the July days rolled along to their own bright rhythm. She came with Toby, never seeming to venture too far from his side. Just a wee mite of a thing — a wisp of a girl child with yellow fly away curls and eyes as big and blue as saucers fashioned from bits of summer sky.

She appeared with him one day. He introduced her simply as "my friend".

"My name's Melanie," she told us, her voice soft and sweet as the petal of a summer rose. "But everybody calls me Melly. I'm in Toby's class. He saw me hanging around downtown ..."

Her voice trailed off into nothingness while Miranda and I stifled a giggle at the idea of Jared having a "downtown".

Toby jumped in to add, "I asked her if she wanted to come to Grandma's. Maybe we can give you guys a hand with the day care kids or walk some dogs or something."

Melly nodded her bright head along with these words, eager to be of assistance, it seemed.

A wistful sort of neglected air clung to her. She resembled a little waif. You could tell no one paid much attention to her. Miranda regarded her with an emotion I could not identify.

"We can always use an extra hand," she told them. "But where's your mom, Melly? Does she know where you are? Should we call her or something?"

Melly shrugged her thin shoulders and replied casually, "Oh that's ok. My mom's working at the store in Guelph today. She gets a ride in early and she won't be back 'til eight tonight. She's pretty tired when she gets home."

Miranda refused to be put off so easily. Right from Melly's first day at Hedgewytch Way, Miranda became her advocate.

"So, who's looking after you? Is there anyone else at home?" she asked Melly.

Melly rose to her full height, of not too many inches, squared her shoulders and replied, "I'm twelve years old. I'm allowed to be home alone."

It might have been comical, the idea of this creature trying to portray herself as so mature, but somehow it just seemed a little sad.

Jenny, who had been unusually silent during this exchange, remarked, "Any friend of Toby's is our friend too, of course, Melly. And we appreciate your offer to help. But we have to let someone at your house know that you're here."

Melly inclined her head and replied, "No one worries too much really. They know I can look after myself. My Aunt Steph's at home now, but she's sleeping. She works nights at the factory. So, I try not to disturb her. That's why I was hanging around today."

The last words came out in a defiant voice. Clearly, Melly did not like being questioned about her home situation. Perhaps it had happened a time too often and she now took it as a personal affront.

Jenny appeared not to notice this and proceeded in her typical easy manner.

"Does your Aunt Steph have a phone number? Maybe I can text her and let her know where you are. Then she'll have my number, as well."

Melly looked doubtful about this whole procedure, but did give Jenny the number, repeating that her Aunt Steph was sleeping and not to be disturbed.

So Melly stayed for that day, and then every day for the rest of the week, running about with Toby in and out of the cottage and studio, scampering through the rambling kitchen to grab a bite to eat.

True to their word, they helped with the day care kids.

"She's very sweet, your friend Melly," Jenny told Toby later in the week as we sat in the orchard among the yummy yellow chairs, watching the little ones play. We observed Melly helping a couple of the younger boys onto the tire swing which hung suspended from one of the apple tree branches.

"Gran?"

"Yes, my dear."

"I don't think her mom cares all that much about her. You know, not like my mom."

"I think you could be right," Jenny nodded, her eyes following the girl shadow. "I've had contact with her aunt though. Only through texting, but at least it's a connection. I'm sure they both work hard. It's not easy being a single mom."

Miranda and I were supervising their lunch later that day, as Melly examined the sandwiches that she and Toby munched on.

"Toby, I think there's an ant in your sandwich."

"Where?"

"Right there."

Toby turned the sandwich over for a closer look.

"Oh, that's just the whole grain bread Grandma buys. It's full of those specks and things."

"All right," the girl conceded. "But it has four black legs. I'm just saying."

It did indeed. We all chuckled.

We spent many hours full of sunshine in the orchard during the days that followed. Toby and Melly added to the sum of happiness found in the lazy hot days. They certainly assisted Miranda and I during our busy hours at the day care. With their help, we were able to take the kids to the old swimming hole and indulge in ice cream at McAllister's ice cream shack. Melly seemed over the moon at this treat. I suspected treats did not play a big part in her little life. She shone when she accompanied us — a bright cheerful presence, never complaining.

Jenny maintained contact with Melly's aunt and, eventually, her mother. She never said too much about them beyond the fact that it reassured her to be in touch with them. And that they didn't mind if Melly hung out at the cottage.

"No doubt," Miranda murmured to me. "No doubt it suits her to have free child care. She doesn't have to go out of her way to do anything."

"Do you know her mom?" I asked.

"No," Miranda shook her head, "No. I don't know her. But I know the look of a child whose mother doesn't give a shit about her."

Miranda didn't usually speak on such a personal level. I knew she had a story. Of course, she did. But she didn't share it. Not yet.

"She does look a little the worse for wear," I agreed, observing her threadbare shirt and too-big shorts.

"I don't think she's well, Molly. I'm worried about her."

"How so?"

"I don't know. I can't put my finger on it." Miranda's thoughtful eyes followed Melly, scampering to and fro with Toby.

The very next day Miranda and I approached the orchard clearing, laden with a lunch basket overflowing with sandwiches and fruit and peanut butter cookies. Half a dozen children scurried about in the grass, Toby and Melly among them. Connie relaxed in a yellow chair, all the while keeping a watchful eye on the kids.

It happened in slow motion. One minute, Melly leapt in mid-flight with the others, shouting with glee. The next, she lay crumpled in the grass, moaning softly.

Miranda and I dropped the basket, running over to the stricken child. I gasped in horror.

Miranda surveyed the situation, never losing her cool. She turned the little body over, smelling her breath and feeling her forehead in one fluid movement.

Connie ran over and squatted beside her. Ragged chunks of breathing portrayed how terrified she was.

"What happened? What happened to the child?" she gasped.

"I don't know," I breathed. I had no clue. But Miranda did. She wasted no breath on unnecessary words.

"Molly!" she barked. "Grab the picnic basket."

I ran in blind obedience, glad to have something to do.

Even to my unpracticed eye, Melly appeared almost unconscious. She only moaned in response to our desperate cries of her name.

It terrified me. My heart banged like a trip hammer in my chest.

"Connie! Get the other children away! Toby, run and get your gran and tell her to call 9-1-1! Molly, open the basket and tell me what's in there."

Miranda called her commands out in a clear concise voice. We obeyed them to the letter.

In the meantime, she flipped over the still figure, addressing her in a low, tender voice.

"It's ok, Melly. You're going to be ok, honey. I promise. We're going to look after you."

Grabbing a napkin and a bottle of water from the picnic basket, she proceeded to wipe Melly's white clammy face. Then she flipped the basket over, as clearly I wasn't acting quickly enough. She descended with a cry of triumph on the bottle of honey nestled within. Jenny had stuck it there because some of the kids liked it on their peanut butter sandwiches.

She tore the lid off and smeared honey on her fingers. Then she gently inserted them inside Melly's mouth, rubbing it all over her gums.

The child gagged a little, but Miranda paid no heed to this. She continued to speak in that low reassuring murmur instructing her to "Swallow! Swallow, Melly! Come on, honey, just swallow!"

Jenny and Toby ran around the corner of the studio as Melly raised her head weakly. She sputtered, honey spraying out of her mouth, and started to sob in feeble gasps.

"What happened?" Jenny cried in alarm, her face as white as a ghost.

"I don't know. I don't know," I could hear myself babbling, but couldn't stop. "She collapsed. I thought she was dead. Miranda—Miranda saved her."

Miranda looked up from her ministrations, never ceasing to utter her low soothing words. Melly seemed gradually to become more coherent.

"Did you call an ambulance?"

"Yes. What do you think happened?"

"I think she's diabetic," Miranda said.

"Diabetic?"

"Yes. I've thought that for a while. I noticed that she's always thirsty and has to pee all the time. One day she had an accident on her way in to the washroom."

"Really?"

"Yes. She was upset about it, so I didn't mention it. But it's been preying on my mind."

"But, but why did you give her honey then?" Connie asked, still ashen and shaken looking.

I frowned.

"Yeah. Isn't diabetes from high blood sugar? Isn't honey full of sugar?"

"Yes. That's right," Miranda confirmed. "I think —"

"Go on," Jenny encouraged.

"I think," Miranda took a deep breath, as we listened intently. "I think there's something else going on."

She finished the sentence lamely.

"What else could be going on?" Jenny asked, not understanding. None of us did.

Where were the rest of those damned nurses when we needed them?

Conversation halted, as the screeches of the unfamiliar ambulance sirens filled our ears with relief. Paramedics sprang from the vehicle, maneuvering their gurney along the cobblestone path and into the orchard.

What a welcome sight they were. Big kindly men approached Melly, using only gentle words to the little broken soul who lay amongst the summer grasses.

They gathered her with utmost care onto the stretcher and wheeled her out to their vehicle. She looked like a tiny ghost swathed in the white sheets, her face pale and terrified.

Miranda climbed into the back of the ambulance. These guys seemed to know her and were quite willing for her to accompany the child to the hospital. Already they conversed in a language the rest of us did not understand, pertaining to glucose and syncope and other unpronounceable words.

Jenny returned to the cottage to attempt to contact Melly's mother and a possible health card.

Hours later, Miranda returned to fill in the blanks of the day, looking tired and disgruntled.

Jenny and Connie wheeled the cart with blackberry tea and chicken wraps onto the porch. We sat and ate and drank, trying to follow Miranda's story.

She told us the whole tale, elaborating on her concerns regarding Melly's fatigue and excessive thirst. One day, she had caught her drinking water from a puddle.

"She was so desperate for a drink, you see. These kids can be overcome with a terrible thirst at times."

Melly had been embarrassed, begging Miranda not to tell anyone. But now Miranda wished that she had acted on her suspicions, thus saving the child from today's trauma.

"But, Miranda, I still don't get it," I said. "Isn't honey high in sugar?"

"Yes." Miranda nodded her head wearily. "It is so, Molly."

Jenny regarded Miranda, her expression unfathomable.

In a low voice, she said, "She was getting insulin somehow. Is that what you think, my dear?"

Miranda nodded, her face a picture of abject misery.

"I'm sure she was. But not in any conventional way."

"I have no idea what you're talking about," I told her. I could see that the others felt as I did, their faces puzzled and uncomprehending.

"I'm not sure myself," Miranda admitted. "But I'm going to find out."

"How?" Connie asked.

Jenny offered Miranda her cell phone, indicating the phone number for Melly's mom listed there.

"You're going to meet with her," Jenny observed. It surprised me that Jenny did not take this task on herself. She seemed to understand somehow that this had become Miranda's crusade.

Miranda merely punched a curt message into Jenny's phone, then replied when it twanged, with two words. She looked up and nodded.

"I'm meeting her at her place. She texted me the address."

"Now?" I gasped. We had been through so much already today that even the thought of any more decisive action made my head swirl.

Miranda nodded again then cast her eyes on me. I groaned inwardly even as I felt her thoughts assailing me.

Come with me, Molly.

I looked around, trying desperately to come up with any excuse. Finding none, I rose with reluctance and followed her down the path, away from the comforts of the porch.

I turned at the corner, as I so often did, to observe Jenny and Connie still sitting there. Jenny gave me a thumbs-up gesture.

I sighed.

Why am I going? I grumbled to myself. *I don't know a thing about diabetes. I'm not the nurse. I'm the ECE.*

"Thanks, Molly," Miranda said, as we approached the little house on the edge of Jared. "I really appreciate you coming with me. I didn't want to come alone."

Her words made me ashamed of my qualms. Still, I felt nervous, with no clear-cut idea of what we were even doing here.

The yard showed obvious signs of neglect. The uncut lawn held various rusty objects in its grassy clutches: an overturned can of paint, several tools scattered about.

Nobody loves this house, I thought. No wonder Melly likes to come to Hedgewytch Way.

Miranda steered me away from a jagged hole in the wooden porch and proceeded to rap on the wooden door. An outer screen door hung in the breeze, full of stains and holes.

"Come in," yelled a harsh female voice.

We entered a dusty kitchen, full of unwashed dishes and clutter.

Miranda cleared her throat, identifying us to the haggard-looking woman sitting at the kitchen table. She might have been pretty once, but now her eyes had dulled in the face of her lot in life, her lips thin and pursed from one too many cigarettes. She lit one now, as she observed us.

"I'm Wanda," she said. "Melly's mom. She's fine by the way. I just came home from the hospital. Probably coming home tomorrow."

I could feel Miranda bristling at her obvious disregard of the whole situation. Miranda, who cared deeply about the little girl, who knew about mothers that didn't love as they should.

"She could have died," she told her, her tone admonishing. "She almost died."

Wanda waved the cigarette smoke away, saying, with a shrug, "I don't think it was that bad. She seemed alright to me."

I stepped forward, sensing that Miranda's words would burst forth in anger any second, and asked hastily, "Did you know Melly was diabetic?"

"Yeah. I guess so. Terry, he's my neighbor on the other side," she indicated her head across the road. "He has a dog that's diabetic."

"A dog?" Miranda gasped in horror. "A dog?"

"Yeah," Wanda looked at Miranda. "You know. Duh. A dog. A pet. The vet said it was diabetic, so Terry got one of those sugar measuring machines."

"A glucometer."

Miranda spat the words out. They fell like pebbles on the ragged corners of the torn linoleum of the kitchen floor.

"If you say so. Whatever. Anyway, one night we were bored, so we used it to take each other's sugar counts. Melly's was 22."

The number meant nothing to me, but Miranda gasped.

"22!"

"Yeah. That's what I said," Wanda regarded Miranda as if she might well be mentally deficient. "I knew that was too high, see, because the vet told Terry that it should be less than 7."

Miranda groaned.

"So, you gave her some insulin?" she asked, almost in a whisper. "From the dog?"

Wanda nodded, stubbing out her cigarette, her brassy hair flopping over her face.

"Uh-huh. She felt ok, so I don't know how bad it really was, but Terry said it was too high, so I figured he'd know. His mom was diabetic, he said."

"As well as his dog," Miranda shook her head, not even trying to disguise her contempt now. "She should have gone straight to the hospital then."

"How did you know how much to give her?" I asked. "I wouldn't have a clue. Didn't the dog need the insulin?"

I felt unable to follow this strange tale. I could feel Miranda's wrath as a palpable thing, but I could not grasp the particulars.

Wanda remained unperturbed. "We just guessed," she said with supreme indifference. "When we needed more, we got it at Shoppers."

"Really? Don't you need a prescription for insulin?" I asked incredulously.

"No. You can buy short-acting insulin over the counter." Miranda's words came out high and strangled. She turned to the washed-out woman sitting at the table. "You gambled with Melly's life. She could have died. A low blood sugar can be just as dangerous — even more dangerous — than a high one. You can seizure and sustain brain damage. You can lose complete consciousness until nothing revives you except for getting glucose into your vein."

Wanda waved her words away with an indifferent flick of her nicotine stained hand.

"What makes you think you can come into my own kitchen and tell me how to raise my own kid? Thinking you're so much better than me," she glared at us, her lips an angry sneer now. "Go have some kids of your own and see how easy it is to raise them with no man around and a shitty job. Get the hell out of my place. I'm blowing this town anyways. Terry and me, we's going to Thunder Bay."

"What will become of Melly?" Miranda asked in despair, deflated now, like a spent balloon. I realized anew how much she truly cared about the child, in spite of — or maybe because of — her illness.

"She'll stay here with Steph. That's my sister. Melly don't want to go so far away and to tell the truth Terry don't really want her along. Now go."

We went.

We picked our way home through the streets of Jared, silent for once. Words alone could never capture the emotions we'd experienced that day and evening.

The next afternoon, when the general chaos that prevailed at Jenny's on summer days had died down to a dull roar, we settled down to relate the whole experience to Jenny and Connie.

"Thank God you were here yesterday, my dear," Jenny said softly. "She'll be all right now, will she? As frustrating as all the rest is, the main thing is that Melly's all right."

"Yes, she will. Diabetes isn't the end of the world. And it's not as uncommon in children as it once was. They have a fine diabetes clinic at the hospital and the staff who run the pediatric program are great. Melly's in good hands now."

Poor Miranda still looked shaken from the whole experience.

"I wish I could help her, Jenny. She's such a helpless little thing. There's so many kids out there who need help, aren't there?"

"Yes indeed, my dear. We just have to help where we can in our own little corner of the world."

Children are also very resilient. They're able to bounce back from events and carry on with living in a fashion quite foreign to adults. Melly came the next day seemingly none the worse for wear after her near-brush with death.

Even now, when I cast my mind back to that second summer in Jared, Melly is the first thing that comes into my mind. I close my eyes and I can visualize her with Toby, running through the orchard grass, laughing in the wind.

They were true kindred spirits, their cheerful natures meshing together and affording them hours of merriment. They were creatures poised on the edge of puberty, still able to take a step backwards into childhood and frolic with wild abandonment. But able, also, to step ahead to accept responsibility, assisting with the children's circle. Not to mention the looming reality of juvenile diabetes.

Melly seemed to take it all in her stride, displaying admirable self-control regarding her dietary restrictions. Although, truth be told, Miranda monitored those aspects of Melly's life. She'd acquired a glucometer, religiously obtaining Melly's blood sugar numbers and acting accordingly.

"Take care of your body. It's the only place you have to live," she told the little girl repeatedly.

Miranda had visited Wanda again, on her own, setting up a few "ground rules", Miranda had acquired an insulin pump for her, after applying for government assistance, and reviewed it with both Melly and her mom on this occasion. At that time, Wanda had again expressed her intention of moving to Thunder Bay with the neighbor, Terry.

"The one with the diabetic dog," Miranda clarified to us, her voice dripping with disdain. "Now she says Melly might have to go with them."

"I thought she didn't want that," I said. "That's what she told us. I thought she was staying with Wanda's sister."

"I actually met Steph," Miranda said. "When I brought over the insulin pump. She seems ok. Kind of tired and stand offish, but ok."

"Life can do that to a single woman," Jenny observed.

"Well I guess it's still up in the air," Miranda explained. "They're going next week. School starts in a few weeks. Something has to be figured out."

I heard the dismay in her words, as we relaxed, reclining in the yellow chairs to gaze up and up into the clear summer sky. The depth of its blue made my heart ache with the sheer beauty of its endlessness.

Toby and Melly chased each other all around the apple trees, making my soul pull with the pain of the whole situation. The thought of losing this girl to Thunder Bay seemed unthinkable. She had walked straight into our hearts in that way children can do when they are so clearly grateful for scraps of attention and affection.

"It won't be the same if she does go, that's for sure," Jenny said, with a heavy sigh.

"No. It will be awful," Miranda agreed. "Just awful."

"What will be awful?" Toby asked, scampering into the midst of our chairs, almost knocking his grandma over in the process. She reached out, giving him a playful swat.

He tumbled into the grass, Melly close behind him, giggling with pleasure.

Miranda averted her eyes away from the child. I knew that Miranda didn't easily form attachments. I could feel her distress at the thought of Melly moving so far away.

"What will be awful?" Toby asked again, with more insistence this time.

Miranda sighed deeply then replied, "It will be awful if Melly has to move."

Toby's beautiful brown eyes dropped in sadness. He turned his chestnut head towards Melly's blonde one, lying amongst the orchard grass.

"Yes," he said softly. "It sure will. I hope you get to stay with your Aunt Steph."

"I do, too," Melly said, her voice low and sad. "I don't want to go to Thunder Bay."

"Thunder Bay is quite a beautiful city," Lizzy told her with reassurance. "It's right on Lake Superior. They have lovely waterfalls and a Sleeping Giant rock that you can look out and see. The legend is that it's a real giant who fell asleep."

Melly shrugged.

"I guess so. I mean, I'm sure it's nice if you say so. It's just that —"

She looked around the orchard, surveying the kind faces of the simple country women who had grown to care about her. She sighed heavily, much too heavily for a such a small soul.

"It's just that I like it here. That's all."

I turned my head, unable to face the naked longing in her sweet, young face.

"Well, honey," Brooke said in a very gentle voice, "you can't stay here. I mean if your mom decides you have to go with her, then you'll just have to go."

"I know."

"Why can't she?" Toby asked. "Stay here, I mean."

"Yes. Why can't she?" Jenny echoed.

Connie shot Jenny a look, shaking her head a little in disbelief. Then a small smile stole across her weathered features.

"They do say it takes a village to raise a child," she said.

"Yes, they do," Jenny replied.

"We might as well be part of the village," Connie concluded.

I regarded Connie, that middle-aged woman, so full of generosity. Generosity, not just of dimensions, but generosity of heart and spirit as well.

Jenny nodded.

"What do you think, Miranda?" she asked.

The question required no reply. Miranda's face beamed like the sun.

Melly stared at them, her face full of wonder.

If this woman, this Hedgewytch, this magical being, wondered why she had to leave then maybe, maybe, she could stay? Maybe Jenny and Miranda could do something so she could stay right here. Here where she'd been happier than she'd ever been before in her short loveless life.

And they did.

Just like that, in the way things happened around the Hedgewytch Way, this happened.

Jenny and Miranda arranged a meeting with Wanda and Steph. They discovered that Aunt Steph had been quite willing to have Melly stay with her, but did not want to leave her alone in the house when she worked the night shift, five days out of the week. Jenny explained that Melly could stay at Hedgewytch Way for these nights, checking in with Steph during the afternoons. Steph agreed to these arrangements. Wanda, it appeared, had been indifferent — a fact that didn't surprise me having made her acquaintance. Jenny informed her that she would set up a bedroom for Melly the very next day.

I could picture that bedroom, as I did Connie's. In my mind, it could be folded up and tucked away until next needed. Except that Melly's would be needed from here on in.

She became a fixture at Jenny's, seeming to enjoy, too, the time with her aunt. We held her right there in our hearts, from that day forward.

When you are a child, it's like you're stumbling about in the dark. You never know who may come your way and enter the path you're walking. For Melly, that someone turned out to be Miranda and Jenny. Because it can go either way, of course. You can meet someone kind. But it's just as possible to meet someone cruel.

It made Toby so happy that Melly did not relocate to Thunder Bay. He loved having her at Jenny's.

"I've heard Grandma say," he told her, "that Abraham Lincoln says, 'Whatever you are, then be a good one'. So, you be a good diabetic, Melly. Be the best diabetic ever."

Several of us overheard these words as he related them to Melly. We smiled at the sentiment.

"We are all meant to shine as children do. It's not in some of us. It's in all of us," Brooke quoted. "There's more to that quote. But that's the part I like the best."

29

"Be the light in someone's world."

LIFE.QUOTE.TODAY

ANOTHER YEAR OF UNIVERSITY LOOMING AHEAD. Another August of busy happy summer days working at the café, helping at the cottage and day care, watching Toby grow and Melly heal and Brooke and Neil fall in love.

Oh yes. That all seemed to be happening. Love lingered in the very atmosphere. All the world loves a lover, and all of that. We had watched Brooke endure Eric Bigg's subtle form of mind torture and we were now thrilled, one and all, with the presence of this handsome charming young fellow who had sauntered into her life.

"She didn't have to go through that love spell that Jenny did for Sara," Miranda observed. "Jenny just kind of produced him for her."

"Well, he did come to set up the website and all that for Jenny," I replied.

Miranda snorted.

"I don't believe that for a second. She engineered it all. I don't know how, but she did."

Matchmaking had its own magic component to it, I supposed, providing you had the correct people to work with. For Jenny, it seemed effortless.

In ancient times, she would have been a wise woman, I suppose — a medicine woman. She always told us that herbs and such were just an old-world way of healing. She said people today are focused on chemicals and prescription drugs. But if we went back to our roots, to the true path of nature, then we would find that way.

"What could possibly be better for a burn than the soothing gel of an aloe vera plant?" she would ask. Or a little sip from cups filled with summer sunshine which may or may not be dandelion wine.

She was ever the caregiver, the sage, the one who hears everyone's truth.

And yet. And yet. Always inside of me existed that ever-continuing question of Jenny, that wall of mistrust and angst that kept me wary of her even as my affection for her increased. A love-hate relationship at its finest. I couldn't have described it even if I'd had to. It stood beyond my layer of comprehension. Miranda couldn't see this at all, which I didn't understand. She held distrust inside of her towards many other beings, but not for Jenny it seemed.

When we were close together, when our thoughts flew to each other, I felt very close to Miranda. But other times she held me at bay.

Someday I would learn her story and I'd understand. I knew this with certainty. I just didn't know when that time would be. While I tended to be an open book, Miranda kept her story close to her chest.

These thoughts fluttered inside me as I wandered my way along the path to Jenny's cottage one late August evening. Miranda had been called in to do some private duty with a demented patient at the nursing home. Verna had a delivery to be made to the cottage and I had volunteered.

I arrived to find Jenny and Toby sitting on the old wooden swing hanging in the orchard. I rounded the corner and surveyed them with admiration. Toby had some funky music on his iPod, their heads bent over it watching an accompanying video, heads bobbing along to the music. A pink polka-dotted ribbon fastened Jenny's hair up, little curls escaping in the humidity, wisping around her cheeks.

Toby spotted me and jumped up to greet me.

"Molly! Molly! Look at this. Granny and I are finding funny videos on You Tube."

He kicked his feet up into the orchard grass. A beautiful long-limbed boy of summer.

It would be nice if boys could stay like this, I thought. *Just innocent and full of joy. Too bad they must go to high school and worry about being cool and impressing other kids.*

I tousled his hair and he ran to get me a tall glass of iced tea with mint picked fresh from Jenny's herb garden.

"Oh, how refreshing." I breathed, sinking into the yellow chair closest to the tree swing. "I brought that delivery from Verna's, Jenny. I left it on the counter."

The day had been hot, but shadows creeping underneath the apple trees lent relief to the evening.

"Where's your sidekick?" I asked Toby.

"She's in the kitchen with Connie. Connie's showing her how to make snickerdoodle cookies. They looked up a recipe that Melly can eat — you know because of being diabetic and all that. So she can have a treat. When they'd done, they're going to bring them out here so we can sample them," Toby replied.

"Yes, he's waiting patiently," Jenny laughed. "Well, he's waiting anyways."

Crickets sang their tireless summer melody. Fragrant breezes wafted through my hair cooling me, making me feel quite contented. Frogs croaked in the swamp over the hill and Toby waved his hands in accompaniment, signaling the air as if conducting an orchestra.

I laughed at his gestures.

"Toby, what are you doing? Are you pretending to be a conductor?"

"I'm just giving the frogs a bit of help with some of their notes."

Jenny grinned, telling me, "His dad used to do that. As soon as the frogs started croaking in the evenings, he would get out this old wand. He'd used it in a school play once when he was small and he kept it forever. Anyways he'd use it to conduct them as soon as they started to croak. He thought it helped them with their song."

"It does you know, Gran. It really does."

Sometimes I felt totally at sea when they were in the midst of their conversations. Like now.

"I get that from him then, don't I, Grandma?"

"Yes, you do, my love."

"Guess what, Molly?"

"What's up, Toby?"

"I might be getting a new grandma."

"Why? What's wrong with the old one?" I asked, bewildered.

"Nothing at all is wrong with the old one," Toby declared with conviction.

"Glad to hear it, my love," Jenny leaned over and tousled his curls, just in case they weren't tangled enough already.

"No, I mean another one."

"Oh really. Well that's good, isn't it?"

"It's fabulous! I'll have three grandmas! I'll have Grandma Joyce from my mom and I'll have Grandma Jenny from my dad and then Neil has a mom too."

"Does he? Is she nice?"

He nodded.

"She is nice. She's really nice. I guess that's why Neil is so nice because his mom is. It must be hard to be nice if your mom is nasty, don't you think so, Molly?"

"I imagine it would be," I agreed. "I was lucky. I had a really nice mom, too."

"Well, I'm like super lucky because I have the very best mom in the whole wide world. And the prettiest too. She looks even prettier lately because she laughs more and smiles all the time.

Not like before. You know. She used to be sad before when Eric would come and not be nice to us."

"I know, honey. I know."

"Anyways, Neil's mom is awesome. I was calling her Mrs. Laidlaw and one day last week she whispered in my ear that I could call her Nana if I wanted to."

"Really?"

My ears pricked with interest. I shot Jenny a quizzical look, but that fine lady just sipped her iced tea.

"Yes, she did. You see she doesn't have any kids, just Neil. She had another boy, but he was killed in a car accident. Just like my dad. And she told me she really likes my mom and she thinks that she is the one. I wasn't sure what that meant so I had to ask Gran."

"You did?"

"Uh huh. And Gran said that Mrs. Laidlaw must think that my mom and Neil are in love."

Jenny's topknot bobbed up and down, affirming Toby's words.

"I did say that."

"Well, that's exciting," I ventured.

"Oh yes, Molly, it is exciting. It really is."

As if he could no longer contain himself, Toby sprang to his feet and cartwheeled away into the grass, ending in a series of somersaults, carefree and full of summer joy.

"It's like that, is it?" I leaned over to inquire of the woman of magic, creaking away on the old swing. "It's a go?"

"It seems to be," she assented. "It seems to be working out just fine."

She looked guileless sitting there in the evening light, as if all this had merely happened around her. But we knew that she'd masterminded things, that she'd plucked Neil Laidlaw up and placed him smack dab into the midst of Brooke's life. And, as a result, Toby's life.

"Of course, I love my Grandma Jenny with my whole heart," Toby joined us on the upswing of his final somersault. He laid his head in Jenny's denim lap and snuggled into it like a little bear.

Jenny's brown hands lost themselves in the tangles of his chestnut curls.

"Of course you do."

"But Gran told me not to worry about giving Mrs. Laidlaw — Nana Ida, I mean — lots of love. She said the more people you love, the better it is for your heart. And that I'll always be her boy. But she doesn't mind sharing me."

"No, I don't, love. I've known Ida Laidlaw a long time and it will do her heart good to get some of your beautiful boy love. Your heart just grows the more people you have to love."

Toby seemed quite content with this reasoning. He started to describe Neil's mom to me.

"She's nothing like Gran. Her hair is kind of red and kind of grey all mixed together. It's really short, too. She doesn't wear it on top of her head like this."

He reached up and flitted his fingers through Jenny's topknot, laughing all the while.

"And she has artheritis ... or something like that — so she doesn't run around and crawl in the grass like this grandma. She moves really slow. But I help her if I can. Sometimes I go downstairs and fetch things from the cold cellar because the stairs are hard on her knees she says. But she's great at playing games. She taught me how to play checkers and *Uno* and even euchre. Hey, Grandma?"

Toby's head popped up, peering into Jenny's face.

"We could play euchre here, couldn't we? Nana Ida says that we can have a progriver—"

"Progressive?"

"That's it. We could have a prog-ress-ive euchre night here and have prizes and everything. She said because you have room here and she just has a small place."

"We sure could."

"And could we ask Nana Ida?"

"Of course."

"Can you play euchre, Molly?"

"Yes. I like playing euchre."

"And Miranda. Where is Miranda?"

"She took an extra shift at the nursing home. So I said I'd make the delivery tonight."

"Miranda's sad sometimes, isn't she?" He looked at me, his little face wise beyond his years.

"Do you think so, Toby?" I asked carefully, not certain of the answer myself.

I contemplated him as he pumped his legs, swinging beside Jenny, the summer evening lighting up his face. His connection to this woman transcended any blood line acknowledged or otherwise. It made no difference how many others entered his life along the way. Her love for this boy grounded him, making him a beautiful being.

"I think so. "

"Miranda is on her own journey," Jenny said quietly.

"I feel so connected to Miranda at times," I mused. "Sometimes I can pluck her thoughts right out of the air. And they seem to be my own thoughts that she's sending to me. Crazy, huh?"

I surprised myself at my own observation. I'd never voiced them before.

"No, not crazy. You're connected, you two."

"We all are!" Toby piped up with glee.

"Yes, we are, my love, and we are all on a path of our own."

"We could look in the seeing mirror, Gran," Toby said eagerly.

Jenny shook her head.

"It doesn't work like that, Toby. People must find their own way. Besides the seeing mirror takes years and years before it sees anything at all. Even then it's just a glimmer you might see."

"The seeing mirror?" I inquired.

"Gran has a mirror in her very own bedroom that sometimes sees things that might happen," he caught Jenny's eye, hastily adding, "But not very often and only for her."

I felt intrigued.

"Is it like the mirror in the hall downstairs that makes you look so much better than you really look?" I asked.

Toby shook his head.

"Oh, no, it's not that kind of mirror. It's a really, truly magic mirror."

"I'm impressed that you know about it," I observed, more than a little curious now.

"Oh, Grandma told me about it one day in a 'weak moment'." Toby made quotation marks in the air with his fingers.

"A weak moment?"

"That's what she called it," Toby declared.

"Very weak," Jenny agreed.

He sighed deeply.

"I suppose that's why it only works for Grandma."

"I suppose," Jenny and I agreed in unison.

I laughed into the beautiful stillness of the summer orchard sunset.

"You know what would be cool?" I asked, caught up in their fanciful notions, "It would be cool to have a mirror that when you looked into it you could see your personality."

"So how you looked on the inside, not the outside?" Toby asked.

"Yes. Like your soul," I replied.

Jenny nodded thoughtfully.

"That's a great idea for your next book, Molly," she said.

I blushed then.

"Oh, I don't know. Anyways, I have a bit of an idea for a story about the power of bees. You know how they're almost endangered now and what we can do to help them."

"Good for you," Jenny nodded approvingly.

"You're gonna write another book, Molly?" Toby asked. "Yay. I know a famous person."

I laughed, feeling my blush deepening.

"'I write only because there is a voice within me. That will not be stilled.'" quoted Jenny.

We turned our heads at the rustling sounds of Connie and Melly bursting into the orchard, laden with a plate of delicious-smelling cookies. Behind them followed Neil and Brooke holding hands and laughing.

"You're just in time for cookies," Melly informed them.

She looked like a different child from the one who had collapsed here on that fateful day. Her clothes fit properly and her hair gleamed from a fresh shampoo. Best of all, her smile lit up the summer evening.

"Now, isn't that serendipitous?" Neil asked.

"I know what that word means," I said. "That's the first one that you guys have used that I know. I won't have to look it up."

"Molly is writing another book," Toby informed the others. "So she needs to know a lot of words."

They turned to me, regarding me with approval.

"Collecting words is great," Neil said. "There's some awesome words that describe something you feel, but can never quite put into words. Like the word 'hiraeth'. Now there's something we've all felt, I think. It means 'a homesickness for a home to which you can never return, a yearning for the past'."

"Yes, you're right. I guess everyone does know that feeling," I observed with a flash of inexplicable sadness.

"Or 'werifesteria'," he continued. "That means to wander longingly through the forest in search of mystery."

"Aw. That's my specialty. And you, Neil dear, you may well be suffering from 'forelsket'," Jenny replied, giving the last word a foreign accent.

"What does that mean?" Brooke inquired.

Jenny giggled. Neil remained silent.

"Well, enough of this," Connie pronounced. "Enough of this 'flumadiddle'."

"Flumadiddle? You made that up," Brooke said.

"I didn't. It means 'utter nonsense'. And that's what it will be if these cookies that Melly and I slaved over don't get eaten up before they're cold."

JARED TIMES

THE MUSINGS OF A HEDGEWYTCH IN SEPTEMBER

Witchy Tip: Hang rose quartz bracelets on the inside of the doors to your home or office to attract only visitors with good intentions.

And if you're outside in this beautiful crowning glory of summer days and you cut yourself, use spiderwebs to help seal the wound. Nature has her own wonderful way of helping us with everything, if we'll only let her.

Some of the best days of the whole year, in my opinion, happen along in this month. The summer is drawing to a close, but she is not yet quite finished, lavishing on us the last remnants of her warmth and brilliance. Another bonus is the mosquitos have gone for the most part, leaving the evenings much more comfortable to sit out.

A maiden born when Autumn's leaves
Are rustling in September's breeze
A sapphire on her brow should bind
'Twill cure diseases of the mind.

From "Birthstones from Days gone by"

Sapphire is such a beautiful birthstone, I think, most desired in its pure rich blue colour, but it can be other colours too — including pink yellow and green. It is believed to bring peace and wisdom to the wearer and encourage truth, loyalty, wisdom, and clear thinking. Especially when worn by those born in September.

September is a colourful time that reminds us of the beauty of change. With the death of summer comes new life. September teaches us never to fear change as new life is always right around the corner. With the harvest coming upon us, we give thanks for the abundance that nature has provided us.

Day and night are equal reminding us of the importance of balance. We celebrate the last of the sun, but welcome the stillness that brings change and strength to us.

And of course, here at Hedgewytch Way, we will be having our last big celebration in the orchard and our last fire in the stone circle on September 22 for Autumn Equinox or Mabon, if you are following the pagan calendar. Always weather-permitting, of course.

Think of your greatest worries and woes, write them on bay leaves and bring them to Mabon to burn them in the fire and start the autumn clean and pure and care free.

Mabon is a time of balance and equality. Day and night are the same length. It borders summer and winter — the last of the growing sun, the moment before the light will be overtaken by night. The energy of Mabon is similar to the special energy that occurs just before twilight, the between-time.

Autumnal equinox is a time of unlimited possibilities. This is the day of perfect balance between dark and night. We must express love and most of all gratitude to the earth and all of its bounty.

We are at the gateway to a new season, a new cycle in the circle of life.

Connie and I have already been up to Madden's Farm for bushels full of their delicious apples that are bursting forth on the trees. There is no better snack than an apple freshly picked from a tree.

We also invested in some of their apple cider so that we can boil it up for Mabon. We'll fancy it up with brown sugar, nutmeg, cloves, cinnamon sticks, orange juice, and maybe some orange zest. We will have it boiling away (toil and trouble) on the stone circle fire in our cauldron. Mabon is not complete without hot apple cider. With maybe some spiced rum to add to it? Not for the faint of heart.

Another pot will hold hot chocolate for those who prefer it. And marshmallows to add to that one.

It's the last orchard spree before May (besides Samhain, which is a whole different thing of course) so bring a ghost story. Bring your best one from when you were a kid even if you must embellish a little. Let's get

our blood flowing. Nothing like a good old-fashioned ghost story for that.

For something different this year, we're going to have a scarecrow making contest. We've purchased enough supplies for five scarecrow making stations, but feel free to bring stuff of your own. Sign up for one of the five teams and you will be given the last summer hour of daylight on September 21st before the sun goes down to create a scarecrow. The winner will receive a yoga pass for two months with our very own Brooke.

Make sure to save the first acorn you see this season and slip it into your pocket or purse to carry for all of fall and winter. It will protect you from negativity during the dark winter months. Then return it to the earth in the spring and say thank you to nature for its assistance.

Acorns are a symbol of security. If you place them on your windowsill, they will protect your house from lightning and if it's there when the moon is full it will draw money for you.

While you're searching for acorns, see if you can happen along a "wishing rock". A wishing rock is a rock with a white line running around it. If you find one and make a wish on it, your wish will come true.

BUT if you find one and make a wish for someone else, ALL of your wishes will come true. There's a very fine lesson in there, methinks. Don't you?

September is such a glorious time of colour and beauty. It leaves us with never ending possibilities for crafts in our children's circle. And now with the extra assistance of Kat and Toby and Melly, we can do so much that we simply couldn't before.

We went on a nature hike and collected all manner of beautiful autumn offerings.

We found pine cones, all different sizes, and we helped the kids make fairies with pine cones for bodies and oak leaves for wings.

We obtained several mini crockpots, by hook or by crook, and filled them with paraffin wax, allowing it to melt for about a half hour. When the wax was all melted, we dipped some of the leaves, stem and all, that we'd collected into the wax. Then we laid them out onto waxed paper that we had on the counter. In a minute or two they, were dry. They turned out amazing. We used some in our Mabon wreaths, but some we strung together with a needle and thread to make a garland.

You can make a thankful tree from them, as well. Just write on each leaf something or someone that you are thankful for. Then fasten them to branches and secure them in a bottle of sand or colourful pebbles. Each person in your family can write on his or her leaf. A beautiful offering of gratitude.

Gratitude has been proven, over and over again, to improve our health, physical and psychological and assist with our self-esteem.

'If you say only one prayer a day make it, "Thank you."'

Another thing to make and use in your Mabon wreath are dried apple slices. Slice them thinly across the centre so you get the star shape in the middle of each circle. Put the slices in a bowl and sprinkle them with lemon juice, cinnamon and ground cloves. Stir them so the apples are all covered, then lay them in single layers on a baking sheet. Cook them at the lowest heat your oven will go to for a few hours. You can hang them up too with the little pine cone fairies. They smell lovely and the leftover ones can be eaten for snacks.

Molly and Miranda bought some plain white plates at the dollar store in Guelph, enough for each of the kids. The kids wrote on them, identifying things and people they loved and drew with different-coloured Sharpies around the edges. We baked them in the oven for 30 minutes at 150 degrees.

They are permanent. What a lovely keepsake.

So, get out and enjoy these last lingering days of late summer. Bask in the warm sunshine on your face and the crunch of the leaves under your feet. Get down on your knees in the garden and plant some bulbs. Always nice to invest in the beauty of the future. Because spring will come again. It always does. The local school are selling them for a fundraiser. Or, of course, our feed mill always has a great variety in stock.

And come to Mabon. Come with your fall hoodies and your ghost stories and your good will. We'll light the sky up one more time and welcome autumn in fine form.

I'm going to sign off with a little something about tea. Any of you that frequent our cottage and yoga studio know that we are prone to different varieties of tea.

Hedgewytch Brews. Here's what's what:

Rosemary; keeps you young
Basil: brings wealth
Lavender: helps you find true love
Thyme: gives you courage
For a headache: ginger tea
For halitosis: black tea
For feeling unintelligent: gingko tea
To help you sleep: valerian tea
For belly woes: peppermint tea
For the jitters: passion flower tea

And here's a black magic cake recipe to accompany any tea for anything that ails you. Just in case you need a little magic to throw into your day.

Black Magic Cake
2 c. sugar
1 3/4 c. all-purpose flour
3/4 c. cocoa
2 tsp. baking soda
1 tsp baking powder
Dash of salt
2 eggs
1 c. buttermilk (which can be made by putting a little vinegar into regular milk)
1 c. strong black coffee
1/2 c. vegetable oil
1 tsp. vanilla

Heat oven to 350.

Grease two 9-inch round pans or one 13x9 baking pan.

Stir sugar, flour, coco, baking soda, baking powder and salt in bowl.

Remember to stir counter clockwise or clock wise depending on what you want

Add eggs buttermilk coffee oil and vanilla beat with beater and pour into pans

Bake for 35 minutes or so. Cool and frost with mocha frosting

3 tbsp. butter
3 tbsp coco
1 tbsp warm water
1 tbsp coffee flavored liqueur
1 1/2 c. icing sugar

Melt butter on stove over low heat. Stir in coco, water and liqueur. Gradually beat in icing sugar.

Enjoy! Stay thankful!

30

"Forgiveness is the fragrance that the violet sheds on the heel that has crushed it."

Mark Twain

"MAYBE WE'RE ALL JUST DOING OUR BEST," Lizzy observed. "I don't think so. I think some people are doing their worst."

These words came from Miranda. She could slip with ease into cynicism. It seemed to be her go-to position.

"How do you know though? Their best could be so much worse."

"And their worst could be better," Miranda answered back.

"Of course — but we don't know that."

The thoughtfulness of Lizzy's words led me to understand that the day for her story had arrived.

"I mean, we don't know when the last beat of our hearts is the last one ever. Nobody knows. I hope that what gets squeezed out of our hearts at the very end is love and not hate."

"Sure, it would be nice to think that, Lizzy, but there's a lot of rotten people out there, don't you know," Miranda told her.

"Well, the world is made up of all kinds of people. And some are definitely rotten, Miranda, I have to agree," Brooke said.

"But sometimes people do bad things when they're not actually bad people," Lizzy continued, her tone bordering on beseeching now.

If she's going to tell us why, doesn't she just get on with it? I thought, exchanging a glance with Miranda. *Why is she beating around the bush?*

"The world isn't black and white," Jenny said. "There's a lot of grey areas and fine lines between right and wrong."

"That's just it," Lizzy pounced on the words.

Jenny nodded with encouragement.

"Spit it out, Lizzy," Connie told her, true to form. "Go ahead."

Lizzy gulped and began.

"I had a brother. There were eight years between us, but we were good friends."

"Who was older?"

"Oh, well — he was. Matthew was the oldest. He would be fifty-five this year if he'd lived. He was so tall and handsome. But he was a daredevil too. He gave my parents an awful time. I was so much younger than him that I couldn't see that. I always took his side — which wasn't hard because I worshipped him. He wasn't afraid of anything. He didn't care what anybody said. He thought that nothing could touch him, that no rules applied to him. I thought he was a superhero."

"He sounds like a bit of a pill, if you ask me," Nora said dryly.

"He does, doesn't he?" Lizzy admitted. "When he was younger, he thought his name was 'chore' because my mom would always refer to him as that."

"That wasn't very nice," Brooke said.

Lizzy gave her head a little shake, in an impatient manner.

"Oh, Brooke, I know that you'd never talk like that to Toby. But things were different back then. People didn't care so much about the delicate psyches of children. I don't think Matt ever suffered too much from her way of talking. She was tough on him for sure, but he was a real handful. And anyways, Brooke dear," her eyes softened towards the young girl, "not everyone is the mother that you are."

"That's for sure," Connie said. "I know what you mean, Liz. My father used to call my sister 'lard arse'. That would be totally unacceptable now."

"And rightly so," Clarisse spoke up. "Young girls have enough trouble with their body images."

"See that's the thing right there," Lizzy said. "Nobody gave a crap about things like that when we were young. And Matt was smart in his own way. I'm sure he knew that he was a chore to my mom. I just don't think he could help it."

The Sunday sun beamed at us as we sprawled in the orchard, some in yellow chairs and some in the fragrant grass smelling of the delicious summer day.

How these days came to pass I didn't know. To this day, I don't know. But somehow or other, a story would be related, a catharsis of sorts and a woman's life would be shared, amongst the orchard grass, the sunny hours, the remnants of tea and goodies.

Jenny passed around the massive blue teapot adorned with silver butterflies, the pot that never seemed to run out of tea. Most of us topped up our cups with refreshing mint tea.

"Nowadays he probably would have been diagnosed with ADHD or learning disability or one of those labels kids get, but anyways that didn't happen in my day. If you didn't do what you were told, you were punished and that was the end of it. No one cared too much if you couldn't sit still long enough to learn to read and write. You just kind of got shoved along in the school system."

"Is that what happened to your Matthew?" Jenny asked, her voice gentle.

"Yes. He attended school every day, but he just managed to coast along. Most days he got into trouble and had to sit in the principal's office. He was smart enough in some ways. He could do anything with his hands. He could fix engines and things that had my dad stumped. He just couldn't learn in the conventional way."

"Too bad he hadn't gotten into a co-op programme or something like that. It did wonders for my grandson," Faye said.

"There wasn't anything like that available in our little country school. Not back then, anyways. He'd help my dad in the garage working on motors and stuff like that. He could focus then. But oh, dear God he hated going to school. The older he got, the more he hated it. He knew he couldn't do the work, so he'd just clown around and get into trouble. A lot of the kids thought he was kind of cool because he didn't care about authority. That just made it worse. He and Mom would scream at each other every morning. It was awful. Dad would leave to go to work, but I was stuck there listening to them. Back and forth and back and forth they'd go, the same shit every single day. He didn't want to go. He hated it. He wasn't learning anything. He was going to quit the minute he turned sixteen. And she would yell that he had to go; he had no choice. He was never going to amount to anything if he didn't get his high school diploma. And on and on it went. Every blessed morning it was the same thing, variations of the same theme over and over until I'd go to my room and stick my fingers in my ears."

We sat in comparative silence, picturing this daily morning ritual. I would have hated it. I hated screaming. I could never remember my mom screaming.

But, I reflected, *I had gone to school willingly each day.*

Lizzy sighed. It seemed to originate way down in her toes.

"I loved them both. But people are just themselves. You can't change them. Lots of times they can't even change themselves. You're just stuck with them."

"Very true," Connie agreed. "When we think about how hard it is to change our own behaviour, we can realize that it's nearly impossible to change someone else's. Believe me, I know."

"It wasn't for lack of trying, that's for sure. I think my mom thought she could make him be a scholar by the sheer force of her own will. It didn't work, of course."

"I used to wish," Faye said in a thoughtful tone, "that I could go back and observe my parents through my grownup eyes so I could understand how our family functioned when I was a child. When you're young, you're so unaware of the chemistry of your own family unit. I think most people would be surprised."

"Indeed, they would," Jenny agreed. "You probably felt empathy for your mom when you became a mom yourself, Lizzy."

"Oh, I sure did," Lizzy grinned. "I used to pray that my boys didn't give me half as hard a time as Matt gave our mom. And yet, you know —"

She hesitated.

"You still took his side?" Jenny asked.

"I did. Because he was my amazing big brother. I loved him to bits. He was never dull, that's for sure. You always felt alive when he was around. All I really wanted was for my mom to stop yelling at him and let him be. But that never happened."

"So, did he finish high school?"

"We-e-ll. When he was about fifteen, he started collecting traffic signs."

"Traffic signs?"

"I know. Weird, eh? He'd ride his bike down the dusty back roads and he'd come back with a sign strapped to his back. You should have seen his bedroom. He'd nail them all over his wall. I remember 'Lovers Lane' and 'Steneville 5 km'. One time he came trudging up our lane carrying a huge YIELD sign on his back. I ran out to help him and he said that this is how Jesus must have felt carrying the cross. I told him there was a huge difference between him and his thefts and Jesus carrying the sins of the world. But it still made us giggle. I helped him smuggle it up to his room. He had them all organized on his walls. It was a sight to behold. They were spread out in a certain order and in between the metal signs were scraps of different posters which he'd picked up on his travels. His whole room told a story. And he kept telling me that someday he was going to travel and see the world for real. Then he'd pick up lots of signs. Maybe he'd write a book and illustrate it with the photos of his traffic signs."

She shook her head at the memory.

"He was one of a kind, that's for sure. There never was anybody else like him."

"I've never heard of that," Connie commented, ever practical. "You can't just steal traffic signs."

"Of course, you're not supposed to," Lizzy conceded.

"Oh, people do it all the time." Miranda piped up, unexpectedly. "I've heard of the Abbey Road sign in London England being stolen more than once as a souvenir of the Beatles. And a South Park sign from Kansas."

"No way."

"Yep." Freddy took up the thread of conversation. "I've heard of it, too. The funniest one I ever heard of was the town of 'Fucking' in Austria'."

Freddy's face revealed no scrimmage of a smile. We all burst out laughing.

"Who would name a town that?"

"Well, of course, it doesn't mean there what it does here. I think it was named after a person — Focko or something like that."

"Freddy Gibson, you're making that up!"

"I'm not. It's a fact. Look it up if you don't believe me. It's not far from that famous town in Austria where *The Sound of Music* was filmed."

"Well, trust you to know that tidbit of information," Nora said in a voice dripping with scorn.

"I know there's a 'Ragged Ass' sign in Yellowknife that's been stolen more than once too, but I won't bore you with any details." Freddy continued. "What sign did your Matthew steal, Lizzy?"

Everyone turned to Lizzy, smiles still lingering on their lips at the absurd turn the conversation had taken. The smiles died, one by one, at the sight of Lizzy's pale face.

"It was a stop sign."

Her voice croaked the words, barely more than a whisper.

"Oh dear," Jenny said. "Someone was hurt?"

"Two people died."

There was a collective gasp, then utter silence.

"We lived in the country, as I've said. There was a sharp turn a couple of concessions over from us. It was an unlikely spot for a stop sign. But everybody who lived around there knew about it and how it could be a dangerous spot. The McMillans up the road had company from Alberta that summer. One morning they decided to go out and look around on their own. It was foggy out. They went straight through the turn and ended up T boned by a cement truck. They never had a chance. They were killed on impact."

"Oh, no," Brooke said, her voice barely a whisper.

"Yes. It was awful. If they'd stopped at the sign, they wouldn't have died."

"Oh dear, how awful."

"Yes indeed. It was very, very awful. Of course, we didn't know right away that it was Matt. We heard about the accident. It was horrifying. Everyone started baking and cooking and bringing food to the McMillans, because that's what they did when there was a tragedy."

"Did your brother get charged?"

"I don't really know what happened and that's the truth. I was only ten and excluded from all the happenings. It was all hushed up in front of me."

"Are you sure it was him?"

"Oh, yes. Positive. He confessed, you see. He was full of mischief and horseshit and wild energy but there was no cruelty in him. He just wanted to have fun and take chances. He wanted to explore that big old world that he'd mapped out on his bedroom walls. He never wanted to hurt anyone. He was broken right in two when he heard the news. Mom and Dad were down at the neighbor's offering condolences when he crept into my room and told me that he had been the one who took away the stop sign. He knelt beside my bed and told me and then he put his head down on my pillow and cried with huge big sobs that tore my heart out. I couldn't believe my big brother who wasn't afraid of anything and who never got upset was sobbing into my pillow. I felt completely helpless. I didn't know what to do. I was just a child. I told him I loved him and always would. I told him I'd never tell anyone for my whole life."

"So, no one else ever knew?"

"Oh no, they knew. I suspect he couldn't contain his remorse and told my parents, but I never knew for sure. He ended up going away to a reform school. I remember the day he left. He lifted me up even though I was getting to be a big girl and he told me that I was his favorite girl in the whole world. He told me to be very good for Mom and Dad. I promised him that I would. And then he was gone."

"Where did he go? What town?"

"I never knew. My parents believed that the least a child knew about upsetting things the better it was. Not realizing that the truth is so much better than the horrible things your mind conjures up. Anyways, he was supposed to come home at Christmas, and he didn't, and then at Easter, and he didn't. I think my dad would have been ok with him coming back for a visit, but my mom was one of those women who could harden her heart like a stone. I begged and begged to be able to go and see him, but I was never allowed. I wrote him letters. I'd give them to my dad to mail, but I never got any answer. I knew he struggled with literacy, but it still hurt that I never heard a word. Then one day my mom told me in passing conversation that Matthew had died," Lizzy's voice broke on the last words. "She was such a cold woman."

"Maybe that was her only way of coping," Connie suggested. "Maybe it was just too much for her to bear."

Lizzy shrugged.

"I felt lost for years after that. My high school years are just a big blur. I hit the books and graduated and moved further south. Then I met Pete at a Junior Farmers Dance one of the girls at work dragged me to." She shrugged and gave a nervous laugh. "The rest, as they say, is history."

Another life story fraught with sorrow and pain. My heart felt saddened for Lizzy whom I'd always regarded as a plain, ordinary country woman.

Lizzy appeared abashed now, not quite believing that she had bared her soul to all of us.

Silence settled in the orchard air, absorbing the heartache of the long-ago story.

"I'm glad you're better now, Lizzy," Brooke ventured. "That was a lot to go through."

"Yes, it was quite a journey. Of course, it helped a lot once I married Pete. He's so solid and down to earth and dependable. And having the boys, of course. My heart and life are full now. And do you know what's helped me find my way through the worst of the memories, Brooke?"

"No, Lizzy. What?"

"You, my dear."

"Me?"

"Yes, you. You and your teaching of this beautiful practice. You and your wise words on yoga and meditation. You and Jenny and all you guys," she waved her arm in a careless fashion at the odd assortment of women perched throughout the orchard. She appeared self-conscious at her own words but she kept on. "I'd never practiced yoga before or anything like that. I used to think it was kind of silly — you know for artsy-fartsy people. Not for a plain old woman like myself. You know? Anyways I had no idea how soothing and comforting it could be. Don't laugh at me but sometimes I feel as if I lost part of my soul along the way and somehow, I found it right here."

No one laughed.

"Like Peter Pan's shadow," Jenny mused.

"Something like that. Brooke helped me stitch my soul back on," she giggled a little at her own flight of fancy.

"It can be a work in progress for all of us," Brooke said. "Sometimes you have to find it every night and hold it close."

"That's ok," Jenny said. "As long as you find it."

"Remember," Brooke said, "The light that you've been seeking, Lizzy, has always been right inside of you, not anyone else."

Jenny nodded as she looked around at us, that sweet smile of hers hovering on her lips as she reached over, retrieving the blue teapot from among the orchard grasses.

"I love what C.S. Lewis said," she concluded, in the gentlest of voices.

"'You don't have a soul. You have a body. You are a soul.'"

31

"I'd rather learn to dance in the rain than worry if I have an umbrella for the rest of my life."

Nikki Rowe

"HEY MOLLY!"

"Come on in. I'm almost done," I called to Miranda, who opened the door to my room after a perfunctory knock.

I regarded her reflection in the mirror as she peeked her head around the corner of my tiny bathroom. And as I did, it struck me anew that we shared a vague sort of resemblance. I'd heard of friends looking alike with no familial connection. Funny how these things happened sometimes for no reason.

"Don't you just hate that job?" she asked, indicating the tweezers in my hand. "I can never get the right angle to see mine properly. And they never come out even."

I surveyed her eyebrows with a critical eye. They appeared to be positioned as two perfect, symmetrical arcs above her blue eyes.

"Well, yours look pretty good."

"Oh, they're great now," she agreed. "Jenny did them."

"Jenny? Plucked your eyebrows?"

"No, no. She didn't pluck them. We were yakking one day last week after yoga. It was that day when you were at the day care centre doing some co-op hours."

"Uh-huh."

I discarded the tweezers. My brows would have to do for now.

"Well, Jenny was saying how she had a natural recipe that worked for facial hair, that's really how they started talking about it."

I grabbed my jacket and we set out to meet the fellows, Keith and Brandon, at Lorna's for supper. I struggled to keep up with the eyebrow tale as we set out into the darkening afternoon.

"Facial hair?"

"Oh, you know, stray hairs that you acquire along the way. I think they come more when you get older, at least that's the gist of what the others were saying."

"Something to look forward to," I giggled.

"Really. Anyways, you know how Jenny always has some recipe for one thing or another?"

"Yeah. Some of them sound pretty way out, I think."

"Anyways, she has this paste she makes to remove facial hair. First, she grinds oatmeal in that mortar and pestle of hers and then she adds some lemon juice and honey. She says some magic words and mixes it all together. Then she applies it wherever there's unwanted hair."

"Your eyebrows?"

"Yup. She shaped them. See."

She turned to me with her brows lifted so I could admire them once again.

"Good job," I observed.

Miranda must have caught a note in my voice. She gave me an odd look.

"You're funny about Jenny still, aren't you, Moll?"

"Am I?"

"You know it."

I sighed. Sometimes I still regretted my words on Beltane, voicing my mistrust of Jenny. Because Miranda had not forgotten them. They lingered between us. How could I explain something to her that I didn't understand myself?

"I don't know," I admitted, shaking my head in frustration. "I really don't. Sometimes I feel myself holding back from her for some reason. I can't help it. It's a feeling I've had when I'm with her since the first time I saw her. Like she's not who she seems to be."

"Well she is a witch. Sorry," she corrected herself. "She always says she's not a witch. That a hedgewytch is a different sort of witch."

"I know, but it's more than that. It's just an odd feeling I get sometimes. I know you care a lot about her, Miranda and I'm glad." I shrugged. "Anyways don't worry about it. It's fine. Life would be pretty dull here if she wasn't around, that's for sure."

"I can't imagine living in this little place without Jenny. It would be black and white. Now it's Technicolor. That's what I think."

"And you get nice eyebrows out of the deal. Maybe next time mine need doing, I'll get her to do them," I said, by way of concession.

We hurried along to Lorna's, happy to be taking time for dinner amidst our busy college semester. Miranda and I had found ourselves gradually winding our way back into the dating world, developing a social life with Keith and Brandon. They both lived in London and often went home on the weekends, as they had jobs and family there. We'd always planned to accompany them sometime, but Miranda and I were stretched pretty thin on the weekend with our own schedules.

The busy days seemed to fly by with a will of their own. The addition of the males filled the days to brimming, until often not one spare moment remained. Because, of course, we didn't want to give up any of our social life, nor could we afford to take time from our work at the café and at the cottage. So the days simply became increasingly piled with activity. Despite Brooke's gentle words reminding us to "slow down and relax and breathe", we rarely stopped to do this. We needed *shavasana* just to obtain a few horizontal moments.

Thursday evenings, like this one, often found us carving out time together for dinner or drinks or both.

The brilliant splendor of the oak and maple trees stood silhouetted, in all their finery, against the achingly clear blue of the fading sky. Living here did make this month outstanding in more ways than one. Getting caught up in the excitement of the witches walk and Halloween (or Samhain) magic seemed to be a way of life now — an accepted flurry of seasonal fun.

"Polish up those brooms. It's almost time to fly."

So commenced the Hedgewytch Column for this month, providing us all with a giggle.

Of course, though, with the October issue of the Jared Times also came the infamous 'Witches Among us' column. This seemed to be affording the guys a source of conversation having perused the local paper before we arrived. This particular article featured another witch hanged in Salem, Massachusetts: a woman named Rebecca Nurse, talking about her age (seventy-one), and how many misguided people in Salem had previously regarded her with affection. Comparisons were drawn between Jenny and the Salem witch. The column continued to describe how Rebecca Nurse regularly appeared in her accuser's homes in spirit form to torment and attack them. It went on to further defame Jenny, accusing her of despicable things — the least of these being black magic.

"Is she really that bad?" Keith queried, folding up the rag and lying it on the restaurant table. "I mean we saw her at that Mayday thing, but I've never said two words to her. She seemed pretty tame, though."

The autumn sunshine had not yet retired completely for the day, leaving a vestige of light, enough to beckon us onto the old stone patio. It felt wonderful to enjoy a beer before parting for the weekend.

"Of course not," scoffed Miranda. "Or Molly and me wouldn't work for her."

"But you always say she's not actually a witch. A headwitch or something."

"Hedgewytch," Miranda and I cried, in unison.

"Whatever. She sounds awful according to this," Brandon observed, pointing at the offending column. "I mean, she sure looks harmless enough. I doubt she weighs a hundred pounds soaking wet. I thought you guys liked her."

"We do, silly," Miranda verified. "You can't take that column for gospel. She's just a country woman trying to make a living with herbs and recipes and stuff."

"What? No magic?" Keith spoke up. "I thought she was a — that type of witch, you said."

"Well, she is, and she does have some magic, but —"

"She does?"

"Yes, she does," I attempted an explanation. In my own perverse way, I wanted to defend her now that she was being criticized. "She does, but she doesn't use it in a bad way. Everything he says — every single thing — is untrue. She uses her magic for good, not evil."

Their faces held similar expressions of skepticism.

"Here." Miranda flipped through the paper to locate Jenny's column. "Here. Read this. This is her column. It's all about home remedy tips and local news and nature tales. That's what she's like."

They skimmed through it, seemingly to pacify Miranda.

"It sounds ok," Brandon admitted.

"Of course, it does. You guys should come out and meet her. Meet her properly, I mean," Miranda told them.

"No thank you. I decline a visit to the local witch. I might come away with my manhood spirited away. Or worse," Keith said, his voice holding a note of jest.

She turned to Brandon who displayed even less enthusiasm.

"What I don't get is that if she's so nice, why does this guy have such a hate on for her?"

"We don't know that," Miranda admitted.

"There must be something to it. You know that old saying 'Where there's smoke, there's fire.'"

Miranda and I exchanged looks. We had no idea.

"And how does this guy even get it in the paper?" Keith continued, warming to his topic. "I mean, you can't just put whatever you want in the local paper. You have to run it by the editor and all that. It can't be a very big staff. I mean Jared is just a little wee place."

"That's true," I mused. "I never thought of that."

"And couldn't your Jenny sue them for slander? Or libel? I never know which is which."

"Which witch is which?" Miranda laughed.

"Something like that."

"I think," I reflected, "that he knows Jenny and knows that she wouldn't sue."

"Why wouldn't she?"

"She just wouldn't. It's not who she is," Miranda finished my thought. "But, Molly, what makes you think it's a he?"

I was going to say something like 'because males can be so hateful.' I caught myself in time, not wanting to offend the males.

I shrugged.

"I don't know. What do you think?"

"I sometimes wondered if it was Joan Payne."

"It could be, I guess. But she's ancient and either demented or really screwed up in the head. This column is written with intelligent calculation. There's some research gone into it, too."

"I always wondered how much of her behaviour is an act."

"Ok. Who the hell is Joan Payne?" Brandon asked. "I'm lost."

"Oh, she's this horrible cackling old lady who lives down the road from Jenny."

"So, she's the witch then."

"No," we replied together, giggling into the suds of our beer.

Keith turned to Brandon and shook his head.

"You couldn't make this shit up," he observed.

How true. But it all seemed as natural as breathing to me now.

"Anyways, Samhain is great to celebrate at Jenny's," I told them. "It's coming up. You guys could come then and see who's who."

"Samhain?"

"Oh sorry. Halloween. *Aka* Samhain. It just means 'summer's end'."

"Oh God," Keith groaned. "They have their own bloody words and everything."

"Molly's right. You should come. Even just come into Jared, because that's where we take the kids on the witches walk."

They said they'd have to see, with a distinct lack of conviction, and we knew that it all held little to no interest for them.

"You're just boondoggling," Miranda accused them, causing both of us to dissolve into laughter.

"WTF?"

"Brooke's new boyfriend has a whole repertoire of words that he uses. They're words that no one's ever heard of before," I explained. "So, Miranda and I are trying to keep up by learning a few way-out words ourselves."

"And using them in conversation," Miranda said.

"Wherever possible," I added.

The guys both shook their heads.

"You're crazy, both of you. Do you even know what a bondoogling is?"

Miranda shook her head, exasperated.

"Boondoggling," I corrected. "Of course. We're not allowed to use a word unless we know it's meaning. That's part of the research. It means to do work of very little value just so you appear busy."

"Hey, we don't do that," Keith exclaimed.

"Well, we might, bro," Brandon put a hand on his friend's arm. "If it means we don't have to go see a witch."

We laughed, returning to our meal and refreshments.

I enjoyed these times. I took pleasure in Keith's company, and we had fun, but deep inside me I always knew how transient my Jared days were. I knew my time here would be fleeting. That these days had been dropped into my life, like a segment from a movie, even as the whole reel continued to unwind into the future.

Keith and Brandon did not ever make it out to Hedgewytch Way, as it turned out. It remained a separate segment of our lives. Which kept it all the more exclusive and unique for us.

We marched through the Samhain preparations with Brooke and Neil and Kat and Toby and Melly assisting with the all the festivities.

We made glow-in-the-dark slime, using white glue and borax and glow-in-the-dark paint. We made ghosts from leaves with white paint and Sharpies and string. We made owls from pine cones. And, of course, we decorated everywhere with pumpkins, filling them with all manner of intentions and magical aspirations.

I could feel a sense of belonging beginning to blossom in me. I allowed myself to surrender to it. It felt so good to be a part of things — the fascination of Samhain, the anticipation of the upcoming Yule season.

Yule which now meant Winter Solstice to me: the longest night of the year, marking the return of lengthening days. A night when Brooke added a special candlelit yoga celebration, telling us we must shine extra bright in the long hours of the night. It meant decorating all the trees at Jenny's and telling lots of stories and Christmas tales to the kids and brewing up delectable spiced drinks in various crockpots.

No dilemma existed this December as to where we would spend that day. We were firmly entrenched in the traditions and activities at Hedgewytch Cottage. I felt secure in this knowledge as the inevitable topic of festive plans came up, one morning after yoga.

"I wish I could just come to the cottage one year with Jamie and the kids," Kerry declared. "But we always have to go to Barrie to see Jamie's parents. I hate it more and more as the kids get bigger. I'd love to stay home for Christmas morning and then come here for a while. But my mother-in-law would have a conniption fit."

I remembered last year that Kerry had voiced her reluctance to spend Christmas with her in-laws, in particular her mother-in-law. What a shame that one person could wreck another's holiday by virtue of their personality.

She looked at Neil, who had just entered the room and heard her last remark.

"I don't think you've got a word in your collection for her, Neil. At least all I've heard you describe are nice things."

"Nefarious?" he suggested.

"Oh dear," she said. "That means evil or something doesn't it? I shouldn't really have said what I did. She's my kid's grandmother. And she's not evil. She's just, just —"

"Odious?" I suggested.

"Yeah. Odious. That's what she is. I'm sorry."

"Don't apologize," Neil said. "Some people are just —"

"Odious!" we all chimed in together.

"It's a good word for some people," Miranda said. "Look at Melly's mom."

She hastened to look around but Melly and Toby and Jenny were away, preparing refreshments. Jenny always chastened us about making ill comments people, reminding us that they would return to us three-fold.

So, it being open season for a short time, we proceeded to throw people under the bus who fit that description. All in good fun, of course.

Because it's true. Some people are just plain odious.

32

"We are the granddaughters of the witches you did not burn."
"Ever mind the rule of three.
Three times your acts return to thee."

H OW THE SUBJECT OF SALEM, MASSACHUSETTS, came to be the topic of the day, no one could afterwards remember, least of all myself.

The greyness of yet another bitter cold winter day had descended upon us. There is nothing joyful about a day like that, dull and overcast. So many such days must be endured before the arrival of spring. I suppose there exists a certain quality of beauty to the winter months, but it tends to wear thin as the days drag on with little sunlight to light their way.

The morning had drifted into a discussion, prompted by Miranda and me, of possible activities for the kid's circle. Our inspiration seemed to be palling with the weather.

"What about origami?" Kat ventured. She had started attending yoga, much to Brooke's delight. She encouraged Kat to tell her friends at school, in an attempt to bring some younger blood to the studio.

"Origami is a good idea," I said.

In my head, I pictured those wayward children, especially the reckless boys, folding paper in precise folds. It would be a nightmare, even with the extra help Kat provided.

I sensed that Miranda shared my thoughts but, not wanting to discourage Kat, she replied, "We 'll look into that."

"What about making some of those cool glass balls for everybody, like I have hanging in my bedroom window?" Melly piped up. She had fallen into the role of passing around tea and refreshments with Toby and Jenny after yoga.

She seemed to glow with an inner spirit and happiness. I sometimes thought about her at night all tucked up in her little bedroom, safe and cared for. And I hoped this arrangement between Jenny and Aunt Steph would continue to thrive.

"Your bedroom window?" Nora asked, in her usual sharp manner.

"Yes. At Jenny's house. In my bedroom."

Nora *harrumph*ed for no apparent reason.

"What kind of a glass ball is it?" Miranda asked her.

"It's a witch's ball," Jenny explained with a grin, adding, "of course."

"A 'witch's ball'? I didn't know that," Melly replied, looking a little taken aback.

"Yes, but it's for good, Melly. A witch's ball is used for protection against evil and bad witches and sickness. Your window faces east which is the best place to hang one."

"Oh, well that's good for me then," the little girl said, appearing relieved. "The sickness part, I mean."

"I've never heard tell of a 'witch's ball'," Verna said, her expression skeptical. "Is that something you're making up, Jenny Smith?"

"Oh no. That's what they're called. But they're called other things too. You might know them as gazing balls or friendship balls or fairy balls."

Several women nodded.

"They're all the same thing," Jenny explained. "Just different names. And they're all different colours and dimensions. It's the beauty of the colours that attract the evil and then they trap the evil inside leaving the home protected. They've been around for hundreds of years."

"I know what you mean by friendship balls," Faye said. "They sell them locally, I think. But they're all molded from glass, Melly. You wouldn't be able to make them in craft circle. Unless you know some glass blowers."

Glass blowers! I felt Miranda's dismayed thoughts beside me.

"But not the one in my bedroom," Melly protested. "It's different than the ones you buy. It's clear and has little flowers inside it. I love it. I love watching it shining in the sun when I wake up in the morning."

"You're right, Melly," Jenny said, never ceasing to dole out tea and cookies. "That is a homemade one. My mother made some for the bedrooms."

"Are they hard to make?" Miranda asked, clearly relieved.

"Oh no. We could manage it, I'm sure. I'll get some of those clear plastic balls at the dollar store — you know the ones that you decorated for the Christmas tree."

"What did we ever do before we had a dollar store close by?" Verna mused.

"It's true," Brooke agreed. "For kids crafts alone. Construction paper and paints and markers are expensive if you had to buy them somewhere else."

"When you have kids, dollar stores are great," Kerry agreed. "It's amazing what you can get there."

"So, what goes into the making of these balls, Jenny?" I asked, trying to retrieve the thread of the wandering conversation.

"Oh, just whatever you want. Little flower petals or herbs or crystals. I have lots of stuff you could use. And the kids can write a little wish or intention on a piece of paper. Then you tie the top with a ribbon and voila, a witch's ball."

Miranda appeared to be mulling this over in her mind.

Then, turning to me, she said, "We could do that. Might be kinda neat."

I nodded my agreement.

"We could make one for our own rooms. Great idea, Melly. Thanks."

The little girl beamed.

"It makes me happy to think your mom made the one in my room, Jenny. I love it."

"Me, too," Jenny said. "The best things are the things the people we love make for us with their own hands and hearts, I think. She made a few of them after we went to Salem one year."

"You went to Salem, Massachusetts?" Nora asked. "Where they hung all them witches?"

"We did."

"I never knew that," Nora said, seemingly affronted that she had not been privy to this information.

"It was shortly after Julian and Buddy died," Jenny explained. "It was a very dark time for both of us."

"So, you went to be rejuvenated by visiting witch's graves?" Freddy asked, with a sideways grin.

"Well, you see, we had just decided to set up shop. You know … the Hedgewytch shop. So not a real witch, but more of a green healing nature witch."

"You always say that," Verna mused.

"Yes, Mama and I decided that right from the get-go, because we didn't want people to get the wrong idea and think of evil spells and black magic. We wanted to be known for healing, not for hurting. But still to have a little bit of magic to get us by. You know?"

"So, you went there to get some ideas?" Faye asked. "Do they have good witches down there?"

"The women that were hung there were really not even witches," Miranda said. "It was just a huge mass hysteria and, because they couldn't explain things, they called it witchcraft. Remember *The Crucible*? We talked about that in high school, right, Molly?"

She turned to me. I gave her a peculiar look.

We hadn't gone to high school together. Had she forgotten that? Just because we had become friends didn't mean we shared a history before last May. In fact, her life before Jared remained an enigma. She never discussed it.

"I don't remember," I said.

"I remember the book," Brooke said. "It was unbelievable what happened to those women."

"Not just women," Jenny said. "Fourteen women, five men, and two dogs. All of them hung for witchcraft."

"Dogs? How the hell could they be witches?" Nora asked.

"The people believed that witches had animal familiars or helpers that they could use to do their bidding. You know, like my Julie."

On cue, as so often happened, Julie emerged from underneath one of the tables at the back of the studio and slunk up to the front of the room. Melly reached down, gathering her into her arms to bestow kisses on her calico head. Kisses which Julie tolerated. Barely.

Nora sniffed.

"She does your bidding, does she, Jenny?"

"No," Jenny sighed. "Julie's not much of a familiar. She has her own agenda. But the people then truly believed that animals could be possessed. One dog was shot when a young girl accused it of bewitching her. Any animal that became sick or injured with no apparent cause was thought to be the victim of witchcraft."

"Didn't they feed the dogs a cake made from the urine of people they thought were witches?" Miranda asked. "I remember something like that."

"They thought that a witch's cake had the power to reveal whether witchcraft was afflicting a person who had symptoms of illness. So, they baked a cake with rye flour and the urine of that person. Then they fed it to a dog. If the dog displayed the same symptoms, then the presence of witchcraft was proved."

"How awful," breathed Brooke. "And utterly unfair."

"It was unfair on so many levels," Jenny agreed. "It was a classic case of scapegoating caused by fear. Because it was such a strict religious community, living in near isolation, they were afraid of the devil and witches who did their bidding. The accusers were young girls, mainly preteens. Because they couldn't explain what was happening to the girls, they blamed it on witchcraft. There was mass hysteria and panic. The women who were accused were hung on Gallows Hill. Mama and I visited it when we were there. There's a sign there that says, 'On this ledge in 1692, 19 innocents were hanged for accusations of witchcraft.'"

"Wow," I felt interested, in spite of myself. "Did you drive?"

"Yes. It's not a bad drive. A full day. But a good one. New England is beautiful in the fall."

"You went in the fall?"

"Yes, for Halloween. Samhain."

"Wow! That sounds awfully exciting," Freddy exclaimed.

"I'd be scared," Verna shuddered. "All those witches walking around."

"October 31st is the New Year, if you follow the Wheel of the Year. The seasonal calendar used to mark the seasonal changes on the earth. So, it's a really big deal down there. The crowds are huge, thousands and thousands of people dressed up in the streets. Mama and I were a little overwhelmed, but excited too. That's where we got the idea for our own witches walk."

"We haven't got thousands coming yet though," laughed Brooke. "I think we had a grand total of forty last year. Not cimmerian enough, I guess."

Verna rolled her eyes and said, "You've been hanging out with that Neil fellow. I can tell. Mr. Wordsmith or whatever he calls himself."

Brooke chuckled.

"I have to keep up with him, Verna. Some of his words are fascinating. And interesting."

"What does that one mean? Do you know what they mean, too?" Freddy asked.

"It means dark and gloomy," Brooke replied. "Like Salem."

"It certainly is a captivating place," Jenny said. "I've never forgotten the sheer enchantment of it. There's a statue of Elizabeth Montgomery in the town square."

I had no clue who this was, but the older ladies nodded.

"Samantha!"

"From *Bewitched*!"

"Yes," Jenny said. "TV's famous witch back in the sixties. And you can go and visit the graves of the witches and read their stories.

Mama found it heartbreaking. She experienced the war and hated any unnecessary loss of life. It's tragic to think that these creatures were misunderstood and falsely accused and not one person believed them. I don't know if they were good people or not, but they didn't deserve to die. Even if some of them were odious."

My eyes flew to Mirandas. How did she know that we had bantered that word around the studio? She'd been in the cottage at the time of the "odious" discussion. Jenny, of course, appeared as innocent as a baby.

"You're right, Jenny," Faye said. "People don't deserve to die that way. History's so often sad when you think back over it all, isn't it?"

"We always hope to do better than our ancestors but who knows what they'll think of us," Verna observed. "Did you meet some real witches down there, Jenny? You and Esther."

Jenny's eyes twinkled in their mysterious way.

"Of course. It's Witch City after all. Even the police cars have the witch logo on them. Some of them are hedgewytches. Like me. Women of nature and the earth. That's where I learned that witches are not a stereotype any more than any other group of people. They just utilize the magic already present. The most important tools for magic aren't crystals or cauldrons, but your free will and your own energy. I learned my first rules of magic there."

"There's rules?" Nora asked. "I never thought you followed any rules."

Jenny took no offense, merely grinning at the waspish Nora.

"You could be right, Nora. Guidelines more than rules, I guess. Things like keeping your thoughts and actions as pure as you can because every action has an equal reaction. And being careful with words, because they're such a powerful magic. Sometimes we lash out in anger and say angry words, giving them more emotion, more power than we mean to. Then they come back to us three-fold. That's why we have to try never to wish harm to anyone if we don't want it back. People that have done wrong will someday see the true horror of their own actions and that will be punishment enough."

"Maybe," Heather said. "But some people never seem to suffer for their own actions."

"We only have to worry about our own actions, really," Brooke pointed out, smiling. "Yoga has its own guidelines."

"I feel like I want to visit Salem now," Freddy announced. "We should all go on a yoga retreat down there."

"It sounds pretty exciting," I agreed. "We can put it on our bucket list. Which I don't have."

"We do now," Miranda said cheerily. "Number one. Go to Salem for Halloween."

"That's where Gran got her mirror," Toby said, adding hastily, "the one downstairs that makes you look good. And the sign that says, 'Come and sit for a spell!'"

"That's right," Jenny agreed. "We got them to start our business with some magic straight from the witch city. Oh look," she pointed through the window at the shafts of sunlight that had broken through the grey day, "We can appreciate some apricity now."

"Apricity?"

"Brooke isn't the only one who's been researching unusual words. I was just waiting for a chance to use it."

"I don't know that one," Brooke admitted.

"It means the warmth of the sun in winter." Jenny said. "Now just look at that!"

The door swung open. In strode the broad striking figure of Neil Laidlaw. He headed towards Brooke, but stopped on his way to tousle the heads of Melly and Toby with long affectionate fingers.

"Speak of the devil," Jenny mused.

"Or the witches," Freddy laughed.

"Whatever," Nora shrugged, in her usual off-hand way, causing us all to laugh.

33

"Kindness is a language the blind can see and the deaf can hear."

Mark Twain

ANOTHER JARED SPRING WHISPERED TO US. We answered with love and hope.

Easter and Beltane passed in their own wonderful way. We welcomed the calendar of Hedgewytch Way as it marched along, everything so familiar now. The inspiration of working outside with the children both at my co-op and at Jenny's continued to inspire me. Tales regaled by our circle of yogis still punctuated Sunday mornings, the sharing of sorrows and joys, of life.

Little did I know that the most monumental tales, the ones still untold, would rock my entire world and leave me changed forever.

Today had found Nora reminiscing, this tale definitely not life-changing. Truth be told, I'd paid little attention to her words, dismissing her as a cynical old woman with little to relate of much interest. This turned out to be somewhat true. Still Nora's story, brief as it was, made me realize anew that every one of us has our own storyline, our own life's tale, unique only to ourselves.

Nora had been expounding on her girlhood years, growing up in Jared. I imagined her always living in the little village, ever crusty, ever grasping for an unsolved crossword puzzle clue.

"Jenny, you were always nice to me," she said, her words unexpected. "I remember that, even as a little girl."

Jenny inclined her head towards Nora.

"I'm glad," she told her, adding, "I always liked you, Nora."

"Really? Some of those kids were just plain mean. They always made fun of me. I was this skinny kid with a great big nose. So, they were loaded with ammunition."

I couldn't look at Miranda. I simply couldn't. Because the thought floated between us, without so much as a glance.

Hasn't changed much!

Nora continued, uncomprehending. Or so it seemed.

"I still am. I know that. But there's not much you can do about things like that. You're just stuck with them. Anyways, we were poor. My mom died young. I lived with my dad and dressed in hand me downs. I remember your mom being very kind to me. Your dad used to always give us apples and carrots from the garden. You come from good people, Jenny."

Jenny demurred, "Thank you, Nora. I think so too."

"Anyways, I came home from school one day and there was a 'For Sale' sign on our lawn. I had no idea that we were thinking of moving. My dad hadn't thought to tell me. I was devastated. I mean, as poor and miserable as we were, at least we had a home. A home where my mother had lived. If we moved, I was sure that I'd lose any memory of her altogether. It's a terrible awful thing for a young child to lose their mother. It just is. It makes a hole in you that never gets filled up again."

Miranda and I looked at each other, exchanging the slightest of nods. We'd lost our mothers, both of us, but this was a topic Miranda never mentioned. Not ever.

Maybe someday, I thought. *When I've known her another two years, I'll hear that story.*

"That's tough," Faye observed. "How old were you, Nora?"

"I was eleven. It was horrible. We did move away, but ended up back here within the year. Because my father never did very well at anything. I hated being the new kid. I had no friends, no connections. At least when we moved back here it was familiar to me. Lots of kids still poked fun at me 'cause I was different, but you never did, Jenny. I don't forget that. Jared was the closest place to home I ever knew when I was a kid. I guess that's why I still hang around here."

"It's a good place," Verna agreed. "I like it here."

"You've been pretty good to me too, Verna," Nora conceded. "I mean, you let me hang around the café working on the crossword with only a cup of coffee going towards your business end. I know I'm a pain in the ass at times."

"At times?" Verna smiled, breaking the ice. Laughter rippled across the studio.

"Oh, I know. I'm just a crusty old woman but I'm grateful really. To all of you. I'm telling you that today. I learned from Jenny that a witch isn't some mean old thing with evil in her heart. You and your mom showed me that witches can be healers and helpers and worshippers of nature. You showed me that your magic and your power are kindness. Brooke taught me to be strong and true to myself. And the rest of you lot," she waved her hand around the studio, her voice rasping a little on the next words, "you're the family I never had before. I've got a place to come at Christmas and Easter and a bunch of friends to spend Sundays with. That scrawny kid with the big nose never thought she'd ever have that much in all her life. She's grateful for it, let me tell you. Listen up because I'm not likely to get sentimental again for another seventy odd years. But I wanted you guys to know."

Jenny stood up and put her arms around that curmudgeon, causing her to squirm and shake her head. But Jenny persisted.

"Don't get all mushy on me, Jenny Smith," she said. "I'm just trying to tell my story, scant and sad as it is."

"Well, I like your story because it's got a darn fine ending," Freddy observed. "You know, ending with all of us and how awesome we are."

Laughter ensued. Freddy possessed that knack.

Just then, the door burst open, allowing a gust of sweet fragrant air to fill the studio. Along with Toby and Melly half-pulling, half-leading a woebegone, bedraggled, very nervous-looking German Shepherd puppy.

Cries of "Grandma!" and "Jenny!" mingled with little yaps from the dog could be heard above the general din of the women, exclaiming and talking.

Jenny stepped forward, placing a tentative hand on the dog's matted fur, then petting it in a gentle manner. The dog stilled.

I'd noticed before the calming affect that Jenny invoked in animals.

She turned to look at the two children who seemed to be fairly erupting with their need to speak.

"Yes," she said. "What do you want to say? Where did this dog come from?"

They looked at each other, then both started to speak at once.

"They said he's a mean dog, but he's not really, Gran. Not really."

"He's not mean to us. He's our friend. He's a good dog really."

"Please can we keep him? Please."

"His name is Rolf."

This last remark tumbled out from Melly, as if this may well cinch the matter, the knowledge that this forlorn creature possessed a name.

"They were going to put him down, Gran!" Toby almost shrieked. "That's not right, is it? He should have a chance for a life. Right, Gran?"

"Who was? Where did this dog come from? Tell us the story. Calmly now, please."

Jenny sat back on her haunches and indicated for the children to start. Melly turned to Toby who, making a visible attempt to speak in a compose manner, obliged.

"Rolf comes from the man who rents the place beside where Melly and her Aunt Steph live."

"He's not a very nice man," Melly interjected.

"And somebody gave him Rolf, but he says he's a bad dog and doesn't listen and he's going to shoot him," Toby's voice rose on a desperate note.

Sympathetic noises filled the studio. Country women tended to be dog lovers. None of them would condone the shooting of a dog.

"Has he bitten anyone?" Verna ventured. "Because you can't have a dog that bites."

The children tripped over each other's words in denial of this.

"No. No. He doesn't bite. He just doesn't do what Ron tells him."

"So he says he's no good. But we can train him, can't we, Gran? Can we keep him? Please? Please?"

"Please?" Melly added.

"Toby," Brooke began. "We can't have a dog in our little —"

"No, Mom. I know that," Toby waved aside this possibility. "I mean here. At the cottage with Gran."

"And I could help look after him. I could run with him and feed him and everything." Melly said.

Clearly these two had hatched up a plan between them.

"Ron just gave you this dog?" Jenny asked.

"He said, 'Here if you think he's so great you take him before I shoot the bastard.'"

Toby turned to his mom and said, "Sorry, Mom. I was just quoting him. That's what he said."

Melly nodded her head vigorously, "He did say that. He really did. Toby only quoted the 'bastard' part."

She caused a stifled giggle as she made air quotes around the "quoted" instead of the word in question. "So, Toby and I took the leash and ran all the way here with Rolf. Because we knew you'd know what to do, Jenny."

"Well, I really don't know, guys," Jenny said thoughtfully. "I don't."

She straightened up, advancing to where Rolf lay in the corner, half cowering, half on guard, eyes wary, body motionless. She knelt beside the dog and stroked his fur. Toby and Melly joined her with caution, allowing Jenny to examine the dog.

"See, Grandma," Toby said, his voice soft. "Rolf really is a good dog. He's just lying there. Ron said German Shepherds are mean dogs."

"Dogs are a lot like people," Jenny replied, never ceasing to caress the dog's head and stroke his ears. "They act as they are treated. If you are kind to them, they will respond with kindness.

"Rolf," she continued. "That's a good German name."

She addressed the dog now, saying, "*Aufstehen*, Rolf."

Rolf rose, tilting his head to regard Jenny as if he understood every word she uttered.

"She's speaking German," Miranda breathed in astonishment. "She's speaking German because he's a German Shepherd."

This appeared to be the truth. Melly and Toby's eyes grew round as saucers, so fascinated were they at this turn of events. Several of the yogis looked on with obvious skepticism, but no one spoke.

Besides, it did seem to be working, whatever language Jenny was speaking.

"*Sitzen*, Rolf."

The puppy promptly sat down.

"*Gipp foos*."

The dog extended a paw to Jenny who shook it solemnly.

"*Braver Hund. Kommen Sie.*"

Jenny gestured to the puppy and began to walk towards the door. Rolf followed at her heels, the very picture of an obedient dog.

"What did she say?" Toby asked of the studio in general.

No one knew. They shook their heads, holding up their hands in a show of bewilderment.

"Who cares?" Melly asked. "I think we're keeping him. She really is magic, your grandma. Come on Toby. Let's go."

The pair scampered out the door eagerly.

A collective chuckle erupted through the studio as the red door closed behind them.

"It's not really magic. Her family is German and she knows the language," Verna stated.

"Aw, yes, that's true. But the magic is inside Jenny. It's not in her words," Nora said, surprising us. "That dog belongs to her now. Like Julie and Hoot and all those little chickadees and hummingbirds."

She surprised us further by offering and proceeding to make the witches relaxing tea for our refreshment.

"It's easy," she said, acknowledging our surprise, "Jenny showed me before. It's just one and a half teaspoons of jasmine flowers and equal amount of passiflora for each cup of water. You boil it and let it steep. It's a lovely smelling tea."

"We'll make a witch out of you yet, Nora," Freddy teased her.

"Didn't you listen, Freddy?" Nora asked scornfully. "A witch can be anyone at all. Any one of us."

We turned as one collective group to watch Jenny and Rolf disappear through the orchard and down the path to the cottage. Rolf ambled along beside her as if he'd done so all his life.

Connie groaned.

"I guess we have a dog now," she observed. "What a place full of strays and misfits. Present company included," she added, with a broad grin.

34

"I survived because the fire inside me burned brighter than the fire around me."

T HE DAY HAD COME FOR FREDDY'S STORY. That's how it happened. Freddy, the clown, always joking and laughing and making light of every situation had her own story. I knew the other nurses enjoyed working with her because she never took herself, or anyone else, seriously.

"Life is a terminal disease and it's sexually transmitted," she'd been heard to declare on more than one occasion.

As shocked as I felt the first time I heard this utterance from her laughing lips, the other nurses hastened to assure us that Freddy never said things like that to her patients or their families. She just used it to lighten the mood on their busy medical floor. Apparently, Freddy's patients adored her. I could understand why. Faced with hospital time, I'm sure it is much more pleasant to be cared for by a cheerful nurse than a crusty one.

So, you'd think that Freddy's story would be light and witty, full of humor and comic relief.

You would be wrong. Dead wrong.

And one Sunday morning, we heard it all. Freddy had given birth to a baby girl. She carried all the tragedy of that birth within her. Why had I never seen this before, this burden that weighed within her?

I guess we'd all just been too busy laughing with her, listening to her jokes.

I leaned forward to catch her words.

"I've thought of wee Emma every day for the past fifteen years."

"She's fifteen now?"

Faye asked the question, her voice gentle.

A web of sadness lay like an unfamiliar mask across Freddy's face.

The silence lingered on and on.

Finally, she managed a reply, barely a whisper, "She died, actually."

"Aw. Poor wee soul," Jenny breathed.

A deep sigh slipped from Freddy's lips before she spoke.

"Yes, Jenny, she was. That's exactly what she was. A poor wee soul who never asked to be born into this cruel world."

The room fell totally silent.

Even now, when I look back, I remember the horror this story invoked in our yoga haven. Freddy, the upbeat one, the funny one, the clown. I didn't want her to have a sad story.

The tears of a clown, I thought. *You never know what lies inside anyone, not ever.*

"The life expectancy of people with FAS is considerably lower than the general population," Freddy continued, as if she were reciting a statistic. "But my poor Emma only lived for five years."

"FAS?" Faye ventured.

"Fetal alcohol syndrome," Sara clarified quickly for those of us (like myself) who had no clue about the meaning of the letters. These nurses overflowed with acronyms.

"I was eighteen, you see. It was twenty years ago. I was a different girl living in a different world. I was raised in a small town up in north western Ontario. It could be pretty bleak there, especially the winters. I mean they can be tough here too, but it's not the same. We were so isolated. There wasn't a lot to do. The closest big city was Winnipeg. We didn't get there too much, my brothers and me. My dad had a law practice there and he'd be gone for days at a time. He was kind of distant even when he was home. But my mom was great. I loved her. I broke her heart."

It seemed hard to reconcile the light-hearted Freddy to this somber girl. The other nurses appeared surprised as well. This story must be brand-new to their ears.

"But honestly I had a fine upbringing. Living up there you saw a lot of poverty, but we always had a nice warm home and enough to eat. I have no excuse in all the world as to why I got dragged down into the mud. I only have myself to blame. I guess you could say I just got in with the wrong crowd. I was always a bit of a tomboy. I could outrun any boy my age and half of the older ones. I could curse right along with them and, by God, I could outdrink most of them too. And then I got a taste for it. I got fond of whiskey. None of that horse piss that passed for beer up there. Oh, no, not me. I liked the hard stuff. Alberta Premium, that was my drink of choice. I never had any trouble getting the boys around town to cough up cash to get me a bottle. There was always plenty to pass around. Sometimes they even passed me around. We were all friends, after all."

Freddy's voice trailed off, her face full of self-loathing.

"You were young, dear," Faye said, in her kind way. "Eighteen is very young."

"Well, look at Brooke," Freddy cried out, her voice bitter and angry. "She was sixteen when she had Toby and look at what a stellar mom she is."

"Freddy, we are all different. We walk our own path," Brooke said, her voice gentle.

"Well, I was a skinny little eighteen-year-old tomboy who was drunk or hung over most of the time. And who never dreamed she'd get pregnant. I'd always been thin, and my periods were haphazard at the best of time. By the time I was sober enough to realize that I really could be pregnant, I was five months along."

"Didn't your mom suspect?" Clarisse asked.

"My mom thought I was just a typical eighteen-year-old out with her friends. I was careful to hide my drinking from her. I'm sure it never crossed her mind that I could be having sex. She was kind of sweet and naïve like that. When Emma was born and it was clear that she had Fetal Alcohol Syndrome, Mom honestly thought that they were mistaken. She thought I might've had a little sip with my friends now and then — her words, not mine — but to damage a child to the extent that my poor baby was damaged was beyond her comprehension."

Outside in the orchard a lark called out. Its song rang discordantly through our little studio where such a sad story unfolded. I suppose the saddest stories always involve children. They are the true innocents of the world. I have never regretted my decision to work with them and help them.

"Anyways, I did slow down my alcohol intake when I found out I was pregnant. I still had some of my Alberta Premium at least once a day, though. By then, I needed it just to survive. Our family doctor saw me at five months gestation. He told me not to smoke or drink, but I just thought he was an old fuddy-duddy. Mom stood by me all the way. My father blew a gasket and yelled at me for being so careless and stupid. But Mom agreed to keep the baby in our house and help me raise her, if that's what I wanted. I didn't really know what I wanted. I was nowhere near grown myself. My mom was just forty and she worked part-time. We had a big house. She didn't seem to think it would be such a bad thing. We knew the baby was a girl and Mom was keen."

"So, your mom set everything up for the baby?" Faye asked. "She sounds pretty sweet."

"She sure was sweet," Freddy's eyes shone with tears. None fell, though. Not yet.

"And then Emma was born. I only had one shot of whiskey that day. She was a huge shock to all of us. Have any of you ever seen an FAS baby?"

She looked around at us.

No one spoke. Several women shook their heads.

"They have some distinct characteristics. They have low birth weights and small heads. Their faces are very flat mid-section."

Freddy took her finger, gesturing from her own forehead to her mouth.

"Their eyes are small and they have short palpebral fissure lengths."

Again, Freddy indicated on her face the space between the inside of her eye to the outside.

"And they have a smooth philtrum. This bit here."

She indicated the groove beneath her nose that ran to her upper lip.

"It's smooth. They don't have this groove here. And their upper lip is thin and flat. And on their hands," she turned her hands over and her finger traced the line across her palm, "they have unusual creases. They're called 'hockey stick creases' because they resemble hockey sticks. And they are jittery and tremulous and easily startled."

Freddy's face wore an expression of infinite sadness.

"They are just poor little tortured souls, tortured by their own condition. They are absolute victims, underdeveloped beings that never asked to be born. It is one of the leading causes of mental retardation. Pregnant women everywhere worry constantly about everything that can go wrong with their babies through no fault of their own. But FAS is 100% preventable."

No one spoke; there being nothing to say.

Freddy picked up the thread of her story, continuing her explanation of fetal alcohol syndrome. FAS. It seemed easier for her to relate the clinical manifestations than to speak of her actual life experience. Even so, it appeared to be taking a toll on her.

"Of course, the most serious is the impaired brain development in the fetus. Alcohol kills or damages developing brain cells. The alcohol passes from the mom through the placenta to the fetus. The alcohol is more concentrated in the fetus and prevents nutrition and oxygen from getting to the baby's vital organs. The baby just can't process it like an adult can. Alcohol is one of the most toxic agents that can affect a fetus. As it enters the baby's bloodstream, it kills cells that are developing, and the type of damage depends on which part of the baby is forming at the time. The brain though —"

Freddy's voice caught in her throat.

"The brain is forming all the time and can be damaged at any time. One drink is enough to stop a fetus from moving or breathing for up to two hours. Even moderate drinking — one drink a day — is enough to cause lifelong learning and behavioral problems in a child. There are new findings that say that drinking alcohol in pregnancy is worse than taking class A drugs."

"Class A drugs?"

Brooke asked the question in a low voice.

"Heroin or cocaine," Sara provided.

Wow, I thought, *that doesn't seem likely. Heroin's a pretty far-gone drug. How can that even be?*

I beheld the abject misery on Freddy's face and realized it didn't matter. The damage to her baby weighed heavily on her soul. And the story had not yet been told in its entirety.

"There is no medication or treatment to reverse or change the physical features or brain damage from drinking while pregnant. When the baby is born, it is already much too late for anything but dealing with the outcome."

Freddy recited this information, her voice remaining detached.

"Obstetrical nurses are trained to recognize the facial features of FAS babies. It's a sad fact that they have seen their fair share of them up there. I will never, ever forget the nurse putting Emma into my arms or the way she looked at me. My poor mom was standing beside the bed and she honestly had no clue what was going on. The nurse said, 'This is one hundred percent preventable. One hundred percent. This baby girl did not ask to be born this way. You did this to her.'"

A shudder passed through Freddy's body as she recounted the words.

"I thought that nurses weren't supposed to be judgmental," Nora observed.

"They're not actually," Miranda agreed, "They're not."

"Ah, nurses are only human, just like the rest of us," Freddy said, with a sigh. "That nurse looked at me," she shook her head, "I will never forget how she looked at me. Sometimes it's hard not to judge."

"Let he who is without sin cast the first stone," Nora piped up. "Even the Bible says that."

"Thank you, Nora."

Nora shrugged.

"It's true. We've all done stuff, you know."

Freddy's sigh seemed to resonate from her tiptoes.

"It's a big thing, Nora. It's big stuff."

"Oh, I know, Freddy," Nora acknowledged. "But you were young. People do lots of wild shit when they're young."

"Yes, they do. That's true. But this is a life. This is a whole little life."

Freddy's voice broke on the last words.

"It's hard to see a poor wee baby like that. And I don't blame that nurse. She'd seen one too many FAS baby — one too many innocent victims of their horrible mothers."

"What happened to Baby Emma?"

Jenny dared to ask the question.

Freddy swallowed audibly then proceeded.

"We took her home, Mom and me. We took her home to our nice comfortable house with the white picket fence and the perennial garden and my two goofy brothers. I've always been glad that she had a nice home for the time that she lived. But my dad barely looked at her. He was disgusted with me, and in turn with her. Every once in a while, he'd get on at me about her father."

She paused.

"And?" Clarisse asked.

"And, Clarisse, my dear, I didn't know the answer to that question. There was a bunch of boys and a few of the wilder girls who hung out together. If someone put a gun to my head, I couldn't have said who was Emma's father, but of course I never told my dad that. I just said I wasn't going to tell him. He talked to me less and less. When he did his voice dripped with contempt. I know he resented the presence of Emma. He just started spending more and more time in Winnipeg. Eventually he got an apartment there. She was a hard baby to look after. She was irritable all the time and often tremulous. My mom was just wonderful. She never made me feel bad. Not ever. And she was so patient with Emma. I'd missed a few credits in Grade 12. She encouraged me to go back and get them so I could graduate. She arranged her part-time job around my class schedule so that Emma never had a babysitter for her first two years.

"Of course, she was very delayed. She didn't crawl until she was a year old. Her motor skills were poor. She would startle and cry at any loud noise. Sometimes even if someone laughed too loudly. But she brought her love. My mom would look at her and hug her and say, 'They all bring their own love, Susan. Every baby brings their own love.'"

"Susan?" Nora snorted.

Freddy smiled.

"Well, Nora, that's my real name. When I first started working in a nursing home up there, I was helping this old stroke recovery guy with his supper which happened to be spaghetti. He was having quite a time with it. I cut up the noodles and told him to 'Have some spaghetti, Freddy' or something like that. Anyways his speech was all garbled, but he managed to say 'Freddy' for some unknown reason. And then he kept saying it over and over again."

"Like they do. Stroke victims, I mean," Clarisse said.

"After that the girls all called me 'Freddy' and it stuck. I never liked the name Susan anyways. I was named after my grandmother and she was a real pill."

"Freddy suits you," Brooke told her. "Did your mom mind?"

"Nah. She wasn't like that. She thought it was great fun. Anyways she loved baby Emma and she taught me how to look after her. When Emma cried and screamed, like she often did, one of us would just hold her and rock her until she settled down. My brothers were good with her too. And she learned to love. She taught me what real love is all about. Her speech was not very good, but she learned to say 'Ma-ma' and 'Na-na'."

Freddy sat back in her chair. Jenny brought her a cup of peppermint tea and a scone. She accepted them, seeming to brace herself to go on.

And the thought filled my mind that I might not be able to bear hearing the end of this story. I felt a little rush of panic, turning my gaze to Miranda. But Miranda's eyes remained fixed on Freddy.

Freddy cleared her throat and continued, "I don't know what I would have done if Mom hadn't been so good with her. It would have been impossible to get anyone to care for her. But Mom cut her work down to two afternoons a week. She insisted I go back to school and get all the credits I needed to go into nursing. Because I knew that I had to give something back to the world. I wanted to help in some way. It was amazing how well I did when I was sober. After that, I never cared if I saw another bottle of Alberta Premium, ever again. I'd done enough to break my mom's heart, enough damage to my innocent baby girl. I wasn't going to ruin their lives any more than I already had. Mom told me all the time how proud she was of me and what a great mother I was. She was ecstatic when I decided to be a nurse. She encouraged me to apply locally, and finally I got accepted at a university that wasn't too far away. It involved long days and lots of studying, but we both knew it would pay off in the end."

"You're such a good nurse, Freddy," Clarisse spoke into the ensuing pause.

"Thanks, Clarisse. So are you. Anyways, Mom asked a woman we knew who lived a few streets over to mind Emma sometimes. It was only for three hours at a time when we couldn't work it out between us. We'd known her forever and she was nice to Emma, but of course Emma didn't like going there. She always wanted to stay home. Laura was good to her though. And Emma learned to say her name as she got to know her. Anyways, I made it to my last year of nursing training. I'd gotten good marks. I was all set to graduate. Then Mom got called into work one afternoon because someone's husband had been in a terrible car crash. It was out of Emma's usual routine, but Mom thought it would be ok. I was due home in less than an hour when she got the call and Laura was willing to help. So, she took Emma over and kissed her and told her that I would be home soon. Mom's car was parked out on the street and she headed towards it. Just at that exact minute the phone rang. Laura went to answer it and for some reason that we'll never know Emma decided to run down the driveway after Mom. A delivery truck was rounding the corner just then. She ran right in front of it. It knocked her up in the air, flat down on the hood and onto the road."

A collective gasp of horror filled the room, the picture these words painted all too clear. The image of a small child hurtling towards the pavement and landing in a crumpled, lifeless heap pervaded the room like a tangible presence.

"My poor mom watched it all, but she was completely powerless. She tried to breathe life back into her poor broken little body, but she just couldn't. It was too late. She died on impact. My poor little girl."

"Your poor mom," Faye's kind eyes brimmed with tears.

"I know. It was awful for her. And for the delivery man. He was barely more than a boy really. I think he was twenty-two years old. It was an accident pure and simple. No blame was laid. But everyone felt broken with grief."

"How absolutely horrible for all of you."

"There are moments that mark your life. Moments when you realize that nothing will ever be the same again. Emma's birth was one of those for me and her death —" Freddy closed her eyes before continuing, "Her death was another. I never knew my heart could hold so much hurt. I didn't think I would be able to go on living it hurt so much. My poor mom never recovered. In spite of Emma's limitations, she'd breathed a wonderful joy and love into our home."

"That," Nora pronounced, with her characteristic way of stating the obvious, "that is a very sad story, Freddy."

A glimmer of a smile whispered on Freddy's lips.

"You're right, Nora. I wish I had a different one. I wish I had a funny one cause that's what I've gotten good at over the years. But I haven't," she shrugged in despair. "That's my story. Sorry, ladies."

Various pacifying murmurs rumbled throughout the room.

"My mom died a year to the day of pancreatic cancer," Freddy said. "I moved down here. And I hold them both in my heart every day of my life. And you, Brooke," turning to our fearless leader, "you're the reason I picked myself up from that sad place. I saw an ad for yoga and it brought me here to this magic place where I found happiness, surrounded by awesome women who all have a story to tell. I mean, of course we do. I know that but this year we've all been talking about our lives, the good and the bad. I remember Brooke saying the reason we sit in a circle is because the energy is never ending in a circle. It's infinite. And I remember Lizzy saying that Brooke saved her and I feel the same way. When I come here, I can learn to live in this moment and feel the goodness that exists here. You said a quote once at the beginning of your class about 'If you suffer it's because of you and if you're blissful, it's also because of you. You alone are responsible for this. You are your own heaven and your own hell.' And I remember so clearly thinking that I didn't want to be my own hell. That Mom and Emma deserved better than a memory that was hell. I wanted to think of them with joy and love. And so, I've tried really hard to do that. Because honestly, girls," she spread her hands out, sounding like the old Freddy, "who wants to be their own hell?"

My heart felt full to overflowing. What a lot of courage it must have taken to tell that sad tale.

Each of these stories wove us closer together, as if entwined with invisible threads of caring and understanding, like a palpable thing. A thing that dwelt here in this quaint yoga studio with its uneven walls covered with funny imprints of children's hands and inspirational sayings.

Maybe everything led here, to this moment when our stories unfolded.

Brooke's smile held all the warmth of her beautiful soul. She knew how it felt to have a difficult story.

"Thanks, Freddy," she said simply. "Thanks for sharing with us."

"I came here one Sunday morning," Freddy said, her tone lighter now, "and you read a quote from Rupi Kaur. I remembered the name because it struck a note with me. It went 'And here you are —'"

Her voice faltered. She couldn't go on.

Brooke and Jenny finished the quote in unison.

"'And here you are living, despite it all.'"

35

"You say witch like it's a bad thing. Don't judge me until you've flown a mile on my broom."

"DID YOU GIRLS HEAR that Joan Payne died last night?" Malcolm dried his hands on his ever-present checked apron, entering the kitchen to relay this bit of village news.

"Old witch that she was," Nora muttered from her usual perch in the corner booth, crossword puzzle in front of her. "Five letter word for witch. C-r-o-n-e."

She proceeded to cackle in a manner befitting to one.

"Had she been sick?" I asked, a little taken aback.

"No, but she was about a couple of hundred years old," Nora piped up.

Verna came bustling in then. She, as usual, had the facts straight.

"Actually, she was ninety-two. Her son is in his seventies now. I don't think she ever had any other children. She hadn't been sick, but she was such a hermit that no one knew her well. Anyways, old Jed McClure checks on her. Apparently, he arranged with Roger when he moved out west to call in once a week just to make sure she was ok. I understand that Joan wasn't too receptive to the whole idea."

Nora snorted out loud. Miranda and I tried, without success, to suppress a grin.

Verna shot us a reproachful look, saying, "I was taught not to speak ill of the dead."

"You'd feel a whole lot better, Verna Snell, if you'd let yourself go once in a while and give your honest opinion instead of always worrying about your business and the opinion of others."

"It's not that, Nora, it really isn't. It's just that Joan can't defend herself anymore."

"She wouldn't have anyways," Nora retorted. "You know fine well that Joan Payne would never have bothered to speak to any of us in a civil manner."

"Well, that was sure our experience with her," Miranda ventured.

"She was unpleasant of course," Verna conceded. "But there was something wrong with her."

"Do you think?" Nora's voice dripped with sarcasm.

"Undiagnosed mental illness or something," Verna went on, ignoring the interruption. "There was no help for these things in her day."

"Well, she had some kind of a personality disorder," Malcolm said. "Anyone with half an eye and an asshole could see that."

"Malcolm!"

Verna's rebuke brought her husband up short.

"Sorry. But there's nobody here except us."

"That's not the point and you know it."

She turned her back to him, addressing Miranda and me.

"Anyways I wanted to let you know that some of us are going to her house later this evening to help tidy up a little before Roger comes back. I guess she was dead in there a few days and the place needs airing out."

My stomach did a backward flip at the thought of this. Miranda, the nurse-in-training, remained unfazed.

"Sure, we can pitch in. Can't we, Molly?"

"I—I guess so."

I could not dredge much enthusiasm into my voice, but neither woman noticed or cared.

Nora said, "I'm going, too. Jenny asked us yesterday afternoon if we'd mind helping a little. 'Helping a neighbor,' she called it, although I can think of another name for her."

"Molly and I weren't at Jenny's yesterday. She didn't need our help, so we went out to the swimming hole."

"Wait a minute," I said, puzzled, "I thought Malcolm said she didn't die till last night."

"Well, that's when Jed found her. But you know Jenny," Nora shrugged. "She knows things like that. She can track the weather better than those weather apps you kids use nowadays. She's always done that ever since I've known her."

"Like me," Malcolm grinned, pointing at the rock swinging on a rope from the cafe's porch.

The sign above it read:

If this rock is wet it is raining.
If this rock is dry it is cloudy
If it makes a shadow it is sunny
If it's white it is snowing
If it's jumping there is an earthquake
If it's gone tornado.

Nora sniffed. "She's better than your old rock, Malcolm."

"Wait," Miranda said. "You said you went to school with Jenny, right?"

Nora nodded.

"For the most part."

"Did you go to school with Roger Payne, too?" Verna asked, curious now.

"He was older than Jenny and me, but we did go to the same school," Nora replied. "He was always creepy. He and Joan never attended any school activities or social functions. And they always lived in that falling-down house at the end of Jenny's road. It's been falling down for fifty years. I heard she has a garden full of poisonous plants."

"Wow. It sounds like something out of a movie. A bad movie."

"It does sort of, doesn't it? But you know what they say. Truth is stranger than fiction. See you girls tonight."

Nora set off on her way, leaving me full to the brim with misgivings about the upcoming evening.

Still, when the time came, I swallowed my doubts and bravely joined the waiting group. Brooke had stayed at Jenny's with Melly and Toby. Freddy alone, of the nurses, was able to come. I felt glad of her presence.

Nora, Dolores, Connie, and Jenny stood armed with buckets and brooms and mops, making a total of seven. We turned to see Neil walking with purpose towards us. He nodded a greeting and proceeded to fall into step with us.

"Thank you, Neil," Jenny told him.

We all echoed our thanks. I, for one, felt safer in the company of this big reassuring man.

"My pleasure," he replied, with a comical half bow. "It's a tough job but somebody has to do it."

There should have been sinister music playing, such as that befitting a spooky movie. It should have screeched from the very trees around us, as we crept with fear and trepidation down the cobblestone path.

It seemed strange indeed to leave Hedgewytch Way and turn to the right. A left turn would lead us towards the familiar comfort of our little village.

Despite my foreboding at the whole endeavor, I could not suppress a twinge of curiosity at the prospect of seeing Joan Payne's abode.

A light summer breeze floated by, whispering among the maple leaves as we passed them.

Jenny stopped for a moment.

"What is it?" Connie inquired.

"Oh. I just wanted to hear what the trees had to say tonight."

"I remember she used to say that even as a young girl," Nora commented. "She'd say that she was heading outside to see what the trees had to say."

"Psithurism," Neil spoke up.

"What?" Nora asked in her abrupt way.

"Psithurism. It means the sound of the wind blowing through the trees."

"Of course, it does," Freddy remarked, with a grin.

Jenny turned now and fell into step with us.

We rounded a corner to encounter a small dilapidated shack-like house decaying into a patch of overgrown plants and vines. The roof gaped with several ragged holes. One of the windows held a large piece of cardboard half covering it.

I shuddered, taking a step backwards. Even Neil looked as if he wouldn't mind turning around and forgetting about this mission. Too bad no one had thought of bringing a flask or something. Alcohol would certainly not have gone amiss right now.

Jenny alone remained calm and composed.

"Interesting choice of plants she's got here," she observed.

Nora said, "I heard she has a garden full of poisonous plants. Is that true, Jenny? Are all these plants poisonous?"

Jenny surveyed the tangled mess thoughtfully.

"Well, let's just say that they can all be used in a poisonous way. Only if desired though."

I felt no doubt that this could well have been the desire of Joan Payne. I visualized her in my mind's eye planting things specifically for an evil purpose.

"Let's see. Belladonna, of course. It's called the witches berry, too, or deadly nightshade. Because if you use it in magical ointments it produces the sensation of flying. It's a powerful poison if you happen to ingest it. Belladonna is, I believe, an Italian word meaning 'beautiful lady'. They used to use the drops of the berry juice to dilate their pupils thus enhancing their beauty. But if you use one drop too many you could go blind."

We gasped. But I felt a pull of fascination, in spite of myself.

Freddy, ever fearless, stepped beside Jenny, remarking as she fingered a tall stalk adorned with purple flowers, "This one's monkshood, I think. My landlady has some in her garden. It's not poisonous is it, Jenny?"

"You're right, Freddy. That is monkshood. But it definitely can be poisonous if used improperly. Monkshood was used to poison arrows and spears for hunting or battle, years ago. It contains aconite which can cause asphyxiation. There was a young actor named Andre Noble that died of aconitine poisoning after eating some monkshood while he was hiking in Newfoundland."

"That's a shame," Freddy observed. "It looks so pretty."

"I have some in my garden," Dolores added. "I had no idea it contained poison."

"Only if it's misused," Jenny reassured us.

"Like so many things," Neil added. "This one even I know. It's a poppy, right? And I know it contains opium."

"You bet. Opium poppies are harmless. It's the morphine and heroin distilled from the poppy's seed head that has the potential to kill. Dr. Harold Shipman was a British serial killer who used morphine as his lethal weapon."

It occurred to me that Jenny held a wealth of knowledge inside her curly head. Neil said as much to her.

"You're a fountain of information, Jenny Smith," he told her.

"Not really, but I do know about plants and their properties. Mama and I studied them extensively before we set up our business. Look at this one here now. Foxglove. I love these. I have them in my own garden. They only come up every second year."

"Digitalis comes from them, right?" Freddy asked.

"Yes, of course you'd know that one," Jenny agreed. "It's used for heart medication."

"Digoxin. It slows and strengthens the heart. But if you don't need that, it could be dangerous too. Slow it too much. Is that what you mean, Jenny?"

"Absolutely. There's a fine line between a therapeutic dose and a fatal one. Then there's this one, Datura. This plant here with the lacy flowers and the pretty scent. They're very poisonous. Datura plants contain tropane alkaloids such as scopolamine and atropine. In some places, it's prohibited to buy sell or cultivate Datura plants."

"Oh, my. It is an evil garden. It really is," Verna observed.

"Exactly," Jenny agreed. "Lily of the valley."

"Really?"

"Oh yes. Lily of the valley can cause burning and swelling of the lips, vomiting and diarrhea. Only if ingested though. And angels trumpet."

"Angels trumpet?" I asked, my head spinning.

"Yes. Like these flowers here," Jenny indicated. "I know the name is lovely, but every part of the plant is highly poisonous. The leaves, flowers, seeds, and roots. They contain toxic alkaloids like scopolamine, and atropine, same as the datura. They can be used in medicine, but are highly poisonous if used without a doctor's prescription. The whole plant is poisonous, especially the pollen when ingested or inhaled. It can cause hallucinations and delirium."

I gazed around, filled with a horrible fascination. All these plants and flowers, typically grown for beauty and pleasure, grew here for nefarious intent, like a double-edged sword.

We turned reluctantly to enter the house. I noticed with a shudder that the door was painted black.

Oh, that can't be good! I thought, pulling closer to Miranda and feeling an echo of her thoughts in my head.

All of us, even Neil, tiptoed with scarcely a sound into the ramshackle house. It seemed somewhat of an anticlimax to actually step inside it. One solitary chair stood in the middle of the kitchen beside an ancient rotting wooden table piled high with old musty smelling newspapers. Linoleum, half ripped up at regular intervals and dark with dirt and soot, covered the floor in some spots. Other areas remained bare plywood. Wallpaper that may once have sported multi-coloured squares of colour, now lay peeled and ripped with layers and shreds hanging from the walls.

The presence of something horrible seemed to have been steeped into the room, like a palpable being. More than the putrid smell, more than the rotting fixtures, dwelt an oppressive air. I shuddered, observing the others. Nora and Verna both looked a little green around the gills.

Jenny proceeded to the stained sink with her bucket, filling it from the protesting tap. The water smelled rancid.

Neil followed suit, declaring, "We'll just have to do the best we can."

"I guess so," Nora said, her tone grudging. "We're here. We might as well do what we can."

Even the effervescent Freddy seemed subdued, but we persevered. Before long everyone had either a mop or broom and some headway seemed to be taking place.

"Well, will you take a look at this?" Connie exclaimed, holding up an old piece of parchment paper. "All these years I've been at your place, Jenny, I've never seen one of these."

Neil rose from his crouching position where he'd been scraping some vile black stain off the linoleum. He towered over Connie. She held the paper up so he could read the words written in ancient black pen. His eyes widened in disbelief. He turned the paper around so Miranda, Dolores, and I might read it.

Despite the weathered paper and blotchy words, most of it could be deciphered. Not that I'd have minded if it couldn't.

It read:

'Poisoned Apple …. One taste of the poisoned apple and the victim's eyes will close FOREVER, in the sleeping death.

Mix together: Belladonna, Henbane, Aconite, Jimsonweed and White Snakeroot. Dip an apple into this brew and let the poison seep straight through it.'

I gulped. Somehow it made everything real, all the bad feeling, all the poisonous plants, all the horrific memories of the repulsive woman who lived here in this decaying building. She really had been evil.

And then, as if clinching the matter, Miranda breathed, "And look at this, will you?"

She held up another piece of paper, a much newer piece, the words standing out boldly, defiant black on the blue lines.

Connie groaned and said, "Oh dear."

I could decipher some of the words, enough to read that it represented the outline to the 'Witches Among Us' column.

"So, Joan Payne has been writing that hateful newspaper article about you?" Dolores exclaimed. "Well, we kind of suspected it, didn't we?"

Jenny gazed at the paper, making no comment. She seemed to be working out something in her head.

A gust of wind blew the battered door open. The whole world seemed to halt as the figure of a man took shape before us. He stood only on the doorstep but something entered the room with him, something hideous and repellent. His body bent into a corkscrew position, but his eyes bulged with a malicious gleam. An X stood on his forehead. A big red faded scar of an X, looking like someone had carved it into his protruding grey skin.

The thought of Charles Manson hit me like a blow. I remembered seeing photos of him and his followers with shaved heads and big X's carved into their foreheads accompanied by scary eyes alight with insanity.

Could this horrible man have any connection to Charles Manson? I shook myself. Of course, he couldn't. I'd just been taken aback by his repulsive appearance and air of malevolence. Charles Manson was in his eighties now, not to mention incarcerated.

This was definitely Roger Payne, another form of evil in the shape of a man. But not Charles Manson. And not a murderer. Hopefully.

Then why the X?

When he spoke, his voice rasped like gravel, sending a chill down my spine. I tried to catch Miranda's eye but she seemed mesmerized by the mere sight of him.

"If it isn't Jenny and her coven." He uttered the words with contempt, his voice thready and disdainful.

Jenny straightened her small frame and stood tall, her voice clear, if slightly tremulous.

"We're cleaning up your mother's cottage. We won't be long."

The others busied themselves with the tasks at hand, purposefully ignoring this wretched, twisted man. But I couldn't tear my eyes away from him. Something discernable lay between he and Jenny. I could almost reach out and touch it. Jenny herself seemed to have changed in front of our eyes in some indefinable way, a change so subtle that the others might not even notice. But I, I who had never trusted her completely, felt it to the marrow of my bones.

"See that you're not," his voice sneered.

Freddy turned from her mop and glared at him, fearless, as always.

"I know you," her voice rang out, clear and true. It brought me back to a semblance of reality.

"I know you from the hospital."

"So what?"

"We cared for you once when you were visiting," she continued. "We looked after you. Now we're helping with your mother's house. That's what neighbors do."

Several moments passed.

I loved Freddy in that moment. I loved her for bringing us back to earth. Her common-sense nature always seemed to make things better. I took deep breaths (Brooke would have been proud of me) and focused on the task at hand.

As I did, those feelings I'd had towards Jenny slowly dissipated like mist in the sunshine. Normalcy settled over me.

This place was playing tricks on my psyche, I thought. *That's all.*

Some bad energy, still undefined, crackled in the air, but I could feel it fading. Jenny resembled herself again. The heinous quality that had filled the little hovel moments earlier seemed to be easing. But it had existed. I had experienced it with every fiber of my being.

"We're almost done here and then we'll leave," Jenny turned to face him, her words even and cold. "And I will not see you again, Roger Payne. Not ever."

She flung these words at the contorted man hovering in the doorway. They affected him somehow, causing him to falter back a step as if assaulted. He opened his mouth to speak, but no words came out.

This resulted in the sight of a gaping old man teetering on the rickety step. He flung Jenny an unfathomable glare, before turning on his heel to walk through the sagging door and disappear down the path, flanked on either side with his mother's poison.

A great collective sigh of relief reverberated through the rotting hovel.

"Wow!" Freddy breathed. "What a pair."

"It's not good for people to live steeped in their own regrets," Jenny said quietly, her eyes still fixed on the departing figure. "They become corroded in misery."

"Or something," Connie muttered.

"Something," Neil agreed. "Something like zemblanity."

"Oh, Neil," Connie's words came out with an impatient bite. I think we all felt a little on edge. "What on earth is that?"

"It's the opposite of serendipity," Neil explained, unoffended. "The discovery of what you'd rather not know."

Freddy grinned. "It was that, that's for sure. I could have gone my whole life without knowing about all of this, this house, the evil garden, that horrible man, and that newspaper."

"Maybe in life it's good to have adversaries to see a contrast in our life. To have someone to push against and define things for us. Things can fester for years. Things can fester forever if we let them."

Jenny's words seemed obscure. They made no sense. Not now anyways.

Later they did. Much later, when everything became known to us.

But right now, nothing seemed clear. Nothing made sense.

The only thing that made any sense seemed to be finishing our task and hastening back to Hedgewytch Way cottage, so dear to us now, so safe and comfortable.

Which we did.

36

"The darkest nights produce the brightest stars."

John Green

"MY EARLIEST MEMORY IS WALKING between my mom and my dad holding their hands. My mom always had my little sister on her hip and my dad held my older brother's hand. I was the 'pickle in the middle'. That's what they called me."

"Nice," I murmured.

"Yes, it was nice."

Miranda spoke softly, the expression on her pretty face one of infinite sadness. Where this memory had initiated, I was unsure, but I studied her intently now. I could feel in her that her story was about to unfold. Somehow, I knew that it would be a tragic one. I'd heard barely a whisper from her in two years about her family or former life. A happy past had eluded her in some way.

We had opted to enjoy our post yoga treats inside the cottage today, due to the increased number of mosquitos after last night's rainfall. This found us milling around Jenny's big worn harvest table, enjoying mugs of mixed berry tea and slices of lemon loaf. Several of the nurses held a glass of black currant wine, explaining this away with the excuse of shift work. Shift work, it seemed, accounted for many justifiable sins. A glass had been offered to everyone, but only the nurses indulged at this early hour. It made no difference to them, they said. They'd had supper at three o'clock in the morning. It could be time for anything now — time for wine, time for sleep, time for anything at all.

Miranda always seemed to hold part of herself back. Sometimes I wished to be more like her, less of an open book. If a thought crossed my mind then out of my mouth it flew.

She looked across the table at me now and repeated, "It was nice, Molly. A nice memory."

I smiled at her with, what I hoped, looked like encouragement.

"I was so happy then. I can remember being happy. Do you see what I mean?"

I didn't really see, but Jenny nodded her head, replying softly, "Yes. So you know it's possible."

"Exactly. That's exactly it, Jenny," Miranda looked at her gratefully. "I knew that I could be that happy. That no matter what it was inside me. The ability, I mean. I can remember love and laughter and family. Sometimes it seems like it didn't happen to me, that it happened to another girl in another family. But I know it really did happen to me. I was that girl. I was the pickle in the middle with my mom and baby sister on one side and my dad and big brother on the other side of me. I was safe and I was happy."

"So, what happened then? Because you talk about all of this as if it was a long time ago. Where's your family now?" Freddy dared to ask.

"My baby sister died." Miranda's words fell from her lips, hard and cold as bullets, landing around the table.

"I'm so sorry," I breathed.

"Thanks, Molly," she said.

"But it was more than that, wasn't it, Miranda?" Jenny queried.

Miranda nodded, taking a deep breath.

"Oh yes, so much more. But that started everything. She, Marcy, only lived to be eighteen months old. God, she was adorable. I can still feel the warmth of her little body pressed up against me when she hugged me. She gave the best hugs. She was so loving. And so sweet."

Her voice faltered on the last words.

"What happened to her?" Sara asked.

'SIDS. That's what they said. Which was the worst because it really means nothing. Nothing to blame."

"Sudden infant death syndrome." Sara rhymed off, but even I knew that one.

"I know what the letters stand for," Miranda nodded. "What I mean is there really didn't seem to be a cause."

"No. There never is," Freddy agreed. "That's the whole thing. They don't really know what happens or why it happens which just makes everything worse. Eighteen months is pretty old for SIDS. Typically, the definition is from newborn to a year."

"That's what we were told, but I guess it's possible. Just not very common."

"It was probably a congenital heart or something that was undetected," Clarisse commented.

"I think that was the consensus in the end," Miranda said softly. "Honestly, though, I never cared why it happened, just that it did. It seemed too horrible to bear. She was still in a crib and Mom and I went creeping in one beautiful summer morning. I don't know why, but this morning brought it all back to me. Just that kind of summer day that seems endless with brightness and light. I remember the sun shining through her window and her little yellow curls spread all over her wee face. Mom was laughing. I remember that very well because I never really heard my mom laugh again. She called out to wake up her little sleepyhead."

Now Miranda's voice did break. I reached across the table and touched her hand. It felt as cold as a block of ice.

"I don't remember much after that. Just a lot of screaming. I can't remember if it was me or her, but the screaming never ended for me. If I close my eyes, I can hear it still."

"Poor wee darling," Jenny shook her head. I didn't know if she meant the baby or Miranda, or both. "Your poor mom," she said. "The hardest thing in the whole world is losing a child. It's the worst pain a woman can ever have."

I remembered Jenny's story about losing Buddy. Her countenance held no self-pity, only compassion.

"Yes, my mom never recovered. She really didn't. I couldn't understand that then. I was only nine and I'd lost my beautiful baby sister. I didn't understand how great her pain was to her."

"Well it would be, wouldn't it?" Connie commented.

"She still had me though," Miranda turned to her, her tone affronted. "She still had me and my brother."

"Ah I know dear," Connie clucked. "I know."

Miranda's shoulders slumped in desolation as she said, ""We were never enough for her after that."

"Now. I'm sure that's not true," Connie said.

But Miranda shook her head, her voice adamant.

"I wish you were right, Connie. But I'm afraid it is true. Nothing was ever the same again. My dad was so sad. I remember he cried. I couldn't believe that my big strong dad could actually cry. But he would hug Jason and I and we all cried together. Not my mom. She didn't come near us. When she found Marcy, she screamed at me to go get the neighbors. Then she breathed and breathed into her little mouth. They called the ambulance and the whole time, Mom was blowing into her mouth and counting out loud. The paramedics had to tear Marcy out of her arms."

"How awful," I felt tears pricking behind my eyes, picturing the horrific scene. But I would not succumb to tears while Miranda's eyes remained dry.

"Oh yes. It was awful all right. It's haunted me since I was nine. Maybe I would have survived better if my whole family hadn't disintegrated after that. Nothing was ever right again."

"Disintegrated?"

"Yes. The mom I knew that morning when I woke up, the mom that tiptoed into Marcy's bedroom with me holding my hand and laughing, she left. She was gone just as surely as Marcy was."

"She left home?"

"Oh, no. No, she stayed there physically. But the essence of her was gone. She started drinking and never stopped. Eventually she just drank herself to death."

I shuddered. What an awful way to lose your mom.

Miranda turned to me, echoing my thoughts, "Yes, Molly. It was awful. She didn't even drink before that. I suppose she must have had the odd drink at parties. But I never saw her drunk. I was just a kid. I guess I was a little sheltered," she chuckled humorlessly, "I hardly even knew what it meant, to be drunk, I mean. Then all of a sudden, she was out and out shit-faced all the time. I don't think she drew a sober breath again. Not really."

"Wow," Freddy breathed. "That's a pretty drastic reaction."

"I kept thinking that she'd get better and be my old mom again. I loved her so much. She was the mom who made homemade cookies and played games. She loved doing stuff with us. She never seemed to get tired of our company. I missed her so much. She was this completely different person. She'd be hung over in the morning and stay in bed. I'd make my own lunch, get myself to school. Then when I got home from school, she'd be so drunk that she'd just be staggering around, saying horrible, horrible things." Miranda whispered the last words, apparently some things being too awful to relate.

"One day she was staggering around and swearing at me. That was another thing she'd never done before. Anyways I started crying. I must have been twelve or thirteen by then. I said, 'I want my mom.' She looked at me and screamed, 'I am your mom.'

"'No, you're not,' I screamed back at her. 'You're not my mom.' She was holding a big bottle of vodka and she hauled off and whacked me across the back of the head with it. I was bleeding and crying and she proceeded to pass out cold."

"My God," Connie gasped. "Where was the bloody Children's Aid? Where was your father?"

"She turned on my father, too. She said if he'd checked Marcy before he left for work that he could have saved her." She put up her hand as Sara started to protest the unfairness of this. "I know that it wouldn't have mattered. I know that now. But she was beyond reason."

"Sounds like she had a psychotic episode," Clarisse observed.

"And never recovered from it," Freddy continued.

Miranda shrugged. "I don't know. It's true she never recovered. My dad would beg her to go for counseling, but she absolutely refused. I can see now that his life must have been a living hell too, but when you're a kid all you can think about is your own little life. I couldn't see how unhappy he was until it was too late."

"Oh, God." My face fell into my hands, anticipating the worst.

Miranda hastened to reassure me. "No, no Molly, he didn't die. He just left. He took Jason and moved to Fort McMurray."

"And left you there?" I asked, incredulous.

"I could have gone. They both begged me to go with them. My dad had a chance at a better job and a fresh start. Who could blame them?"

"Why on earth didn't you go, then?" Connie asked.

Miranda sighed deeply. "I couldn't leave my mom."

"Really?" Verna looked dubious.

"Oh, it's true," Sara said. "Kids love their moms and always want to be with them. Even if they are —" she stopped whatever word had been on her lips and substituted, "not very good ones."

This made no sense to me, but Miranda nodded.

"It's true, you know. It's only now as an adult that I realize how much better things would have been for me if I'd just left with Dad and Jason. I lost complete track of them both after that. I think they were glad to see the ass end of us. And Mom never knew if I was there or not. I ended up looking after her. Nobody looked after me. I was twelve by then, still in public school. I didn't want to leave everything and everyone I'd ever known." She shrugged, observing with great sadness. "I just couldn't leave."

She gazed at the assortment of faces, all wearing identical expressions of empathy and compassion. She shook her head apologetically.

"I'm sorry. I'm going on and on. I don't know what's gotten into me."

"It's no worry, child," Connie assured her. "You don't say enough half the time. It's nice to know a little bit about you."

"Not a very nice story, though," Miranda said, her words heavy with her old sorrow. "I wish I had a better one to tell you guys."

"It's ok," Freddy said. "I felt the same way when I told my story, Miranda. It's always nicer to have a happy one. I wish that for everyone. But then we wouldn't be who we are. And we all talk more at certain times. Wait till you work night shift and you haven't slept for thirty odd hours. You tell the other girls things you wish you hadn't when you wake up the next day."

"Oh, yeah. And believe me, you wish you hadn't heard them either," Clarisse laughed. There seemed to be no offense taken between this lot.

Jenny resembled a wise little owl perched in her favorite chair, her big eyes wide with kindness, her topknot fastened with a black and white polka dotted ribbon.

"You go on, Miranda dear," she told her. "Talk all you want."

"You should start charging for this time, Jenny," Sara joked. "It's better than therapy, I think."

"Ah, no. That's not the point, you see."

Jenny didn't elaborate as to what the actual point was, but I supposed that it was just this. This camaraderie, this fellowship. I'd never thought that in this day and age there would exist such a place where all types and shapes and sizes of women connected on a Sunday morning, putting away their cell phones and links to the outside world to come together like this. In such an incredible way. You could almost believe in magic. A magic of sorts, anyways.

Jenny turned to Miranda with expectation. No one else spoke. In a moment, she continued.

"There's not much more to tell. After Dad and Jason left, she just deteriorated more and more. I wanted so much for her to be my mom again. I never stopped wanting that. I guess I was a naïve child. Once when I was about thirteen, her skin colour kind of changed. It went a funny yellow."

The nurses nodded, as if they'd been waiting for this part of the story.

"Jaundice."

They said the word in unison. I almost chuckled. Miranda would be one of these beings before too long.

Miranda nodded.

"Yes, jaundice. Even her sclera turned yellow."

"The whites of her eyes," Freddy explained, in an aside to the rest of us.

I shuddered. It sounded awful.

"I was so naïve," Miranda repeated. "Even at thirteen I was so unworldly. One day when she was standing beside the kitchen window in her nightie, I could see her belly was all swollen up."

"Ascites," This remark from the refrain of nurses, as they shook their heads sadly.

Freddy translated again.

"Ascites is when your abdomen gets very bloated from liver failure."

"Yes, she was in liver failure, but I didn't know that. I went up to her. I remember being so happy and putting my arms around her and saying — saying —"

"Ah," Jenny said gently, "you thought she might be pregnant."

Miranda nodded.

"It sounds silly now. I mean I should have known better. No one came to our apartment ever and her only lover was named Vodka," she smiled weakly. "But I was a stupid kid. I was so bloody lonely. I can remember feeling overjoyed as I asked if she was going to have a baby. You see, I thought maybe then we'd be a family again. Oh, I thought it would be so nice to have a baby around again."

We waited. No one asked but no way in hell would this scenario end well.

Miranda continued, her voice flat as she explained, "She slapped me away and told me that she'd had her baby. That baby was gone and she had taken everything with her. I asked her what she meant by everything. Like an idiot. She said she took all her love. I said that she still had me and she slapped me away. She had no love left for me or anyone, she said. Why the hell hadn't I gone with my dad and left her in peace."

Stillness fell over the room.

Jenny approached Miranda, enveloping her in her arms. Miranda did not pull away as she may once have. Everyone registered astonishment to witness teardrops dropping from

Jenny's eyes. Landing like little pearls amongst Miranda's thick brown tresses. I'd never seen Jenny so moved. Nothing seemed to affect her as the telling of this pitiful tale had.

"I'm so sorry, so very, very sorry that this has happened to you, Miranda. Something like that should never happen to a child in this world."

Miranda allowed Jenny to hold her. She looked diminished somehow now that her story had left her. The remnants of her tragic childhood lay around us in shards of sadness.

"When I got to high school, they sent me to the guidance counselor because I was so withdrawn and detached. Or so they said. Anyways, the guidance man told me that I was broken and nothing could fix me. I never forgot that. He said it was just too late to fix me."

Jenny returned to sit in her chair. She shook her head in a world-weary gesture.

"Don't believe it, my dear. It's never too late to fix anything. I'm a hedgewytch. I know many ways to fix many things."

"I wish I could believe that," she whispered. "I've been almost happy here, these last two years. I thought I'd die when I first got here but now it's so different. It's almost like I'm meant to be here."

"Of course, you're meant to be here," Jenny replied firmly. "You're supposed to be right here with all of us."

And so am I, I thought.

How these years in Jared would play out, I couldn't fathom. But I knew that somehow the end of them would hold paramount significance for Miranda and I. Maybe around the bend of the next year, which lay as yet wreathed in obscurity.

37

"Always keep that place where the magic grows inside of you, alive."

Anonymous.

T HE WEEKLY POST YOGA *TÊTE-À-TÊTE* had hurtled full tilt into an ongoing exchange of gossip and dialogue. Even a little more than usual. Perhaps this had been caused by the unseasonable bout of bright delectable sunshine, nature's last gift to us before the winds of autumn blew the warmth away into winter's waiting arms of ice and snow.

Miranda and I had been running a little late today, slipping into the studio at the last possible moment. The ladies seemed to be picking up a thread of conversation from before the class. Or maybe it was from last week. Or last month. It wouldn't be the first time subjects for discussion had become meshed together to run on endlessly.

Ravens appeared to be the topic for today. Who knew what precipitated these things?

"Clarisse is having raven trouble," Freddy told us, by way of explanation.

"Ravens or crows?" Miranda asked, for no reason I could discern.

"What's the difference?" I asked.

"Ravens are bigger, I think," Freddy replied. "They're in the same family as crows, anyways. They're smart birds," she smiled and gestured to Clarisse, "They've been outsmarting Clarisse's husband."

Clarisse rolled her eyes.

"It's not bloody hard to outsmart him, let me tell you," she said. "I was just saying that they've been getting into our garbage bags. Not a little bit either. They drag them along the ground and peck away until there's big holes in them. Then they get at the insides with their beaks until there's stuff strewn all over the road. I usually work on Tuesdays which is our garbage day, so I was unaware of all this. When I get home from a twelve-hour shift, they just let me lie on the couch and moan about my aching legs. I never knew we had this bird problem. But last week I had time owing, so I had Tuesday off. Bert and Chris, our son, were going on and on Monday night about this big plan they were hatching which involved ropes and pulleys and arrows. I didn't know what the hell they were talking about. Usually I like it that way. Whatever they want to do on the farm is up to them. That's the way I look at it. I just tune them out. I've got enough to do looking after my patients. But this sounded kind of serious. When I asked them, they told me about the problem with the garbage. I was always at work, so I had no idea. All this garbage flung everywhere. Well, they would fix them. They had the whole thing figured out."

She chuckled, shaking her head at the plight of males.

"Did it work?" I ventured to ask.

"The whole bow and arrow and pulley device?" Clarisse asked, making elaborate gestures with her hands in the air. "I don't know. Because I intervened and told them that I would go down to Canadian Tire first thing in the morning and buy a couple of big trash cans that snap down. Which I did. And guess what?"

"No more garbage problems?" Brooke asked.

"Exactly!"

"We'll have to give you more time owing days off," Freddy laughed. "See how many more problems you can solve."

"Well, honestly, it's just a matter of common sense."

"Common sense is not always common," Verna remarked. "And men look at things so differently than us. They really do. Malcolm does things in the kitchen sometimes that I just shake my head over."

Miranda and I hid our smiles. We knew this to be quite true, first-hand.

"Well I'm glad you found a solution," Heather said. "Ravens are a huge problem to farmers. They have been for years around here. They're responsible for lots of livestock deaths, baby lambs and calves. The little calves are just laying down or sleeping and the ravens will come and start pecking their eyes out."

Miranda and I both shuddered but the local women seemed unsurprised.

"It's true," Lizzy agreed. "One of the telltale signs of a raven attack is pecked-out eyes."

"Dear God," Miranda said, "No wonder they call a group of them an 'unkindness of ravens'."

"They do?" I asked, thinking that this sounded made up.

"They do," Dolores confirmed. "They're smart, too. Really smart. They can mimic humans and other birds. I read somewhere that they can communicate with hand gestures."

"And they can recognize faces and remember them. I heard they can even mimic human speech," Freddy said. "I wonder if that's true. They're supposed to be some kind of magic. Do you think so, Jenny?"

"Oh yes indeed," Jenny relaxed a little, having handed out her last slice of blueberry loaf and cup of peppermint tea. "They're said to be the guardians of sacred and secret mysteries. That's because their eyesight is super keen and, because they're associated with psychic powers, their feathers can be used to aid clairvoyance. They have different warning calls for different animals too. If they have a carcass and they can't crack it open, they make the call for a wolf so the wolves will come and do the work for them. Afterwards they eat what's left over."

I can honestly say that I'd never given much thought to these birds in my life. Save for feeling annoyed with their incessant cawing at times. I'd never again be able to view another one without thinking of all these facts. I could have happily gone about my day not knowing these tidbits of information.

"They don't sound very nice," Clarisse said, echoing my own thoughts. "Maybe I should have let the guys rig up that pully thing and take a few of them out."

"There's an old crow counting rhyme. I can hardly remember it from years ago," Verna said thoughtfully. "It's about when you see them together and what it means. 'One for sorrow, two for joy, three for a girl, four for a boy.' I can't remember the rest of it except for seven. It's about not telling something."

She shook her head in frustration.

It was Nora who finished the rhyme. Nora, the crossword star and queen of useless information. She rattled off the whole poem with no hesitation.

One for sorrow
Two for joy
Three for a girl
Four for a boy
Five for silver
Six crows for gold
Seven for a secret never to be told.

"'Seven for a secret, never to be told.'," mused Verna. "That's it, Nora. Good for you, you old brain. Must be all those crossword puzzles you're always working away at."

"Must be," Nora agreed, shrugging modestly. "It's just an old superstition."

"There's lots of them about ravens," Jenny said. "Throughout the years the raven has been associated with the medicine of magic. Their colour is the colour of the black hole in space that holds all the energy of the creative source. Some believe that ravens are a symbol of our dark or shadow self. That it's just as important to explore your dark side as your lighter side to achieve balance."

I surveyed the group of women.

Did we all have a dark side? Some more than others, of course. Not being psychic, I couldn't be sure, but I had felt only goodness from this bunch. No evil.

And what I felt for Jenny? That wariness and sense of mistrust. What would that be called? Not evil surely. Misgivings. That seemed to say exactly how I felt about her. I harbored misgivings.

I turned my attention from my thoughts to the conversation where Jenny seemed to be describing a spell to banish personal troubles. Apparently, it involved enlisting the raven's help to perform it.

You were to collect sunflower seeds, as many seeds as you had troubles. Then you take them outside to a tree that you feel close to. You place a dish of berries or other seeds in the limbs of this tree. You examine each one of your troubles and place them inside each sunflower seed, getting the negativity inside the shell of the seed. Once you've loaded up the seeds with all these problems, you place them into the dish. The crows will take each seed and crack it open, getting rid of your troubles. They'll be happy because they'll be paid in food. When they're all done get the dish back and don't forget to thank the ravens.

"Well that sounds nicer, to let them take away your problems. Nicer for them, I mean, than to do some of that other stuff. Like pecking the eyes out of baby calves," Miranda observed. "I used to know a girl named Raven when I was in school. She was dark and mysterious just like her name."

Since the telling of Miranda's tale, she had casually made several references to her earlier life, something she'd never done before. It made me happy to think that she would share things with us now, no matter how small.

The door swung open then and Neil entered in a gust of autumn air, several brown leaves sweeping along beside him. His broad face wore a worried expression, unlike his usual happy-go-lucky self.

"There's a child missing in Jared," he announced.

Some of the women stood up, the rest turned to face him, everyone on high alert.

"Who is it?"

"A little girl visiting the McArthurs. Their granddaughter. Her parents are visiting from Toronto."

"So not one of our kids then," Nora observed.

Neil looked at her and answered, "No, not one of our children. But she's somebody's child."

Nora looked contrite.

"I didn't mean it like that, Neil. I really didn't."

Neil nodded. "I know. I'm just worried. This never happens around Jared."

The women started clucking, shaking heads.

"Maybe she's just wandered off," Brooke said. "How old is she, Neil?"

"Only five."

"Well, we'll all have to help look for her."

"Oh, Brooke," Neil rushed to her, pulling her into an embrace. "I knew you'd say that."

"But we do, Neil. We can't leave a wee girl outside just wandering around."

"Of course, we can't," Verna agreed briskly. "Come on, ladies. Let's show them what Jaredites are made of."

Jenny and Connie had uttered no words, but proceeded to spring into action. They bustled around the kitchen, organizing things, pulling out backpacks, and filling them with non-perishables. The rest of the women followed suit, putting away dishes and mugs, wrapping up leftover cake.

Neil straightened up chairs and tidied up. Brooke came to join him, taking his hand.

"We'll find her, you know," she said, gently.

She opened the heavy wooden door and, one by one, we filed out, armed with compassion and the determination that a five-year-old girl would not be lost on our watch, in our village. We would ban together to help, in the wonderful way that women do when the cause is desperate. And a lost child was the ultimate in desperate situations.

The glory and brilliance of the chrysanthemums now lining the cobblestone path beckoned in the autumn breeze like yellow flags waving us on, encouraging us.

"I know I'm getting long in the tooth," observed Nora as she marched along beside Heather and Verna. "But I always wanted to stay in reasonable shape. I wanted to be able to hurry if I had to. You never know when you might be called upon in an emergency — to save a child's life or something."

Miranda and I, who were walking behind them, caught the remark and dared to exchange a grin at the thought of it. But Nora appeared to be serious. I felt a surge of affection well up inside me for the funny old woman.

Hopefully we would save this child's life, I thought. *If it comes to that.*

So, the afternoon began with hope and purpose. But as the hours waned down and afternoon melted away into dusk, hope began to fade. There was no sign of the little girl. She had seemingly vanished into thin air.

Apparently, the parents had been having a cup of tea after church on the front porch of the grandparent's house. The little girl, Emma, had been playing happily in the grass, tumbling and somersaulting around to the back yard. They could hear her laughter and cries of glee. Until they couldn't.

We marched up and down the streets. No one had seen a little girl in a pink shirt and navy leggings. But then most people had been inside having brunch or taking it easy on this Sunday.

It was unheard of to think that she'd been abducted. Everyone kept saying that nothing like this had ever happened here. Never.

Miranda and I returned to the rooming house with heavy hearts, as the last strands of light lingered in the sky. I tried with desperate effort not to think about how dark and still the country must seem to a little girl who had spent her life in a big city.

Some of the women had been openly weeping as they departed to their respective homes. Neil led a despondent Brooke and Toby home, as Jenny and Connie took Melly to Hedgewytch Way.

Melly had whispered, "I know what it's like to feel lost and all alone. I feel bad for Emma."

Then she gave Miranda a quick hug before following the other two women.

It took me a long time before sleep came to wrap her arms around me and let my mind ease a little. I tossed and turned, trying to take my mind away from this terrible thing that had happened right in our midst. Morning had almost broken before I fell deep, deep into an intense slumber.

I saw it then so clearly, as clearly as if I were at a cinema, the picture rolling out in Technicolor in front of my eyes. I saw row upon row of cornstalks, miles of them. And in the middle, traipsing down the centre of two rows, a woman. I could only see her back, but I knew her. I knew somehow, in that funny way of dreams, that she was a part of me. She wore khakis and her hair was piled on top of her head, curls sticking out every which way. A dog trotted beside her, a German Shepherd whose head reached almost to her shoulders and a funny looking tri-coloured cat lurked around her ankles, ready to spring into action. I just couldn't for the life of me remember who she was.

I awoke with a massive start to find the alarm on my cell phone banging away and Miranda knocking on my door. I felt utterly disorientated.

What the hell had just happened. Was it really 8 o'clock?

My mind cleared quickly as I registered the news that Miranda offered to me.

Emma had been found, safe and well. A little scared, but she would be fine.

She had wandered off into the neighbor's cornfield and supposedly fallen asleep in the heat of the unseasonable sun. Unused to this, being a city child, she had advanced further and further into the field until she was quite far away from any civilization.

"Who found her?"

"Jenny." Miranda told me. "Jenny found her at the crack of dawn. I guess it was bothering her, so she got Rolf and they headed out. They kept walking in the corn field till they found her. She was all curled up on the ground — dirty and scared, but ok."

"Wow. Did she have Julie with her too?"

"The cat? I don't know, Molly. Why do you ask?"

"Oh, I don't know. I had a dream. Kind of. But really real."

Miranda listened intently, so I continued.

"I dreamed I saw Jenny and Rolf and Julie walking down the rows of corn searching for Emma."

Miranda shrugged.

"Well, that really happened. Maybe you had a vision."

I didn't know. I just felt glad that Emma had been found.

An air of happiness had consumed the whole village, so different than the one of despair which enveloped it yesterday.

Miranda and I walked to the café and were greeted with many cheerful waves.

A crisis averted. A happy ending for our little village.

"Look, Molly," Miranda pointed. "There's a bunch of those ravens they were talking about yesterday. Before all this other shit happened."

I counted them. They lingered on the sidewalk, thinking about Clarisse's garbage maybe? Now safe in the confines of the metal can.

"Seven of them," I told her.

"Seven," she repeated. "Seven for what? I can't remember."

I turned the rhyme over in my head before I got to the number.

"Seven for a secret never to be told."

"Whoa," Miranda shuddered a little. "Sounds ominous."

'Seven for a secret never to be told.'

But the big secret, the secret living here in Jared. That secret was to be told. I knew it. I could feel it.

Seven for a secret that would be told.

But when?

38

"Happiness is an inside job. Don't assign anyone else that much power over your life."

Mandy Hale

"SO, I WALK THIS LINE EVERY DAY. This cancer line."

"Sorry. What?" Brooke seemed a little taken aback.

I cast my gaze to the aggrieved-looking woman who had joined us for yoga. She'd never come out before and I didn't know her. She sure looked like she could use a little more Zen in her life, though.

She wore the sallow, pinched look of the chronically ill. Her face had fallen into bitter lines, her eyes dull, and her whole body bespoke of defeat. A scarf, the universal sign of baldness from chemo, covered her head.

"The cancer line. The line between chemotherapy and cancer," she replied in a voice that implied we knew very little indeed.

"Oh, that line," the nurses nodded in sync now, Freddy, Irene and Clarisse. This they could understand.

These Sundays remained my favorite times, the time when the day rested and so did we. A stretch of an hour or two with no immediate commitments spent in the company of women who grew dearer to me as time progressed. This morning we were indulging in lemon echinacea tea and banana bread.

"Yes, that line," the woman dropped her head and sighed deeply.

"Why do you continue then, Betty?" Verna asked.

"Why?"

"Yes, why do you do it? If you're so unhappy about it."

"You," Betty's words had turned hostile. She pointed an accusing finger at Verna. "You have no idea at all what it's like."

"You're absolutely right." Verna agreed. "I don't. I'm sure it's hard."

"Hard? Hard?" Betty's tone rose several octaves. "It's a terrible way to live."

"The chemo is so strong that it kills the cancer cells that are multiplying in your body," Irene explained, her voice gentle. "So, it stands to reason that they kill some of the good cells, too. Your body is fighting hard."

Betty peered, unsmiling, into Irene's earnest face.

"It's poison, that's what it is. It's bloody poison they pump into my veins. Think about it. You lose your hair. You lose weight. You throw up all the time. And it destroys your immune system which is the bloody thing that helps you survive. It's poison shit as far as I'm concerned. And my doctor thinks going to yoga and saying '*om*' a few times will fix me up."

"He probably just thought that it would give you more peace of mind," Brooke said. "That's what yoga does. It teaches you to live in the moment."

"In the moment," Betty snorted. "How easy everything is for you young people. What's your biggest worry? Where you left your cell phone?"

Brooke blushed. I thought of all the worries and responsibilities that she lived with.

Miranda and I exchanged a look. And thoughts. We had gotten pretty good at this telepathy thing.

Who invited her? She qualifies as odious, for sure.

All the women seemed a little taken aback by the venom in Betty's voice. It seemed so out of place here in Jenny's cozy cottage. Freddy answered in her forthright way.

"Brooke has a lot of responsibility, you know. And the practice of yoga does help. Of course, it's an ongoing thing. Lots of patients have been helped through many issues with a combination of medicine and yoga."

Betty peered at her, her beady eyes wary.

"I've seen you there sometimes, at the hospital."

"Yes, I go to oncology when they're short," Freddy said. "I know some of the chemo patients."

"I don't know if half you nurses know what the hell you're doing. You always seem to be making a joke about everything."

"'Laughter is the best medicine,'" Freddy quoted, apparently unoffended. But I could sense Miranda's indignation. She loved her fellow nurses.

"That's a load of crap," Betty observed. "It's downright insulting to laugh and make jokes around sick people. I heard you making fun of that lady, the one who had a stroke. Her name's Mary and you call her —"

"I call her Eileen," Freddy finished the sentence. "I call her Eileen because she leans to one side. She doesn't mind, you know."

"How do you know she doesn't mind?"

"Because Freddy's patients love her," Clarisse jumped into the conversation. "They all love her. She's an excellent nurse."

"Oh, you would stick together, you lot. We're just victims lying there while you pump us full of poison, laughing and calling us names."

"It's not like that," Freddy said, a tinge of annoyance creeping into her voice. "It's not like that at all."

"Maybe not from where you stand. But from where I stand that's just how it is. Chemo on one side, cancer on the other. What the hell do you call that?"

"I call that the choice of life over dying," Clarisse ventured.

Betty rose to her feet, surveying our little group scattered around Jenny's table.

"Well, I call it crap," she pronounced. "Pure crap. I'm leaving. And I'm not coming back. Bunch of cliquey women thinking you can make things better by balancing on one leg."

She turned and departed, leaving a silence in her wake. A silence that didn't last long.

"What a disagreeable woman," Verna said. "I think that's the first time I've ever seen her. I've never seen her at the café."

"No, I haven't either," Nora agreed, who spent almost as much time at the café as Verna did. "I think they only moved here a couple of years ago and she doesn't get too involved in Jared life. She doesn't seem to like anybody."

"Ah, well, maybe she's not feeling well. I mean clearly she isn't," Brooke said. "That's likely why she's so unpleasant."

Clarisse shook her head.

"I bet she was always that way," she declared. "Illness doesn't usually change your whole personality. It just exacerbates it."

When the non-nurses looked quizzical, she added, "makes it worse, more pronounced."

"It's true," Irene agreed. "Lots of patients have a wonderful attitude no matter how sick they are. And the grouchy ones usually have been grouchy all their lives."

"Born grouchy," Nora said. "Like that one."

"Some people are just like that," Heather agreed. "They feel better when they've given you all their troubles and bad stuff to process. Like my daughter-in-law. She calls me and tells me all the trouble she's having with Sebastian, my grandson. All the rotten things he says to her and all the problems at school. I don't know if she feels better or not, but I'm left with this horrid weight on me, worrying about him. And there's really nothing I can do about it. I mean they live in Saskatoon. I'm just left with the worry of it all."

"That's where your yoga practice can help you, Heather," Brooke said, pleased that it could be of use to someone today. "Try to remember not to take things personally. Her complaining and trying to wreck your day says much more about her than it does of you. Stay true to your inner self."

"I just tell her that it's all going to be all right," Heather replied.

"It's all going to be all right in the end," Freddy quoted. "And if it's not all right then —"

"It's not the end!" finished Irene, Clarisse, and even Miranda, with her.

I laughed.

"I never heard that before," I said.

"We say it at work when things go wrong," Freddy explained. "More to save our sanity than anything."

"I like it," Brooke said. "I'll have to remember that one."

Brooke collected tidbits of sayings and poems, interspersing them into her yoga classes.

"I think that quote came from John Lennon," Jenny said.

"It may have, but they said it in that movie, too. The one with Judi Dench that was on at the movies quite a few years ago now," Verna added.

"I love Judi Dench," Heather declared. "I loved her in those James Bond movies."

How easily sidetracked these women were!

"Me too," Freddy said. "But they killed her off in *Skyfall*. That wasn't very nice. She's one classy lady. I love her acting."

"*The Best Exotic Marigold Hotel!*" Verna called out triumphantly. "That's the movie they said that in."

"I saw that movie," Heather said. "I don't remember that saying."

"I do," Verna declared, "Because Malcolm would say it to me in the kitchen after that when things went wrong. It was the hotel manager that said it in the movie."

"Neil taught me a word that means 'something that makes you forget grief or suffering'," Brooke said. "I think it's pronounced 'nepenthe'. Like that."

"That Neil and all his words," Nora said, shaking her head, "I never heard anything like it."

"It's unique all right," Brooke agreed, unable to keep the affection from her voice.

"I wish there really was such a thing as that," Freddy said. "That nepenthe thing. It would be great."

"It would," I agreed.

I'd like to forget about Moira and Tod. I enjoyed Keith's company and we had fun, but it was nothing like the mind-blowing waves of love that used to rush over me when Tod and I were together. I knew it never would be, that Keith would always just be a guy to hang out with.

"Nepenthe," Brooke said dreamily. "A fictional medicine for sorrow. A drug of forgetfulness."

"I think after all," Jenny said. "that patience alone will look after all the bad things."

"What do you mean?"

"Well, patience is, in essence, a magic power. Not everyone has it, but when you do, it gives you power over your own life. I think, anyways."

"I don't know," Heather said. "I think patience is a lot like other things. You've either got it or you don't."

"I think you can cultivate it," Brooke said.

"You would," Heather replied, her smile taking the sting from her words.

"No, it's possible," Clarisse spoke up. "When I first started working as a nurse, I didn't have as much patience as I do now. I've had to make myself be patient. It's hard, but you can do it if you have to."

Neil entered the kitchen then, ducking so as not to hit his head on the bunches of dried herbs hanging there.

"Well, are you ladies solving all the world's problems today?" he asked in his cheerful, boisterous voice.

"We really are," Nora said. "We're even quoting you, Neil. You and your never-ending supply of words no one has ever heard of."

"I find it interesting actually," Verna said. "You being a logolite, or whatever you are."

Neil grinned.

"A logophile. There's actually quite a few of us word lovers, but not enough to get the word into the dictionary. It comes from a Greek word 'logos' meaning speech or word and 'philos' meaning dear or friendly."

"Well I'm glad you're one. I love all your words," Brooke declared.

She linked arms with him, and waving good byes to us, they departed.

This, of course, led to more discussion, this time the subject being the budding romance happening in our midst.

I smiled as I thought of the range of topics covered in the Hedgewytch kitchen today.

Miranda and I had volunteered our hand at assisting Jenny in the manufacturing of sachets, so we turned our attention to the herbs and material laid out on the counter waiting to be fashioned into something beautiful and hopefully functional.

"Just follow my lead," Jenny instructed us. Therein lay the hope.

Miranda and I mused together over the chart laid out for us, written in Jenny's distinctive hand.

"For sleep or to induce sleep – try lemon balm or cowslip

To calm the nerves – chamomile or violet leaves and flowers or cowslip

To lift the spirit – try mints, any of the mints or heather or sweet cicely

To cure a headache – try lavender or chamomile

To keep away evil spirits – rosemary

To invite trouble – mugwort."

"Invite trouble?"

"That's just a chart," Jenny said, waving aside the implication. "I don't have any mugwort."

I let myself wonder about that. Why was it written as such by Jenny herself if she never wanted to invite trouble?

We busied ourselves with the task at hand, our olfactories overwhelmed by the redolence of the herbs mingling together around us. Jenny had tags of coloured paper, with words of wisdom to adorn each sachet. Julie had curled herself up in the bay window, looking about with a general air of disdain. Every once in a while, she turned her head our way and Jenny would throw her a kiss. Which she tolerated from her mistress. Rolf had sprawled his lengthy body in front of the fire, his mighty head thrown back in a position of total relaxation. Periodically he would let out a contented moan, no doubt dreaming of a chase in which he was the victor.

As I worked with the sachets, I listened with half an ear to the conversation which showed no signs of dying down. During the grey winter months, it was pleasant indeed to have female companionship and a warm fire.

Snippets of comments floated over to us, causing us to grin or shake our heads.

"Being inside with kids all day is a type of prison really. You talk about learning patience. That can draw on your last scrap of patience."

"You young people have no idea how lucky you are to be able to just look at something and read it without squinting at things from a mile away or having to run for your glasses."

"Oh Nora. You don't want to sound like that horrible Betty now, do you?"

Pauses in the conversation were punctuated by one or the other of them declaring that they must go now. That they had a lot to do at home. But no one actually rose to their feet.

"That's a God-awful schedule that day, day, night, night. I don't know how you do it, Irene. Always coming off the night shift."

"Hey, did you guys hear that Dr. Victor took our advice and ordered some gin-soaked raisins for Mrs. Connelly at the home?"

"Oh, that's good."

"What?" I turned to Miranda. "Gin-soaked raisins? Is that a joke?"

"Oh no," Jenny said. "They give them to the people at Jared Home. Mama used to get them. She swore by them."

"What are they?"

"Well, that's what they are," Miranda explained. "Exactly how they sound. You just take golden raisins and soak them in a bowl of gin. The gin has to be made with juniper, because I think it's the compounds in juniper that have an anti-inflammatory healing effect. Anyways, you soak them and then take nine a day. And it helps. It really does."

"I find that hard to believe," I said, feeling skeptical. "It's probably a lot in their heads."

Miranda shrugged.

"Even if it is, it's better than taking drugs. Some of those arthritis drugs have terrible side effects."

So many different ways to look at things. Such a varied perception of life, right from medication to beliefs. The more I knew of all these assorted ways, the less I knew what I thought myself.

Sometimes I fought against the Hedgewytch ways of life. Other times they came to me without even asking. Like the night I saw Jenny and Rolf saving the little girl. So clear that I might as well have been standing beside them.

And then it happened one night in February, one cold winter night that crackled with white magic.

I didn't know for sure what had happened, but I knew to the bottom of my soul that something had.

I didn't know where I went or how, but I went somewhere, somewhere beyond the realm of my bed, my everyday life. Somewhere far away. Or so I thought. But maybe not. Maybe I didn't go far at all.

However, I knew with certainty when my eyes fluttered open, with the kiss of the sun lingering at my blinds, that I had been away. That I had travelled someplace else. Like a huge yearning inside me, I could almost remember. Almost. But it stayed just beyond the edges of my mind, teasing my consciousness, never revealing itself. Only snatches of memory came to me. The lushness of the green meadows tickling my feet. I ached at the loveliness of the flowers against my legs and the whisper of the warm breeze in my hair, brushing my cheeks.

I felt myself drifting through the darkness like a shadow, like a whisper.

If it happened before then it could happen again. Couldn't it?

I could sense the truth of my life here closing in on me. I did not know what that truth was. I only knew that before I had finished in Jared, it would all be clear to me.

39

"What if I read to you a story,
Starting 'Once upon a time',
And you realised that it was your life
Spelt out on every line ..."

erin hansen

THE END OF THE STORY came with swiftness and unexpectedness one lush summer evening.

Miranda, Jenny and I alone lingered on the porch of Hedgewytch Way.

It turned into the end of the world. The end of everything as I knew it.

Or maybe, just the beginning ...

40

"Witches seek the sacred knowledge the rest of the world has already forgotten."

Dacha Avelin

A DAY HOLDS THE POWER FOR SO MANY POSSIBILITIES in its twenty-four hours. And you can't know what will happen within them. Once in every so often a day is given to you that changes you forever, you and the world you knew only yesterday. So that your world is never, can never, be the same again.

This day came for Miranda and me in May. It dawned like any other, with the warmth of sunshine and the promise of spring. We were both busy as ever, busy every day with college and working and everything else on our plates, busy as only young adults crave to be. We didn't want to miss out on one second of life.

The last chore on our list found us at Hedgewytch Way, helping seven children into rubber boots and jackets. When they had departed with their respective caregivers, we loaded ten dozen packages of lavender cookies into our baskets for the Corner Café.

"You're alone?" Miranda observed.

"Yes. Unusual, isn't it? Connie's away in Guelph for a few days."

Jenny gestured for us to follow her out to the porch. We needed little encouragement to sit and partake of a cold beverage before trudging back to town. We gratefully accepted tumblers of raspberry lemonade.

"Where's Melly?"

"She and Toby have gone to Guelph too. Brooke and Neil took them to the cinema with Grandma Ida."

"You didn't want to go?"

"I had things to finish up here. And it's good for them to have time together. I'm so lucky. For years I had Toby almost all to myself."

"Do you mind?"

"Mind?"

"Sharing him."

Jenny cocked her head, smiling a little.

"No. I don't mind. It's so good for Toby to have Neil in his life. Neil is a good, solid, dependable man. They don't grow on trees."

Miranda and I exchanged a smirk. Didn't we know it?

"They're going to be just fine." She said the words with conviction.

"You know that?"

"Yes, I do."

Miranda shot her a quizzical look and asked unexpectedly, "Do you know anything about us?"

Jenny seemed to ponder the question carefully.

At that very moment, my eyes fell on Jenny's broom which always leaned against the outside of the purple door. Today it stood upside down, it's bristles pointing skyward. I remembered with a flash of clarity that this meant the witch who lived within wanted no company.

But why? What was going on?

"About us?" I croaked.

"Yes." Miranda replied. "About Molly and me."

Jenny considered this a moment longer before turning to face us.

I could feel my heart accelerating like a trip hammer inside my chest. My breath seemed to come to me in ragged gulps as the awareness dawned on me, with utmost certainty, that we were on the verge of discovering something monumental.

Jenny took a long drink of her lemonade before replacing it on the wooden table with great resolve.

"I do," she replied, her voice barely a whisper.

She cleared her throat and with more conviction declared, "I do."

The evening around us kept pace with the crickets and the soft mellow breezes. But for me it stood still, silently waiting.

"Honestly, I don't quite know how to begin," Jenny's gaze had shifted out to the shadowy corners of the trees. The air lay redolent with the perfume of her beloved lilacs.

"Is it a big thing?" I ventured, not recognizing my own voice.

Jenny nodded, her topknot bobbing up and down.

"Oh, yes. It's a big thing. It's a big thing for all of us. It's funny you know. I've thought about this day for so long, and now I have no idea how on earth to begin."

I looked at Miranda, uncomprehending. I could have reached out and grabbed the letters of her thoughts as they drifted towards me.

WTF??

"Do either of you girls have a photo of your mother on your phone?"

I shook my head at this unexpected question. My cell phone held no photos of Mom. They were stored in a flowered box at the back of my cupboard. Remembering how Miranda had described her mom, I felt quite sure that she wouldn't either.

But she surprised me by answering in the affirmative, thus proceeding to flip through the files on her iPhone until she conjured up a photo and tapped it to life on the screen.

"It's an old one," Miranda said, a wistful note to her voice, "before she started drinking. But it's how I like to remember her."

A wave of shame swept over me. My phone held no photo of a mom, who had been the best mother ever. But Miranda had close to her, at all times, a picture of her abusive alcoholic mother. I mentally sent an apology heavenward.

I pondered the irony of this while Jenny extracted the iPhone from Miranda's hand. She donned her little half-moon reading glasses, studying the screen, her expression unreadable.

I took a refreshing sip of my raspberry lemonade.

Without a word, Jenny passed me the phone. I had to tap it again to bring up the image of Miranda's mother.

The world stopped. It literally stopped on its axis.

I gaped open-mouthed at the photo of Miranda's mom, uncomprehending.

I turned to Miranda, staring. The whole world had decelerated into slow motion.

"We have the same mom!"

I felt that I should scream these words, this observation, but only a raspy whisper materialized from my lips.

My eyes locked into Miranda's blue ones. Why had I never noticed that she had my very own eyes? Those eyes stared back at me now, clearly doubting my sanity. I handed the phone back to her. My words fell from my mouth in a garbled rush.

"Our moms. Our moms! We have the same mom, Miranda. That's why we can read each other's thoughts. That's why people always think we might be sisters."

This knowledge seemed beyond any comprehension. I shook my head, unable to take it in.

"We're sisters! We are! We must be!"

"Molly," Jenny intervened, laying a quietening hand on my arm. "Molly, are you quite sure that really is your mother? Didn't she have a little birthmark just on her right cheek almost underneath her eye?"

How did she know that? How could she know that?

Wordlessly, Miranda tapped the phone back to life, handing it to me again. I scrutinized the photo and had to acknowledge that indeed this wasn't my mom. The woman smiling up from the screen looked like a mirror image of my mom, like a reflection or something. She bore no birthmark on her right cheek.

"I don't get it," Miranda murmured. "I just don't get it."

Neither did I. I had no words. I turned to Jenny, knowing that she held all the answers inside her.

"We'd better have something stronger that raspberry lemonade," Jenny said, attempting a small laugh.

She opened the old wooden cupboard that stood haphazardly on the porch, withdrawing a bottle of dandelion wine and three goblets. The cupboard got used a lot in the warmer weather — one end leaning at a crooked angle, looking as if it might fall over, but never falling.

Miranda and I sat in a confused daze as Jenny poured us all a generous portion of the golden liquid. She raised her glass and we all clinked our glasses together, prolonging the moment of the great revelation.

For how could it not be a great one? A huge one? This secret that originated from a time long ago, a time of our mothers and some unknown identity.

Jenny inhaled deeply, shutting her eyes with the effort of the words she must speak.

"A long time ago ..." she began.

"Yes, yes, a long time ago," Miranda's words came out in a strangled, impatient voice.

"I have to tell it like a story, because that's what it is. My story."

"Go on."

"Ok."

Our words mingled together, filled with eagerness and trepidation.

"A long time ago in the year 1969, the world was a different place. It's hard to imagine now just how very different it was then. People talk about the sixties and hippies and free love. But in the day to day life of ordinary families, values were very rigid — especially in small farming communities."

"Like Jared."

"Yes. Like Jared. Families attended church every Sunday. People didn't live together before marriage. And if a woman happened to get pregnant, she married the father of her child. That's the way it was. There are lots of teenaged mothers nowadays. I'm not sure why because birth control is readily available. But when I was a teenager, if you became pregnant, it was a huge disgrace to your parents. To your whole family. It was almost unheard of."

Miranda and I exchanged baffled looks. Where was this going, this story of Jenny's?

"I was born in 1953, so I was in my teens in 1969. I turned sixteen on May eleventh of that year."

The summer hush of the country had descended on the evening now. The whole world waited with great expectation to the culmination of Jenny's story.

"My parents were good, hard-working people, right off the boat from Germany. Well, you girls know that. You knew my mom, especially you, Miranda. She was very sweet. I loved her very much, but she was a typical wife of those times. She followed my father's lead on everything. He was the head of the house, no question about it. His word was law."

She let out a deep sigh, seemingly lost in memories of yesteryear.

"He was a good man. He was a good dad to me, but he was always very strict. I think that when you live through a war, it does something to you. It makes you strong, but also very tough inside. When he made up his mind about something, there was no changing it. Never. My mom was always easier to get around. Maybe her mind was more open because she had the gift of second sight."

Jenny took a long gulp from her goblet, adjusting the ribbon around her topknot. The next words tumbled out, having been trapped inside for all these years.

"When I was fifteen years old, I got pregnant. It wasn't a wonderful teenage romance. It wasn't even a beautiful interlude to remember. I was raped."

"Raped!"

"Yes. I'm telling you this because I am telling the whole truth to you girls. It's your right to know. No one around here knows anything about this, least of all who the father was."

"Are you going to tell us that too?" Miranda breathed the question.

"Do you want to know?"

Did I want to know? What difference could it make now? We wouldn't know the person from that long ago anyways.

But Miranda nodded eagerly.

"You know Joan Payne who just died, of course?"

"Of course."

"Her son Roger raped me."

The words fell separately like stones into the warmth of the surrounding dusk, dropping there, leaving shock and horror in their wake.

"I was coming home from school on the first day of grade ten. It was a beautiful warm day, sunny and bright. I never was as happy and carefree as I was that day. It was that kind of happiness that comes only with childhood. Roger was a year older than me, but he wasn't in school. He was always creepy. Well, you girls saw him that night we were cleaning up. He's still creepy. He used to leer at girls much younger than himself. You know where the road from town branches away into our road? He was hanging around that thicket of oak trees there. I always loved those trees before that day," she said, lost in her memories. "I used to listen to what they said when the wind whispered in their leaves. Anyways, I said hello and tried to walk past him, but he reached out his big hairy arm and grabbed me. He was a huge giant of a boy then, nothing like how you saw him last summer. He's all wizened up now. Anyways he seemed massive to me then. I was never a very big person."

I shuddered, picturing it all. Jenny, not even five feet tall, and the looming figure of absolute corruption.

"He pulled me behind those trees and threw me down on the ground. I'll spare you the horrific details. You'll just have to imagine how awful it was. I was naïve and sheltered and that day was the end of innocence for me."

Somewhere during the telling of Jenny's tale, Miranda's hand had crept into mine. I squeezed it now.

"What did your mom say?"

"My mom wasn't home that day when I got there. This was unusual, but I remember feeling glad. I was in no condition to speak to anyone. I was shocked and still terrified. My blouse was ripped.

My skirt was grass stained and my underwear were bloody. I ran straight to my bedroom and lay on my bed sobbing. When I looked in the mirror, I didn't recognize my own face. I was as white as a ghost and it was like the light had gone out of my eyes. I got out of my clothes and scrubbed up as best I could. We only had a dug well then and we always had to be very cautious about how much water we used. I almost ripped my skin off trying to remove his smell from my skin. For days and days, I could still smell him."

"You didn't tell your mom and dad?"

"No. I was so ashamed. I didn't want them ever to know. Nowadays, the police would have been called and he would have been arrested, but things were so different then. A girl was somehow made to feel that if such a thing happened to her that she was 'asking for it' in some way. I felt that it must have been my fault or this couldn't have happened to me. I was absolutely distraught. My parents had the orchard out back here, of course, but in those days, they had two hundred additional acres to farm and forty head of cattle. The fall was a busy time for them. And I just kept to my room, using Grade ten homework as an excuse. Mama asked me a couple of times if I was ok, but I always assured her that I was fine. I just thought that it was an awful experience I would have to put behind me. And I tried desperately to do that."

"Did he ever try anything like that again?"

"No. I took to riding my bike to school. It took me quite a bit longer, because I could walk out to the main road in Jared and catch the bus. I didn't care. I would have biked further than that if I had to. I felt more secure with some means of escape. About a month later, I heard that he'd headed out west to work on a ranch. Maybe his mother suspected something and sent him away. I never knew. I was just so relieved to hear that he was gone. It was only then I could actually breathe properly since that first day of school.

"Well, I thought that everything would be all right then. I thought I could just carry on and eventually I might even forget the whole thing. Then I started to feel unwell. My food didn't taste right, and I was exhausted all the time. I thought it was just the trauma of the rape catching up with me. It was December when I realized that I was pregnant. I remember lying in my bed and putting my hand on my belly. I could feel the swell of it underneath my hand. I wanted to die then. I really did. I wanted to curl up in my bed and use all of my willpower to end my life. But of course, it doesn't work that way. I knew that this wouldn't go away by just ignoring it. This was something that would only grow and grow until there would be no way to hide it."

I shuddered as I pictured that young girl of so long ago, surviving in the aftermath of rape, alone and terrified. Lying in her bed with a growing baby resting under her hand, not knowing where to turn next. Miranda's hand remained clutched in mine, her eyes agog with the telling of Jenny's tale.

"What did you do?" she asked.

"I wanted to just tell my mom. I thought that maybe I could make her understand. But I knew it would be very hard on her and we'd just have to reiterate the whole story again to my father. So, I waited until after supper the next night when we were sitting by the fireplace. Mama had the Christmas lights along the mantle. I always loved how they made the room glow. That's why I still hang them there now. And into this beautiful family scene, I laid my bombshell of a story. I was so scared that my knees were knocking together. I told the whole story of the rape and how I was trying to put it behind me and then how I had just discovered that I must be pregnant. I'd had no formal test. You couldn't buy a pregnancy test at the dollar store then like you can now. But I hadn't had a period since August. And by now it was evident."

"What did your parents do?"

"Well, they responded true to their own fashions. People usually do, I think. Mama was stunned and said very little, but she did come to sit beside me and held my hand. My dad ranted and raved and yelled. First that he would kill me, then Roger, then he was going to do the whole world a service and kill Joan Payne. I just sat and cried and cried. I was fifteen years old. I was a child really. I had no idea what to do or what was going to happen. I honestly don't think that my parents did either. But when I went to bed that night, I felt a little better from the sharing of that horrible story. After a while Mama came up to my room and lay beside me in my bed, just holding me. Eventually my dad came up to my room too.

411

He was still angry, but he said that he could see it was not my fault and he was sorry that this had happened to me. He would always love me he said. Which was kind of a big deal for my dad. He wasn't very demonstrative. And I knew the news was killing him inside."

Jenny got up and returned with a plate of vegetable wraps left over from the day care centre. She refilled our glasses. Clearly, she thought that we needed fortification. We began to nibble absent-mindedly.

I thought about all of this, having no idea what could be ahead in this tale. Because I knew that she had no child that was forty-five years old — at least not one that I'd ever heard spoken of. And how on earth did all of this tie in with Miranda and me? My head swam.

"We didn't have any family to turn to. Both of my parent's families were back in Germany. We had friends, of course, but none close enough for a secret of this magnitude. My father wanted me away from Jared. He wanted me to have the baby and give it up for adoption. That was the way of the world then. Teenaged girls did not keep their babies. If an unexpected pregnancy occurred, it was dealt with, but never discussed openly. These subjects were strictly taboo. So, they sent me to a home for unwed mothers in Toronto after the Christmas holidays. I expected to hate it but, in some ways, it was a relief. All the girls there were in the same boat, so no one judged you. The nuns ran it and they were strict, but I didn't mind strict. Some of them were cold and stern, but others were kind enough. I remember one, Sister Roberta. She seemed to take a shine to me. She'd been raised on a farm herself and she would sometimes sit in the evenings and talk about country life and how she still missed the outdoors and the wide-open spaces. When I told her we had an apple orchard, we'd talk about the pink blossoms and the beautiful perfume in the spring air. Because I stayed until spring."

I reflected on this, as Jenny paused to take a bite of her wrap. I pictured a young girl torn from her country home, forced to spend months in the big city as her body changed in subtle, terrifying ways.

"It wasn't so bad really," she continued, "I missed my mom and dad something terrible. And I was homesick all the time. I'd never been away from home before. And it wasn't feasible for them to visit. But when I look back on that interlude at the home, there was something so special about it because —" her voice caught a little, "because that was the only time in my life that I had my babies with me."

"Babies!" Our voices rose in unison.

Miranda's eyes widened into saucers, mirroring my own.

"On May eleventh, 1969, I turned sixteen years old. And I gave birth to twin baby girls."

41

"All of us labour in webs spun long before we were born."

William Faulkner

"TWINS! TWIN GIRLS!"

I stared, slack-jawed, at Jenny. Miranda looked around, startled, as if half expecting to see two little girls materializing in the evening shadows.

Her thoughts flew by me in the dusky air, thoughts of wonder and puzzlement. But I knew there remained much of Jenny's story to tell, the big story of her life. She'd waited so long to tell it.

"Yes, two perfect, tiny baby girls. Two pieces of my heart and soul. They came a little earlier than they should have, so they were very small. When I looked at them, I didn't think for one moment about Roger Payne. I just thought they were two miracles of life. I'd kept them safe inside my body. They'd heard my heart beating inside of me, beating just for them. I felt I would melt with love for them."

The sadness of her long-ago loss covered Jenny's face with sorrow. Miranda squeezed my hand.

"My parents came to see me that day," Jenny continued, "because it was my birthday. May eleventh. And by some peculiar twist of fate, it was also Mother's Day that year. My parents already had arrangements made to visit me because of those two things. They didn't know that I'd given birth until they arrived. I wasn't due for another few weeks. I knew they were extremely upset about the whole situation, but they still tried to show their love for me. They simply didn't know how to react to this news. It had been decided when I entered the home that the baby would be given up for adoption. There was no question about it. There was no mothers allowance or subsidized help from the government in those days. And there was never any other choice in my parent's eyes."

We had settled back into our chairs now. I saw the first star of evening winking across the sky. Somewhere in the distance an owl hooted. *Was it Hoot?* Jenny wouldn't be there to hold him on her arm tonight. She still had much of her story waiting to unfold.

"They were clearly astonished by the news of the early arrival and the status of twins. I didn't know what to say either. The birth had been traumatic for a sixteen-year-old child. And I was unprepared for the hormones gushing through me. Not to mention the attachment I felt. The love. I felt like I couldn't hold it all inside of me. My mom hugged me and wished me a happy birthday. I, in turn, wished her a Happy Mother's Day. They'd brought me a card, but my dad said they'd waited to see what I needed for my birthday. He said that he could walk to the store and get me a gift there. What did I want for my sixteenth birthday?"

Miranda and I exchanged unhappy looks.

"Uh-oh," Miranda breathed.

"Yes indeed. I looked at them and said that what I wanted for all my birthdays for the rest of my life was to keep my babies. Dad turned on his heel and left the room. Mom sat down on the bed beside me and started to cry. She cried and cried. She said that it wasn't possible — just not possible. She said it broke her heart to give them up, but Dad would never consent. She said that it was better this way, then they'd have two parents and a home. She said I was too young to be a mother. I was only sixteen. She said maybe it would be different if there was only one. I pounced on her words. Could I keep one? I'd do all the work myself. They wouldn't even know there was a baby in the house. On and on I sobbed and pleaded and begged. My poor mama just cried all the harder. Finally, she said, 'Jenny, they are a part of me too. They are my granddaughters. This is very hard. This is the hardest thing that we'll ever have to do. But you must think of these little ones. They must have a proper life.' Dad came back then with a shoulder bag for me for my birthday. He looked at us, his look was very stern as he asked us what the matter was now. Why was Mama crying so? 'Jenny still wants to keep the babies, Fritz,' Mama told him as I cried 'Oh please, Papa, please,' reverting to my old childish name for him. He put the bag down on the bed beside me, kissed my forehead and took Mama by the arm to stand her up. He looked at me and said only 'No, Jenny, you cannot keep them. It is out of the question.' Then they both hugged me and went home to Jared. They never even saw the babies."

"Wow!"

Miranda's eyes glistened with tears. I felt as if my very breath had been consumed by the sorrow of this long-ago tale.

"Nowadays it's not uncommon to see teenaged girls with babies. I don't always think that it is the best answer, but who really knows what's best? I know that giving a baby up and never seeing them again leaves your heart just one big empty ache. It's always there. It never goes away. Each year on my birthday, I would think 'They would be one and then two. They would be walking and talking and starting school.' I never mentioned them at home, but simply continued with high school and tried to study hard. That was the old-fashioned way. 'Least said, soonest mended.' It's an old adage." She sighed from the bottom of her soul. "One we know now doesn't work. When you don't speak of things, they just fester inside of you. But whom could I talk to about it? Certainly not my father. He'd taken up our life just as before. Business as usual. I knew it was hard for him, but he was of the mind that we should just put it behind us and carry on. My mom agreed, but it was much harder for her. She'd never been sad before, my little mom, but I sensed a big sadness in her now. We both shared the same longing, I knew. One morning I got up early and found her sitting in her chair by the kitchen window drinking a cup of coffee. I came into the kitchen and gave her a hug. She seemed so lonesome sitting there somehow. She turned to me and I could see that she'd been crying. She said, 'It's hard to think that we could walk right by those girls on the street and not even know them, isn't it, *LiebesKind*?'"

Jenny said this last with her German accent. I'd noticed that whenever she quoted her parents her words became slightly guttural, obtaining a faster tempo than her usual manner of speaking. I realized then what a captivating storyteller Jenny was. Usually she listened to the stories of the lives of others.

"Dear heart, dear child."

I had been distracted for a second and glanced my question at Miranda.

"Jenny was defining *'liebeskind'*." Miranda explained. "Your poor mom," she added softly.

"Indeed. When she said those words to me, I realized how sad she was too. She hugged me so tight and told me that we must have faith that the nuns had found them a good family and that they were being raised by good people. It was then that she talked to me about *hellsehen konnen*."

Another German word spoken in that distinctive voice.

"What's that now?"

"What did you just say?"

The questions spilled out of us simultaneously.

"Oh, sorry, girls I was getting wrapped up in my story. I've gone over it in my mind a million times, but this is the first time ever that I've told anyone."

"Really?"

"Really. No one knows, not even Connie. My husband knew, of course, but besides him."

Why us?

Miranda's words danced past me.

"Oh, you'll see." Jenny said assuredly, startling us with her perception.

"What is that 'h' word?"

"*Hellsehen konnen*?"

That German accent slipped from Jenny's lips again. Tonight, she had become a magical person who spoke words in another tongue. She'd turned into a little faerie from another time with a story both old and sad.

"That is a German word meaning 'the second sight'. Have you girls ever known anyone who had it?"

"Not really."

"Sometimes I thought that my mom did," I said slowly, "but it's not unheard of on the Island."

"Well it does exist," Jenny went on. "My mom had it and I believe that her mom before her had it as well. Mama didn't make a big thing about it. It was more little things — like knowing the phone was going to ring or knowing what was going to happen before it did. But only to a degree. She downplayed it, probably because of my father. After he died, she encouraged me to work on it. It was Mama who invented the whole concept of the Hedgewytch Way. We'd always been knowledgeable about herbs and natural remedies, but she thought there was lots more we could use in our enterprise. My husband was all for it, too. He didn't understand an ounce of magic, but it always fascinated him. We conjured up the whole idea of the Hedgewytch Way and here we still are. But I'm getting ahead of myself. I'm sorry, girls."

Miranda gently reminded Jenny, "You were telling us that Esther told you to use *hellen—hellse*—whatever that frigging word for second sight is. She told you to use that to do what? Track your babies?"

"Not exactly. It doesn't work that way. It's not an exact science, you see. Maybe it's different for everyone, but for me it was something that came only at certain times. I couldn't predict them. It isn't like my spells with candles and herbs or my recipes with spices and essential oils. This is something that comes to you on a wave like a big beautiful gift. You can't summon it. You just feel it. I looked down into those tiny perfect faces and I willed myself to keep their essence inside of me. I did, too. I felt them all my life. Sometimes I wasn't positive that it was them, but usually I was. And that gave me the strength to keep going especially in those first few years. I might have given up on life entirely if not for the feeling that they shared this world with me."

"How did you feel them when you didn't even know where they were?"

"I can't explain that part to you. I really can't. Perhaps if Mama were still alive and strong-minded, she'd be able to. But I can only tell you how it was for me. I knew they were both adopted as soon as they were big enough. And they weren't adopted as twins. They went to individual families. That was the first thing that I felt about them. I asked Sister Roberta and she confirmed it, even though she wasn't supposed to. So, I knew that for sure."

"Why couldn't they stay together?" I asked. I felt sad for twin baby girls who had to be separated, without their knowledge or wishes, first from their mother then from their sister.

"I honestly don't know. I had no say in any of it, of course. I just kept kissing their faces and telling them that I loved them over and over again. I couldn't stop hoping that somehow, in some part of them, that they'd remember all the love I poured into them. I didn't get to name them, of course, but I thought that if I ever got married and had a baby girl, I would name her Star. Don't you think that's a lovely name?"

Startled by the question, Miranda and I nodded uncertainly.

Jenny's voice had become dreamy, a little faraway.

"Star. To shine like a beacon over your whole life." Jenny shook her head a little. "I never had another little girl though. But I always thought of the twins as being my little stars. And they did shine for me in a way. Because I felt them every day."

"With your second sight?"

"Yes. Do you remember the mirror in my bedroom that faces the east window? The one Toby calls my 'magic mirror'?"

"As opposed to the one that makes you look good downstairs?" I laughed.

"Exactly. Well, in the magic mirror I could sometimes see my girls."

"You could?" Miranda gasped.

"Yes. I know it's hard to believe, Miranda dear, but it's quite true. Like I said before, I couldn't summon them or anything like that. It only happened sometimes, and always in the first light of morning. I'd gaze into that mirror and I'd see them just as plain as I see you right now."

"In the window, you mean? They were a reflection?"

Jenny shook her head.

"That's the thing. Not in the window. If I looked at the window, there was only the eastern sky. And I had to look at the mirror in a certain way. I couldn't look right into it. I had to let my eyes get soft and kind of unfocused. Then I'd look out the sides of them. If I turned and looked directly at the mirror, they would evaporate into the image of the sunrise." She sighed deeply. "It's awfully hard to describe. But it's the truth. A mirror has the reputation of being a soul catcher because it can draw in solar energy. This energy can be stored in a mirror."

"Do you know for sure it was them?"

"As sure as sure can be. And the mornings that I saw them I was so happy I could burst, but sad too, of course, because I missed them with all my heart. But I knew it was them. I knew every fiber of their beings. They were a part of me and I was a part of them."

It was a lot to absorb. I felt completely overwhelmed.

"So, you watched them grow up?" Miranda asked.

"Yes. In a manner of speaking. I can't explain it really. I can see you girls are having a hard time understanding it. They would just come into the mirror. First they were babies, then toddlers, then little girls. They came more often when they were small. As they got older, not so much. Once they didn't come for almost a year. I was almost desperate with longing until they came at last. And I was able to find peace in my heart knowing they were alive and well in the world."

"Did you know where they were? Could you speak to them?"

"No. It didn't work that way."

Jenny stopped talking now. She opened her little cupboard, producing some lavender cookies, her expression unreadable. She seemed preoccupied, almost nervous. It must be hard to tell someone about this phenomenon when you really didn't understand it yourself. Especially when you'd never told anyone before.

Why hadn't she? I wondered, all of a sudden. *And why us? Now?*

The answer dwelt somewhere just outside of my comprehension. I simply couldn't reach it.

"So, you were able to watch your girls grow up." I ventured. "Do you still see them?"

"Sadly, no. They're both dead now."

"Wow. They both died young then?"

"Indeed."

"Did you see that too?"

"I didn't see it in the mirror, no. But the world felt lighter, different to me. If it's true your life flashes before your eyes just before you die, I hope they got to see my face on that very first Mother's Day when I had them. I hope they saw all the love I had for them in my heart. But there was something else."

We waited, both of us, scarcely daring to breathe.

"Something else?"

"Yes. Something wonderful. You see I didn't just see my twins in that mirror. Each of my girls had a daughter. Sometimes I was able to see them, too."

"A daughter? Like your granddaughter?"

"Yes. Two of them."

Jenny leaned forward, fastening her intent gaze on our faces. Some bit of knowledge dangled just outside of my awareness, something I could almost fathom, but not quite. Gazing at Miranda, I could see that she shared my perplexed expression.

"Molly. Miranda." Jenny took our hands in hers. Miranda and I still clutched each other's hand. We had become a circle. I shivered in anticipation, although I had no idea of what. She spoke in a gentle, deliberate voice.

"How do you think, Molly dear, that I knew about your mom having a birthmark underneath her right eye? It was a little like a tiny teardrop wasn't it?"

I nodded dumbly.

"And why do you think I knew what they both looked like? Why do you think people wonder if you girls are related?"

I couldn't grasp it all. I shook my head, confused, trying to comprehend her words and their implication. But my mind wouldn't allow it.

"Our mothers — Miranda and me — our mothers are —"

"Your twin girls," Miranda breathed in awe.

"Exactly."

"So, we — Molly and I — we're cousins! First cousins!" Jenny nodded.

"Then you —"

"You —"

"You're our grandma!" The words rushed out in unison.

"Exactly." Jenny repeated.

She fell back into her chair; the telling of her story having exhausted her. I regarded her with new eyes. She shone in a different light. For the first time ever, I felt no animosity towards her. And I knew.

"This is the reason I didn't trust you, isn't it? Why I never felt at ease with you. Because I knew you were holding back on me."

Jenny nodded.

"Yes, my dear, it is. Some people can feel the magic and some can't. No amount of trying can change that. You feel these things so deeply that you felt it in me and didn't know what it was. So, it made you uneasy and mistrustful."

"And we're here," Miranda marveled. "We're both here in Jared, of all of places in the world we ended up here together, with you."

"Did you instigate that, Jenny?" I asked. "Did you make that happen? You always tell us that you're not really a witch."

"I do say that," Jenny admitted. "And I'm not. Not really."

Jenny's eyes twinkled then. They actually twinkled, little sparks seeming to leap from them.

"But," she concluded, sounding like the old Jenny now, "but that's not to say that I don't have a little bit of magic at my disposal."

42

"You had the power all along, my dear."

Glinda, good witch from *The Wizard of Oz*

T HE TWINKLING OF JENNY'S EYES shot into the warm velvet of
dusk, drifting around us, as my whole world whirled around me.

I couldn't grasp all this. I couldn't take it in. Was this reality, or
was this just a dream — an illusion? I didn't know. I couldn't tell.

I felt dizzy, as if I might fall right off the end of the earth. I
turned to Miranda, who looked just as shocked as I did. I could tell.
Of course, I could tell. She was my cousin, even closer than a first
cousin really because our moms had been twins. Twins! Jenny's
twin girls! My mind seemed to burst, my head nearly explode with
all this new information.

Jenny, true to form, just sat in gentle silence allowing us to
struggle and become aware of this new information. Facts that
had come to light. Family who had emerged from images of loving
friends.

We sat as such for what seemed to be a long while. Then Miranda silently rose and sat down in front of Jenny. She placed her head in Jenny's lap, hugging her knees. With a tenderness beyond words, Jenny placed her hand on Miranda's loose brown curls and stroked them.

Miranda had needed this love, craved it, for so many years. This love, this grandmother love, it had been here all along. We just had to find it.

Events had been set into motion over forty years ago. They'd been spiraling towards their destiny when some day they would all come together.

Today.

Jenny raised her head to look at me. She held out her other hand. I got up and sat beside Miranda in front of her.

"Oh! My two girls. I've longed for you so much."

"Why did we have to wait so long to know all this, Jenny?" Miranda's voice cracked a little.

"It wasn't time yet."

"Oh, you and your timing," Miranda groaned. "I wish we'd known before. I really do."

"It wasn't time. It really wasn't. Things must happen in the right order. Just like you telling us your story. You couldn't do that until you were ready."

"I suppose."

I remembered how sad Jenny had looked as Miranda recounted the tale of her mother's decline into alcoholism. At the time, I'd thought her sadness had been all for Miranda, but now I realized with a shock that she'd been hearing the story of her own daughter. A heart-breaking story.

"No one else knows this?"

"No one even knows that I had the babies. My parents were very private people. In the sixties, things like that were very hushed up. Adopted children had no knowledge of their birth parents. I don't even know if my girls were told that they were adopted."

Miranda and I looked at each other and shook our heads. If our mothers had known, neither of them had shared the knowledge with us.

"How could you have waited for all these years? Weren't you awfully impatient?"

"At times. But I just stayed right here and loved you with all my heart."

The answer came soft and simple, sounding so much like an echo of my mother's words that a shiver tumbled right through my soul.

"Tell us the rest of the story," Miranda said, her voice scarcely more than a whisper.

"There's not much more to tell."

"But your life didn't end when you had our moms."

"I felt as if it did. I felt as if I would have given anything, anything in the whole world, if only I could have kept those two tiny pink bundles. Those two shining stars. But you're right, of course. My life wasn't over. I had to keep living. I came back and took up my old life of school and farm chores. But it was never the same for me. The rest of the girls in my class seemed so frivolous and childish. I'd given birth. I'd crossed over into a different land and there was no crossing back. Not ever. It's our experiences that shape us. The other girls were still in the merry round of homework and sock hops and crushes on boys. I'd been raped and impregnated and given birth to twins. I felt like I inhabited another planet."

"Didn't you tell a girlfriend or anyone?"

"No. I never did. I had a few friends at school, but none that I could trust with such a huge truth. I can't stress enough how much of a disgrace it was back then. It's hard to imagine how humiliating it would have been if word got out. Not just for me, but for my folks. And I was ashamed. Deeply ashamed. I told no one. I studied hard and graduated with honors and I got a job as a secretary in a law office in Guelph. That's where I first met Julian."

"Your husband?"

"Yes. He restored my faith in everything. In life and in love. I started to get my joy back. It took a while. It didn't happen quickly. But one day I woke up and I was surprised to find I was looking forward to the day. I'd always been a happy kid, but after the babies my joy disappeared. Julian, well, he brought it back for me. He was a little older than me and quite handsome. He came into the lawyers on business for his mother. His dad had just died and she was having a hard time coping with finances and bills and so on. His dad had done all that stuff. She didn't know anything at all about the state of their affairs. Julian was very patient with her. I noticed that first. I always admire patience in a person. I loved my papa, but patience was not his strong suite, not by a long shot."

"So, he was handsome and older and patient. Wow, what's not to like about that?"

"Nothing. He was very easy to like. He was pleasant to talk to and cheerful."

"And ..."

"And nothing. I simply was not interested in any romance at all. After the horror of Roger Payne, I was quite sure that I never wanted to have sex again. And after having had my babies torn from my body and my life, I was quite sure that I never wanted children either. So why would I care if Julian Smith was handsome and cheerful and kind?"

"Why indeed?" Miranda and I queried at the same moment. We immediately linked our baby fingers, crying, "Jinx!"

Jenny smiled at us, indulgently.

"I know it sounds silly now. But at the time I was firmly convinced that I'd spend my life living with mama and papa, working at the office and helping on the farm. This didn't displease me. It seemed the sensible thing to do."

Jenny chuckled now, deep in her memories.

"But that Julian Smith. He had other ideas for me. The second time he came in with his mom, he brought me a bouquet of posies. He said they were for my desk. That was all. There was no request for a date. The next time he came was a week later. He had no appointment. He just said that he thought I might need some fresh flowers. He did that eight more times."

"Eight times!"

"Well, ten in total, if you count the first two bouquets. By this time, I was looking forward to seeing him, in spite of myself. The big thing about Julian was that he was so genuinely nice. He just was. He was nice and kind through and through. When he brought me the tenth bunch, he turned to leave and then he came back to my desk and grinned at me. 'Ye-e-s,' I said. And he said, 'Will you go out with me? I'd really like to take you out.' "

Miranda and I waited expectantly.

"Where was your first date?"

"We went to the show."

"Do you remember the name of the movie?"

"Yes. It was *Paper Moon*."

"*Paper Moon*? I've never heard of it."

"Of course, you haven't. You weren't born for another twenty-two years. This was 1973."

By this time, Miranda and I knew enough not to question how Jenny would know the year we were born.

"Was it a good movie?"

"Oh yes. It was. I love those good old movies. It was with Tatum O'Neil and her dad, Ryan O'Neil."

The names meant nothing to us and were of little interest.

"And you hit it off?"

"Like I said, the thing about Julian was his inherent niceness. He had a comfortable kind of easy-going personality. He was never any different from that. I thought when I told him about my trauma and my giving birth that he'd run a mile. I told him the whole story one night. He was quiet for a while. Then he took my hand and told me that he was very sorry I'd have to go through all that. And that he wanted me never to be hurt again and would I marry him."

"And you said yes. Of course, you said yes."

"Not right away. No."

"But you just said that he was the nicest man ever."

"And handsome!"

"And kind!"

Jenny laughed at the two of us.

"It's true. He was all those things. But I'd been hurt so deeply, physically and emotionally, that I thought I'd never be able to have a normal life with a man. I thought that would be my punishment for what had happened to me."

"But that wasn't your fault!" I cried.

"I know that now. But for a long time, I felt only this horrible guilt. People used to be made to feel guilty for so many things. We know better now. But after a few months, I allowed myself to fall in love with him. My parents liked him. They appreciated that he was good to me. I think all three of us had been stuck in a tunnel of sadness after the babies, but Julian helped us come out the other side of it. He was from Toronto, but he'd drive up and often helped my dad on the farm while Mom and I made supper for all of us. Then we'd eat together. It was then that Julian and my dad built that circle of stones in the centre of the orchard. Lots of nights we'd light a bonfire and sit out there. We'd lived with heartache for so many years that I think we were all surprised when it started to ease and we felt better. We started to have happy times again. In the winter, we'd sit at the old table and play euchre."

"He sounds nice," I said. "I wish we could have known him. He would have been our grandpa."

As soon as the words left my mouth, I knew them to be false.

Miranda shook her head.

"No. Oh, God, you mean that miserable dirty man that came to Joan Payne's house last summer was our grandpa?"

We shuddered simultaneously.

"He is no more your grandfather than Eric Biggs is Toby's father. Neil will be the father that Toby carries in his heart. When he finds out about Eric, it will mean nothing because we must let the bad ones go completely. Julian would have been a wonderful grandfather to Toby if he'd lived. Don't get bogged down by thinking that we have to give bad people credit. Just let them go. If you want to think of a grandfather, think of Julian. Roger Payne will rot in his own evil ways. When Julian came into my life, I chose to face the light."

I knew that I'd have to do some heavy-duty thinking about all of this in due course. I made a mental note to go over it all later — not to dwell on it, but to understand it in my mind, enabling me to move on.

Miranda seemed to be of the same mind.

"So, you liked him. Your mom and dad liked him. When did you decide to marry him?" she asked.

"Let me see," Jenny pondered a moment. "We were married in '75, so I guess it took me a couple of years. We were married right here on this property ... in the orchard actually. In May. On my birthday."

"And our mom's birthdays," I breathed.

"Yes, and of course it was Mother's Day," Jenny smiled. "But this was a happy day. A glorious day. The apple trees were all in blossom and they smelled like heaven. Even though my dad grumped a little that we weren't getting married in a church, he came around. Julian knew a minister in Toronto who was happy to marry us outside so the ceremony was still very Christian."

"Wow. It sounds wonderful," Miranda observed.

I nodded. I could picture how amazing it must have been.

"Oh, yes, it was one of the best days of my whole life. It was a small wedding. Julian's cousin played the guitar and sang, "Only Yesterday" by the Carpenters. Do you know that song?"

Miranda and I shook our heads.

"Well, it told our story perfectly. You never hear that song anymore, but the odd time I do, it sends me right back to that perfect day in May when I married my wonderful husband."

"Do you have any pictures?" Miranda asked. "I've never seen one at your place, only pictures of Toby and Brooke. I'd love to see one of my — my grandparents."

The last word came out in a shy whisper, but it caused Jenny's face to light up with pleasure.

"Aw," she breathed in pleasure. "Aw, my Julian would have loved you. I've had three years to get to know you and love the people you are. He would have loved you too. His heart could hold lots of love. I do have pictures, but they're away in my Grimoire."

"You have a Grimoire? You witch, who's not really a witch, but just a bit of magic, so we hear now," Miranda laughed as she tripped over her own words. "I thought a Grimoire was a book of witchcraft?"

"Well, it can be," Jenny admitted. "Mine is not a conventional one. It's more like a scrapbook, really. It's got two little locks from my baby girls taped on the first page and every day that I saw them in my mirror, I made a note of it, what they were wearing, and how old they were. And little observations that I knew would be important. Like the day you girls came to Jared. That day made my whole life worth living. Anyways, I have my wedding picture stuck in there. I'll show you it to you sometime if you want to see it. There's a lock of Buddy's hair too, but for the most part I made him his own scrapbook. I'm making one for Toby too. And Melly. Just a little record of some of the highlights of their lives."

"Tell us more," Miranda begged, child-like. "Tell us more about your life."

Jenny laughed.

"There's not much more to tell. Julian got employment in Guelph — which was wonderful. I didn't want to move to Toronto, and he was ripe to leave the city. We both wanted children, but Buddy didn't come along for four years. And I never was able to conceive after that, much as I longed to. Julian and I would both have liked a houseful of children, but it didn't happen like that. Still, we loved Buddy with all our hearts and so did my parents. He filled a hole in my heart that had been empty so long. His full name was Julian Fritz after the two men that loved him best in the world, but we called him Buddy from day one. It suited him."

"You told us how when he was little everyone would call 'Hi Buddy' to him," I remembered.

"Yes. Like people do, you know. Like 'Hi little fellow,' but he didn't know that. He just thought everyone was his friend."

"That's awesome," Miranda said.

"It really was. No wonder he was such a happy little guy. My poor dad died when he was less than a year old. I was always glad he got to know him a little. He would hold him and tell him stories in German. I'm sure my dad felt heartbroken over the twins, as Mama and I did. We never really got a chance to talk about it because he died so young and so suddenly. Not that it would have made any difference. It wouldn't have brought my babies to me. By then they were far away, leading lives that had no connection to me."

The story had been told — the old, old story of heartache and sorrow, love and joy. Nightfall had crept over the porch, absorbing the tale and sweeping it away. Above a full moon had risen over the trees, shining with a white dazzling glory.

I had no idea what hour it was. Time seemed to have hovered over the little cottage, standing still while long ago memories could be brought forth to form their tale.

We knew it was time to go, however reluctant we felt. We hugged Jenny and started on our way down the cobblestone path.

As we passed beyond the trees, our shadows lingered along beside us, illuminated in the moonlight. I looked down at those shadows. They were holding hands, swinging them like long lost friends. Or long-lost cousins who had just found their way back to each other.

43

"When we speak of magic, we should speak of those moments that were the purest, when the stars were bright and when laughter was loud. Those are the most magical moments in life."

T HAT MAY EVENING CHANGED OUR LIVES FOREVER, of course. Life seemed to flow then, like a beautiful golden river, coursing along, gathering all the history and memories and merging into the future, leaving in its wake all the loss and sorrow and joy and hope.

Many times, I thought of Miranda's words, her wish to have known and understood sooner the relationship between us. I couldn't help but look back on the time already spent in Jared when I'd felt suspicion and mistrust towards Jenny. It seemed such a waste now.

But the future shone so brightly that it seemed wrong to feel regret. I tried to look ahead. However, sometimes, that too made me uneasy. This was our last year. Miranda and I would both graduate soon. We would seek jobs wherever the prospect of employment took us. I always knew that Jared, however beloved it had become, would be merely an interlude in my life, a stop on the way. I wouldn't settle down here.

When I look back over my life now, that last year of university still stands out in a glory all its own. After wandering along trying to pick up the remnants of my soul, after losing my mother and experiencing betrayal by my dearest friend and boyfriend, my path had finally become defined. Defined with family, a past … and a future. I had ceased to be rudderless, bobbing around with no ties to the world. I had a grandmother, a cousin, a whole community of yogis and friends.

People always talk about "finding themselves", but I really did find myself that year. I found a piece of myself in Jared that I never even knew had been missing. But when I found it, I became whole.

Somewhere along the way after that, Miranda and I both shed the male friends we'd been hanging with for the last couple of years. I'd enjoyed Keith's company, but I'd always known that he and I were just pals, not really going anywhere concrete in the path of life, not ending up together. So, gently, I let him go.

Life seemed so full now, so joyful. Even the dull days came fraught with warmth and companionship.

And the magic. The magic seemed everywhere. I never knew if Jenny created the magic, bringing it to our attention until it became a tangible thing, or if the magic had been inside of me all along. Now that I knew my rightful ancestors, I realized that I could have that bit of magic in me. As could Miranda.

It wasn't like a TV show where you could cast a spell with your fingers to make an inanimate item change right in front of your eyes. It was a substance much more inherent — a feeling, a knowledge that this enchanted energy really did exist.

"Remember what Jenny told us a long time ago," Miranda reminded me. "Magic isn't good or bad; it's not black or white. It's both together. Just like nature. The good and bad is in the heart of the witch. It's in her energy and thoughts."

"Well, I guess that makes us good witches, too, then," I laughed, twirling her around, laughing merrily together.

We twirled and laughed through Mabon and Samhain, Yule and Imbolc. The months flew by.

Change, that bittersweet companion of life, reached out her slender fingers and drew us into her arms.

Freddy became a baby buddy to newborns whose parents, for whatever reason, could not be with them to provide all the contact they needed. It fulfilled something inside of her.

Sara and Jamie, the receiver of that magic spell for love which seemed so long ago now, eloped and moved to Ottawa, both having obtained nursing positions there.

Lizzy surprised us all by breaking out of her farmer's-wife mode and volunteering with troubled youths at a local centre. I hoped that this would mend the part of her that had been damaged and hurt by her brother's careless actions so many years ago.

Connie brought her partner, Gail, around for us to get to know. Something had come free in Gail's life and they were now a couple, open for all the world to see. Their love for each other shone in their faces, a wonderful thing to behold. Connie still helped Jenny, but her days at Hedgewytch Way became less and less, her overnights almost nil. I smiled to myself, remembering my vision of Connie's bedroom wrapped up like a parcel and tucked underneath the stairs.

Nora, of all people, took over Connie's position at Jenny's. She blossomed in her role as assistant — not to mention she became much more successful at solving her crossword puzzles. Maybe some of the magic had rubbed off on her, too.

Or maybe we had learned to observe the "kalokagathia". That's one of Neil's words, of course. It means "the good and the beautiful in a person".

Miranda saved a child's life. An eight-year-old boy had been flying a kite that had become tangled in the hydro lines. His heart had stopped. Miranda performed CPR on him, single-handedly saving him. Our Miranda was a hero. I almost burst with pride.

I had written another book that had been published and distributed in the stores around town. This one, also a children's book, depicted how they could find magic in everyday life and nature. All they had to do was look for it.

And we opened our hearts to each other completely. No more hesitation existed between us — or Jenny. It made me happier than I'd ever been in my adult life. Light and love flowed through me, enveloping Miranda and Jenny and spilling over into the rest of my life.

Our Sunday yoga sessions became more and more dear to me as the year slipped past. We had started to apply away for employment, knowing our days here were becoming numbered.

One such morning in early spring, I felt particularly sentimental. Gazing around the room, I thought of all we'd shared over the course of my time here. All these women with their own unique life's path. We gathered together in comradeship and affection, acknowledging all the revelations we'd shared, judging none.

"I have an announcement," Brooke said. "Listen up. I don't want any gossip. I'm going to tell you all at once, so you better get it straight."

Her grin took the sting out of her words.

I wondered for a moment if she were moving away with Neil. What a blow that would be. But things didn't always stay the same, no matter how much you may wish them to. And then, with a pang, I realized that if she did leave it wouldn't affect me anyways.

You could have heard a pin drop in the studio. Everyone waited with bated breath. It wasn't Brooke's way to be dramatic — quite the opposite — but now she seemed to hesitate.

"Actually, I have two announcements."

Toby could bear it no longer. Toby, who had been barely ten when I'd first met him and now was a tall handsome youth. Today he acted much younger, as he jumped up and down with excitement, Melly at his side, fairly dancing with the suspense of telling us the news.

"Can I tell, Mom?" he begged. "Please!"

Brooke said, "That might be easier," adding, "I'm no good at these things."

"Brooke and Neil are getting married," Melly screeched. "I'm going to be the flower girl and get a new pink dress and throw flowers all along the ground for them to walk on."

"My mom is having a baby," Toby yelled, trying to make himself heard over the excited Melly. Once she started, there seemed no way to stop her as she went on to describe every detail of the upcoming wedding, whether accurate or not. "A baby! I think it's a boy and I'll have a brother. Yay!"

Brooke sank into a handy chair, blushing wildly, amidst a host of cries and exclamations and hugs from her adoring yogis.

"We're very happy," she said. "I'm happier than I ever thought possible. I'll have to do some research and figure out how to modify my yoga poses for pregnancy."

"Oh, that's nothing to worry about," Connie snickered. "Some of us old girls can show you how to improvise for weight gain around the middle. Present company excepted, of course."

The wedding had been decided on for May before Brooke lost too much of her girlish figure.

The preparations happening at Hedgewytch Way surpassed anything I'd witnessed ever. For weeks and weeks, Miranda and I helped with cooking and baking and making decorations. Every day, one or another of the village women would come and offer their assistance.

The wedding day dawned clear and pure, the sky a curtain of azure, the sun glowing with all its brilliance and warmth. But of course, it would be. Jenny had put out 'into the universe' a spell for perfect weather for a wedding day.

We barely touched the ground with our feet that morning, so excited were we, as we sped up the path, our dresses flowing behind us in their plastic wraps.

Neil had arrived earlier than us even, putting his nervous energy to good use, dragging chairs out to form rows in the orchard and helping Jenny with numerous last-minute tasks.

"I'm suffering from 'cingulomania'," he called to Jenny, on one such journey back and forth from the kitchen to the orchard.

"That sounds serious," Miranda observed.

"Ah, it's not so bad," Jenny laughed. "You'll be able to do that soon."

"Do what?"

"He wants to hold Brooke in his arms," Jenny explained. "I think he is suffering from ustulation, myself."

Neil grinned, hoisted two chairs up on his broad shoulders and left the room, chuckling away to himself.

Miranda threw me a rueful look.

"I'm gonna miss all their silly words," she said.

"Me too."

It didn't seem that there could be one single person inhabiting the streets of Jared that day. Everyone I'd ever known or seen appeared right there in the orchard, lined up on the masses of chairs. I had no idea where they'd all come from but, in true Hedgewytch fashion, everyone had a chair.

Neil stood at the entrance to the orchard, calmer now, and cutting a very handsome picture indeed in the tuxedo he'd donned after performing all his chores. Beside him stood the most beautiful man I'd ever seen. *This must be the best man.* Our eyes met, and I knew beyond any certainty that he was my destiny. I didn't doubt these things any more. I had magic in my blood. Jenny winked at me just then.

Of course, he was.

Neil's uncle and aunt played the guitar and sang "Perfect". Toby and Melly walked side by side through the orchard, he carefully holding a pillow bearing the wedding rings while Melly scattered flowers along the way looking like a princess in her taffeta pink dress, her yellow curls dripping with flowers.

All brides are beautiful. That's a well-known fact. But Brooke's beauty surpassed earthly bounds, a vision floating in wafts of white lace, a sapphire necklace nestled at her creamy throat. Her brown hair gleamed in the sunshine, woven through with lily of the valley from Jenny's garden. There wasn't a dry eye in that crowd as she drifted over the grass. She had eyes only for her man, who had tears pouring, unchecked, down his own cheeks.

Just as the minister spoke the words, "I now pronounce you man and wife," we turned to behold Connie and Gail strolling down through the apple trees, hand in hand. Toby and Melly, who had stealthily doubled back to the cottage, strode now in front of them, Melly strewing more flowers and Toby bearing another pillow sporting two plain golden bands. Both wore grins like Cheshire cats, having pulled off the secret of a double wedding.

When the women reached the front of the orchard Brooke and Neil held out their hands drawing them forward, towards the minister. And so, it happened that Connie, too, got married on that beautiful day in May. The measure of happiness had climbed off the charts with all the love exploding into the air, filling it with jubilation.

Some days stand out like beacons in your life, never fading, no matter how many more pass in their wake. Even now I can close my eyes and feel the utter purity and joy of that day. I can smell the perfume of apple blossoms drifting above us, waving their own benediction of beauty. I can hear the laughter and gaiety, not marred by one negative word. And I can picture Dan, standing there under the trees with his best friend Neil, looking like my handsome prince who had come to take me away.

For that's what he was. His name was Dan Storms. He hailed from Salmon Arm, British Columbia.

He asked me to dance and we never stopped dancing. We danced and laughed together, as the afternoon faded into evening, which then surrendered to the velvet darkness. The stars came and sparkled down as the music and laughter carried on and on, no one wanting this enchanting day to end. We all knew there would never be another like this. I held that night in my heart forever.

Jenny wore a red dress with a handkerchief hemline and marvelous red shoes. Various bracelets adorned her tiny wrists, including some made by the village children, and she wore white lilacs tucked inside her topknot. She twinkled with a lifeforce all her own. The children dragged her up and danced with her for hours and hours.

I drifted past her on the orchard grass, in Dan's arms, satiated with wedding wine and happiness, as she danced between Melly and Toby performing some peculiar dance steps known only to the three of them.

"I'm so happy, Jenny."

I breathed the words to her as we floated past each other.

She stopped to linger for just a second, long enough to take my face in hands that perpetually smelled of lavender, and say, smiling, "I know, my dear Molly. It's your time now."

44

"One day I will be an old
woman with long silver hair,
magical tattoos,
eyes full of light and life,
and lots of laugh wrinkles.
My children's children
will lay out with me
under the stars."

A ND THE REST, AS THEY SAY, IS HISTORY.
We surrendered that beautiful May day to the old orchard, leaving only vestiges of laughter and love to linger there in our wake. I thought that years and years from now, the apple trees would still hold memories of that glorious wedding in their loyal hearts.

Then we had to leave Jared behind. How very wonderful it would have been to stay, safe and cozy, with a village so familiar to us now that we knew every nook and cranny of it. As we did with the people there. But we had to leave. We'd always known it. The day had arrived too quickly. I wasn't ready. But perhaps, I never would have been.

We had to let Jenny go. We had to have faith that we'd all be together again, Brooke and Neil and Toby and Melly and the new baby and all the yogis who had grown inside of my heart, laying down deep roots there. Funny Freddy, kind Faye, crusty Nora, wistful Heather, brisk Verna, loving Connie ... and all the others. The stories of their lives had woven our heartstrings into a web of female love and friendship.

In one of those funny quirks of fate, I moved to British Columbia while Miranda obtained a nursing position in Halifax — a coveted post in the neonatal intensive care.

"You're only four hours from my home!" I cried. And we vowed to visit my beloved Island together. But perhaps not to see Tod and Moira. I hadn't evolved that much yet.

I accepted a part-time job in Vernon at a primary school and another part-time position working with autistic kids in Salmon Arm. With Dan, of course. My true love.

Miranda found hers in the halls of a hospital in Halifax: a doctor tirelessly saving the lives of little souls who couldn't fight for themselves. I knew he would have to be very special to see what I saw when I looked at Miranda. The mirror of myself, all my imperfections, my hopes and dreams.

Sometimes, if I missed everyone too much, I would cut an orange in half, hollowing it out but leaving the centre core intact. Then I'd pour vegetable oil, with a drop of lavender, into it just below the stem. I'd light it and let it burn, allowing it to bring me back in my memory to those Jared days. And whatever visions that would lead me to.

One night I saw Jenny standing beside me, as clearly as I'd seen her the night she made the cornfield rescue, just before the edges of sleep receded. I woke in fear that perhaps something had happened to her, but when I texted her in the morning, she only said that she had been "checking in" with me. I thought maybe I had appeared in her magic mirror.

Well, she was my grandmother after all.

I loved her without abandon. I felt myself starved for stories from "home", as I now thought of Hedgewytch Way. I longed for news of Brooke's baby and Toby and Melly. Melly, who grew into a creature of grace and beauty, a wonder of a girl who remembered to listen to the words that breezes whispered into the summer leaves, who danced with flowers, laughed with butterflies, and found magic everywhere. She never stopped loving Toby, either. And he never stopped loving her. But that's a story for another time.

Some days, when I felt negativity around me, I lit a black candle in front of my bedroom mirror and said, "Any dark or evil force may now return unto it's source. May my home and I be free, safe and well. So mote it be."

Not with Dan present, though. He seemed on board with my smidgens of magic, but I didn't want to scare him with the big witch guns.

I realized I was pregnant when I'd lived in Salmon Arm for three years. And why was I not surprised when Miranda texted me within the hour to inform me that she also was expecting a baby. She and her good doctor had never managed to get married, only engaged, between their busy schedules. Still they were both ecstatic about the new baby.

"If this baby is a boy, I have to call him Buddy," I told Dan one evening.

We lay entwined on our cozy couch, our German Shepherd, Calvin, nuzzled between us. Sometimes, I would regale Dan in laughter with the tale of Rolf and how Jenny trained him. We spoke only English to Calvin.

"Of course, you do," Dan agreed. "We do."

I fell in love all over again.

Miranda was pregnant with a little girl, our due dates within a week of each other.

Miranda and I promised each other solemnly that we would reunite in Jared with our babies as soon as everyone could safely fly. Four years was too long to be away.

We would all come together again at Hedgewytch Way. Back at Jenny's.

Back where it all began.

JENNY'S GRIMOIRE

This is the day!

They are coming today!

I'm happier than beyond my own wild expectations.

A beautiful May sunrise greeted me in my magic mirror.

And two perfect babies. So tiny but still, I'd know them anywhere. My heart knew them even before they were born.

Perhaps we really can have heaven here on earth. My heaven would be all the glimpses of my loved ones I've had in this mirror. And here they are today on my birthday.

Buddy, full of joy, a friend to everyone along the way.

Star, to shine like a beacon over all our lives.

And today is the day.

I can hear the magic loud and clear.

Buddy. Star.

They are coming today.

ABOUT THE AUTHOR

Barb Bissonette is a retired medical nurse of forty years at Soldiers Memorial Hospital in Orillia, Ontario. She completed a mission to Dominican Republic with the Sisters of Charity to work among the people living there. She loved nursing, but has always enjoyed reading and writing. As a child, she would write poetry and short stories. Barb belongs to the Muskoka Authors Association. Her favorite person is — and always will be — Lucy Maud Montgomery, the great Canadian author.

Barb has had three novels published with Strategic Book Group: *Among Little Faces*, *A Winter Town*, and *Leave a Light on for Christmas*. She has always believed in the everyday magic that lives inside each one of us — the kind of magic that happens when you close your eyes and wish with all your might and believe with all your heart.

You can find out more about works and world of Barb Bissonette on her website *BarbBissonette.com* and her Facebook page *Barb Bissonette Writer*.

Manufactured by Amazon.ca
Bolton, ON